The Ghost

A Skin Art Story

J Shaffer

ACKNOWLEDGMENTS

I suppose a good place to start is with my mom and dad. This was all their fault, blame them. It was kicked off in 1977 when they pulled into a drive-in theater somewhere in Alabama, seeing it as the best way to bring their 2-year-old to a public showing. The movie in question was this cheesy sci-fi epic called *Star Wars*. Don't feel bad if you've never heard of it; it seems no one else has and I sometimes wonder if I made it all up. Anyway, that led to a life of poor choices when deciding how to spend my free time and what to be interested in over the next X amount of years.

I also need to thank Tatum Preston. If she hadn't so willingly- or foolishly, you decide- said she'd read my writing, I don't think I'd have ever gotten past writing page 2 of this book. Then there are the Ebrahimi sisters: Victoria and Yasameen. In my opinion, both are amazing and wonderful, and they've given me quite a lot of assistance as readers for my work.

Next is my editor, Rebecca Dobrinski. In addition to the Wonder Woman-esque feat of making it seem like I might've stepped into an English class at some point in my life, she also gave me one of the most assuring comments about my work. It really made me feel like this wasn't as dreadful as I feared, and that people might like this thing.

I would also like to mention my cousin, Ashley Owensby. The drawing didn't make it here, but it's progressively finding its way onto my arm. And, speaking of art work, I absolutely need to thank Marylin G, who produced the cover art. Let's be honest, it's most likely the reason you even bothered to look at this book at all, so check Facebook and Instagram for more of her work.

Chapter 1

Yet another sleepless night found Gina sitting on the roof of her building. The pot was not having its normal effect; she was exhausted but felt no closer to going back to sleep.

She watched as a storm rolled in from the west, as they usually did. The clear night sky gave way to dark clouds as they swallowed the few stars visible over the city lights. As storms went it was considerably tame, with barely noticeable flashes of lightning and low, muffled thunder. The cool breeze fell over her and broke the stifling early-August Southern air. From the ground below, she could hear a car's soft rumble as it ambled down one the few remaining cobblestone roads in Birmingham. If only for a moment, it was enough to make her forget the dream keeping her awake tonight.

Gina couldn't remember the first time she had the dream, a nightmare really. It had always been with her. Almost without fail, it preceded something major in her life. Still, it had never been as frequent or vivid as it had been the last two weeks. All the screams and blood and fire and the woman with a head full of bad brains were typical. The long hallway with doors to nowhere- that was new. And so was the man with no eyes and hands of dead light; he particularly unnerved Gina.

The rains fell and pitter-pattered gently against the tin roof on the patio lean–to. When the sound pulled her from the unsettling thoughts, she realized she had been on the roof for nearly two hours. Drowsiness crept back in. As tempting as it was, Gina decided against falling asleep in the hard-plastic lawn chair. Willing her weary legs to move, she shuffled downstairs to her apartment.

She crawled into bed and drifted off to sleep as flashes of lightning softly illuminated her apartment. Assurances that tomorrow would be a good day and the dream would soon be a distant memory bounced through her head. It was just a phase; she was simply worried about something silly, that's all. Once she figured that out it'd all go away, right? At least that's what she kept telling herself, like a mantra to ward off evil.

Sleep was hard won, though it didn't help Gina to convince herself the sense of dread darkening her thoughts wasn't ridiculous or misplaced. In the deepest parts of her mind Gina knew something big and bad was on its way. And it had her square in its sights.

The bus station was just like all the others He had been in before: worn and greasy-looking, with a mix of smells screaming misery, fear, anxiety, and destitution. Just like the rest of the world, He concluded, except somehow places like this were honest about their sorry state, almost reveling in their bluntness. It was as if these places understood they were part of a sick and emaciated world yet felt absolutely no shame. In a way He could almost respect that. But then that was the way the Adversary and all associated with it worked: make one think itself worthy of notions like respect or love or admiration or mercy.

And just like the rest of the world, He found a little aspiration and expectation mixed in to the mood of this bus station. However, these types of places made it easy for Him to ignore them. It was as if they belonged to those who had no idea what such things truly felt like but had once heard of them. If He thought about it, He might find it quaint in a way. Sadly, they were all wastes, so this quaintness was pointless in the end. Besides, that also was the way of the Adversary. It tried to make Him think its slaves and façades had feelings, real ones. They did not, but He often wondered.

He brushed past the bus driver, now chattering to a cop, as He gathered His bags. The driver recognized Him as a passenger, perhaps, but could barely place Him despite spending much of the last two days staring at Him in the rearview mirror. Every time the driver looked at His seat, she first thought it as empty, only to suddenly see Him sitting there. It unnerved her, and she was glad to see this passenger leave. However, if one asked, she could not exactly say why. As soon as He walked out of her sight, she could not remember precisely what so disturbed her in the first place. She would have a strong need to sleep with a light on until the day she died but would never really fathom why.

The driver was not alone. Most people who encountered Him quickly forgot or had trouble recalling anything about Him or what He looked like. His presence, on the other hand, no matter how momentary the experience, stayed with them. Eventually it might grow into a low-level paranoia that never went away, or merely a dull sense of unease shrouding everyday life. That was one of the gifts allowing Him to perform His great calling, ensuring the Adversary and all its kind that judgment was coming. The "people" in this dead world never understood the exalted errand assigned to Him, but they felt it. Few could pursue Him or put together any of the pieces allowing them to stop Him.

None, that is, with the exception of one.

The Hunter was already here- the entire city soaked in its stench. He could not tell exactly how long the Hunter had been here. Possibly a day, but that was doubtful. Likely, it was a few hours. That one could always chase Him down and never forgot what He looked like. Being able to recall His appearance had not helped, though, the few times the Hunter tried to enlist others to help track Him down. Unfortunately, removing the Hunter was not His job; that task would eventually fall to another like Him. Until then, the Hunter would be yet another challenge to overcome.

He stuffed His knapsack in a coin locker, preferring to keep a smaller satchel with Him, and then stepped out into the night. On the streets, He felt the iniquity of the place. He was sure there were good people, perhaps, trying to live in this moral squalor. Sodom had Lot after all. It was not for Him to decide if that was enough, though, so He ditched those reflections. He walked a few blocks, intuitively knowing where they would be. And sure enough, He found them.

Several blocks filled with lights, sights, and sounds promising pleasures that should be avoided, but drew in the flies with its rotted honey all the same. He walked among the sick and degenerate throngs as they sought false indulgences. The bars and nightclubs pushed all manner of paltry intoxicants and insinuations of hollow sex, while parlors whispered pledges to make their dupes anew with ink and steel and other unthinkable "art".

One stood out among the rest. She was skinny, but she showed the first hints of a budding temptress beneath her girlish veneer. Her hair was a natural brown, contrasting with the dyed colors of her compatriots. Her attire was a barely modest remnant of her waning innocence. Given the slightness of her friends' clothing, that was sure not to last long. She already had too many rings in her ears and she covered her face in a whore-mask of make-up. She could not be more than 15 and already she was speeding into harlotry.

She would ultimately lead many men, and probably women, astray with her charms and body. He found His hand absently reaching inside the satchel and wondered where He would put the new tick mark for her. He pushed that from his mind and focused on her. Would His knife start at her throat this time? No, lower would be better but how low? Sometimes He really wanted to taste the panic in their stink, a small compensation for His loyal work. And He could almost taste hers.

Too soon! He shut His eyes and snapped back to reality. The Hunter would be on Him too quickly if He started now. As might the police, for that matter. Although incapable of stopping Him, they could still be a major impediment. There was much to do in this city, He could feel it. The longer He could work without intrusion the better.

There was something special awaiting Him here. In good time, all would be revealed. He could wait, but not for long, and it was unlikely that He would have to. Until then He would explore the city and know it well. He gave the girl one last look before merging into the crowd.

Chapter 2

A couple days passed and the dream subsided as it always did. It could have been the drinks from the night before that did it, or maybe all Gina needed was just to relax. Maybe now she could get back to her normal, easygoing life. At any rate, she'd had a good time at the club: listening to her best friend spin music as the throng danced around her, feeling the verve of the mass spill into and through her. Gina had heard of phenomena like the St. John's Dance and bacchanalia. In that club she understood the experience. Nothing mattered except moving and feeling. The harder the mob danced, the harder she did and, it seemed, vice versa. She found it odd to only remember bits and pieces of the night before. She didn't think she drank *that* much. All she really remembered was the dancing.

Regardless, she was alive and well and going to be late for work. Fortunately, she didn't have far to go to get there. Her father's shop was just below her apartment. In fact, her father owned the whole five-story building. He once told her the building was over 100 years old, dating back to the 1880's. Originally it housed a grocer on the ground level, an accounting and law firm on the next few, and a doctor's office on the fifth floor. Now the first level was home to her father's tattoo and piercing parlor. A seamstress rented the second floor. The last few floors had been converted into apartments with Gina occupying the top one.

Over the bathroom sink Gina shoved aside the residual haze as she washed last night away. She brushed her teeth, put on some deodorant, and tried to comb the knots out of her hair before deciding she'd push it back with a white Alice band. She noticed the dark blue highlights in her black hair- really only visible when the light hit just right- had begun to fade. The black color wasn't holding up either. She briefly considered going back to her natural white-blonde; it'd be so much easier. She had nothing against her natural color, but she had colored her hair for as long as she could remember. To be more accurate, her mother started coloring Gina's hair when she was very young. She was oddly steadfast about it, in fact. Dismissing such thoughts, she dabbed on a wine-colored lipstick and smudged some black liner under her eyes. The kohl contrasted with her pale skin and made Gina's striking light blue eyes stand out all the more.

Dressed now (and ignoring her jeans were fitting a little tighter than they did before) and as ready as she could be, she made her way to the door. Out of the corner of her eye, Gina thought she saw someone, a small girl, sitting on the top of her couch. Looking directly at the sofa now there was no girl, but she did notice someone was sleeping there. Try as she might, though, Gina couldn't remember inviting any of her friends to crash at her place last night.

She slipped her bag from her shoulder, letting it drop silently to the floor. Reaching down, her fingers wrapped around the baseball bat leaning against the wall near the door. She held the bat loosely by her side as she warily approached the couch. The person's face was buried in cushions and obscured by the sheet. A few ropes of dreadlocked hair poked out from under the covers. These locks were dark, not the bright, electric colors sported by the few goth-ravers she knew. Gina decided to go for broke and nudged the sleeping form with the fun end of the bat. She repeated this a few more times before the shape stirred and the sheets lowered enough for her to see a face.

Not fully awake, but realizing all was not right, his gaze swept across the room a few times before settling on Gina standing over him, and particularly on the bat in her hand. Her face was a mix of caution and curiosity, accentuated by a many-pierced eyebrow raised high up on her forehead. Really seeing him now, she noticed his thin face with sharp features and clear hazel eyes. The stranger's hair was deep brown with gold-like highlights, kept in shoulder-length dreadlocks. His skin tone was dark, from sun exposure or naturally or both- she couldn't really tell. His facial characteristics made it hard to discern race or ethnicity. She definitely didn't know him, but there was something that made him more than a complete stranger.

"Did we sleep well?" she asked, trying to keep her voice calm and smooth.

"Uh... yeah," he slowly started before regaining some composure. "I guess so." His eyes darted to the bat once more before he slowly pushed himself up into more of a sitting position.

They stared at each other for a moment, both wondering what the other would do next. Glancing once again to the bat in her hand, he began mapping out the best course of escape, just in case, and how to maximize the retrieval of his few but inexplicably scattered gear in the brief moments he would have to depart. She stood between him and the door, making escape all the more difficult. At the same time, in Gina's head, the night before flashed a little more clearly. The recollection of talking to this guy jumped to the fore. She remembered meeting him at the bar, learning that he'd just gotten into town and didn't have anywhere to stay.

There'd been something odd about that last part, going beyond sharing details with a complete stranger. It was the *way* he explained it, like he expected there to be some push or sway to his words. Like he thought he was Bela Lugosi in *Dracula* or something. That struck Gina as a little sketchy, but she was usually quick to pick up on whether or not someone was trouble. She really didn't get that trouble vibe off of him and figured the sketch-factor was just from him being travel-weary.

At any rate, at least Gina now remembered inviting him to crash on her couch. "Wait! We met at the club last night. You just got into town and all," she affirmed, putting him at ease. "Sorry, but I don't remember your name." She stuffed the bat under one arm and held out the now empty hand.

He lightly shook her hand. "Dez. The name's Dez."

"Dez? It's nice to meet you, um, again. I'm Gina and this," she said waving her hand to indicate the apartment, "is my castle, my Batcave, or whatever." She hoped her crooked smile conveyed a sense of humor in the comment and not simple dorkiness. His wry grin assured her he recognized the attempted wit. Simple dorkiness was still a strong possibility, though.

"Anyway, I was just on my way out." She was mildly happy she could get away from the previous awkwardness. "Gotta get to work," she added in a stilted, clumsy tone.

"Alright, um, I can get my things pretty quick..." he began.

"Oh no, that's not what I meant. You can hang out here for a while. No need to rush."

"You hardly know me." Given the circumstances, they both appreciated the absurdity of the statement even as he said it. Still, Dez soldiered on. "I mean I could steal your shit."

Gina quickly took stock of her apartment: a few pieces of fourth-hand furniture, no television, a decent enough stereo and a bunch of CDs, various stacks of books and comics. She owned a small fortune in art supplies, but used paints and charcoals weren't big on resale value. Her laptop could be a temptation, but it was in her pack and going with her. The stereo might net someone $150, maybe. Still, the nearest pawn shop was several blocks away and the equipment was bulky, heavy. All things considered, stealing her shit really wasn't worth the effort. She looked back at him and shrugged.

"Yes, you could," she agreed with an affable smile.

Grabbing her backpack and stowing the bat to its spot, she started toward the door and explained that, if he was hungry, he could find cereal and the necessary accessories in the kitchen. It was small enough she didn't feel any need to tell him where he might find any of it. Gina pulled a key from the ring hanging off the pack, told him how to lock the door and where to bring the key when he decided to leave. With that she hurried along the short hallway and ran down the stairwell, leaving a total stranger in her apartment. Her cavalier attitude about her meager possessions started to fade, particularly when she thought about her collection of comic books. Some of those were worth quite a bit of money.

Gina pushed those thoughts aside. She didn't get any bad juju off Dez. He seemed okay. Gina was rather confident in her ability to assess people's character. It had never failed her before. There was a first time for everything, she supposed, but there had been far worse times in the past for it to have bitten her in the ass. In the building's small lobby, Gina thought about checking her mail but figured it could wait until later. She strode out onto the sidewalk, took six steps and arrived at work.

Bells above the door announced her entry into a spacious waiting area with a few comfortable-looking, if drab and threadbare, couches and chairs. Magazines that mostly detailed various forms of body art were available for anyone waiting. Gina smelled freshly brewed coffee lightly masking the sterile smells of assorted instruments fresh from the autoclave. The sweet sound of Jenny Lewis' voice drifted from a few speakers barely covering the faint hum of a tattoo machine coming from a backroom. A young woman with dark and unruly brown hair pulled back into a bushy pony-tail tried to straighten the magazines into a semblance of order.

"Someone's late," she said with a smile and sing-song voice as Gina strolled through the door. Gina met the chirpiness with a practiced grumpiness and a middle finger before giving the young lady a quick wink as she headed behind the counter.

"Morning, Michelle," she replied with a cheerful grin. Michelle was one of Gina's oldest friends, though they drifted apart some over the years since high school. She had gone off to college for a short time but that fell apart. When she returned home she spent most of her time trying to figure out what to do next, unexpectedly getting married in the process. After recently finishing cosmetology school Michelle started working at the parlor, just doing odds and ends until she found a job at a shop somewhere. Gina hoped this would lead their relationship back to its earlier closeness.

"I thought you and Jacob were gonna meet up with me and Quinn at the Loft last night. Something come up?" Gina asked as she tossed her backpack in a cubby hole and poured herself a cup of coffee.

"We ended up at the Panic with his sister," she answered with a slight scrunch of her nose at the word "sister", as if it left a bad taste in her mouth. Gina nodded with understanding and sympathy. That was a battle Michelle and Gina had many a chat session about.

"Any improvements?" Gina queried, already knowing the answer but faking optimism all the same.

In response Michelle turned her thumb down and stuck her tongue out. "That woman's never gonna forgive this sassy black girl for corrupting an innocent white boy."

"Sassy? I thought black women were saucy?"

"Nope, that's Latinas and I think it's spicy you're thinking of."

"Good to know. Nothing's more embarrassing than getting racial stereotypes mixed up," Gina said with a depreciating roll of her eyes. "Well, better luck next time," she encouraged before going to the back to get her room ready, and almost ran into a mountain.

Under normal circumstances Gina called this mountain "Papa". Most everyone did, though for her it was because he really was her father. He was tall, just over six and a half feet, with black hair that had faint streaks of grey, and dark blue eyes. At first glance his slight frame wasn't apparent due to his height, thus people tended to be alarmed of him initially. The legion of old and faded tattoos that covered much of his body, coupled with his general biker-like attire, only added to the intimidation factor.

Currently, said mountain looked at her with an expression that usually reduced Gina to a dribbling, apologetic idiot as far back as her memory served. She tried not to say anything at all. It didn't even matter if Gina had done anything wrong or not, the look always had that effect on her. Before she could inevitably start tattling, about anything and everything most likely, the mountain's expression changed. With some mirth, he unhurriedly said, "You're late."

Annoyed now, Gina declared with faux-umbrage how she would begin arriving late more often just so she wouldn't have to go through this "indignity" when it did happen. Frankie hugged his daughter tightly and kissed the top of her head- not an easy action given he was well over a foot taller than her- before letting her go to her work room. As she walked past one of the other studios, the needle's hum stopped and someone within started to point out Gina's tardiness but was cut off by her formidable insistence to not continue; underscored with an itemized list of which body parts were in jeopardy if her warning went unheeded.

Frankie soon poked his head into her studio. "So, how'd Quinn do last night?"

"She was awesome!" Gina said, glowing with delight for her friend. "The crowd really liked her set. I think she'll get the chance to do more at the club."

"Good to hear!" he returned. "It's been awhile since I've seen my other kids. What all have they been up to?" Frankie had a habit of "adopting" Gina's friends as his own and they tended to return the favor.

"Other than the DJ gig, Quinn's seeing some new guy."

"Good! It's about time she got back out there again," he said. Then his voice turned sour. "Anything I should be worried about?" Frankie asked with a gruff, steady tone that meant he'd probably be talking to Quinn's mom later that night. Given Quinn's past relationships, there was reason for concern.

"I think he's okay," she started. "Kinda boring but that's probably what she needs, for now at least. He's gotten work done here before and works up at the auto parts store near the house, so you probably know him."

"In that case, I guess I need to call Becky and tell her to pretend not to like him," he said with a knowing grin. "What's the boy's name?"

"Harris. Other than that, Quinn's good and Suz is just, um, Suz." Gina had only known Suz for a few years now, meeting her after she'd moved to the city, but they became fast friends. She was originally from some small town in Tennessee, though Suz never really talked about her hometown. By all account, she had a seriously rough time there. How rough exactly Gina didn't know; Suz never really went into it, and none felt right to pry. All the same, given what a disaster her life was at the time, Gina couldn't imagine it being trifling, so she couldn't find it a surprise that she rarely brought it up. With help from Gina, Quinn, Frankie, and others, Suz had straightened out a lot. Still, she often leaned towards crazy.

"Not sure if that last part is a comfort or cause for concern to be honest," Frankie replied with a smile. "Well, I'll let you get back to it. I think you got an appointment in half an hour."

"An hour!" Michelle idly corrected from the front of the shop.

"In an hour, then," Frankie corrected. "Don't forget family dinner tomorrow night. Your aunt's cooking." Gina shuddered.

Gina's aunt, April, was Frankie's much younger half-sister. Frankie was 17 when April was born and she barely a year old when he had a falling out with their father and left home. He didn't see his baby sister again until 13 years later at their father's funeral. Frankie's older brothers, at best, ignored April's existence but Flora, Frankie's wife, came to adore April so Frankie tried too as well. After spending several years pretending, Frankie did come to care for and love his baby sister, and they became close. It probably helped that April was the only member of Frankie's family who did not regard his daughter as a freak or embarrassment.

After Flora's health began to deteriorate, April, along with her daughter Cinnamon, moved into Frankie's home to help. When Flora died Frankie found the house to be less lonely with them there, so he asked April and Cinnamon to stay. April's situation at the time was bad anyway, primarily due to a messy divorce from her deadbeat husband who was also a shitty father to Cinnamon. Accepting Frankie's offer was a no-brainer. Plus, April helped to take care of Gina and her younger brother, Trevor, and Cinnamon became more like a sister to them than a cousin.

It had been over a year since April was laid-off from her job at a bank and she was having little luck finding employment other than waitressing, which she was reluctant to go back to. In the last few months April had focused her attentions towards improving her cooking skills, with debatable success, both to keep from falling into a funk over fruitless searches and to make up for her lack of income. However, its use as a distraction had started to wane so she was considering biting the bullet and waitressing again.

"It's just spaghetti, so she probably can't mess it up too bad. Anyway, Trevor's bringing that girl he's been seeing," Frankie said.

"I'll be there with bells on then," Gina cheerfully said with a mock salute. Trevor had never had a girlfriend before. He was 16 and had so far been more interested in music and games. She hardly saw that as a big deal, though one would think otherwise to hear some of his friends talk about it. Said friends mostly lacked girlfriends themselves, she noted. Still, Gina was curious to meet the one who'd finally caught her brother's attention.

It wasn't long before Gina had her room set up. With a bit of time to spare, she went to the other room and talked a bit to Bruce, one of the other artists at the shop. He had opened the store early for the client he was currently working on. Frankie never minded if they did that, but normally Bruce stuck to strict hours. Gina only needed to look at the legs of the olive-skinned beauty in his chair to know why he broke routine. Whether the customer realized it or not she was walking on Bruce's kryptonite.

Until recently Gina and Bruce had been seeing each other. They both knew it wasn't likely to lead to anything serious, but there had been an undeniable draw between them ever since they met. How they waited as long as they did neither could fathom a guess. Still, they didn't see the lack of a future for them as anything except friends as a reason not to indulge, if only a little, in their mutual attraction. At the same time, they felt it would complicate things when it eventually burned out if everyone knew, so they kept it private. This had a side benefit of adding an extra layer of excitement to the whole affair.

It did fizzle out, though Gina still harbored some quixotic feelings for Bruce. Not knowing if he felt similar, and concluding it didn't matter either way, she kept it to herself. That didn't make it easy for her to see Bruce showing interest in someone else. Not even in light of her being the one who broke things off.

Gina was about to leave her colleague alone when Michelle called from the front. She found Dez waiting at the counter, Michelle had a look in her eye that would have been ingeniously insinuating in high school, but for someone in their mid-20s was just too obvious for decency. A slight rise in Gina's eyebrow and subtle drop at the corner of her lip told Michelle to forget the thought, but both knew that would never happen. She resigned herself to spending the rest of the day dodging neon-casted allusions.

"Here's your key back," Dez said handing it over the counter. Gina could almost hear Michelle's ears perk up. "Thanks for the cereal. Um, you're outta milk by the way."

"Oh, thanks." Had Gina not felt the mountain fall in behind her then she might have noticed Dez scrunch up his face at the word "thanks". She glanced back; the look on his face told her Frankie had seen Michelle's very specific glee over a man asking for Gina.

"Hello?" Frankie said in a friendly voice reminiscent of a story about spiders and flies. "Who's your new friend?"

"Papa, this is Dez. Dez, this is my Papa," Gina answered, relieved Dez appeared at ease with the situation as he extended his hand out. She hoped her father would see this as a sign that nothing "adult", as he would put it, was afoot. Frankie shook Dez's hand. Gina's relief grew; her father believed a lot could be told about someone by their handshake. Frankie would take Dez initiating the exchange as a good sign. That relief evaporated with...

"It's nice to meet you, sir. Your daughter was kind enough to let me sleep at her place last night..." Dez winced at both the realization this was not the smartest thing to say at the moment, and at Frankie's tightening clutch.

"He slept on the couch," Gina injected quickly, somehow managing to keep her voice nonchalant. Frankie's grip eased while his verbal response was strangely reserved.

Noticing the bag over Dez's shoulder, which Gina observed had a clear lack of any of her possessions, Frankie asked, "You from out of town?"

16

"Yeah, I just got in last night."

"Where from?"

"All over now, but Vancouver originally," Dez answered. "Just going where the muse takes me, you know?" Frankie relaxed more. Like Gina, Frankie generally had a decent sense of people. He also liked helping people out where he could. The two traits usually played well together.

"You got a place to stay while you're here?"

"Not yet. I was gonna look around for a hotel room or something today. Any suggestions?"

"Well, one of the third-floor apartments is available upstairs. It's not the greatest in the world but it's furnished, and I could probably cut you a deal on the rent," Frankie said. "We can go take a look if you want."

Dez accepted and Frankie went to his office, grabbed his keys, and the two went to check the apartment. As they left, Gina's appointment came in.

The rest of Gina's work day progressed as normal. She worked on several clients, two of whom were new. She adored most of her regular clients, but she really loved getting new ones, especially if they never had any work done before. That gleam they got in their eye showing they were hooked and would want more always gave Gina a bit of a buzz. A six o'clock lull was livened up when Jacob, Michelle's husband, brought in pizza and cola for everyone.

It was later in the night, just after closing time, and Gina was advising a young girl looking to get her first tattoo. Michelle had long finished straightening the shop and storing equipment from the autoclaves but had stuck around with Jacob talking to a few people they knew from around town. She was saying her good-byes and walking out the door with Jacob when they almost ran into Dez. The three exchanged apologies as Michelle sent Gina a knowing look and Gina returned an evil one.

"See you at the Panic?" Michelle quickly asked Gina.

"Probably. Quinn's dropping by in a minute. I'll see if she up for going."

"Bring your new friend!" Michelle cheerfully yelled from behind the closing door as her husband dragged her away.

Dez waved to Gina as he took a seat in one of the chairs. He had changed clothes and freshened up. Like the outfit he wore earlier, the ones he had on now were practical and meant to be sturdy while staying comfortable. Dez had mentioned traveling so Gina reckoned that probably meant walking and hitchhiking as well as buses and the like. He picked up one of the magazines from the table and idly thumbed through it.

Gina finished her discussion with the girl and set an appointment for the following week. She was obviously excited about getting her first tattoo as she practically skipped out the door. Gina turned the sign on the door around to "Closed" and locked the first lock. She turned off most of the lights and grabbed her backpack from its cubby hole behind the counter. Dez stepped outside as Gina turned on the alarm, locked the door completely and helped her pull down the heavy metal roll-cage.

"That girl said something about 'the Panic'," Dez cautiously asked. "What's that?"

"Michelle? Yeah, it's a bar we go to sometimes," Gina answered. "A lot, actually." She continued with a slightly worried look on her face. For some reason her brain picked that moment to calculate the amount of money she and her friends had spent in that place and promptly shut down. "We'll probably go in a little bit. Wanna come along?"

"I don't know. I'm pretty hungry. I haven't eaten anything since at your place earlier. That's why I came down here: to ask if there was anywhere nearby to get something to eat."

"Well, the Panic doesn't actually serve food, but there's a place next door and they take orders from the bar. We can head down there as soon as..."

"Hey, lady, how come you look so scary?" someone yelled from behind Dez. He and Gina looked around and saw a young woman approaching them. She was fairly tall and curvy. She walked with a slackened air about her and wore a pair of red plaid capri pants, a faded Green Lantern shirt and old green and white Keds. Her hair, half colored black and the other bleached white, was pulled back in a loose ponytail, the two halves separated by a part in the middle. Her skin had a slight tan to it that highlighted her thick, dark eyelashes and warm brown eyes, and her wide smile lent her a charming glow. She wasn't wearing any noticeable jewelry, but the lobe of her left ear had a large star tattooed on it with a smaller one just behind it. Inside the cartilage of her right ear was a series of seven circles that decreased in size as they climbed. Gina stepped past Dez and hugged the woman tightly. "You scare the men looking so scary like that!"

"Because I like my men all scared-like!" Gina returned dutifully. They laughed a little and Gina turned to Dez, who had a very confused look on his face. "Sorry, old television show. Dez, this is Quinn. Quinn, Dez."

They shook hands and Dez noted, "You were the DJ at the club last night, right?"

"Yup, that was me," Quinn replied. While her voice was filled with happiness over being recognized- even in such a minor way- it was also tinged with apprehension.

"You were pretty good."

"Thanks," she took the compliment, her face glowing some as she did. This time Gina caught Dez's cringe at the word. She filed that under "Weird" but didn't think this the time or place to find out what that was about.

"Oh yeah, what'd Ferris say? You gonna get to spin at the Loft?" Gina asked.

"Maybe. She's looking at other DJs, but she may give me a night or two a week," Quinn said with an unconcerned attitude. Given Quinn's previous excitement about working the Loft, this left Gina a bit confused. Quinn saw this play out on her face and continued with a smile. "But Quentin wants me for a party he's got coming up at his place."

Initially Gina didn't seem to register the weight of what Quinn said, but surprise soon crossed her face enough that her eyes almost shot out. "Quentin? Holy shit, really?" Gina hugged Quinn tightly. Dez had no idea what they were talking about but could figure out it was a big deal. Gina, remembering there was someone uninitiated, explained, "Quentin's this guy that puts on a lot of parties; big ones!"

"Yeah," Quinn continued, "and people he gets to work for him have a habit of getting noticed. Like Porn God 39 and the Atomic Muffs a few years back. That's just entertainment-wise."

"The take away, I take it, is Quentin picks you up and you go places," Dez finished the thought.

"Pretty much," Quinn said. "I'm not the only DJ for the night though. I think he has, like, four or five others lined up. He'll probably start me early before a lot of people get there."

"Whatever, that's still awesome *and* that means we celebrate!" Gina cut in. "We need to get Suz. She at work?"

Quinn nodded. "Talked to her earlier. She'll meet us at the Panic a little later." Quinn looked sideways at Dez and then back to Gina. "You warn him about Suz yet?" Gina shook her head, a wicked grin playing at her lips.

"Well, that should be fun then," she said with a smile that quickly matched Gina's.

The Panic was the type of bar most people would never notice unless it was pointed out to them. The phrase "hole in the wall" only began to scratch the surface. In a movie, it would be frequented by some broken-down detective to drown his sorrow and self-pity before the place got shot up by gangsters or a problem-ridden blonde bombshell in a red dress walked in to kick off the plot.

On the way over, Dez found out the bar's full name was "Ye Ol' Moral Panic" though it originally had the uninspired moniker of "Mike's Pub". Its name change had to do with a local religious group's sad attempt at resurrecting Prohibition in the city and the owner's vocal opposition a decade earlier. Said resistance included some choice assessments of religion in general which were not well received by other local religious communities. The "Ye Ol'" part was simply to give the place some character.

Photos- some framed, others not; some professional, some simple Polaroids; all some stage of faded- covered the walls, telling a history of happiness and enjoyment, pain and loss. There were a few with a seeming place of prominence over the others; cherished soldiers of the tribe who were lost or celebrated or both. These were joined by bumper and band stickers of various measures of cleverness haphazardly slapped across a portion of wall or along a runner board, over table tops and stool seats or the back of a chair. Dated announcements, most long out living its heralded event, could be seen beneath it all; layers of history caked over another further back to some gilded, half-remembered age. To some it would come off as mere kitsch, but the regulars knew it was more than that: they were the Panic's battle scars, well-worn and deserved from decades of fighting the good fight.

Dez found the place relaxing. At least, once he got past Harold the bouncer it became easygoing. Although Harold was barely five and half feet tall, he seemed to be just as wide. Dez knew some of the doorman's bulk, maybe even most, had to be fat rather than muscle, but he had no desire to find out the ratio; he had the feeling people rarely did much bouncing once Harold decided to throw them out. While the bouncer's size was intimidating enough, what made him even scarier was, with a combination of clothing and his dark skin, the man found a spot by the door allowing him to blend in, making him almost invisible. Dez believed no one Harold's size should be allowed to hide that easily. Despite all this, it became apparent Harold was the friendly sort with everyone (with the ladies a little more so) so long as they didn't cause any trouble.

Gina and Quinn greeted the pair of bartenders, one a short doll-faced girl with large green eyes and thick brown hair and the other a middle-aged man with a demeanor suggesting his middle fingers were not given the opportunity to bend as often as the others. At the bar Michelle, Jacob, and Bruce were having a jovial and lively conversation with Mike, the male bartender and also the establishment's owner. A fourth person was sitting with them. Her bearing, combined with her physique, would make even serious bruisers rethink messing with her. She was introduced to Dez as

21

Marcella, and that she worked with Gina at the shop, mainly as a piercer but also adept at various beading and scarification practices.

They ordered food and drink from Mackenzie, the doll-faced bartender, before grabbing a booth. The women were telling Dez how they'd met when Mackenzie brought their orders. Dez was starting in on his bacon-cheeseburger and fries when he urged the two to continue their story. "It was like a week into kindergarten and I had these big, ugly-ass glasses to fix a lazy eye, right?" Quinn began. "Naturally, I was a serious target for all the mini-sociopaths.

"Then this little albino girl with a bad dye job shows up one day," she said nudging Gina.

"I am not an albino!" Gina protested. "And my hair got better."

Quinn waved her hand, light-heartedly dismissing her friend's protests. "So, I'm thinking my problems are over. I mean; spooky pale girl *has* to trump funny glasses girl. Oh, how wrong I was."

"Served you right," Gina half-heartedly pouted but Quinn ignored her.

"So, it's lunchtime and I'm backed up against a wall by these three mutants when all of the sudden creepy albino girl just... appears between me and them (I mean, like, *poof* from out of nowhere). Then she orders them to 'back off' and 'leave her alone' with this serious voice." Quinn did her best to playfully imitate said voice, lowering it into a mocking bass pitch.

"We're all five-year-old kids but she's still head and shoulders shorter than us. Those kids were scared shitless anyway. They never picked on me again and us two weirdos have been friends ever since." Quinn finished, throwing her arm around Gina's shoulders and squeezing tightly.

"So what's your story, Dez?"

He swallowed the bite he was working on. "Not much to tell; pretty boring really," he answered, an obvious attempt to avoid the question. Gina wanted to give him the benefit of the doubt. He had been traveling on his own for some time and, she imagined, probably had to play things close to the chest a lot. Still...

"Well, bore us to death then," Gina threw back with a pleasant smile before slipping a few fries into her mouth.

With a tight, defeated grin Dez took a swig of his beer. "Alright. You know I'm from Vancouver." Gina nodded.

"What made you leave?" asked Quinn.

"Nothing to keep me there." His answer was a bit too fast. Rehearsed and repeated countless times, if only to himself.

"No friends or family?"

Dez answered with a slow shake of his head. "I had a few friends but..." He took a moment to think about what he'd say next. "Well, my parents and sister were killed in a car crash and after that... I just couldn't really deal with anything there anymore."

"And now you just go place to place to, what, find yourself or something?" Gina suggested.

"Something like that," Dez laughed. "Passé, I know."

"A little Kerouac, I guess, but not *too* cheesy," Gina replied with a smirk. "What do you do for cash?"

"I pick up an odd job here and there; washed plenty of dishes and cleaned more than a few nasty-ass toilets," he offered with a small grin. "Spent most of a winter in South Dakota chopping firewood once and sold painted seashells from a stand right off the beach in Florida a few summers ago. For the most part, though, I play my guitar and sing here and there."

"That's cool. We could probably help with that," Gina stated, Quinn nodding in concurrence. "If you want."

"That'd be great!"

"What's that?" Gina pointed to a tattoo on Dez's right arm, on the inside of his forearm. It was of a red and white heraldry shield. A gold lion stood to one side and a black bird on the other. A lop-sided crown sat at the top. Across the bottom the name "Lucy" was written on a scroll-like banner. "Who's Lucy?"

"Lucy was my sister," Dez's expression sunk. "We were pretty close."

Hoping to change the subject slightly, Gina quickly pointed

out, "That shield looks Spanish. Is that where your family's from?"

"It is," Dez replied with some puzzlement. He shook it off quickly. "Well, my mom's side of the family is originally from Spain, but they moved to Portugal quite some time before she was born. How'd you know that?"

"A lot of people want heraldry stuff for tats; by now I've done enough research I can figure a little bit out; like the country and such. I mean, I know that the crown means some kind of nobility. I couldn't say how high, but I know it isn't royalty or anything like that."

"You say stuff like that and still wonder why people call you a dork," Quinn said. Dez surmised ridicule such as this was clearly the means the two women chose to show affection.

"What about your dad?" Gina said, ignoring Quinn's jab.

"Not much to say there. He was from Jamaica. Moved to New York and met my mom. Both were fresh off the boat. They never married but they had me and my sister after moving to Vancouver. They made a good living as musicians, but never got famous or anything."

"Your sister's name was Lucy? Wait, is 'Dez' short for 'Desi'?" Quinn asked. Gina, her face brightening with amusement, picked up where she was going with it.

"Yes," Dez sullenly admitted, trying his best not to look at them as he did. "Well... yeah. My mom had a freaky obsession with *I Love Lucy* for some reason. It drove everyone crazy but..." He left the thought hanging and neither Gina nor Quinn wanted to pry.

The bar started to fill up with more people of various cliques and walks of life. A few people came over to the table to say hello to Gina or Quinn or both. Most gave Dez a friendly welcome, if not merely a polite one. With the distraction, Dez took the opportunity to turn the flow of conversation back towards the two women.

He learned that Gina had been adopted by Frankie and his wife, Flora, when she was quite young. They later had a child of their own, Gina's brother Trevor, but they never treated either any differently. Flora died some years ago, though Gina didn't say from what.

The subject of Quinn's family was dodgy, but she made out as if it had always been just her and her mother. A cousin got Quinn involved in DJing while she was still in high school. Although she did nothing to bring attention to it, Dez noticed the pinky and ring fingers of Quinn's left hand were missing. In their place was a long-healed and ragged-edged scar along the knuckles. He didn't mean to stare at it and felt ashamed when she caught his gaze. It was easy to guess she might be used to it, though, when she gave him an odd smile. With that action he also saw other scars on her nose, lip, and ears; all smooth and straight, as if something had been ripped away. Dez thought these scars might be why she wore no jewelry. Over the years Dez learned how to discern narratives and when to stop asking questions. Sadly, some stories seemed far more common than he once thought.

The cause could have been completely innocuous, like some sort of accident, but there was something in the way she looked down and away, hiding behind her hand before smiling; like she was attempting to disarm a bomb before it exploded. The missing fingers probably told him more about Quinn's past than she was comfortable with, even if it was inexplicit.

He wasn't sure how to excuse his intrusion, not sure if he even should. It became immaterial when Quinn excused herself to talk to someone at the bar, leaving Gina and Dez to make small talk. Initially they chatted about music and books, but soon shifted back to the tattoo on Dez's arm. Gina was suggesting how she'd go about touching it up when something else clearly caught her eye, causing a smile to slowly spread across her face.

Dez followed her gaze to a trio of women at the door. They were crowded close around Harold, who was immensely enjoying their attention. It wasn't long before two of them, one blonde and the other raven-haired, headed to the bar. The third made a beeline towards their booth.

This one's hair was deep purple and neatly framed her strong, striking features and high cheek bones. A tattoo of a demented-looking white rabbit in a purple suit surrounded by flames decorated her left shoulder. Starting just below her right elbow, a pattern of swirls, loops, dots, and circles made its way down and around her forearm, over her wrist, and continued over the back of her hand and down her fingers. A silvery stud jutted out below her lower lip. She was simply dressed in a baggy pair of overalls, an old tee shirt with the graphic long faded into obscurity, and worn-out sneakers. Her outfit had likely been chosen for comfort rather than style, but it may as well have been a gown of the finest silk on her. Words like beautiful, gorgeous, babe, or pretty could be easily and honestly applied to her but none even began to approach the truth of her presence. She was simply indescribable, which made her dangerous in Dez's mind.

There was only so much trouble beauty could get someone out of, however, and what this woman had was better than diplomatic immunity.

She slipped easily into the booth and cavalierly laid her head on Gina's shoulder. The action was exceptionally familiar, almost as intimate as a deep kiss in greeting. Gina gently touched her head against the woman's and wrinkled her nose.

"You stink," Gina said in a long, joking tone of voice. Despite the jest, Dez noticed their new companion had a strange and heady scent, lacking those certain qualities usually associated with perfumes and soaps. Her scent wasn't offensive; instead it was as enthralling as she was. He couldn't imagine this was how she naturally smelled, yet it was the only conclusion he could draw.

"I'm sure I do, doll," she responded lazily. "I'll just rub up on you, get your good smell all over me," she cooed as she rubbed against Gina's shoulder, both laughing. At this point, she seemed to finally acknowledge Dez's existence. "And who might this be?"

"This is Dez," supplied Gina.

The woman stretched her arm across the table. "Suz. Pleased to meet *you.*" Dez immediately identified with every gazelle on earth that ever had a cheetah look their way as he shook her hand. "And where did we come from, Dez?"

"All over," Dez began. Gina found the reclusive act amusing, and a little cute, but she saw no point in humoring it now.

"Dez is from Vancouver and is a modern-day Kerouac

despite a tendency towards gainful employment."

"And possibly being in possession of talent," Quinn added as she wrapped her arms around Suz's shoulders before plopping back down in the booth next to Dez. "Which we'll find out soon enough," she said before turning to Dez.

"Talk to Nate over at Demon Aether," she said handing him a slip of paper with an address. "If he's not there, you can talk to Wendy. They'll hook you up with a gig to play or serve coffee or both if you want."

"Cool. Appreciate that," he said taking the paper and studying it. "I'll check that out in the morning."

"And where are you staying while in town?" asked Suz.

"Downstairs from her," Dez pointed to Gina.

"In your old apartment," Gina said to Suz.

"Old 3A?" She said with a bit of nostalgic glee. Dez nodded. "Just remember to jiggle the handle on the toilet if it rains. It always stuck when it rained for some reason."

Exchanging more small talk, Dez learned that Suz danced at a local strip club (or "gentlemen's club" as she cynically corrected) called the White Rabbit. Dez could tell she had little trouble attracting attention and, more importantly, that she was fully aware of this ability. Further, she really knew how to use it to her advantage; something he figured gave her an edge in her occupation.

Over the course of the conversation, Dez gathered Suz was good at projecting an air of inanity to obscure a crafty intellect; with her looks, people probably expected her to be lacking in the brains department and she was more than happy to let them keep thinking that. Throughout the conversation, she talked a lot but said very little, especially about herself. Dez wondered how often anyone realized an exchange of information with Suz was severely lopsided in her favor. Then again, he wasn't bad at that game either. He learned a lot in the past few years and he'd like to think he was good at that game. However, he got the feeling Suz was in a whole different league.

Soon the four of them joined the others at the bar. They spent several hours celebrating Quinn's good fortune, with everyone getting to know the stranger in their midst. Dez warmed to everyone, far more than he usually did, and they seemed to take to him as well.

After all this time, he had never really given much thought to moving from place to place. He no longer had a home or much else keeping him tied to one location. All he had in Vancouver was long gone and nowhere else he'd been had much to offer. Here, though, he starting to think he could settle down. The last few years were beginning to wear him down. It made him happy to think, maybe, once he was done, he'd have some place he could call home.

If any place could ever be home.

If he'd ever be allowed a home of his own.

Chapter 3

He had been in town for a few days now and felt comfortable enough with the city. He knew his way around and where he would likely find his quarry. The Hunter was undeniably here- He could feel it in His bones- but they seemed distracted. Maybe the Almighty was working directly on the Hunter, giving explicit aid in this virtuous mission. Was this a sign He was close to being elevated? If that was the case, then He needed to remove all concern and doubt and concentrate solely on the task.

He found a park near the city's central library where, with school still out for summer, many young people chose as an easy place to socialize. In His experience, at such places He would find many would-be whores looking to catch the attention of some unsuspecting boy or man in order to drag them down into the flames with her. This one was no exception. Most of them lingered on the sides, their culpability and eagerness hardly diminished by their passivity. Any of them would make a fine selection and He could no doubt save some unwary fool a few troubles. Future marks, perhaps, because all of them paled to the true wolf in sheep's clothing.

As with many- all, if He were being honest- of His marks who had come before, He found her arousing. Sensations stirred in ways He would rather not think about. He interpreted this as a sign the Almighty had chosen a suitable mark; one that truly embodied the Adversary's baseness and deceit. She was pretty and slender, with a body suggesting she went to great lengths to keep fit. The body is of course a temple, He had to concede, but He found it obvious she did so only to make her enticements of weak flesh that much easier. Her long golden hair gleamed in the afternoon sun, making her all the more noticeable.

Even her displayed hobbies and interests were geared toward enticement. Most of the boys congregating in this park seemed to be into skateboarding, among other similar activities, and she had latched onto this sport to worm her way into their graces. Although she showed remarkable skill with the hobby, He found it brazenly obvious she was only pretending to enjoy the pastime, either as a participant or an observer.

Naturally, her efforts paid off. The boys crowded her like little flowers straining for the sun. They raptly listened as she spoke, or at least acted as if they did. Whenever she performed a trick on her skateboard, the boys devotedly ooh'd and aah'd as if her talent was amazing, despite their actual intentions being wholly evident. Over the last few days He heard a passing comment from one boy or another about how much they'd like to sleep with her, but she seemed to not reciprocate any such desire. This was a common piece of chicanery used by harlots: pretend to be above and beyond those desires so males would want them more. Fruit need not be forbidden to be craved, after all; just simply out of reach. He lamented how these young boys lacked awareness of this, but what upset Him more was how they likely wouldn't care even if they were.

As is often the case, the other girls flocking to this place engaged in niceties to her face, but quickly reverted to spitefulness when out of earshot. Frankly, the banality of this fussy process was tiresome, and He wondered why He bothered being so selective. Correcting any of them would greatly improve the state of the world, in his opinion. Although their seductive ways were bad enough, He found a female's lack of earnestness far more offensive than her potential or actual promiscuity.

Yet judgment was not His commission, nor was it His place to question.

He was drawn from His thoughts by a fast moment of

excitement. The kids suddenly started leaving. It was not clear why; the young were often slaves to their most immediate and ephemeral cravings. He tried to follow their movements through the chaos. They collected their belongings and jumped about, piling into various vehicles. He had no idea where they were going and, after noticing she was not leaving with them, had little care. She waved to them as they pulled away, watching them drive away before returning to her skateboard.

He waited a minute, made sure no one was paying any attention to Him or her. Satisfied, He stood, drew a charming smile across His face, and approached her.

Little more than an hour later He was back at His lodgings. The water ran over him, taking the blood from His body and making it disappear down the drain. He held her in His mind. Her face; the look in her eyes; the golden hair between His fingers; the skin giving way. Finally, her warm blood splashing across His lips. He could still feel her body against His; could still taste the last of her breath in his mouth.

He did have to admit the thought of elevation in the eyes of the Almighty had made Him overzealous with this one. He dragged her body down several blocks, forcing the people to look at the exposed instrument of the Adversary. He pleaded with them to reject their inequities, to give themselves back to the Almighty. In the end they could only gawp or turn away, if they even acknowledged His lessons at all.

He had to consider that, perhaps, He had gone too far, or expected too much. What was done was done, however. No use fretting over it now.

He made the celebratory mark on His thigh and discarded her body in the trash in an alleyway. He probably couldn't remember which dumpster if His life depended on it. That was more than she deserved but she was still one of the Almighty's children, fallen though she was, so He felt some shame. Between thoughts of the girl and the soap making things a bit slippery, He almost spent himself right then. It would have been disappointing if that had happened. He really wanted this one to last.

But, like always, it did not. She had already been forgotten, expunged from His mind. Still, the need came on again fast and hard. The Almighty wanted more. He would just have to find another one, but that would not be too difficult.

It never was.

It wasn't long before the body was found.

Although people reported the spectacle of a man dragging a young girl down the street, and cops responded to the confused and baffled accounts as well as they could, it took a garbage crew to find her remains in a dumpster early the next morning. The details started pinging various databases across the country. It was all quite familiar: the state of the body, age of the victim, no concern about concealment by the perpetrator, confused and contradicting eye witness accounts, physical evidence that would soon be deemed useless. It was a story that popped up throughout the United States, even in areas of Canada and Mexico, over the last several years. The bodies would suddenly pile up in one place and just as abruptly stop, only to start up somewhere else.

Once a connection was made to link the various cases together, law enforcement agents eventually started calling the perp the Ghost.

Sara Post spent five of the last six years chasing the Ghost. Before that, her life had mostly been about following in her dead father's footsteps: ROTC, the Navy, and now the FBI. Although in her first year in the Bureau she worked on many important cases, none ever felt like they mattered until the Ghost case. It was a puzzle that had yet to be solved, but she came closer than anyone else so far.

Less than a year ago, she was positive she had caught the Ghost. After years of inconsistent witness accounts, reports placed a suspect at the scene of one murder. His name was Desiderio Salvia. The more Sara dug into Salvia's past, the more he fit the pattern. What's more was his sister, Lucille, was among the early victims. There were many before her from Washington, Oregon, and Idaho, with the earliest known in Northern California. All places within relatively easy travel from Salvia's residence in Vancouver. Through his itinerant lifestyle as a musician, he visited those states often.

After his sister's murder, Salvia fell off the grid, popping up every now and then. And each of those times would coincide with the Ghost's work. Then there was the Marsh case from West Virginia. Ellen Marsh was only 13 years old. As was usual with the Ghost, she had been viciously tortured, both before and after death, much of it sexual in nature. Salvia was seen hastily leaving the location where Ellen's body was found, and physical evidence placed him at the scene. While it wasn't much, it was enough to bring him in on suspicion.

The local cops picked up and detained Salvia, though not for very long. Additional eye witnesses soon came forward and placed another individual at the scene as well. The reports about the other individual fell more in line with the cases involving the Ghost. They contradicted each other, and wildly so. Most said Salvia followed this ambiguous person and possibly chased him away, albeit too late for the Marsh girl. However, the girl's body had not been defaced to the same extent as prior victims, suggesting the killer had been interrupted, probably by Salvia.

Salvia was released, but Sara couldn't let him go that easily. It was the closest anyone had come to identifying the Ghost. She became obsessed, letting other cases slip. Her supervisors eventually placed her on administrative leave. Despite being only a couple months- which included time spent in therapy- Sara found herself relegated to low-profile cases. She wasn't supposed to have access but, whenever a case that looked like the Ghost popped up, she managed to flag it and gather as much information as she could without bringing too much attention to herself. Sara had been in the middle of updating her own database on the Ghost with this most recent case when her uncle called.

Sara was close with her uncle, William. She always had been. He was her father's brother and, with her mother no longer around, when Sara's father detached from everything but his career with the FBI, William did what he could to fill the role of parent to her. When her father died, Sara barley mourned his passing, seeing little need to grieve for someone who had largely become a stranger to her while her "real" father stood by her side. Sara never told him as much, but William did better than his brother had in a long while. Later, when she was forced to take leave from the Bureau, her uncle was the only person in the agency fighting for her; even after it was clearly a losing battle. When the inevitable came, William was the only one who kept Sara focused and composed. Although she kept a detailed catalog regarding the Ghost, William tried to swing her attentions to other things. With his insistence that her fixation on the Ghost would only work against her in the long run, William helped Sara see her way through.

This was why his call requesting her archive on the Ghost struck her as so odd. Early the next morning, Sara found herself sitting in the waiting room of a Central Intelligence Agency director's office. She knew the CIA dealt with law enforcement, in theory, but usually at international levels. Why would they need her files on the Ghost? True he was dangerous and had strayed outside of the U.S. borders on several occasions, but he was hardly a threat to national security. Furthermore, nothing suggested the Ghost had ties with anything within CIA interests. Granted, the current ethos insisted on a higher level of cooperation between the various agencies than in times past, but that didn't make this meeting any less peculiar.

Especially since they specifically wanted *Sara's* profiles and collections on the case, not the FBI's.

Sara was looking over a few of the reports when the secretary announced the director would see her now. Gathering her things, she moved towards the door when an energetic young man in a military uniform almost bowled her over as he left the office. At just at five-foot even, Sara was used to people almost running over her. Had she not been preoccupied with her papers, she might have seen him coming. From his uniform she could tell he was a Marine. Only slightly taller than average, to her he may well have been a giant. Although it had grown out some, his hair still had the familiar Marine "high and tight", making it too short for her to tell its color. Although it was obviously flushed from excitement, his skin was pale- leaving Sara to guess his most recent post kept him out of the sun, but she noted it made the deep blue of his eyes gleam. He affably apologized to Sara before turning to shamelessly flirt with the receptionist.

No accounting for taste, she thought, side-eyeing the exchange as she gathered herself. The assistant's auburn hair, soft green eyes and pale, freckled face would have been alluring to her but something about the woman struck Sara as "off" in a way she couldn't put her finger on. That said; she was rather eye-catching so if the man found her attractive Sara wasn't going to hold it against him.

Once in the office, Sara found the director standing near the door, waiting to greet her. "Sorry for the delay, Agent Post. My son dropped in unannounced." With persistent pride, he vaguely indicated the door and the young man she passed on the way in. "He had some news he was quite thrilled about and couldn't wait to tell me." His gaze lingered on the door a moment longer before he really looked at her.

"Well deserved, I'm sure," she replied evenly. Mentally, she added *Hope whatever it is gives him some time out in the sun.*

He smiled at that as they shook hands, then she took the seat offered her. Still somewhat uneasy about this, Sara couldn't help but expect a reprimand awaiting her for this meeting. The absence of her uncle, who promised he would be here, made her trepidation even worse. With a deep breath, she pushed those worries aside since there was nothing she could do about them.

The director was in his late 40s, maybe early 50s, but he seemed to keep himself in good enough shape. Combined with his thin-rimmed glasses, his light brown hair had a few streaks of gray that gave him a classic, intellectual look, and an obvious cheerfulness from his last meeting broke through the business-like demeanor he might have been trying to affect. This helped put Sara at ease.

"I'm Director Nelson Lowden," he introduced himself as he

went back to his desk. As he lowered into his chair slowly, staring off into the distance. "You know, I think I met your father once or twice. A good man as I recall."

"Thank you," Sara mumbled. "He was," she quickly, and blandly, inserted after a noticeable second had passed. Lowden, however, didn't seem to detect her clumsy assertion.

"He and your uncle were almost twins," Lowden mused instead, eyes squinting as he studied Sara. "I'm guessing you take after your mother more." She acknowledged by nervously running a hand through her black hair as he dismissed the small talk with a wave of his hand.

"I had your file sent over yesterday; impressive read," he announced as he picked up the folder from his desk. "Let's see what we have here," he idly emitted while flipping through the pages within. "Sara Post. ROTC in high school, high marks; went into the Navy upon graduation but resigned under alleged Section 654 violations in 2002." Lowden raised his head and gave Sara a thoughtful though humorous look. "Let me take a shot in the dark. You never told, someone asked, yet *you* were the one in violation."

Sara knew it wasn't a question. Even if it had been she wouldn't have answered it. It was a touchy subject for her, a fact Lowden swiftly picked up on. With a cynical shake of his head he dropped the subject.

"Applied to Quantico after graduating Cornell, placing in the top five-percentile at both; entered the FBI in 2008 but placed on disciplinary action in March of this year due to excessive actions in the course of duty, creating an obstruction to resolution." The corners of his mouth drooped into brief deliberation before he closed the file and let it flop down on his desk.

Whatever misgivings he might have after reading her profile were quickly put out of mind. "Anyway, I'm sure you're wondering why you're here." Sara nodded tentatively. He jutted his chin out to indicate the briefcase and expandable file folder she brought in with her. "I take it those are your documents on the Ghost?"

"It's a lot I know," Sara replied, still not sure how to

respond to the situation.

"Well, your uncle did say you were thorough. Especially with this case," Lowden gave a disarming smile to indicate there was no judgment in his words. "That's good. I think we may need to know as much as we can on this Ghost person."

"Why?" Sara blurted. She regained her composure and continued. "I mean, you're CIA. The Ghost is a serial killer not a terrorist..."

"I appreciate that this seems like an unusual request... and, you're right: this person does *not* fall under the purview of *this* organization. Under normal circumstances it would stay an FBI matter." He paused a moment to make sure she processed his response. "These may not be normal circumstances, however. I'll be more than happy to explain that, and you might like what I have to say. But I need to know the details before I can make any determination."

Sara accepted that she'd have to play the game to find out its purpose. Lowden decided to start simple. "How many victims are we talking about?"

"This recent one will make 38 confirmed with an additional 23 at a high level of certainty though unsubstantiated." Lowden raised an eyebrow. Sara continued. "That we know about. A lot of girls within the Ghost's profile go missing every year. Given the erratic nature of his movements and the difficulty in tracking him..." she let that point hang in the air. Lowden took in a breath before asking Sara more questions.

They talked for about half an hour before William arrived. He apologized for being late and greeted Sara with a warm smile. The combination of her familiarity with the topic and William's presence put her more at ease. It wasn't long before her concerns about reprimands faded away.

Sara went over all her files on the Ghost in great detail. Every so often a question from one of the men would lead her on a tangent, leading to more questions. She found it difficult to follow the logic of their inquiries. While they seemed interested in finding the Ghost, the methodologies on display were far from usual. Ultimately, Sara had no idea what the purpose for this discussion was. In the end, it was well into the afternoon before the interview was over. No one in the room was left with very cheery outlooks.

"So, is this a 'normal circumstance'?" Sara asked after a moment of uncomfortable silence and it seemed the two men had finally run out of questions. Lowden and William exchanged quick glances that certainly translated well in some language, but only left Sara annoyed.

Finally, Lowden replied, "Not in the least." Despite his firm tone, Sara doubted the answer was the result of the gruesome nature of the subject.

"You think there's more to this than just some sick freak, don't you?" Still with no clue what the men were aiming for, this conversation began to grate Sara's nerves.

Lowden considered his approach for a moment and then sat up straighter in his chair. "Sara, what do you know of psychic phenomena?"

Sara waited for Ashton Kutcher or Alan Funt to jump into the room and tell her she was the unwitting butt of a televised joke. When that didn't happen, she decided to see where this would lead. "You mean like those guys who think they can conjure the first letter of your dead grandpa's name?"

Lowden and William both had a small chuckle at that. "No, not those guys," Lowden smirked. "No. What we're talking about are *real* psychics, Sara," he said it casually as though commenting on the weather. "Not those spoon benders or anything like that. We're talking about the *legitimate* ones." Once again, this was delivered with a disarming laugh meant to lighten the mood.

"Then I would have to say that I do not know anything of the subject, sir," Sara deliberately uttered each word separately. Her eyes cut over to William who gave her an easy smile. She was getting pretty upset, but she doubted her uncle would play such a tasteless joke on her.

Detecting her impatience, Lowden attempted to reassure her. "Agent Post, we're not having a bit of fun at your expense and we're certainly not trying to embarrass you. Your work is impressive. In fact, I'd say your uncle's glowing description was a serious understatement," he said, rounding the desk and placing a hand on her shoulder. "You've been patient enough, so I'll cut to the chase. But this'll seem beyond belief."

"Just trust us that it's the truth, Sara," William interjected.

Lowden cleared his throat and began. "You may be passingly familiar with the incident in Roswell, New Mexico, back in '47. Many claim an unidentified craft of alien origin crashed there and the U.S. government has spent over half a century covering it up..."

"... and doing such a bad job of it that almost anyone with a library card or internet connection can easily expose it," William glibly added.

Lowden chuckled softly and proceeded. "I doubt I need to tell you that it wasn't an alien spacecraft, nor was it a weather balloon, but something *did* happen that night in Roswell'" He paused a moment to give her a chance to ask questions. When none came he went on. "You'll have to forgive me if I can't tell you *what* exactly but suffice it to say it scared the living shit out of the few people in Washington who knew.

"Of course, it wasn't exactly anything new. There've been reports and accounts like this going back to humanity's early days. Myths and religions have been built around it all, some still going strong today, but none of them ever got it right. They couldn't, I guess, until now since this was the first valid documented evidence that there is far more to it all than we could have ever fathomed. Since then we found that psychics, witches, ghosts, and all the stuff that goes bump in the night are real. Hell, probably even God!"

William elucidated. "Mostly. They at least have some basis in fact, even if the stories don't get it right."

Lowden looked like he might disagree, but let it slide. "The government tried to look into it further, but most of the agencies at the time had their hands full dealing with communism and the general paranoia of the next decade. Finally, an organization was founded in '53 that was meant to specifically investigate all things paranormal."

"Sort of like the FBI except instead of criminals you, what, chase the Boogie Monster?" Sara said incredulously with a small huff of laughter. "Got Bigfoot locked up in Gitmo yet or is that case still open?"

"Agent Post... *Sara*... I understand your skepticism and that's good," Lowden replied. "Uncertainty helps keep one objective in light of the situation. People find out one thing exists and before you know it they're spreading pepper in their yard and leaving milk out for the Wee Folk."

"Yeah, because that'd just be crazy," Sara jeered, gathering her files. "I'm sure you have a pack of werewolves somewhere you need to chase down so I'll just get out of your hair now." She stood to leave.

"Sara, please!" William softly took her shoulder and turned her to face him. "I know how this sounds. I thought it was a joke when I was first introduced to it and I had a good reason to think otherwise."

With her uncle's pointed words, a memory was dredged up from the recesses of Sara's mind. She couldn't remember how old she was, but she couldn't have been older than six or seven. Her parents were throwing a 4th of July party; neighbors and their kids were there, and it was a nice day. At some point her dad asked Sara to check in on her uncle in the guest room, see if she could coax him down to join the party. He had been staying with them for a few weeks after being hospitalized with a serious injury. Sara had known her uncle had been in some foreign country before then, she wanted to say somewhere in the Middle East, but she couldn't remember where. She did know it was the reason why he was discharged from the military.

During those weeks she saw little of William, even though they were usually inseparable during his visits. He stayed in his room day and night. Occasionally he'd sit at the table for breakfast or dinner, but he rarely ate more than a few bites and looked as if he'd hardly slept.

And he was always jumpy.

She remembered waking up a few times to hear William and her father talking in her father's office. William always sounded anxious during these discussions, but she never heard what they were about.

She did as her father asked and went to his room. Sara had her uncle wrapped around her finger- if anyone could get William to join the party it would be her. She could hear her uncle moving about the room; she knocked but he didn't answer. Maybe it was too soft for William to hear or maybe he ignored the knock. Sara opened the door anyway and saw her uncle standing before a mirror wearing only a pair of pajama pants. She watched him as his fingers held open one of his eyes, studying it intently before doing the same with the other. He then drove up his eyebrows, pushed in his cheeks and pulled at his lips. She saw the nasty scar that ran across his chest, shoulders, and down his back.

Sara didn't say anything, just closed the door and told her father that William was sleeping. A week later, some men came to the house and asked William to accompany them somewhere. Sara's father wouldn't allow it without him going too. When they returned both men seemed to have aged 10 years in the few hours they were gone. They talked only to each other for the next few days.

However, it wasn't long after her uncle seemed to get better. He was soon honorably discharged from the military and brought into the FBI, but he didn't talk about his work. Although he never treated Sara differently William was never the same. He became distant- not always but often enough- like he wanted to say something but could never quite figure out the words or knew it'd do no good. Her father, on the other hand, emotionally drifted away over the next few years. It eventually chased her mother away and left Sara starving for approval that never appeared. Her dad died in some unfamiliar and lonely hospital room. She was with him until his last breath, but if he recognized or appreciated that act of devotion Sara surely couldn't say.

Now she wondered if this was what her father and uncle had gotten wrapped up in. Did she lose her family because literal monsters were real? A part of her wanted to believe it all, especially if the Ghost was in some way involved. Fairly accomplished, Sara prided herself on her achievements (even if they did sometimes run within the mundane). The Ghost was her one failing, in her mind at any rate. That she had come closer than anyone else to catching him made it all the worse. If the Ghost had some power- some preternatural ability- no one could have guessed at, well it might put a sugar-coating on the bitter pill.

Sara sat back down. "Okay... say there are monsters and what not out there; what does that have to do with the Ghost?" It occurred to her that the moniker given to the killer may have been unintentionally apt. "Is he a ghost? Can ghosts kill people?"

"No, not a ghost and, as far as we can tell, ghosts can't really hurt people. Not physically anyway," Lowden replied. "We think he may have some rare psychic ability allowing him to alter people's perception and memory on a mass scale, if only limited to him."

"Maybe it's just that my experience is limited to a few crappy late-night movies here, but wouldn't that be a common thing for psychics?"

"Not to the degree evident in the Ghost's case. The psychics we've come across tend to have very low levels of ability. Not to mention a narrow scope. For example, someone who displays telepathic capability might glean a stray surface thought or two but nothing from long term, or even short term, memory and they certainly couldn't control anyone," Lowden explained. "Beyond that, there's no evidence to date that any psychic is much stronger than what we've seen."

William made a noise. It erupted from the back of his throat and to most it would sound like an attempt at stifling a cough, which is what Lowden evidently took it for since he pulled some lozenges from his desk and threw one to him. Sara, however, recognized it as the sound her uncle often made when he disagreed with something, but wasn't going to voice his opinion.

"How many psychic psychopaths have you come across?" inquired Sara, ignoring any misgivings she had about her uncle's reaction to what was just said.

"A few but they were hardly any worse than a run-of-the-mill psychopath," William, now recovered, answered. "And their abilities weren't exactly an aggravating factor in their psychosis or danger," he added as he slipped the tablet into his mouth.

"Unlike here if we're right," Lowden adjoined. "A psychotic

with the ability to move about as he pleases; with no way to track him until he starts killing; can kill with a crowd of witnesses and still walk away with no one able to agree on even the basics of what he looked like." He shook his head once before keenly staring at her. "Agent Post, you know this guy better than anyone. Whether he falls under our domain or not, the Ghost needs to be stopped. We're offering you another chance to do just that."

Sara played at taking time to think about this. She wanted another crack at the case, officially, and without having to scavenge about for new information. She wasn't sure about this whole psychic deal, but she had no qualms playing nice with deluded loons if that's what it took. "Okay. I'll go along with you on this one. Can't say I buy all the talk about witches and goblins yet, but I'll go along for now."

"A chance is all we ask, Agent Post," Lowden said happily. "Given your inexperience and understandable doubt, we'll pair you with your uncle on this case. Sound good?" he offered with an easy smile.

"Sure," Sara answered. William's presence might help with the insanity of the situation. "We'll start with the latest murder," she said looking at her uncle.

"Agreed, what's the location?" William asked.

Sara handed him her file on the most recent killing. He silently read the city's name and felt his stomach drop.

It just had to be *there*.

It was over 20 years ago, and William had been given his first real assignment with the Agency. Initially, he'd hoped it to be therapeutic but that hope died quickly. He stayed in the surgery theater's observation room, sitting next to Dr. Andrei Basov, a scientist who defected from the Soviet Union in the late 1960's. William wasn't sure of which scientific field Basov was involved or where his expertise lay, but he had heard terms like "brilliant" and "genius" thrown about often and quite casually in reference to the man.

43

William's preferred term for him, on the other hand, was "unhinged", though that was only when he felt like being charitable.

Basov watched intently, his face a stone mask, as nurses ran wildly about the room. One collapsed in a corner, begging unseen phantoms to leave her alone. Another had been taken from the room, blood spurting past the scalpel she abruptly drove into her own neck. There were several moments over the last few hours when William felt reality was unraveling around him; dire voices whispered to him from the edges of his consciousness as a familiar and dreadful shadow shuffled about in a far corner of the room. He was warned this might happen. That *she* had a way of getting inside a person's head and playing with their mind. Somehow, he managed to push all of it away, noticing all the while her eyes were raptly locked onto him from the table where she was strapped down.

Source 715K was in the midst of giving birth, but if she felt any pain it was impossible to tell. She was still. She was silent. Her only apparent reaction was an eerie calmness that stood in direct paradox with agitation and panic that permeated everyone, with Basov seemingly the sole exception, around her.

Then, with a crooked smile and croaked laugh, she decided to let everyone within the room feel the birth pains. William, falling back against the wall, had never felt anything like it before (or since). Basov doubled over, almost vomiting, while the delivery doctor fell to his knees, screaming and clawing at his abdomen. Possibly acting on prior instructions, a nurse managed to inject a sedative into 715K. Even then, 715K was still awake although the effects of her more worrisome abilities faded. William shook the last of the pain away and helped Basov back to his feet, intentionally pulling him up rougher than was needed; for reasons he couldn't fully quantify William found himself repulsed by the scientist. The delivery took several more hours with all present enduring disturbing occurrences the entire time.

At last, the baby was born. "It's a girl," the doctor shouted out over her shoulder. Perhaps someone was supposed to be taking notes, but none remaining bothered.

She was having trouble breathing and was rushed to a side table. Basov hurried into the delivery room to interject his opinions over the doctor and nurses trying to get the baby's lungs to work. William was supposed to stay by Basov's side. However, he felt a remnant of 715K's manipulations lurking within the delivery room, waiting for him to come near. He stayed just inside the doorway, willing himself to no longer see that malignant shade. Then William looked at the woman lying on the delivery table, truly seeing her as a human being and not a test subject.

She was young, how old exactly William couldn't say. He doubted she was older than 20; suspected she was much younger. The operation was need-to-know only, and William's need was low, so he knew very little of the project or its subjects. He would learn more later, but for the moment all he knew about 715K was that she was like every other subject: young and disowned by family, assuming she ever really had one to begin with. In short, she was deemed someone who wouldn't be missed because no one cared to know she ever existed to begin with.

He took in the sluggish way her head moved about now, a line of drool pouring from a corner of her mouth. One eye lazily twitched opened and closed while the other stayed wide open but idle and unfocused. He had never seen eyes so pale blue before and nearly lost himself within them. Suddenly he heard a voice in the back of his mind, tiny and from far away. He couldn't understand what it was trying to tell him, but he knew he wouldn't like it if he had.

Knew, no matter what he did, it would play a role over the course of his life in some way.

William found it odd to see 715K as dread incarnate just a moment ago when he considered her so peaceful and soothing now. From across the room she focused in on William, her one good eye meeting his. After a distressing, prolonged moment of scrutiny, seeing through him or beyond him as he was now, she gave him a sad, almost admiring, smile.

He snapped back to the here and now when the baby began crying. Basov muttered excitedly in Russian as the doctor checked the girl's vitals. William kept watching as 715K lazily turned her head in the general direction of the sounds her child was making. After a moment she began to giggle, low at first but rising in volume until it became a wet, maniacal cackle. The baby abruptly stopped her wailing and turned her head towards her mother's laughter.

The mirth stopped as white foam began to sputter from 715K's mouth and her body convulsed. A nurse tried to hold her down, to prevent her from harming herself. The doctor hurried to her side, shouting orders as he went. Basov instead walked calmly over to William. The scientist mumbled something, but due to his accent, thickened now with excitement, William didn't comprehend. The scientist's face twisted with annoyance as he reached into William's jacket and pulled the gun from the holster within. Basov fired a single shot that caught 715K just above her idling eye. The nurse holding her down was now covered in the young woman's blood and trembled with fear and confusion.

The baby cried again. This time everyone in the room felt its fear and anger.

William didn't see the girl, referred to as Subject 178, or Basov again until almost three years later. This time he and another agent had been sent in with a team of contractors to eradicate the project. It seemed Basov had decided the girl was a weapon he could use for his own gain. The facility housed a couple other Agency research projects and the teams working on them, not just Basov's. Unfortunately, those teams were to be neutralized as well. The progress on those could be saved but it'd take some time before they were started again. It disgusted William to kill innocent people, especially the doctors and nurses and general staff. But given what went on in the facility he could hardly look at many of them as being totally innocent.

That consideration assuaged his conscience to some extent. Beyond that, he had his orders. That's what he told himself.

William was mildly upset he was not the one who found Basov. Apparently, the scientist tried to use an intern as a human shield, not realizing the intern was to be put down as well. Most of the project's workers had been eliminated, but Subject 178 was nowhere to be found. Eventually William discovered her hidden away in a side lab, a nurse huddled protectively over her. Within were a pair of the mercenaries, dead and apparently killed by each other. The nurse kept herself between William and the girl. He tried to fire, but the same pale blue eyes he lost himself in a few years earlier looked at him now from over the nurse's shoulder.

She might have been a living weapon, a danger to all, but all William could see in front of him at that moment was a young girl who hadn't hurt anyone. Not without cause at any rate, he considered as he glanced down at the body of his fellow agent.

He lowered his gun, swiftly crossed the room, and grabbed the nurse's arm. She started to scream as he yanked her to her feet, but he assured her that he wasn't going to hurt her or the girl. Instead, he was going to help them get out. It was insane, and he really didn't know why he was doing this. He didn't know *how* he was going to do it, either. It just seemed right. Later, when he looked back on that day, it seemed he had been working off a plan he devised long before then.

More precisely, he had been working off a plan that had been devised for him.

William stayed ahead of them, guiding them through the carnage of death and fires he and his team created. He got them to a service exit where he knew three stationed contractors waited to catch anyone attempting to escape. He told the two to wait while he sent the others away. With a story about how Subject 178 was reportedly pinned down on the north side of the facility and back-up was needed, he was certain it wouldn't work. The lie was weak, he knew it, but there was something fixed to his words, like something else was simply using his voice, giving it credence to the hired guns. As soon as William was sure they were gone, he headed back to retrieve his charges.

William gave his instructions to the nurse, where to go, what to do, etc. As he spoke he again found something correcting his directions mid-sentence. Something else was providing information to him. His instinct screamed accusations that, somehow, it was Subject 178's doing, but she was barely three years old. Besides, he had worked hard practicing techniques that would shield him from her influence.

That's what he told himself.

He stood inside the door and watched as the nurse walked away with 178. His eyes never left them until they were pulling away in a car, rounding a turn, and disappearing from his sight. No one else saw them leave. William later found out the three he sent to reinforce the north side had been mistaken for staff and were gunned down through friendly fire. An explosion in Subject 178's room left the place such a wreck that no bodies could be retrieved. Between the other agent radioing she was cornered in her room and her expected capabilities, no one questioned how such a fiery and all-consuming inferno occurred.

Not even when considering the team had not been supplied with explosives. All were presumed dead.

Over the next few months William kept tabs on the nurse as best as he could. She made it frighteningly easy. She gave her name as Alma and, though she largely did as William told her, she made some mistakes. He expected that; Alma had struck him as a person who was decent at heart and people like that almost always underestimate the depths unscrupulous people will sink. As such, they can never imagine routes open to those with little to no conscience. William covered their tracks for them easily enough, but anyone really looking would see right through the façade.

Still, she did impress him. Alma managed to place the child with a young couple. As far as they knew, the girl was a year younger than her actual age. William didn't know if that was a bit of cleverness on Alma's part or simply a guess. He kept track of her over the years, saw she did alright in school and made friends. Most importantly, she never exhibited any abilities other than those of a normal girl. A few strange occurrences happened around her, but nothing worthy of grabbing the wrong attention.

It wasn't long after 178 was placed with her new family, the one who gave her the name Gina and seemed to genuinely care for and love her, that William had an opportunity to approach them. The girl was away with her new mother, but the father was home. The conversation was terse, as William expected.

Were you told of what your daughter can do?

We were told that she was... special. We've seen a little of what she can do.

Special? More than you can ever imagine and if you want to keep her and everyone around her safe, you'll see that she contains it, never uses it.

Couldn't we teach her to use it right?

Maybe but then they'd know. They'll never go for her, not at first. They'll go for you and your wife.

If it'll keep her safe, I'm fine with that and I bet my wife would be too.

You can be sure they'll bank on that. With you gone, what would she have to keep her human?

She is human.

Not to them. To them she's a weapon that can either be used by them or by no one. So long as she's alive, she can be used by someone else, in their mind. Teach her well, Mr. Shields. Teach her to be kind and compassionate or whatever you want her to be but if you want her to be safe, you'll teach her to keep what she can do to herself. You'll teach her to forget it if you can.

All in all, William had hoped that she would get to live out her life as normally as she could. Then again, his lack of belief in coincidence rivaled that hope. Now, sitting in Lowden's office a score of years later, looking at the city his niece pointed out, he knew whatever chance Subject 178 had at a normal life was now likely shot to hell. A killer had chosen *her* home to play in and if the Agency's suspicions about him were correct, it might be beyond what they could bring to the table.

Chapter 4

The girl smashed the over-sized buttons on the small plastic guitar with an exuberance that wasn't as pretend as she insisted. She overdramatically jumped about the cleared off area of the living room, striking rock star poses at particularly harder "chords" while making exaggerated faces. She rocked her head back and forth or side to side slightly, not wanting to take her eyes from the screen. Her dirty blonde hair managed to swish about all the same. Despite her earlier claims about the game's stupidity Gina got the impression her cousin's mockery was just a typical teenager method of masking her enjoyment with something supposedly so juvenile.

"I wished they'd put some P.J. Harvey on here," Cinnamon commented as she dipped down at the knees while pulling on the whammy bar as the game prompted, her mouth open in a silent, ferocious scream. A smirk crossed her face as she stood back straight. Currently she was "playing" "Only Happy When It Rains" by Garbage and doing well as far as Gina could tell. "That'd be cool, don't you think?"

Gina kept the smile her cousin's reference invoked small. She knew this suggestion meant Cinnamon had been listening to that artist a good bit recently, as Gina had prompted not too long ago. Gina had heard the girl play guitar for real a thousand times, alone and in the band she and Trevor put together. She found the girl's talent and presence grow more impressive with each passing year. Along with her gift with the guitar, Cinnamon's singing voice was primal and more than a little fearsome. Often Gina would put forward an artist or band she felt might inspire or encourage her cousin's talent.

"Any ones in particular?"

"I'd go for 'Rid of Me'," the girl replied as the game's song concluded. Cinnamon watched as her score tallied and the computerized audience cheered. The higher the score got the bigger her smirk. "I fuckin' love that one."

"Me too, but I think it takes too long to get going as far as this game goes," Gina replied. "Some Rollins Band would be cool, too." Cinnamon looked at her with one eye squinted, a look indicating she was considering her older cousin closely. Pointing her in a certain direction could sometimes be a uncertain effort in the last few years, Gina had found. Finally, the girl shrugged, presumably in acceptance, as she pulled the guitar controller over her head.

"When's Trevor getting back?" Gina asked. "I can't wait to meet his little girlfriend. Since she had to cancel coming to dinner the other night I'm really curious now."

"He'll get here soon I guess," Cinnamon answered blithely as she leaned the plastic guitar against the TV stand. "He called just before you got here and asked if he could bring Mason over too. So, you know, they'll probably fuck off at his place for a bit before they head back here."

"Mason, huh? Well, that explains a few things."

Trevor's friend Mason had a crush on Cinnamon since the day she and her mother moved into Frankie's house. He was a good kid in Gina's opinion, but he tended to put girls off by trying to be something he wasn't- such as *anything* other than a total geek. He generally annoyed the piss out of Cinnamon, although not nearly as much as she claimed.

"What the fuck's that supposed to mean?" the young girl demanded as she plopped down on the couch next to her cousin. The question was rhetorical since she already knew what Gina was hinting at, the two having had this conversation many times before.

"He's not that bad once you get him to calm down is all I'm

saying."

"Fuck that and I know where you live and make good grades in chemistry is all *I'm* saying!" Cinnamon retorted, her laugh making it clear she enjoyed the teasing.

"Then why'd you wear that *Buffy the Vampire Slayer* shirt?"

"What of it?"

"It's only one of Mason's favorite shows."

"So?"

"So, he'll have to comment on it and..."

"Fuck off!"

"Language, Cinnie!" April, Cinnamon's mother, shouted from the kitchen. The cousins looked behind them, seeing her standing inside the kitchen, and snorted. Being just short of six feet, April may have been tall like her half-brother and inherited the same open blue eyes, but she lacked the firm gravitas Frankie's voice carried. This usually mitigated any warning or threat to members of the family. April once tried to keep her daughter's vocabulary clean of vulgarisms, but recognized it was a losing battle around the girl's ninth birthday. She still made a show of it from time to time. Given Cinnamon's life so far, April was glad her daughter's prevalent use of foul language was her only real vice.

"Tell me, what's Trev-bear's girl like?" Gina asked to bring the subject back to what she really wanted. "What's her name again? Jen?"

"Sweet Jen, yeah."

April had started attaching the word "Sweet" to Jen's name, from what Frankie told Gina, and it somewhat stuck. She explained that it was to distinguish her from one of Cinnamon's friends, also named Jen- April had no cute monikers for *that* Jen, but she made up for it with more than a few dirty looks.

"She's cool. Into bugs so, you know, that's creepy," the younger girl emphasized with a knowing look before going on. "But she's nice as can be all the same. Kinda quiet, probably 'cause her parents are serious fuckin' asshats. Half the time she looks like she might jump out of her fuckin' skin and run away."

"Skittish, huh?" Cinnamon answered with a careless shrug

of her shoulders. "I'm sure *you* do your level best to keep the poor dear relaxed," Gina smirked. That got Gina a light punch to her upper arm and called a "fucker". She was hoping to get a little more information about this girl from her cousin, but April called Cinnamon to help get dinner on the table. Having to resort to another source, Gina went out to the garage where her father was working on another one of his projects. Other than cars and tattoos, Frankie's hobbies fluctuated too often for Gina to keep them straight. She was at the garage door when the squeak of breaks from the driveway told her she could get the information first hand.

As they walked in the house, Trevor was explaining his theory on how the character of Grandpa Joe from *Willy Wonka and the Chocolate Factory* demonstrated behavior far worse than any of the supposedly horrible kids.

"...only lay his ass up in bed for 20 years, doing nothing but smoking and bitching about cabbage, while his daughter worked her fingers to the bone doing everyone's laundry but can suddenly jump up and do a song and dance when Charlie gets a golden ticket, and that's just for starters. Listen to the song, 'I Got a Golden Ticket'? Not 'Charlie's Got a Golden Ticket' or even 'We Got a Golden Ticket'? Hell no! The fuck with Charlie and everyone else, Ol' Grandpa Joe's the one with a golden ticket and gonna get him some chocolate!"

Trevor broke off his diatribe when he saw his sister. He smiled and hugged her as if it had been months or years since he last saw her instead of just a few days. He stood head and shoulders above her; his hair, faded red same as their mother's, seemed short but was just where he hadn't styled it in his usual mohawk, instead letting it fall around his head. He was wearing an old work shirt from some mechanic's shop which once belonged to someone named "Doug", who likely outweighed Trevor by a good 70 or 80 pounds. She greeted Mason with a hug as well and told him she thought his hair was growing back nicely from that 4th of July incident that inspired him to shave his head.

Finally, Trevor introduced her to Jen. She was as nice as everyone had said, and pretty to boot. She was just a touch taller than Gina, with thick, wavy dark hair and honey-colored eyes. Her body was thin and compact, likely from her years dancing ballet, as April had mentioned. Smiles came easy to the girl, but Cinnamon was right, she did seem nervous and jumpy. Gina wanted the chance to get to know her a little more, but her aunt announced dinner was ready. After offering to retrieve her father from the garage, Gina softly patted Jen on the shoulder hoping to put the girl at ease.

Turning toward the garage, she suddenly found herself standing in the maternity ward of some hospital. There were several newborns asleep in bassinets as a nurse jotted notes in a logbook at a nearby desk, the calendar above her displaying year 1997; 15 years ago. Gina stood over a baby wrapped tightly in a pink blanket. The tag attached to the small bed bore the name "Holt, Jennifer" scrawled in thick black letters across it.

A tall thin man- grey of face and hair and dressed entirely in black- slid into the room. His gait was odd, leaving Gina mildly disturbed, but he moved as fast as he did silent. He made no effort to go undetected by the nurse, but she failed to notice him all the same. The man lightly pressed his fingers to the nurse's neck and her body instantly slumped over to the desk, her pen clacking to the floor and rolling away. The action was quick, giving Gina no time to warn the woman. The nurse's chest continued to move up and down though, indicating she was still breathing, still alive. Making his way to the baby beds, his steps made no noise despite the hard soles of his shoes. He stopped when he read the baby girl's name and stood at the opposite end of the bassinet from Gina.

"What's going on?" Gina asked, her pulse racing, hoping he would answer but he didn't even register her existence. She tried to knock the man on the shoulder but found she couldn't move. Her breathing came in hard gasps and her heart pounded harder as he leaned over the baby, studying her for a moment before muttering something too low for Gina to catch. He seemed distressingly joyous.

"What are you doing?" she demanded loudly, her voice breaking, as he held his hand over the sleeping girl's chest.

Something skittered out from his jacket sleeve and landed softly on the baby's forehead. The dark shape seemed to dance over the infant as Gina tumbled away from the scene and found herself in a strange bedroom.

She looked about and determined the room had to belong to a young girl, five or six years old. It was night and the only light was from a dim lamp on a white and pink desk. Coloring books and crayons were spread out over the desk's surface, toys and dolls lined along the back of the surface, and a pair of tiny ballet shoes hung from the foot of the bed.

From somewhere outside the room, Gina could hear shouts and cursing, a man and a woman in another room. The man was screaming while the woman spoke in hushed whispers. She couldn't make out anything being said, but she could tell as loud as the man was, the woman's words were somehow worse. A shuffle from the corner behind the bed brought Gina's attention back into the room. A small girl with wavy dark hair and tear-rimmed honey eyes huddled between the bed and the wall. She was scared and crying but trying to keep from making any noise. Gina wanted to hold her, tell it'd be okay, take her away- wanted to just do something, but she couldn't move.

She realized the shouting had stopped. Heavy footsteps thumped outside the bedroom door, growing louder and louder. The door slammed open, but Gina fell away again to find herself back in her father's home. Right outside the door leading to the garage with Frankie standing in front of her.

"Geez girl, you scared the hell out of me," he was saying with a small laugh, towering over her and holding her by the shoulders. Seeing the distress on his daughter's face Frankie worried a bit more. "You okay, baby doll?"

"Yeah?" Gina said, not really comprehending what her father had said, not quite sure if she was really where she appeared to be. "Yeah, I'm fine," she choked out a few seconds later. It was a lie, she was anything but fine. Nothing like this had ever happened before, not that she knew what "this" was. She recalled enough to know it had something to do with Jen, but what exactly, Gina couldn't fathom. Every instinct told her to tell her dad about what just happened, as she usually would, but she didn't know how or where to begin. It was so foreign Gina couldn't even begin to put it into words.

"Dinner ready?" Frankie asked; concern growing greater on his face as Gina just stared at him.

"Um, yeah," Gina replied uncertainly. "You can see me? Hear me? I'm right here, right?"

"Yeah. You sure you're feeling okay?"

"I don't know. Maybe I just need some food in my stomach," she weakly smiled, hoping to convince herself as much as her father. Frankie agreed with that, in his experience he didn't know of much that couldn't be solved with the application of food. By the time they began to eat, Gina had mostly collected herself, with credit for that going to a shot from the bottle of good whiskey Frankie kept in the garage.

April and Frankie sat at the ends of the table, and Mason made sure to sit across from Cinnamon. Gina found herself opposite from Jen. Not even remotely sure of what happened, Gina couldn't help seeing the scared little girl huddled behind her bed every time she looked at her brother's girlfriend. Did any of it occur or was this the start of a nervous breakdown? As April talked about something or another, Jen glanced over at Gina and found nothing but a hard stare. Realizing what she was doing, Gina tried to look away, but her eyes promptly fell back to Jen, who could only offer an uneasy smile.

Gina felt like kicking herself. Trevor seemed to really like this girl and Gina wanted to get to know her. Now she was probably putting the girl on the verge of pissing herself by acting like a complete oddball. Through the fog of self-recrimination Gina realized April was asking her something.

"Huh?" Gina bit her lower lip to bring her back to the here and now.

"I was asking about why your new friend wasn't able to make it tonight," April repeated. "What was his name again?"

"Dez," Gina answered as Cinnamon interrupted with a turn-about-is-fair-play comment regarding Dez. Gathering herself, Gina met it by complimenting her cousin's shirt. Mason's conspicuous reaction was enough to keep Cinnamon from making any other such comments for the night. "He was gonna come along but, I don't know, he was acting a little weird this afternoon. Just said he wasn't feeling up to company tonight."

"How do you mean, 'acting a little weird'?" Frankie's tone was wary. Dez was living in one of the apartments Frankie owned and it wouldn't be the first time someone had trashed the place or worse. That was a concern, certainly, but Gina knew Frankie was far more interested in the safety of her and the other people living the building.

"He was just, I don't know, kind of agitated. Asked about the girl they found and if any others had been killed the same way recently."

"That happened not too far from the apartments and the shop, right?" Trevor asked.

"Don't talk about that!" April cried. "I think about that... that girl was the same age as my baby," she said reaching out to Cinnamon, who was not a big fan of the parental anxiety happening next to her. April was concerned for Cinnamon's safety, but she knew her daughter could take care of herself. Her reaction had a bit of the melodramatic mixed in simply to annoy her child.

"Fuck sake's, mom. Someone trying that with me would get their ass kicked up between their teeth."

"I thought she was killed down near the library? That's about ten blocks away from the shop," Frankie put into the conversation.

"Did they ever say what the girl's name was?" Jen quietly asked.

"She was last seen down there, probably killed there, but the body was found across from Bug's Lounge," Mason answered.

"That jazz club? It supposedly happened in broad daylight; how did the body get that far without anyone seeing?" from Frankie.

"I don't think so. They probably won't because she was a minor, I'd guess," Trevor answered Jen.

"I know you can take care of yourself, baby, but I still worry," April said to Cinnamon.

"Not necessarily," Mason said about Trevor's speculation but what other possibilities existed in his mind he never said.

"World's full o' self-absorbed fucktards, Uncle Frank," Cinnamon said, ignoring her mother. "Probably no one gave two shits about the girl."

"I don't think you should use that word," Jen kindly advised Cinnamon.

"People called the cops. From what I heard they saw the guy carrying the girl, but all the calls gave messed up descriptions," Trevor said, probably repeating something he got off a website.

"What word? Fucktard?" Cinnamon asked Jen.

"Yeah," Jen answered.

"Like I said: fucktards," Cinnamon said in general. "What's wrong with fucktard?"

"I just think it's just a bad word," Jen answered. "Well, not 'fuck'," she said in a low and wavering voice, "but the '-tard' part is."

"She has a point, sweet pea," Frankie quietly said to Cinnamon. The girl nodded a reluctant acquiescence. April may not have had a bearing on Cinnamon's vocabulary, but Frankie had a good amount of success in that arena.

"Don't worry, Mrs. Pratchett. I'll make sure Cinnamon's safe," Mason said to April. April smiled and patted Mason on the shoulder. Everyone knew if the situation arose Mason would more likely need Cinnamon's protection rather than the reverse, but April appreciated the sentiment. Cinnamon stuck her arm out towards Mason, one finger raised at him. It wasn't the finger the girl would normally have raised. Instead it was her pointer finger, held loosely upward.

"Wha... What are you doing?" Mason asked her, his voice trembling a bit.

"I think she's wishing you out to the cornfield, dude," Trevor answered with mock seriousness.

"Are you?" Mason played at being worried, shifting a bit in his chair. "Are you wishing me to the cornfield?"

"I think so, son," Frankie said with amusement behind his

words.

"Aw man! Why're you wishing me to the cornfield?"

April pleaded with her daughter to stop wishing Mason out to the cornfield as Trevor and Frankie started talking about other episodes of *The Twilight Zone*. Gina's attention slipped back to Jen; particularly how rivulets of red started spreading out across her white blouse. The girl gave her another kind, nervous smile, but her eyes betrayed how she'd rather keep her interest on the conversations going on and not her boyfriend's weird sister staring at her *again*. Gina shut her eyes tight, hoping the action would bring her back to her senses before totally freaking the poor girl out and ruining something nice for Trevor.

She opened her eyes and found only her and Jen sitting at the table. The room was dark but there was a peculiar, low illumination about them. Outside the wind howled and thunder raged. Jen's blouse was soaked with red and Gina could hear blood trickle to the hardwood floor beneath the girl's chair. She was not bound or held down in any way, she just sat there with a sweet smile across her face. Lightening flashed, and Gina saw the man standing behind her for the briefest of moments. It was not the same tall, thin man from before; this one was younger and naked. Another flash and Gina saw the scars that tick-marked the man's body and the glint from the knife he held in his hand.

Even in the dark Gina could see the man's eyes. They were dead and wild, a sinister storm seethed behind them while his twisted mind was the calm eye of that storm. He barely moved his knife hand, but she was a thin line spread across Jen's throat. The young girl continued smiling as blood cascaded from the slash, pouring out from her mouth and coating her teeth, as her head fell back at a ghastly angle. A light grew from within the man, starting as a muted yellow radiance from the pit of his stomach and growing to a fiery and blinding white brightness. He rejoiced; screaming praise and ululations as the light consumed him completely. Then, as rapidly as it begun, all was dark again. Across from Gina, Jen was propped up in her chair reminiscent of a child's doll coming to rest after having been carelessly tossed aside. There was no spark to be found within her; just a morbid life-like shell left behind. The man was gone but his malignant specter remained.

The hand shot out from the gloom and spun Gina around in her chair. Those eyes were even with hers; dead and wild, a seething storm. She felt his mouth cover hers, their lips fusing, and his hands grope madly at her body. Then Frankie was holding her by the shoulder, shaking her gently. Everyone at the table was looking at her: April rose from her chair to get Gina a glass of water; Mason held her arms to keep her steady; Cinnamon and Trevor repeatedly asked what was going on; and Jen was asking how Gina was feeling, accompanying her concern with a genuinely kind yet desperate smile. Gina felt sick to her stomach, but she felt better knowing the girl showed honest concern even though she had to have been freaking her out all night.

April was returned with a glass of water, which Gina drank in huge gulps until Frankie told her to drink slowly. After a while Gina apologized, throwing out a half-assed excuse about not sleeping well recently, must've had a fainting spell or something. She excused herself to lay down in the living room. After dinner Trevor took Mason and Jen home, the girl going out of her way to give Gina a warm goodbye.

Gina could still feel the specter hanging about; its wicked hands on her, mouth locked with hers. As April and Cinnamon cleaned up, Gina dug her phone out from her backpack. She called Quinn first, getting no answer but leaving a message. Then she dialed Suz, a few rings and someone picked up, there was unruly laughter and people talking loudly from the other end.

"'Lo?" Suz's purring voice cut through.

"Hey, it's me."

"It *is* my lucky night then," Suz's grin could almost be seen over the phone, which made Gina feel a little better.

"You at work?"

"I am but not for too much longer."

"Need a ride home?"

Suz hummed. "Well, Chastity was going to give me a lift, but you know I always play loosey-goosey with my plans." Gina smiled, some of the worry lifting away from her. With her next words, Suz nearly drove all her trepidation away. "Especially if I think you'll come calling."

"Cool," she replied in a small but pleased voice. "See ya in a bit."

Chapter 5

Between his years in the military and having lived in Washington D.C. most of his life, William was used to heat and humidity. He wasn't prepared for August this far south, making him feel every single one of his years the moment they stepped off the plane. Their arrival in the mid-afternoon meant they were probably getting the full brunt of the heat of the day as well. His shirt instantly fixed itself to his skin. He hoped for a breeze, but when one came along it felt more like a blast furnace, making him instantly regret that wish. Sara seemed to be fine with it though. Then again, she also didn't appear to notice anything not pertaining to the Ghost. As such, she was greatly annoyed when her uncle asked her to hold his suitcase while he took off his coat and loosened his tie.

A car was waiting for them. It wasn't long before they were on their way to the local police precinct managing the case. Once there, the atmosphere was mixed- the local police detectives on the case resented the presence of Federal agents, but the grisly nature of the crime made them glad to give it to someone else to handle. Not to mention the pressure they were under to solve it as fast as possible. The victim turned out to be from a family with a few prominent city attorneys, and the media was not being kind to the local cops. Still, they gave some resistance at first, which only annoyed Sara.

In the end, the locals gave over all the reports and evidence they collected after dwindling fuss. There was a surprise, even to William, when Sara asked to see the remains. The medical examiner's report was included, and Sara had no training necessitating seeing the body first-hand. However, she insisted, claiming there were particulars of the case an M.E. might not look for or notice. An officer was assigned to drive them the several blocks to the county morgue, his annoyance at this task obvious. She spent half an hour with the remains, alone as she demanded. When she was through Sara found William waiting for her in the outside hallway.

"What was that about?" he asked with more concern than anything else. She could tell he was already wondering if bringing her in on the case was a mistake. It pissed her off, but that anger was blunted by William's apparent concern for her well-being, not her capability. She also appreciated he waited until they were alone to question her instead of calling her competency into question in front of an audience, an experience Sara was regrettably well acquainted with.

"I needed to see the body."

"Why? I've been over the files too; there wasn't likely anything to be found by examining the body that the examiner didn't already have in their report."

"To remember what I'm doing this for," she elucidated after some self-conscious hesitancy. "The only break we've ever had was after I viewed the body of the victim before Ellen Marsh. Seeing that brought clarity; made it certain what it was about, that it was more than just another case."

She took a deep breath; the humid air and stale exhaust of the parking garage almost made her choke. She let out a nervous laugh. "Or maybe I'm just being stupid and superstitious. Either way, I just hoped to get whatever it was again."

"Okay," William took her shoulder in hand. "Let's get started then."

They headed back to the police station and were given a spare office. By now it was late into the evening, though the sun remained well above the horizon. Their bodies were still on Eastern Time instead of Central and William was beyond starving.

A nearby Chinese place delivered dinner, but Sara hardly touched hers except when William insisted.

It was well after sunset when they checked into their hotel room. The room was cheap and rather cramped, but it was clean as well as near the station, the crime scene, and anywhere else they might need to go. William was really feeling the mugginess and needed to take a shower. He was, physically and emotionally, drained. He worried his niece was putting too much of herself into something she might never be able to finish. Should the Ghost vanish again, especially if Sara once more came close to catching him, what would that do to her?

He had seen such obsession before in his brother, and to what that led.

Then there was the assignment; the things the Ghost had done were ghastly, but William had seen worse. However, those had mostly been done by... entities... that could hardly be called human, regardless of their appearance. The Ghost, as far as anyone could tell, was human even if a very sick one.

On the flight down, he thought a lot about the move he was about to make, not that Sara's company gave him any distraction. For his niece's sake he had only one wild card to bring in on this case.

Finished with his shower William dressed in more casual clothes- dark slacks and a white button-up shirt- that were indistinguishable from his business attire to anyone other than William. With the heat he decided against a jacket, but he wasn't going to leave his gun behind. There was no reason to suspect Subject 178 was a danger, but nothing to assume she *wasn't* either. And with someone like him showing up on her doorstep, she'd be justified in thinking the worst. Even then he wasn't sure how much good his gun would do. She could probably twist him like a balloon animal long before he even knew he was in danger. All the same, it gave William some confidence to have it on him as he secured the holster to his belt.

He told Sara he was going out for a drive to clear his head before trying to sleep. In response, she made a noise that might have been an acknowledgment or just clearing her throat. When he left the room, she didn't look up from whatever she was reading.

She expected as much already, but Dez was turning out to be alright as far as Gina was concerned. He acted a little peculiar, a little aloof, a few nights before. He explained how, despite moving around for a few years, it usually took him a day or two to acclimate to a new place. She suspected this was hardly the full story, especially with his pointed questions about that murder, but she couldn't really dispute it.

Besides, it wasn't so bizarre to be unbelievable. Plus, whatever had been troubling him appeared to have passed, so Gina was willing to give him the benefit of the doubt.

The night before Dez came up to the roof to hang out with her and Suz. Soon after Quinn and her new boyfriend, Harris, came over with booze. Dez opened up with some stories about things he'd seen and done while traveling. He told them about having been, for all intents and purposes, taken hostage by a biker gang in Corpus Christi which later led to him being inducted as an honorary member of said gang. There was also the time he accidentally kicked off a brawl at a St. Patrick's Day parade in Boston which engulfed several city blocks before it was diffused. They really liked the story about him getting caught up in a post-game riot in Detroit that ended with him handcuffed and sharing the backseat of a cop car with a rabid fan; a fan who then proceeded to dismantle the car from within, and mostly with his own forehead. Dez could only watch and hope the guy didn't notice him in there too.

They mostly felt Dez was exaggerating many of the details, but they let that slide. He had an engaging way of telling a story that made even mundane events seem epic to the point it was hard to tell what was real and what was embellishment, but they were entertaining nonetheless.

Dez also played music for them, singing songs either he or his parents had written. Gina fell in love with more than a few of

66

them. He also knew many well-known songs, to which Harris and Quinn sang along. Gina already knew Quinn had a decent singing voice, though Harris' talent was more enthusiastic than pleasant. However, Dez's voice imparted a distinctive, underlying quality to whatever song he sang. His voice was still in her head when she went to bed the night before and remained long after she woke up. It was comforting and, though it didn't let her forget the things she saw during dinner at her dad's house, it alleviated their impact.

She hadn't dare tell anyone about what happened; not even Suz who was willing to accommodate almost any amount of insanity without judgment. What could she say? Nothing was coming to mind; or, at least, nothing she could think that'd go over well. Fortunately, everyone bought her claim about lack of sleep and Trevor said it didn't squick Jen out too much.

Currently, however, Dez wasn't exactly sure what he what he had gotten himself into. It started out with him asking if Gina could take him to get groceries, and now...

On the one hand he really, really, *really* wanted to look but on the other he had to wonder if he could ever look Suz in the eye again if he did. He tried to appeal to Gina sitting next to him for some indication of what he should do but found no help. She was engrossed in discussion with Chastity, the dark-haired girl who came into the Panic with Suz the other night. Dez thought her name was Raven, but that turned out to be the blonde instead. Chastity asked Gina about getting tattoo work done and Dez fast discovered how no other subject could keep Gina's attention more than that. Once she started, not even Armageddon could demand precedence.

That it gave Gina ample opportunity to handle the dancer's leg was another sign that she'd be no help in Dez's quandary. He didn't think Gina was into women, though the possibility was obviously there. She certainly took almost every opening to flirt with women. He asked Gina about that the night before. She was hesitant at first but eventually she answered.

"See, when I first started as a tattoo artist I was weirded out about touching women in... um, certain places. On their arm or something was fine but, you know, *other* places not so much. Then someone suggested flirting with them to break the tension and it worked well. I guess I do it all the time now just out of habit.

"So long as they're cool with it," she concluded. "They usually are," Gina added with a crafty smile.

On stage, Suz strutted and prowled as soft multi-colored lights bathed over her, lending an unearthly splendor to her already striking appearance. Dez knew the song playing was "Superstar", an oddly appropriate song in his opinion, but he didn't know whose cover it was. It certainly wasn't The Carpenters. He couldn't hear her thick-soled boots over the music but could feel them thumping against the platform's top. She leapt up the pole so fast Dez barely caught the action until she was twirling, upside-down and hanging from her locked ankles, down its length until her head slowly came to rest on the stage. He thought she might be stuck for a moment; her silky babydoll tumbled down until her breasts were almost uncovered, lights glinting off the silvery ring in her belly-button, then she kicked off from the pole and rolled into a crouching stance. Her wicked gaze washed over the men sitting or hovering at the stage; quickly settling on the first to become aware of his lecherous gaping and avert his eyes.

Target selected she crawled and glided leisurely over to him. Her arms rested on his shoulders as she leaned in, bringing her face in close to his, her cheek a hair's width from his. Her scent enveloped him as she moved, and his eyes were locked with hers, their lips almost brushing together. She could feel his mouth open and his pulse race. He got brave and his tongue darted out to try to find its way into her mouth, but she pulled away; the right corner of her mouth making a devilish smirk; his money in her hand, clearly seen as she playfully wagged a chastising finger at him. He sat there looking ridiculous, even if he didn't feel it, as she moved on to the next guy.

Dez was no stranger to strip joints. He'd seen many dancers on one stage or another and generally found them to be dreary places. The White Rabbit did nothing to change his mind about that. However, Suz's performance was extraordinary on many levels. Almost everything she did could be found in any typical routine, but she avoided moves Dez considered absurd. Her enticements and outfit were common, but she was on a higher scale of graceful than Dez had ever seen. She readily pulled off maneuvers on the pole he imagined required a good deal of proficiency and athleticism. It might not, it might have been a simple trick as far as Dez knew; but, even if that were the case, he didn't think it would take away from how incredible he found Suz's performance.

What really caught his attention was that she never actually removed any clothing other than the babydoll, which had been over a smaller, gauzy shift underneath that she kept on. It wasn't a full-nude club, just topless, and pasties weren't required so there was plenty of skin to be seen in the joint. There were moments when her body was nearly exposed, but she'd pull back or swing away before it ever happened. Regardless, her lack of nudity didn't seem to affect her ability to relieve anyone of their cash. They handed it over, or held it out for her, or simply stacked it on the edge of the stage for her to collect at her leisure.

Her set continued with a song he had heard many, many years before, but didn't know the name of it or the band. It hardly mattered though since it too was a different version. When he originally heard it, the music was fast and hard with a male singer while this cover was slow and slinky with a female vocalist. The third song, "Glamour is a Rocky Road" by My Life with the Thrill Kill Kult, gave the set a suitably fast-paced ending. By then the dark-haired dancer was being paged to see the DJ and Gina returned her attention back to Dez.

"You look uncomfortable," she wryly noted; her eyes cutting towards the stage as Suz disappeared through a curtain at the back.

"I'm just not a big fan of strip clubs," Dez answered weakly as he raised his beer to his lips and drank. That was true enough, but not really the problem at the moment. The DJ announced the next group of dancers as the music, or what passed for it, started again at an unnecessarily loud blare. It was bad enough the volume was deafening, but it also had all the melodic value of severe head trauma and the lyrics were, if one wanted to be kind, asinine. The girl who replaced Suz was hardly a match, but what she lacked in style and grace she made up for with an enthusiasm that put others at ease.

"We won't be much longer. Thanks for being patient. I had to give Suz a ride to work but I didn't mean to stay this long."

"Didn't she sleep over the night before too?" Dez asked. Once the question left his mouth he realized it sounded so accusatory.

"Yeah, things have been a little weird lately," Gina answered. If she caught any subtext in Dez's question or was offended it didn't show. "Suz's just been good enough to keep me company."

A newly-arrived and gregarious group of guys in kilts approached the stage, wasting no time getting to their fun, cheering loudly as the dancer on hands and knees shook her backside at them. A few of them showered cash on her lower back. Gina puckishly asked Dez if he wanted to find out if the men were wearing anything under their kilts. He gave a definite negative on that idea as she downed the last of her Jack and Coke, the third of what was supposed to be only one. They intercepted Suz on their way out. She had changed into a shiny pair of black hotpants and high-heeled shoes, showing the tattoo on her left leg and foot that matched the one on her right arm. They were saying their goodbyes to her as the kilted men begged Suz to join them; a proposition she would only agree to if they weren't wearing anything under their kilts. A condition they were more than happy to show they met, much to Dez's unease and Gina's amusement.

When they set out a little over three hours earlier to take Suz to work, Gina promised to take Dez somewhere he could buy groceries. He had been able to get some immediate items at a corner store near the apartment, but they didn't last long. Gina needed some things too, so it wasn't a bother for her, not that it would have been anyway.

Dez didn't even realize Gina owned a car until earlier that night. The night they met they were dropped off by Quinn's boyfriend. Later they took Quinn's car to the Panic. He really hadn't known Gina to leave the building much at any rate, so it never crossed his mind she might have a car. On first seeing it, a

1969 Mustang Mach 1, Dez could only laugh at the thought of such a short girl like Gina driving it. It was very nice, obviously cared for and ran well, but he just couldn't imagine how she was even able to see over the dash. It wasn't long before Dez realized how wrong he was in his initial assessment. While Gina could see over dashboard just fine, she claimed she drove the car by "feel" as much as anything else.

When they got back to the apartment, Gina parked in the garage on the backside of the building. Hers was the only car in it, though it could fit three, maybe four if they were small. With their hands full, Gina and Dez took the elevator at the end of the hall up to their respective floors.

"I didn't mean for that to take so long, at the club or the grocery store," Gina, by way of apology for the sidetrack, told Dez as he stepped off the elevator at his floor. "It's been weird the last couple days and I just needed the distraction."

"No problem," Dez smiled with a casual shrug. The motion was slightly hampered by the weight of his grocery bags. "You know, if it helped."

"It did," she replied. "I might hang out up on the roof again later on if you'd like to join me."

"Sure. Give me an hour? I need to put these away and check some things first."

"Sounds good. See you in about an hour." She dragged the inner elevator door down, bringing the outer door with it, and pulled the lever to one side. The elevator lurched into motion again. It jerked to a stop when she pulled the lever back to center once it reached her floor. It took her only a few minutes to put her groceries away. With the better part of an hour before meeting back up with Dez, Gina thought about maybe taking a shower. She'd already taken one earlier, before taking Suz to work. Still, between the residual tension of the last couple days and mugginess, she thought it might feel good to take another. At the very least she needed to change as the stale tobacco, old alcohol, and heavy mix of several types of perfume smell of the strip club clung to her clothes.

Just as she finished slipping on a new shirt, there was a

knock at the door. Thinking it might be Dez she went to open it. As she placed her hand on the knob an uneasy feeling crept up her spine. She didn't feel threatened but the distinct impression that she wasn't going to like what she found on the other side was there all the same. Making sure her baseball bat was within easy reach, Gina unlatched the locks on the door and opened it enough to leave a bit of slack in the chain.

She peered out the crack and saw a man in casual clothing, his demeanor relaxed. His hair was short and copper-colored, setting off his greyish-blue eyes. Due to his boyish face, particularly the charming half-smile he wore, he seemed like he could be in his early to mid-40s, but Gina got the sense he was quite a bit older. It was his eyes- his looks might have correlated well to his age, but his eyes had seen way too much of what life could dish out.

"Gina Shields?" he asked.

Before leaving D.C., William pulled as much information on Gina Shields he could without alerting anyone. This was mostly limited to things like her driver's license, social security number, and a few bits and ends such as school records. Studying the photo on her license, he could still see the little girl from decades earlier, even under that black mess of a dye job. Her kind eyes and easy smile certainly didn't look like someone who could kill with a stray thought or once would have been regarded as a tyke bomb.

He really didn't want to bring Shields into this. The way she was brought into the world by far more than earned her the right to live her life without ever dealing with something like this. He hoped the freshness of the Ghost's crime here and Sara's detailed, thorough explorations of the killer would be enough to give his niece what she needed to bring him in. That it'd be enough, so Sara could move past it all.

It soon became obvious that, if his career had taught him anything, it could never have been that simple.

The local police did all they could, mostly did everything

right, but it was clear they were out of their element. Just like all the other police departments before them. The Ghost would get away and keep killing. The Agency had a few psychics working for them and it would be nothing for him to bring them in on the case. Lowden made sure to have one or two on stand-by. Sara's files showed how that likely would have been fruitless too; there were several instances where psychics and mediums offered information to police departments investigating the Ghost. The extreme majority of them were simple frauds passing off parlor tricks and chicanery as preternatural power and looking to boost their status, but William recognized a few of the names, knew they were legitimate. None of them were any more reliable than physical evidence or witness reports. If they weren't any help then, William saw no reason the Agency's psychics would be any more help.

But Shields: she was something different, something more. He remembered shortly after Subject 178 was born, someone asked Basov how she would differ from the psychics already available. The scientist responded by saying to compare those psychics to Subject 178 would be like comparing a candle's light to the sun. William assumed it was another of his arrogant boasts, until that day his team was given the order to "close" Basov and his facility. It was clear Subject 178, now Gina Shields, could have destroyed all of them, erased them from existence, without even looking up from her coloring books.

And here he was, sweltering in a car in the middle of the night outside her apartment building looking to open Pandora's Box, all for the sake of his niece's sanity. If he lived, he mused, he should at least get a coffee mug or a hokey t-shirt out of this.

William knew Shields' apartment was on the fifth floor. From the street he could see the lights were out, so he decided to wait. How long he had been waiting he wasn't sure and the heat was making his eyelids heavy. He caught himself nodding off a few times before a car matching the one registered to Gina pulled into the alleyway next to the building. A few moments later she appeared from around the corner. Her license said she was only five-foot-four, but from William's point of view she looked shorter.

No, not shorter; she looked young, much younger.

He still saw the little girl calmly looking back at him as she was rushed from the destruction.

That memory was rudely shaken away as he saw who emerged from the alley with her: Desiderio Salvia. William had seen where there was supposed to be a tab on his location ever since the Marsh case in West Virginia. According to the files, his current whereabouts was supposed to be somewhere in Maine. He doubted Salvia's presence was mere coincidence, but he'd look into that later once he figured out how to bring it to Sara's attention without throwing Gina in her sights or putting her on the Agency's radar.

They seemed friendly and were carrying several plastic bags as they walked into the building. William gave it a few minutes before following them. In the squat lobby, which was only a slight depression before a small set of steps leading to a hallway, William saw a row of locked mailboxes. As he already knew, the sole box for the fifth floor had "Gina Shields" scrawled with a Sharpie marker on a white card. The only thing designated for the second floor looked to be a business instead of an apartment. Judging by the mailboxes, none of the two third floor apartments had anyone living in them. Of the fourth-floor flats, only the one was occupied.

At the end of the hallway William could see an elevator. It looked ancient and undoubtedly made a lot of noise when used. He decided the stairs would be a better, quieter approach. He climbed to the third floor and peered into the hallway. He could see the doors to the two apartments on his side of the well-lit hall and at the end was a large window looking out over the street below. Having watched the building for some time, waiting for Shields to return, William knew the window led to a fire escape.

He crept up to the first of the two doors and listened in to see if he could hear anything. Someone was moving about inside, and it wasn't too long before William heard a few notes from a guitar flowing from within. He was confident this was where Salvia resided, and the other would be vacant. Still, he made sure this was the case before moving on. Hearing nothing from the next apartment he made his way back to the stairs and up to the fifth floor.

Once there he could see only one door but there was a spot, more of an impression, on the wall further down that was probably where another once stood. Again, he listened at the only door just as he did on the floor below and could hear someone moving about: someone barefoot walking rapidly across hardwood floors, a noise that might have been a door or drawer slamming closed. It went silent and William knocked. Whoever was within quickly walked to the door, the knob clinking as someone on the other side took hold of it, but there was hesitation. After a moment, knowing there was someone on the other side of the door but it not opening, the back of William's neck started to grow tense. He kept his arm and fingers loose, letting the muscles relax and willing should he need to pull his gun. Finally, he heard a lock being undone, followed by two deadbolts, though he could only see one on his side. The door slowly opened, a chain preventing it from going too far, and he could see pale blue eyes framed by black and blue hair looking back at him.

"Gina Shields?" he asked.

"Yeah," her answer was slow, cautious.

"I'm sorry for disturbing you at such a late hour," William began. "I'm Special Agent William Post with the F.B.I.," he said, holding a small wallet with his identification up for her to see. "Do you have a moment to talk?" he presented it as a polite request, but underneath was the promise that "no" was not a response that would be accepted.

"Sure."

"Mind if I come in?"

"Can I see your ID again?"

He smiled at that and held the wallet closer to the door. She could see an identification card and badge. She made a show of scrutinizing it, but it was readily apparent to William that she wouldn't have been able to tell a fake from the real deal. After a few seconds she pushed the door closed a bit, sliding the chain away and invited him in. He stepped inside and made a quick scan of the apartment.

He quickly saw where a separating wall had been knocked down, combining two units to make a single larger one. He saw no television but there was a stereo and hundreds of CDs. A set of shelves was packed tight with books and many more were in stacks and rows on the floor. Several long white boxes were piled in a corner between the shelves and a threadbare couch. A disorganized cloths rack served as a closet in a corner, with a pile of dirty clothes on one side and a basket of, presumably, clean garments on the other. Under that were several pairs of shoes lined up in a row of everything from boots to sneakers to pumps to sandals. Next to the unmade bed was a small dresser with a mismatched mirror sitting atop it. The mirror was cloudy to the point the reflection was worthwhile only in the center but stuck in the frame were enough scraps of paper to make that the only part unobstructed anyway.

Some of these scrapes were ticket stubs, but others were notes and photographs. One picture had Gina, roughly aged 12 or 13, with a woman whose round face was framed by long, faded red hair. They were smiling and in front of a sign that was obscured by the frame. The woman, Gina sitting next to her, held a young boy in her lap. Another was a Polaroid that had Gina, still roughly the same age, with a brown-haired girl of a similar age. They were hugging another woman who was tall with long wavy blonde hair, a slinky black dress and thick pancake make-up to give her a hammy corpse-like appearance. The white bottom of the photo had a quick message signed by someone named Creeper McShaw.

A third was more recent. In the center was a tall woman in a small white shirt, the tale twisted into a knot at her stomach. Her hair was up in pig-tails, held together with green and silver ribbons, and she was wearing a black robe with a similarly colored patch. To her left she was tightly holding Gina to her. Gina was dressed in purple and red and seemed to be a cross between a clown and a nurse, both of the demented variety. On the other side was another woman, dressed in a green suit with question marks and a matching bowler hat, trying but largely failing to step out of frame.

Turning away from the mirror and its pictures William

considered it wasn't exactly the type of place he imagined her living, but then he really wasn't sure what he expected to begin with.

"So, can I get you anything to drink?"

"A glass of water would be nice. If it's no trouble, of course."

She walked to the kitchen while he stayed by the door. He took the opening to get a look at her now. As his information said, she was short, but she also had a curvy body that looked strong and tough. At first glance her light complexion might make one think her ill, but there was an evenness indicating good health. If it weren't for some sharpness to Gina's chin, her jawline would give her face a perfect U-shape that worked well with the wide flare of her nose. Her thin, dark eyebrows were accentuated by a single curved barbell on the outer edge of the left and a set of three small silvery rings adorning the right, while the left portion of her lower lip sported a similar ring.

Her left arm, wrist to shoulder, was covered by a tattoo of flames with many peculiar, alien eyes staring out from behind them. At first William thought Gina was wearing rings on several of her fingers but he soon realized all but one was inked, and more adorned a few of her toes. On her right wrist was a band of weaving, concentric circles of red and black ink matching another covering her left knee. Further up above on her right thigh, a scarlet and gold lion crawled up her leg and was visible from under the leg of her shorts. William wouldn't be surprised if Gina had many more tattoos and piercings that could not be seen for her clothing.

She returned with a glass of water and handed it to him. "So, what did you need to talk about?"

He took a big sip before setting the glass down on the counter. He really did not like this crushing humidity. "You've no doubt heard about the murdered girl found not too far from here?"

"I have but the cops already came by and asked about that," she answered truthfully. "It was really too far away so I probably didn't have anything that could help with that." William gave a respectful and calming smile.

"I've already read their reports, Ms. Shields," he replied. "It wasn't much but I wouldn't say that you couldn't be of any help," he finished. She inched a little closer to the door and, he then noticed, a baseball bat that was propped up next to it.

"How do you mean?"

"This may be a little hard for you to believe," he started, grasping too late how that phrase always made what came next nearly impossible to accept no matter how sensible. He soldiered on anyway. "... but you have abilities that no one else has."

"Abilities," she repeated. "What's that supposed to mean? You mean, like, superpowers or something?"

"Something like that, yes." His expression was serious, but Gina watched him for a few moments longer, waiting for him to crack.

"Oh, for fuck's sake, that ID was pretty good. Seriously, I'm impressed you kept a straight face, but you'll need to leave before I call the cops. And I mean *real* ones," she started to walk over to the counter where her phone was and had a wry smile on her face making it clear she would only humor him long enough for him to leave.

"I know how this sounds, but this is real," William insisted. Long ago he had been trained to keep psychics from using passive sensory abilities on him; to resist mind reading and block other powers. He had trouble with it initially, but by now it was second nature to keep these defenses up. He could turn it on and off like a switch. He let those barriers drop.

Her phone was in her hand now, her fingers hovering over the buttons, but she didn't move to dial any numbers. Her hands suddenly twitched, as if electricity surged from her fingertips and up to her brain. So far what had made Gina most uneasy about this man was that she didn't get anything off of him; no sense of what his intentions might be, whether he was honest or decent, depraved or deceptive. Agent Post had been a total blank. She had never met anyone she couldn't get at least a vague sense of and that scared her some.

Then suddenly she could read him the same as anyone else. What he was saying sounded crazy, but he wasn't lying. He was telling the truth, or what he understood to be the truth. Also, he wasn't out to hurt Gina, not deliberately at least, but she could tell his intentions weren't wholly benign either. Now that she was able to get an impression of him she, strangely, relaxed some.

Her next words were slow and deliberate. "Okay, say I believe you, what 'abilities' are you talking about?"

"It's hard to say exactly but they should be somewhat standard: telepathy, pre- or post-cognition, empathic resonance just to name some. Maybe psychokinesis."

"See, I've never done any of that. Wouldn't even know how truth be told."

"No? Let me take a stab: would you say you've always been a good judge of character?"

"Sure."

"Empathic resonance. You can feel the emotional state of others; know if they're lying or what angle they may be playing at." Her mouth opened and closed a few times, words caught in her throat as she tried to come up with something to dismiss what he just said as normal. He could tell it was hitting close to home, but she wasn't really buying it just yet. "You ever think or dream of something that later happened?"

"Who hasn't?"

"How often do you?"

She paused a bit. "More times than I like but it's never anything specific," she admitted guardedly. Honestly, Gina had never dwelled on it much. Really, she just figured she merely remembered the times her dreams seemed prescient, forgetting about the times it didn't. She thought about it now for a moment, her lower lip slipping beneath her front teeth as she did. "It's more of a sense, an idea, that something bad is about to happen. I don't know what exactly; just that *something* is gonna happen."

"How?"

"I have this dream; it's always the same dream. Well, it's more a series of images, you know?"

"Images of what?"

"People dying, mostly. No one I know... I don't think I know them anyway... but they're always dying, being killed by this... guy," she said, unsure if that was the right word or not, but not coming up with anything better.

"If you think about it I'm sure there would be other... unusual ... occurrences that have happened before."

The memory of Jen at the table, throat slit, and the tick-marked man with the dead eyes immediately barged into her mind but also the visions of the maternity ward and the scared little girl huddled behind her bed. William could tell by the look on her face that disbelief was making way for provisional credence. "If you'd humor me I think I could prove it beyond a reasonable doubt."

"And how do you plan to do that?"

"Let's take a ride," William said taking a step towards the door. Gina shot a firm-jawed, raised-eyebrow look at him as she took a half-step away from him. She might be buying into his claims a little, but this was a bit more than she was willing to swallow. "You said you were a good judge of character; what are you getting as far as my intentions go?"

She considered him for a minute. She didn't think her photo would end up on a milk carton but, even considering her more recent actions, riding off into the night with a complete stranger didn't strike her as the smartest move to make. Finally, "Okay. But first..." she said as she walked over to an end table next to the couch. She opened a drawer and pulled out an instant camera. She quickly held it up and snapped a picture of William. The flash blinded him briefly. The picture spat out from the camera and she pulled it free as she made her way to the kitchen counter, flapping the photo along the way. "Now I have a picture of you, so if anything happens they know what you look like," she said as she shoved the photo and camera on the counter.

"Alright, does that mean you'll come with me?"

"Not yet," she said as she rummaged through another drawer, producing a pen and a pad of paper. She scribbled with the pen on the paper some to make sure there was ink in it before writing a note out to someone. She asked William for some information about himself: his full name, his home address, the make and model of his car, the name of his boss, and a few other tidbits. She put the note next to the photograph and then pulled on some socks and sneakers.

"Now," she declared, "I am ready to be a complete and utter idiot. Lead the way."

Chapter 6

Gina had read a lot of books in her life, particularly those with tales of adventure. It occurred to her how many of them started off with some mysterious visitor showing up to tell the protagonist they possess some wonderful but singular power they must use to defeat some great wooly evil harming the land. Even with having a great family, she suspected her attraction to such stories stemmed from her being adopted. Gina long doubted she would discover she was the last of some royal bloodline, complete with castle and a secret fortune, or be shuffled off to a secret school for wizards. She probably wouldn't even get a little dog and a neat pair of shoes out of it but finding herself in a darkened alley with some guy who claimed she had superpowers seemed about right, in a weird sort of way.

They ended up across from Bug's Lounge, where the girl's body was found. Yellow police tape was still there but it had been torn down by someone and left trailing across the sidewalk. The dumpster had been taken away as evidence but an outline of it and the body inside were there. She could see some faded brownish stains on the ground, both in the alley and the sidewalk, that Gina was certain had been the girl's blood, though she hoped it something else, no matter how gross.

Since the city banned smoking indoors a couple years earlier, several people stood around out front of Bug's. A few noticed Gina and Agent Post milling about the alleyway and she could hear some of the comments being made. Some were quietly inquiring about what they were doing but those were drowned out as others gleefully offered some rather base possibilities. The body of a raped and mutilated 15-year-old girl had been found in this alley. The killer had taken her several blocks to dump the body here, in broad daylight, and people had wondered how such a thing was possible. Gina wasn't sure, but she a rising hunch that some people were able to honestly assume that someone would choose this alley just a few nights later to get their freak on might have gone some distance to explain the event. At the very least, she could put any worries about what would happen if Agent Post turned out to be a deranged killer who had chosen her as his next victim to rest. Given the palpable high-minded dispositions of the people across the street, she would definitely die with an appreciative audience on hand.

The only downside she saw was that she had no way to let it be known she wanted her obituary to make note her murder received a fucking golf-clap.

"You know, when someone tells me they're gonna prove something to me beyond a reasonable doubt, I tend to like a little more 'prove' with my 'reasonable doubt'," she told Post as he set a high-powered lantern down in the center of the crime scene.

"Here," he said, motioning for her to come closer with one hand while indicating where a dumpster had once been with the other. "Stand here. Tell me what you feel. What you sense."

Gina dragged herself over to the spot. It felt a little morbid standing there, her shoe next to a large stain. She stood there for a minute; eyes closed and concentrating. Finally, "You know, I think I am sensing something, that I'm feeling something. I'm sensing a god-awful smell because I'm standing where a dumpster used to be and I'm feeling like a complete git for it."

Post, hooking his fingers in his belt loops, ignored the remark as well as the stink eye she gave him and turned slightly away from her. She could tell he was upset though she didn't think it was with her; it was the situation he was annoyed with. He ran his hands through his short coppery hair as he thought. He went back to the car, fished something out from the backseat, and returned with a file folder. Flipping through it, he pulled out several large photos to hold against the light of the lantern. As he flipped through them, Gina moved to stand over him to could look too.

She could tell they were of the alleyway but had probably been taken in daylight. The first few contained dark pools with tiny plastic numbered markers next to them. Others had the same markers next to various objects of interest. Some were of the girl's body, which compelled Gina to straighten and turn away. It was one thing for her see this type of stuff in a movie, no matter how gory or life-like, but it was something else to see it for real. She didn't dare look back until Post made a noise to signal he found the one he was looking for. He held it up, slowly turning in place; looking between the image and the alley as it was now. Then he walked towards the wall near the opening to the street. Compared the snapshot again and pointed to a spot on the wall.

"Put your hand here."

Gina studied the spot. She couldn't see anything out of the ordinary. "Why?"

"One report said that the killer smashed the victim's head into the wall here. She was stabbed repeatedly down by the library and the blood loss weakened her. By the time they reached here, she wasn't going to live, but the examiner's report said that the blow to the head was what ultimately killed her," Post explained. "I'll be honest, I don't know much about this stuff, but if this is where she died her resonance might be strongest here; strong enough that you might able to get something."

"What was her name?"

That confused Post. "What does that matter?"

"I don't know it. She was a minor, so the news didn't release her name. I wanna know her name."

"Christina Walker," Post told Gina, still mildly confused but willing to work with her.

"Okay. If I'm going to go along for this ride, you have to start calling her Christina, not 'the victim' or 'her' or 'the girl'. The killer dumped her in the trash as if she was nothing, that doesn't mean we should act like Christina was nobody too," Gina said as she put her hand on the wall.

It was daylight, there were people walking by; some minding their own business, others gawking. Gina was near the wall as a girl, Christina, had her face smashed into it next to her. Her blood splattered onto Gina's face. She could hear bones crunching, the last of Christina's breath leaving her body in a tiny, rattling, pathetic wail, but all that went through Gina's mind was how pretty the girl's hair was, a lovely strawberry-blonde. Then she realized Christina's hair wasn't that color, rather it was just soaked through with blood. Christina was pulled away from the wall, her face a bloody and broken mess. Half-open as they were, her eyes changed.

Dimmed.

Gina fell back from the wall, slapping at her face to wipe the phantom blood away. A light rain began to fall. She coughed, her stomach queasy, and she doubled over. Post moved to hold her steady, but she pushed him back, the movement making her crash into the opposite wall. "No. No. No. No. No. No. No. No. Fuck you!" Gina cried as she slapped him away.

"What? What happened?" his hands out in a placating fashion, hoping to calm her down.

Gina leaned against the wall and slid down into a sitting position. She vaguely realized she might be sitting in something revolting and she'd have to burn these cloths, but she didn't really care right now. After a moment, tears welling up in her eyes, she pointed to the spot on the wall. "Your examiner was right. That's where she died."

"Did you see the killer?"

"Huh?"

"Did you see the killer?"

"Why are you asking me?" her voice was tiny and cracking as she tried to choke back sobs. "There were like... a hundred-people standing about! Didn't they tell the cops what the fucker looked like?"

"Sure. They told us what he looked like," Post said with a little laugh, crow's feet and other stress lines tarnishing his boyish face. He opened the file again, flipping through the pages until he found the pages he was searching for. "Here's one. 'Medium build, brownish hair, average height'. Helpful."

He turned the page. "Here's another. 'Medium build, blonde hair, average height'. It's a surprise he hasn't been brought in already."

He found another report. "Oh, I like this one. 'Black guy, tall, maybe early 20s'. Or this one: 'short, Asian descent, bleached blonde hair'." He closed and handed the file to Gina. "All the reports are like that! And not just for this one."

"This one?" she carefully took the file in her shaking hands, not bothering to open it.

"This is hardly his first rodeo. He's done this all over the country for years. We have no idea how many girls like Christina he's killed," he pointed to the spot on the wall as he spoke. "There's upwards of 40 confirmed, but there could be hundreds more." After staring down at her for almost a minute, letting his words sink in, Post reached down for her hand. Slowly, she took it and let him pull her up. His help was far gentler than his present demeanor suggested possible.

Post towered over her but scrunched down so he was eye level with Gina. "This time, we might be able to stop him, but I need your help."

"If I can do this, then, there *have to* be others like me that can too," she hoped that was true. It would mean she could just go back home, throw these clothes away, and forget this ever happened.

"There are others, yes; but, not like you," Post answered. His voice was apologetic. "Like I said, I don't know much about this stuff but someone who did once told me that you would be so much more than the rest."

She studied him, trying to find the least hint that he might be lying or just taking the piss and finding none.

Post continued before she could say anything. "Granted, he was a depraved madman, but I think he might have known what he was talking about in your case."

That got a fast, reflexive chuckle out of Gina. She didn't really find it funny; she just wanted a reason to laugh. Any reason not to think about witnessing Christina's death. He took that as a sign she wasn't completely demoralized, which was good because, if his suspicions were right, what he was going to need her to do next was far worse than look at a crime scene.

Gina stood in the dreary hall while Post was inside talking to someone. She thought about running but figured since he knew where she lived her chances of staying not found were nil. She could see through a small window on the door that the discussion between the guy in the lab coat and Post was looking heated. If her experience with the agent tonight was worth anything, she'd be willing to put money on him getting his way. She figured this would likely amount to a negative for her, which made it all but guaranteed to happen at this point.

She tried to take her mind off the conversation happening on the other side of the door- as well the unpleasant wet spot on the seat of her pants. which was drying far too slowly- by taking in her surroundings. She got as far as the sign with "**MORGUE**" printed on it and decided to start mentally listing the states and their capitols instead. She was on Augusta, Maine, when the door slammed open. Lab Coat burst past, clearly livid, with Post behind him the picture of serenity. Lab Coat got to the end of the hall and turned back to Post and Gina.

"You have half an hour! No more!" he yelled. Gina was hardly a fan of Agent Post, but she had to admit his response to Lab Coat's decree- acknowledgement, dismissal, and indifference all silent and all at once- was rather artful.

Gina expected the morgue to be icy. Instead the temperature inside was quite comfortable, making the place even more unsettling. She also found it disappointing, though she could only wonder why.

Maybe it's best if I don't know why.

Post led her through a large room with several metal tables. On two of them were bodies, one was hastily covered up by a young student who then rushed out past them. The other must have just come in and had not been attended to yet. Gina was glad the tables were not their destination. What little encouragement that realization brought evaporated when they turned a corner and she was faced with rows of small metal doors on the walls.

"Wait here," Post told her as he went back towards the entrance. She knew he was only gone a few moments, but it seemed like hours with her just standing there knowing what might be behind any one of those cold doors. A chill crawled from them, or so she imagined, traipsing through her body so casually she felt violated. She thought she could hear a tiny voice calling to her from behind one the doors. Her eyes drifted over to it, searching, coming to rest on the one marked 38 when Post appeared beside her, causing her to jump with fright.

"Jeezy-creezy! Do I have to put a freaking bell on you?" His face was blank, but she thought she could see a bit of humor in his eyes. "Oh, you thought that was funny?" she demanded, but he had already started towards one of the doors. "Creepy fucker," she grumbled at his back.

He stopped in front of the one numbered 38, took hold of the handle and opened it. Cold air blasted out from the compartment and brought goose-pimples to Gina's skin. Inside she saw a metal slab with an opaque white bag. She instinctively knew what was in the bag, though she tried to pretend otherwise. Post dragged the slab out, the sound reminding Gina of being six and riding the roller coaster with her parents. She was scared, but they were there thus she knew nothing could hurt her.

But her parents weren't here with her now. Instead, she was alone in a morgue with a puzzling and unrelenting federal agent.

A small clang brought her back to the present; she realized the noise was quiet, but its reverberation leant it an ominous quality.

Post drew the zipper on the bag down along one side. Gina saw tufts of stringy but beautiful blonde hair spill out past the opening. She wanted to turn away but didn't. She forced herself to look. At some point Post had slipped on a pair of gloves, but Gina didn't notice until he reached in and pulled the girl's colorless arm out from under cover of the bag. He looked at Gina as if he expected her to do something, but the only thing that came to her mind instantly fell into her "Not Gonna Happen" category.

"What?" she asked.

"Take her arm."

"Hm, not gonna happen." He gave her the look again; the same one he gave her when he asked if he could enter her apartment. "Fine. Do I get gloves too?"

"Sorry," he apologized as he shook his head. She gave him credit for having the decency to mean it.

She took several deep breaths to psyche herself up before taking hold of Christina's lifeless hand. Everything she'd read described dead bodies as cold and clammy, but that came nowhere close to describing what this was truly like. It was unsettling, but not nearly as much as Gina would have suspected. A stray thought crossed her mind, wondering about all those books and movies about impressionable young girls falling in love with vampires and if that was what it was like to fuc...

He stood over her, the air around him heaving with malice. *Your fault.*

She tried to get away, but he was just so strong. Once the knife went in the first time she knew she would not live to see another day. There were so many people nearby. She screamed for help. Some looked at them, but most just kept their heads down. The knife went in and out, in and out, in and out, in and out, over and over and over and over.

Brought it all on yourself.

She saw blood, her blood, streaming down her body and pooling at her feet. He yanked her closer and started walking away with her. She had to see what he looked like. The sun had been in her eyes, blinding her but now she might see him.

You made me do this.

She struggled to look up, look at him. It was hard, but she managed to raise her head enough as he looked down at her. His face was waxy, like a bad disguise that'd later be tossed away in some cheesy spy drama. Their eyes met; they were such a beautiful deep blue, like the ocean.

Why weren't you true?

From beneath the bridge of his nose a second pair of irises with strange pupils slid into place below the normal ones. Then a third pair emerged from his temples, and a fourth and a fifth. She tried to scream but all she could achieve was a sad whimper.

You must be made to pay for your sins.

His droopy mouth split apart in a ghastly sneer to show row after row of needle teeth, ropey tongues slithering behind.

Gina let go of the arm and retreated a few steps. Post stepped around the slab but stopped dead in his tracks once he saw the change in Gina's face. It twisted in ways that should not have been possible and he could swear her eyes became five-in-one for a moment. A creaking laughter streamed from her mouth, low at first only to gain in volume. Post took hold of his gun, loosening the holster's locking strap, but refrained from drawing it.

"What do you hope to accomplish?" They were Gina's words, issued from her mouth, but it was not her voice. It tittered and grated, creaked and croaked. "You can't stop me, you must know that! *He* won't let you! There were many that could have, could have stopped me so easily. But they didn't. They didn't for the same reason you won't stop me: because you know that these are your wages. You brought this on yourselves. Just like that whore," she said pointing towards the body on the slab, "brought this on herself. You wallow in this fallen world..."

Gina screamed in her own voice as she fell to her hands and knees.

She stayed there for several moments, her body rising and falling with deep, shaky breaths. Post dropped his hand from his gun and started to walk towards her. Her hand shot up, palm out, suggesting it was in his best interest that he stayed back. She rose to her feet and lifted her head. "What the fuck did you do to me?" she hissed.

When no answer came from Post, she asked again, louder. "What the fuck did you do to me?"

Again, no answer. Again, she asked, now a shriek. *"WHAT THE FUCK DID YOU DO TO ME?"*

There was a timbre to her voice now causing Post to take a couple steps back. The room shook and all the metal doors except 38 scrunched inward with a sickening sound. Tiles on the wall and floor cracked and shattered and popped. Post found it hard to breathe, as if his lungs were being crushed within his rib cage. Then it all stopped with a crash on the other side of the wall. Gina stood there, taking in huge gulps of air. Post took a cautious step forward, then another and another and another until he was standing before her. She looked at him, her eyes a mix of anger, confusion, fear, and supplication.

Quietly, he said the only thing that came to mind. "You do deserve an explanation." He knew it was a lame response, but it was all he had.

Cheap shoes scuffed the floor nearby. "What the hell did you do to my morgue?" Lab Coat was back, his assistant beside him. They took in the room. His face was of pure rage; hers one of bewilderment.

Gina cut her eyes towards them, disregarding Lab Coat and his assistant as she brushed past him as if they didn't even exist. Post moved to follow her, stopped beside Lad Coat but didn't face him.

"You've a mess to clean up." Lab Coat blustered for a reply, but Post cut him off. "And a good explanation for this to come up with. One that doesn't include me or the girl if you know what's best," he said calmly before leaving to catch up with Gina.

They sat in Post's car across from Gina's building. The rains had apparently become heavier while they'd been at the morgue, making the streets wet, but had since moved on. They sat in silence; she held him in her seething gaze, her finger absently running along the lid to the cup of coffee he had bought to steady her nerves. She had already told him all she had seen at the morgue, so it was time for him to tell her what was going on. He was trying to figure out where to start but it all required more clarification than he could provide.

"The beginning would be nice," she had said but that was open to interpretation.

"Okay. It started off as a joke."

"A joke?" she repeated incredulously, her voice venomous. "Yeah, it sure is pretty fucking funny."

"A joke. Sort of: back in the '50s a French newspaper published an article about a program launched by the U.S. government to use psychics in a new initiative to fight the Cold War. Clairvoyant spies and psychic soldiers, you know? It didn't take long for the Soviets to hear about this, so they immediately devised their own program.

"Unfortunately, by the time the Soviets found out that the article in question had been an April Fool's joke, a hoax, the U.S. learned of the Soviet program and started one for real."

"So... my life gets turned upside-down because of a stupid prank? Great; that's just fucking lovely."

"No. Your life gets turned upside-down because there's this psycho going around killing young girls," he took a deep breath. "Your life gets turned upside-down because this tired, old man can't see his niece drive herself crazy trying to catch this psycho." His voice was so small. So far from the cool and commanding tone she had been exposed to all night.

He couldn't look at her when he said it, had turned away from her. While William could hide his face from her, Gina could feel the defeat and regret weighing the man down. She could touch his fear that he was on the verge of losing something special to him, and the greater fear that he already had.

For the first time that night she saw an old man instead of the authoritative Federal Agent. The anger she had for him faded a little. She put her hand on his shoulder and he looked back at her.

"She's really that important to you?"

William studied her for a few seconds. Gina had every right to be enraged; to hate him to his very core. His issues didn't have to be of trouble to her, but there it was. She didn't feel sorry for him or pity him. She was just concerned, genuinely concerned, about his motives. She really wanted to do something to help.

Teach her to be kind and compassionate or whatever you

want her to be but if you want her to be safe, you'll teach her to keep what she can do to herself. You'll teach her to forget it if you can. His own words from so long ago echoed in his head. He had to hand it to Frankie and Flora Shields; they did a far better job of following his advice than he did. "She's all I have. Her and the Agency and the last's hardly a thing to have."

"The Agency? You mean the F.B.I.?"

"No."

"But aren't you...?"

"Officially, yes, but..." he paused. "All you need to know about the Agency is that you need to stay off their radar."

"How?" she asked, trepidation and disbelief was in her voice. He knew how he should answer that, but it'd only be ridiculous given their activities tonight.

"I'll do what I can with that." *You'll teach her to forget it if you can.* He wasn't sure if his younger self was taunting or chiding him. "But, you'll have to learn how to control what you can do now that it's out of the bag. You might need it if the Agency discovers you're alive."

"That I'm alive? What does that mean?"

"Officially, you're dead."

"If that's the case then why am I not?"

"A woman named Alma took you away."

Gina didn't need any special powers to tell that that was hardy the full story. "That's all huh? Was this Alma lady a superhero too?"

"No, just the regular kind who put her life on the line to see a kid she barely knew to safety and into a family that obviously loved you." That shut Gina up for a moment. Still, there was more he wasn't telling her. An image of a man with no eyes and dead light for hands came to her.

"You were there too." He caught this was a statement and not a question.

"Yeah."

"Were you supposed to kill me?"

"Yes."

"And?"

"And... I didn't," he evenly admitted. He shook his head. "I couldn't."

"So, you're just a regular kind of hero too?" A tiny smile played across her face.

"Not remotely." He appreciated the gesture, but he couldn't humor her like this. Her smile stayed anyway.

Both were quite for several minutes. When she spoke again, her question was quiet. "This guy that's killing people? Can you catch him?"

"I don't know."

She nodded and started to get out of the car. Post put his hand on her arm. "There's one more thing you need to know." She gently pulled the door closed again.

"Okay."

Post nodded towards the apartment building. "You know someone named Desiderio Salvia."

"Dez? What about him?"

"He's connected to the killer."

Gina felt her stomach drop at that assertion. Her mouth opened and closed a few times, trying to process this information. "Huh?" was all she could manage to get out of her mouth.

"Not too long ago, in West Virginia, Salvia was arrested on suspicion of being the killer. Witnesses placed him at the scene of the crime, but he was released because they were so conflicting. Like all reports regarding the Ghost..."

"The Ghost?"

"That's what he's referred to, the killer," Post explained. "All reports about the Ghost have only one thing that's consistent: inconsistency."

"You think Dez might be the Ghost."

Post wrinkled his nose at that. "I don't know. His sister was one the victims..."

"His sister?"

Post nodded as an answer. "Whether that makes it more or less likely he's the Ghost I don't know, just be careful around him is all I'm saying."

Gina chewed her lip and then nodded before getting out

the car. Post gave her his card with his contact information. He watched as she crossed the street to her building. At the doorway she turned back to him and gave a small wave goodbye before going in. She made her way up the stairs, zombie-like, trying to get a handle on what she had just been told, what she had done. For some reason she had an easier time accepting she had superpowers than she was wrapping her head around the possibility of Dez being a serial killer.

She paused at the third-floor landing and considered going to Dez's apartment but thought better of it. After all, what was she going to say? *So, stabbed any good people lately?* She continued to her own apartment. Inside, a note had been shoved under her door. She opened it and saw that it was from Dez.

Waited on the roof for you. Guess you fell asleep or something. See you later.

-Dez

That plan had been forgotten, but after what she was just told Gina thought that might have been a good thing. The note was crumpled up and tossed in the trash. She changed into some bed clothes, made a cup of tea and tried to read a book, but it was no use. She tried drawing and listening to some music, but this too was no use. She found it impossible to relax.

The box under the couch was retrieved and Gina took loaded her pipe. Grabbing a lighter she headed up to the roof. Once there she tried to shake the rain water from one of the plastic lawn chairs but gave it up for futile. Another wet ass was the last thing she wanted after the night she'd had so far. Seeing that the other chairs had been no less drenched she settled for leaning back against a dry spot on the wall of the old tool shed. The bowl lit, she inhaled the smoke, holding it for several seconds before exhaling the smoke into the air. The air was still so it hung thickly in front of her for longer than usual.

As it dissipated Gina saw her standing by the edge of the roof.

At first Gina thought Suz might have decided to drop by after work. It might have been Quinn, however; the company of either would have been greatly appreciated by Gina. It didn't take her long to realize this was neither Suz nor Quinn, though. This woman was completely unfamiliar. All Gina could see of her was her back, but she could see she was dressed in a greyish slip of a dress that ended mid-thigh and a pair of dingy high-heels that had probably once been white. From her shoulders hung a pair of broken costumed angel wings and a plastic tiara worn on her head. Gina shuffled carefully over to her.

"Hello?" she asked tentatively. The woman jumped, turning to face Gina. Now that she was closer, Gina could see that her skin was a shifting purple-grey and black that reminded Gina of an oil slick on the surface of a body of water. The surprise on her face let Gina see her eyes clearly: they lacked irises and pupils and resembled smoky pearls, highlighted by the dark streaks that ran unevenly down her cheeks. The angel wings were not just broken but tattered, as was her dress. The thin straps for both the dress and wings had been melted into her flesh, lined by never-healing scars. The tiara was warped and wilted and fused into her skull. She pointed to Gina, the action jerky as if several attempts at it were made, discarded and tried again in rapid succession.

"You can see me?"

Her words hit Gina in the pit of her stomach like a hammer. It was a singular voice, though it seemed like several layered atop one another, none going in the same direction. It went forwards and backwards and sideways and up and down and left and right. It was at once fast and high and slow and low and even and measured. Gina grabbed the ledge to hold herself steady, nausea working its way through her whole body. If this new person noticed Gina's distress she didn't show it.

"Oh my god, that was *so* clichéd I know but what else can ya say? I mean, it fits right? It so totally fits," she seemed to be addressing the universe instead of Gina at this point.

"What the absolute...?" Gina swallowed back a bit of vomit that threatened to climb up her throat.

"Most people can't see me," the woman gently explained as

if Gina was simply slow on the uptake and not in agony. "Because I'm dead," she went on.

That blow was softer than the last, but Gina was sure she was going to throw up now. She reached the garbage can in time and really wished she had eaten a bit more earlier. Once she was sure nothing else was coming up, she stepped away from the can. *Is the world... breathing?* She thought as the air was moving in and out, contracting and expanding around the woman.

"What was that?" Gina tried again, her voice wobbly and weak, still holding on to the garbage can.

"Looked like corn," the woman drily replied as she leaned in close, looking in the trash can. Again, her words were fast and slow, in reverse and fast-forward at the same time. That one wasn't so bad, and Gina was beginning to suspect the woman's movements and voice were more like the gist of those things as opposed to the real deal. Thinking like that made it easier for Gina to handle it at least.

Wiping at her teary eyes, Gina shakily muttered, "Things went... wrong. *Really* wrong."

"How so?"

That was better. Now that the world was going back to how it was supposed to, to the extent that it could, Gina was becoming less concerned with the wrongness of this woman. She had other questions now.

"Sorry, I don't mean to be rude..." Gina paused and changed tact. "No, I *do* mean to be rude: who the fuck are you?"

"No, *I* should be the one who's sorry!" The woman exclaimed, her hands pressing against her chest. There was the hint of a Southern accent in her voice. It wasn't thick, but it was just enough to give her speech a certain character. "It's been so long since anyone saw me or tried to talk to me... well, anyone alive that is. I have to say other dead folk don't have a lot of new things to talk about. It's probably because they never get out that much. I don't know why. I mean I guess I get it but just because you're dead don't mean your life's..."

"Hey!" Gina yelled. The woman stopped her stammering. "That sounded very intriguing and all, and any other another night

98

I might've been okay with letting you go on with the zany ramblings, but I've had a *really* trying night," Gina tried for a no-nonsense glare, settling for a weak, pleading smile. "So, I ask you: could you please just give straight, uncomplicated answers?"

The woman thought about this. Dejectedly, she agreed. "Okay."

"Great. Now, who are you?"

"Angela Mooreland. And you?" she replied, holding her arm and hand out stiff as a board. Gina regarded it warily then figured since she'd already touch one definitely-dead person tonight, touching a more deadish person couldn't make matters any less fucked than they already were.

At least, Gina consoled herself, Angela was holding out her good arm, and not the blackened one with what looked to be charred flesh and a lot of bone showing through.

Gina gingerly took it. She could feel the woman's hand against hers but more in her mind rather than against her skin. Looking at it she could see Angela's "skin" reacting to being pressed to Gina's but her own seemed to not even register the existence of Angela's. Always a sucker for a good ghost story, Gina had expected one's touch to be the icy chill of the grave, but it felt more like her hand had merely been asleep and the feeling was returning now the circulation was going again.

"Gina Shields."

"Pleased to meet you, Gina Shields."

"You can just call me Gina."

"And you can just call me Angie."

"Okay, Angie, I take it you're a... ghost... or something?" Gina put a slight pleading on the "or something" part. She wasn't sure if she was ready to deal with ghosts yet.

"I guess so. Not many people around to talk about it but I guess that's a good enough word for it."

"Aren't you supposed to be bound to, like, where you died? Did you die here?"

"Most ghosts stick to the place they died or somewhere important to them I suppose, but as far as I can tell they don't have to if they don't want to. It's easier to stick with such a place, I guess, but not as much fun if you ask me."

"So, you go where you want?"

"Pretty much."

"Then why are you here on my roof?" That came out a little harsher than Gina intended, but the ghost didn't seem to notice. She wondered if Angie was just so excited to be talking to someone that she'd let any amount of rudeness slide.

"Because of them," Angie said as if it was obvious.

"Them who?" Gina demanded even though she knew she wasn't going to like the answer.

Angie waved her arms out in a sweeping, encompassing motion before pointing to several places in fast succession. "Them."

Gina looked about once more.

There were dozens of them. Maybe a hundred. Maybe more.

They were everywhere. They lined the roofs of the nearby buildings and crowded her own. The ones on the other roofs faced hers while those near Gina faced the stairwell. How she didn't see them before now she didn't know, but she wished she could go back to *not* seeing them. They were ghosts like Angie, but they were all younger girls, or had been when they were alive. As far as Gina could tell, none could have been older than 17 when they died. All the ones close enough for her to really see showed dreadful and grievous wounds: bashed-in heads, gouges torn from torsos, mangled faces, and more.

Near the door to the stairwell Gina saw a skinny girl with what might have once been beautiful blonde hair and a face that she only recognized from seeing it slammed hard into a brick wall.

"Christina?" Gina whispered. Not far from her, Gina spied another girl that would have had dark skin in life and familiar facial features; one that might have been in her apartment some days prior. "Why are they here?" she whispered to Angie.

"Hard to..." she started loudly before Gina hushed her.

"Keep your voice down," she hissed out the command. "I don't want them to know we're here."

"They probably already know," Angie patiently suggested.

"They probably just don't care. Like I said: dead folk? Not the most sociable of people."

At that, one glowered bitterly toward Gina. Her matted black hair stuck fast to her skull and blue eyes looked out from a boney face. Her skin, or what would pass for it, was thin and translucent where it still existed but Gina had the impression it had been milky white in life. The girl antagonistically snapped her teeth at Gina before turning her attention back to the stairs when another shade bumped into her.

Gina wasn't so sure about the not caring part, but she also felt pretty stupid now. She quietly asked Angie to continue. "Right, so as I was saying, it's hard to tell why they're here. Most ghosts stick with something that was important to their life."

"What could be important to them *here*?"

"Don't know," Angie easily admitted. "They look like they were murdered," she leaned in closer to one nearest her. "Pretty brutally I might add. From what little I've been able to gather, ghosts of murder victims sometimes stick with the person who killed them if they were never made to pay for it. You know, the whole 'I can't rest until the bastard what killed me is brought to justice' thing?" She scrunched up her face, looking skyward, her fist balled and shaking at the heavens as she said it. She relaxed then and, making a motion that Gina interpreted as an eye roll. "Kinda boring if you ask me."

"Then why did you follow them?"

"Hello? Dead," she said pointing to herself. "It's about as thrilling as it sounds," she glanced about at nothing in particular. "Especially in this town."

"So... their killer is probably in this building?"

"Probably," Angie said. "Not 100% but I think it's pretty likely. You have someone in mind? Someone in the building right now?" she asked, the possibility of some form of excitement perking her interest. Gina nodded, and Angie bounced a little, clapping her hands.

Gina took this in and rolled it around her brain. If these were the spirits of the Ghost's victims and they were hanging about because their killer was here, then it seemed to fit with Dez being the Ghost. She debated about whether she should call Agent Post with any of this when Angie pointed out there was a disturbance among the ghost girls over on the other side of the roof. Gina watched as they mechanically shuffled to one side to fall back into place once again. Some briefly acknowledged the source of the commotion before returning to their vigil of the stairs. Finally, the newcomer got to where Gina could see. It was another girl. She couldn't have been older than 12 and she would never get any older.

"Looks like another one down," Angie commented softly. One of the ghost girls, the familiar dark-skinned girl, automatically patted the newcomer's back before standing stock still once again. Disappointment crossed Angie's face. "That probably means your suspect is innocent then. If he's still in the building, that is."

Maybe, Gina thought, but he still had a load of questions to answer.

William returned to the hotel room to find Sara asleep sitting up in a cross-legged position against the headboard of her bed. He moved the files and reports surrounding her to the table and placed her laptop on his bed. Gently, he laid her head down on the pillows and pulled the covers over her. It reminded him of the Christmas when she was six and she wanted to stay up to see Santa Claus but was asleep by 10:30. Cradling her in his arms, he took her up to her bed as her parents started putting presents under the tree.

She murmured disjointed facts about the Ghost: dates, names, and locations.

The information he got from Gina wasn't a lot to go on. Had she been seeing the Ghost for what he really was or was it just a residual cognitive hallucination from the victim. He could hear Gina admonish him in his head. *Her name wasn't "victim", it was Christina Walker.*

Considering they might have been off about assuming him to be a psychic, William rolled through all he'd done with the

Agency, all that he'd seen and investigated, for other possibilities. There was that thing he ran into once in Las Vegas years ago, but it didn't quite match. Sure, it wore human skin to hide among people, but it didn't kill. It only used the skin of people who'd already died instead. They could be dealing with something similar, which could be the reason for all the inconsistent descriptions. But this explanation only led to far too many questions making it all the more unlikely. Maybe some sleep would help him figure out how to use the new information and how to give it to Sara.

For now, he was too tired to do more than slip off his shoes, secure his gun some place safe, and lay down. He went to put Sara's laptop on the table but noticed he brought it back from sleep mode when he moved it. The screen was nothing more than a video player with a paused image of what looked to be a tiny restaurant. William was more than a little bit of a Luddite and accidentally made the video play as he attempted to turn the laptop off. There was no sound, but he saw people coming and going quickly, so he assumed it was set to run at a faster speed. He was trying to stop the video when *something* caught his attention. He backed the video up and played it again. Once more *something* but he couldn't determine what, the video was playing too fast. He tried to get it to play at normal speed, maybe even in slow-motion, but that was beyond his technical expertise.

Deciding to let Sara sleep and point it out to her in the morning, if she didn't already know, he put the computer aside and lay back on the bed. He drifted off to sleep quickly, he could always do that, but it was rare that his sleep was restful. This night would be no exception.

Chapter 7

She spent the rest of the night tossing and turning with little sleep in between. Initially Gina thought she might be able to deal with this better if it had come on slowly, a little at a time, but she knew that was a lie. There was no way she could have been okay with any individual part of this, though it hardly made things easier to take in one go. It was bad enough that there was a serial killer out there killing young girls, but the possibility he had supernatural abilities made it even worse. More, a guy she just met- and was really beginning to like- was mixed up with said killer.

The cherry on her sundae? She also had some sort of barely controlled superpowers allowing her to see some hinky stuff, trash a room better than a doped-out rock star, and apparently had a murky history having to do secret government projects.

On top of it all, she was supposed to be dead.

And, speaking of dead people, there were ghosts. She had no idea how many geists of the killer's victims were out there, silently watching her apartment. Well, Dez's apartment, but that didn't make her feel any less weirded out by it; and for more reasons that mere proximity. It was certainly the creepiest of creepy developments without even considering they were also decomposing.

Then again, Gina was finding she preferred the spooky quiet ones as opposed to the talkative one who invited herself into the apartment.

Gina was trying to be understanding about the whole thing. It had probably been some time since Angie had anyone to talk to, especially someone who had more to talk about than their death. Plus, Angie was nice enough to peek into Dez's apartment to make sure he was there, providing some proof- and comfort- he was not the killer. However, Gina was finding sympathy for Angie wearing thin as the latter kept her awake by constantly asking questions such as who was the current President, Clinton or Bush; whether Nirvana was still a cool band, or had they sold out.

The sun rising made things less gloomy, but also amplified the weariness in Gina's muscles. The tension of the last several hours faded, and she was having a hard time keeping her eyes open, but she was also finding it impossible to keep them shut thanks to Angie's nattering. She finally asked the ghost to leave and drifted off to sleep once the wraith was gone. The clock on her phone showed 11:38 when she roused once more. She was still physically exhausted, emotionally drained, and figured no amount of coffee would do her any good. She started a pot anyway. While it brewed she called Michelle to find out if she had any appointments waiting for her.

"Nope," Michelle answered immediately, the exact amount of time she needed to recall all their schedules from memory.

"Good. I'm not feeling so hot this morning. I think I'm just gonna take the day off," Gina told her.

"No problem. I'll let Papa Frank know when I see him," Michelle replied. "Do you need me to bring ya anything?"

"No, but thanks. I just couldn't sleep for shit last night," Gina said, knowing that Michelle was likely to drop by anyway. They exchanged good-byes and hung up. The coffee wasn't finished brewing but Gina went ahead and got her cup, sugar, and creamer ready. To pass more time, she decided she'd run down stairs and get her mail. She opened her apartment door only to find Angie standing there. In the sunlit hallway she looked less substantial than in the dark of night, but the supplicating expression on her face was visible enough.

"Have you been standing there this whole time?" Gina

hissed, hoping no one else was around to hear her, once she got over the initial shock of seeing Angie again.

"Possibly," the wraith responded with an expression that might have been confused acceptance. "Probably. I've been in this spot since you told me to leave."

"That was quite a while ago."

"I'll have to take your word on that," Angie apologetically told Gina. The living girl took a deep breath and told the sullen ghost she could come in, mildly regretting it as slight nausea rolled over her from seeing Angie's herky-jerky flow as she rushed in, seemingly moving in reverse while still moving forward.

Gina gripped the doorknob for support with one hand, her other on her stomach as if that'd fix the sudden queasiness. "The fuck is the deal with that?" she weakly gasped.

"What's the deal with what?" Angie wondered as she looked about in effort to track down the object of Gina's query. Her voice reverberated throughout the room and made reality warp slightly accommodate her presence.

In answer, Gina pointed in Angie's general direction, waving her hand up and down to include the whole of her. "That! You!"

Gina knew that was hardly clarifying. She took a calming breath as she shut her door.

"When you speak it comes out all forwards and backwards and everything and before and after you say it. Then there's the way you move. It's all..." Gina shuffled her body in weird motions, trying to impersonate Angie but was only making herself look silly judging by the wraith's amused look. Gina gave up on that and went for a simpler starting point.

"What's with the outfit? The tiara and the wings?"

"That's easy!" Angie said. "I died at this Halloween party some frat guys were throwing. I was an angel." Her face screwed up in contemplation as she looked down at herself. "A sort of slutty angel, I guess, but still an angel.

"Anyway, I think some asshole doped my drink and I was blacking out when someone took me to a room upstairs. I don't know what he was gonna do with me *exactly* but, since he dropped me and ran away without a second thought when someone yelled that the house was on fire, I doubt chivalry was at the forefront of his mind." Angie said it casually, obviously having had a while to come to terms with it all.

"Not a bet I'd take either," Gina muttered, though Angie didn't seem to hear that.

"It was smoke inhalation that did me in, but I think I caught fire a little before I expired completely," Angie continued, holding her blackened arm out. "Got myself singed just a bit," she commented cheerily as she displayed the grisly sight.

"Yeah, just a bit," Gina warily repeated as she took in the nearly skeletal mess.

"I guess I had a nerve or two still twitchin' when that happened, but I was mostly out by then. Good thing too because I bet being on fire would've been a total bitch!

"As for the rest of it I did talk to this one other ghost. I'm not sure what he was in life, but he sounded pretty smart; he probably knew what he was talking about. He said something about a space-time dilation effect around ghosts because of all the residual psychic energy." Angie screwed up her face in confused thought. "Or, something. I think I may be saying it wrong. Anyway, I had no idea what any of it really meant. Come to think of it he was really into energy and kept asking if we could mix ours. You know, like he wanted..."

"Yeah, I get it," Gina held her hand out in front of her to stop Angie from continuing. "I really do get it. Thanks." Still curious, Gina asked, "So did you, um, live...," she said that word as delicately as she could, "...around here?"

"Yup! Born and raised and died right here in Birmingham," Angie answered. "I have a sister that lives not too far away. At least I think she still does," the ghost went silent for a second, sadness turning her face to stone. The moment was brief; Gina barely caught it before the wraith perked back up. "Anyway, I was a student at Montevallo when I bit the big one.

"I didn't even make it through one semester, but I hear that not an uncommon college experience. One way or another," she finished with a measure of casualness. The comment struck Gina as being more than a little defensive.

The coffee pot made a gurgling noise, signaling it finished brewing. Gina went to the kitchen and poured some into her cup. She was scooping sugar into the cup when Angie spoke up.

"So, you're a psychic."

Gina looked up to face the ghost and found her leaning against the counter, her elbows resting on the surface and her head planted on her palms. None of the items Angie's body brushed against seemed in any rush to acknowledge her presence. Gina, for the sake of her endangered sanity, did her level best to ignore it all.

"Sort of, I guess."

She tried a few times to start the story, stopping and going again, and starting over before settling on just heedlessly blurting it out. "This federal agent came to the apartment last night to talk about one of the ghost girls on the roof. Well, not the ghost in *specific* but *why* she's a ghost now. Follow?" Angie shrugged out what might have been an affirmative.

"Okay, so he tells me I can help with the investigation because I have these, um, powers. I guess psychic works, but he said some scientist had something to do with my birth once told him something about candles and sunlight when talking about me and other psychics..." Hearing herself talk made Gina shut up as she tried to recalibrate her speech to sound less crazy.

Before she could take the story back up Angie took a long look at Gina. "So... you're, like, *super* psychic?" she said, stretching the words out slowly as she talked.

"Maybe," Gina answered shyly, as if saying it aloud would rip time and space apart or, more likely, certify her as insane.

"So... what can you do?"

"I'm not sure really," Gina started. "I can see ghosts apparently, but I'm not sure why I haven't before."

"That's not surprising, really."

"Oh yeah?"

"Yeah, that guy I was telling you about earlier, he also said that even people who were 'attuned' to see ghosts rarely did. I guess the livings' subconscious are set on permanent ignore or something by default when it comes to the dead."

"Does that mean you've never been seen by another psychic?" Gina asked, a feeling of morbid pride growing within her.

"A couple here and there," the shade answered, deflating Gina's ego a little. "One just wanted me to help her scam people in fake séances. That was sketchy, but she didn't want to have anything to do with me once she found out I couldn't pick stuff up or make the walls bleed or anything like that. I split when she started swinging burning clumps of sage around to exorcise me."

"Does that work?"

"Sort of. I mean, would you stick around if someone started brandishing burning clumps of anything at you?" Gina conceded the point. "Another one, well, I don't think he could actually see or hear me. I don't think he was even psychic. He kept telling people that my name sounded like it started with a 'K' or 'J' and wouldn't repeat my answers correctly. A few times he acted like he was talking to a man and not a girl. I'm not 100% sure he really believed he was talking to the dead or if he was just another scam artist. There are a lot of both out there."

"You can't throw plates around or make a hallway seem way longer than it really is?" Gina took a sip of her coffee. "None of that haunted house legerdemain?"

"Nope."

"Can you do anything spooky?" Gina asked with a playful grin.

"Well, I can do this..." Angie said as she took a few steps away from the counter.

She stood still for a moment, her eyes closed. She put her hands to her face and ripped it away from the skull beneath as a gaping maw of gnarled teeth snapped outward. The ghostly flesh fell away from the rest of Angie's body and her broken cardboard wings burst out into sprawling, blackened streamers of flayed and bloody flesh. The wraith had transformed into a screeching, nightmarish abomination grasping and snapping at Gina. It lasted for only a few seconds before Angie's visage stood meekly in the middle of the apartment once again; a strange, greasy-looking vapor slinking out from her in a thin haze.

Sheepishly, Angie adjusted her jaw to sit correctly as she waited for Gina's reaction.

Without realizing it, Gina had thrown herself flat against her refrigerator, the coffee cup dropped and broken on the floor, the dark beige liquid soaking into her socks. She took a few deep gulps of air, made her heart resume beating, and collected her thoughts. "Well, that... was certainly... um," Gina said with a weak smile as she took a dishtowel from the sink and dropped it down over the spilled coffee. She pulled her socks from her feet and took them to the bathroom.

"But if no one can see you, how's that any good?" she asked from the other room. Her voice cracked only a little.

Angie started to follow but the sound of the living girl pissing made her stop. The wraith knew death affected one's social norms almost to the same degree it does one's ability to continue living, but not completely. Most would probably prefer not to hear such sounds, but Angie kind of missed having to take a piss. It was annoying in life, but she often found herself appreciating the things like that now. She stayed outside the door.

"Not with the living but it can be useful with the odd ghost. People who were touchy-grabby assholes in life aren't any bigger on self-reflection in death and can usually find even more ways to justify their behavior. Being dead is the ultimate pity party, you know."

The toilet flushed, and Gina washed her hands. "Awesome. It's not bad enough you're dead; you still have to deal with douchebags. So, did you just figure that out on your own?"

"Oh no!" Angie said as Gina brushed past her to go back to the kitchen, her shoulder tickling from the slight contact. "I had a roommate for a little while. She'd been around for, well, I'm not sure how long but a long time and knew a good bit. She taught me a few things. I could have picked up more from her, but she could be a bit, um, tiresome so I moved out."

The dishtowel had absorbed most of the spilt coffee now and Gina wiped up the rest and threw the cloth into the sink. She began picking up the broken pieces of the cup. "Can you do anything to the living?" Gina inquired as she tossed the pieces into the garbage can. "No demonstrations needed, by the way."

"I can make people feel things."

"You mean emotions? Like make them feel scared?"

"Scared, yeah," Angie replied. "But other feelings too. It helps if they're already heading that way, then all I have to do is give them a little nudge, but I can make them feel any way I want. Maybe even give them an impression or idea of why they feel what they're feeling. I can also hop on for a ride in living people. I can't make them do anything and it's kinda hard. I can't do it for long either but it's the closest I get to being alive again."

"That's genuinely disturbing. None of that with me or my friends or family, by the way," Gina warned, to which Angie quickly agreed. With the mess cleaned Gina got another mug out and fixed a new cup of coffee. "There was that new girl on the roof last night and I think I know a couple of the others." She took a sip. "Can they talk?" Gina asked, nodding her head up towards the ceiling.

"Doubtful," Angie answered ruefully. "Well, not in any way useful at least. I've been watching 'em and ones like them, they're not..." she struggled to find the right word. "Whole," she uncomfortably settled on.

"Whole? What do you mean 'not whole'?"

"See, they've mostly moved on or there's really not much of them left anymore," she explained. "That last part often happens when death is sudden or pretty traumatic. The ones upstairs are still here but not on their own. And we're lucky they aren't either. I've seen what it's like when a ghost like them is here on their own steam. It ain't pretty," the wraith shuttered. Gina thought of the dark-haired one, the way she snapped. She could feel anger and spite cascading from her. She'd hate to see that one off a leash.

"Something is keeping them here," Angie continued, "which is probably true of all ghosts, but whatever it is isn't part of them. It isn't of their making. Something outside of them is doing it." Angie turned her head towards the ceiling. "*Someone's* keeping them here."

Although she assumed it had happened to her plenty of

times before, Gina let the feeling of being thwarted by metaphysics sink in. Being fully aware of it only made it even worse. She picked up her phone and dialed the number on Agent Post's card. It rang a few times before going to voice mail. She left a message telling him he could expect a new body to be found and what the new girl would look like, but she didn't have any more information. She wondered if she should say something about what she saw with Jen earlier, but decided against it, for the moment, and ended the call.

"You said all of those girls on the roofs are connected to this serial killer?" asked Angie.

"Yeah."

"Can't you just use your psychic mojo and see what this guy looks like, where he is?"

"Tried that last night a little; it didn't work all that well," Gina answered as a sickening chill ran up her spine. The urge to wash her hands again crept into her mind. "Besides, as far as I can tell, others with more experience than me have tried and failed so I doubt I'd be any real help."

"But you're super psychic, right?" Gina gave the shade a dismissive look. "How long have you been at this?"

"Counting last night? A day." She started to drink more coffee but amended herself first. "Not even that really."

"You never knew you had powers before yesterday?"

Gina caught Angie's face twitching on that last word and realized it happened whenever the ghost said anything regarding the passage of time.

"Not exactly," Gina lowered herself to the couch. "I think I may have used them before without knowing." A foggy memory of her and her father sitting in an ice cream parlor flashed through Gina's mind. He was telling her something very important, but the words wouldn't make themselves known to her fuzzy recollection. "I think I've always been like this but I just... sorta forgot."

"Forgot? It's not like we're talking about car keys here," Angie said as she took a seat next to Gina, the cushions remaining undisturbed. "How do you forget something like that?"

"I don't know!" Gina barked harshly. She took a deep

breath, calmed down. "Maybe it was intentional; like there was a good reason." Holding on to that possibility a moment, a notion came to her. "That agent said something about scientists and a facility, like a laboratory. He talked about something he called the 'Agency' and said I needed to stay off their radar. Maybe that's why I forgot what I can do."

Angie nodded. At least, for the sake of her lucidity, Gina imagined the motion the ghost made to be a nod. "Well, something had to kickstart it again; any ideas what?" the shade replied.

Gina slowly bobbed her head, her lower lip pressed under her upper teeth, as a hazy memory filled her mind. Her thoughts went back to the night she met Dez.

They were at the bar talking, he was telling her about having just got into town, but the *way* he spoke was weird. It was like he was placed an odd spin to his words, articulated his speech in a manner that emphasized at peculiar points. It felt strange; left her a bit foggy even now as she merely reflected on their meeting. His utterances snaked through her mind, making her agreeable towards him and eager to help him out.

It wasn't abrupt or forceful, just coaxing and alluring. It didn't hurt she probably would have helped him anyway, but it abruptly stopped. More than just stopped- the words retreated in the most direct way possible. She remembered hurting a little; but, then it was over, and she was fine. Dez seemed shaken when it happened, started to walk away even.

However, she had assured him it was okay. That she probably just drank a little more, or a little faster, than she should have.

Maybe.

"I think Dez might have somehow tripped it up."

Angie's excitement was rousing fast now. "How?"

"Don't know," Gina shrugged. "I know he's not *the* psycho but that doesn't mean he's not *a* psycho," she winced at her words. "I don't think he's a bad guy, but there's way too much about him that I don't know and he's not telling."

Another thought occurred to her then as she looked at Angie closer. "You know, I should be way more freaked by all of this; visions, me being a psychic, shadowy government agencies, serial killers." She scrutinized Angie a touch more intensely. "You...

"But if Dez somehow made all of this kick in... I don't know, it's like I've been too busy trying to keep a lid on that to be terrified. I should be going full-tilt, rubber-room crazy but I can't even say I've really been all that alarmed."

"If it's something that's always been a part of you then it may have spent all this time getting you ready for it," Angie offered. It was a stretch; even her voice gave lie to any belief the geist might have had in the thought.

"Maybe," Gina murmured doubtfully. Regardless of the reason why, the rest of what Post told her seemed more pressing then. "The agent also said that I should develop my powers in case *they*..." she supplemented the word with a spooky voice and wiggling creepy fingers, "... come for me."

The wraith smiled with enthusiasm. "Then that's what you should do. Especially since you have someone living below you who you have no idea what they're about."

This reaction set Gina on her heels. "Why do you care?" she guardedly probed.

The ghost barely took any time to consider her reply, though she was more entreating in tone. "I have a problem that I could use a medium on... and you could be that medium."

They stared at each other for a long beat. "Maybe?" Angie meekly added.

After a moment Gina replied, "Well I certainly appreciate the honesty." She drank from her cup, turning away from the shade.

"I don't mean right now," Angie hurriedly persisted. "You've got other things to deal with... I get that... and you hardly know me. I may not even be the type of person you'd wanna help out in the first place. All I ask is think on it; give me a chance. Please?"

Gina did take a minute to consider it. Her parents raised her to do what she could to help people in trouble. Granted, whether it extended to people who were already dead was something that never actually came up, but with recently available data it seemed like it might still apply.

"And if I decide I don't want to do what you need?"

"No harm, no foul!" Angie declared, excitement looking bizarre in her solid grey eyes. "But first, we need to get you up to speed with your psychic stuff."

"Fine," Gina finished her coffee and put the cup down on the table. "How would you suggest I start improving my... powers?"

Angie thought about this for a moment, the thrill slowly draining from her face. "What can psychics do?"

Gina shrugged. "Read minds. See the future. Move things with their brains."

"Okay. I'm not sure I have a mind in the traditional sense so trying mind reading is out for now," Angie responded uncertainly.

"I might have already done the 'see the future' thing and I've done the 'see the past' thing," Gina supplied with a shudder. "I'm not really up to do either again."

"That leaves moving things with your brain!" The wraith finished, pointing to the coffee cup Gina just put down. "Give it a shot."

"I'll try," Gina agreed. Angie excitedly opened her mouth to say something. "Don't Yoda me!" she quickly interjected, guessing at the shade's incoming remark. The ghost was dejected but she yielded.

Gina closed her eyes, sitting up with her back straight. She took a few deep breaths and thought about the cup moving across the table. She stayed still for an uncomfortable amount of time, her back beginning to ache, before opening one eye and looking at the cup.

It was in the same spot before she closed her eyes.

She sighed. "See, I don't think I can do this; *any* of this!"

"Oh bullshit!" Angie yelled as she rose up to hover over Gina. "Most psychics couldn't see me even if they wanted to and gave it their damnedest. Yet here you are having a conversation with a dead girl you didn't wanna have without even trying!" With it a few inches from Gina's face, the ghost's visage started to slip back into the skeletal maw, eyesockets blazing with a sinister green light. Gina fell away, sinking into the couch cushions as the cup and a few books on the table flew up at the ghost, though they harmlessly flew through her and crashed into the wall behind. The table itself jumped an inch or two off the floor, landing skewed before tumbling over onto its side. Other objects on the table fell over or slid off onto the floor.

Angie's face instantly returned to normal, a satisfied smile across her lips, as she sat back down next to a terrified Gina.

"See, you just needed the proper motivation," she said amiably.

Gina wasn't pleased, but her attention was more on what happened with the table, the cup, and the books. After standing the table back up, she started to pick up a small toy that had fallen from it when Angie made a chastising noise. Gina looked up at her; the ghost's face was stern.

And becoming a bit skeletal.

"Fine!"

Relaxing a little, Gina tried using her mind to pick up the toy. It took a few minutes, and more than a few tries, but the toy soon sat in the center of the table. Thrilled with herself Gina tried, and succeeded in, picking up other objects from the floor and putting them on the table. Each object was easier than the last and she was quickly manipulating several at once.

She moved on to trying other uses of this ability. She got pretty good at picking out a CD, taking it from its jewel case, and playing it on her stereo. She collected the pieces of the second broken coffee cup and threw them away in the trash without getting up from the couch. She tried making herself a third cup of coffee from across the apartment but realized not being able to see what she was doing was a major impediment. She moved on to folding and hanging clean clothes from the laundry basket, but couldn't get the finer manipulations of the action, resulting in clothes balled up or twisted in loose knots on the floor.

At some point during the training she joked to herself how this would probably make getting rid of those 15 or 20 pounds she wanted to lose that much harder. *I was at least getting some exercise walking to the fridge* she thought before regarding to her disastrous attempt to pour coffee with her ability. She'd at least have to stand somewhere in the middle of the apartment to see what she was doing, even if she didn't have to set foot in the kitchen to do so. That was something.

"Psychics can see things remotely, can't they? Like faraway places or around corners or other rooms?" she asked the ghost. Angie gave a tentative agreement and Gina smiled as she patted her belly. "Yeah, they do," she hummed to herself.

Sara's eyes popped open at the sound of the door closing. Shooting straight up into a sitting position, the feeling of a forgotten bad dream quickly dissolved, leaving a disconcerting residue in her bleary mind along with an uncertainty of her surroundings. Awareness swept in quickly but remembering the cheap hotel room provided only cold comfort. William was already showered and dressed, setting coffee and breakfast from a nearby fast-food joint on the faux-wood table. She looked at the time on her cellphone. It was already after 10.

"You let me sleep this late?" she accusingly groused, digging sleep from her eye with the heel of her hand.

"You needed it. It won't do any good if you fall out from exhaustion."

She knew he was right, but she didn't want to admit it. Still, Sara thought she could've gone with a little less sleep.

She grabbed a few pieces of clothing and went to the bathroom. The morning heat was hardly any less oppressive than the day before, so she opted to take a cold shower. It was less than 15 minutes before she was sipping cooling coffee and eating lukewarm food every bit of faux as the table she was eating it from. Having taken only a few bites from his breakfast, William was drinking coffee while flipping through a newspaper. The front page reported on the 15-year-old victim. Scanning it from the other side of the table, Sara could see it didn't have anything new to add to previous reports beyond a mention that the FBI was now involved.

William peered over the top of the paper and saw Sara was eating less than she was reading. He didn't need to ask to know which article she was perusing. "Sports or funnies?" he dryly tested. She suddenly perked up, mildly surprised by the question before realizing the jest in which it was offered. She sank back some in embarrassment, but William told her what she was looking for without judgement.

"Nothing we don't already know, obviously, but the paper doesn't seem to be the biggest fan of the local PD," he said as he folded the paper and slid it across the table. Her hand reaching for it, he pinned the paper to the table under a couple of fingers. "I do want you to take a look at something first."

He grabbed Sara's laptop from the dresser where he left it the night before and put it down in front of her as he pulled his chair over beside hers. "I noticed this last night when I tried turning the thing off," he explained. Sara, knowing her uncle's troubles with almost any technology invented after 1990, let a soft smile cross her face. The video player was still up.

William started the video. "What's this of?"

Sara watched it play. It was still set to fast-forward, but she recognized it immediately. "This? It's just security footage from a camera in a restaurant near where the Ghost first encountered the victim."

"Christina Walker?" William clarified, hearing Gina's voice in his head before he realized it.

Sara glanced at him strangely, her brow drawn. "Yeah." Sara never knew her uncle to personalize a victim, he always said it disrupted objectivity, but she ignored it and continued. "Local PD hoped they might get a look at the perp but the view to the street wasn't right."

"I saw something strange on it last night, but I couldn't get it to play in any way but fast-forward. Can you slow it down?"

"Sure," she blurted with a small laugh. He may as well have asked whether it was possible to tie a shoe given the tone of Sara's response. "Do you have a time mark?"

He told her about the moment he wanted to look at. She stopped the video, made an adjustment, and started it back again a few seconds before the mark. It was playing at a normal speed for a moment when Sara saw the oddity just as William was about to point it out to her. She rewound the video and played it again, now in slow-motion.

The film was grainy black-and-white, so fine detail wasn't possible. It showed the normal business day of an eatery- people walked in, ordered food, and left. Some ate there, some didn't. That's mostly what they saw until a little more than half-an-hour before Christina Walker's life ended. The recording showed one individual enter the eatery, order and eat their food and leave, as typical; but it was as if someone went behind them and scratched the person out with a ball-point pen. Every frame was like that: dark, squiggly lines gouged into the recording over the person like an angsty kid marking out hated people in their yearbook.

"Is that him?" Sara croaked. Whatever kept human witnesses from remembering any details about the Ghost, regardless its source, it was now clear his abilities extended to electronic witnesses too. "Is that the Ghost?"

Sara watched the clip over and over again, hoping each time the scribble would forget to obstruct her just this once. If they weren't unsettled by the circumstances enough, they soon realized the obfuscating scrawls were different with every play-through. Something was actively involved with each attempt to see the Ghost on the film instead of a passive application at the moment of recording. The Ghost may as well have been in the room with them right now, laughing at their wasted efforts to find and stop him. Sara might have sat in the chair all day watching the recording if her phone hadn't gone off.

She looked at the display. "Local PD," she said to William as she answered the call. Less than a second later Sara was grabbing a pen and paper from her bag. "What time?" She jotted something down on the paper. "Where?" More jotting. A pause. Writing. "We'll be there shortly," Sara said as she hung up the phone.

"What is it?"

"Another body was found this morning; about an hour ago. The locals think it's our guy."

Within 10 minutes they were parked half a block from an abandoned apartment complex. They pushed through a small crowd trying to see what was going on. Uneasiness washed over William, but he assumed it was apprehension of what they'd find within. A cop stopped them at the yellow tape, but quickly let William and Sara through when they flashed their identification.

"The place has been set for demolition for... well, as far back as I can remember... but there's some problem regarding zoning. Probably just the owners trying to get the place tore down on the city's dime," one of the local detectives told them as he walked them to the crime scene. "A lot of kids sneak in and trash the place. Squatters take up residence. That's how the body was found: squatters." He said pointing out a young, nervous couple talking to a uniformed cop.

As they walked through the complex, William and Sara took in the detritus of a forgotten society making its way as best it could in the vacant area. There were bottles everywhere, broken or not, the fumes of their dried contents swirling into a sour, stagnant mixture in the air; ripped trash bags with their rotting contents spilled out; discarded articles of clothes, shoes, and furniture mixed in with a few used needles and condoms. Few of the windows had unbroken glass, if they had any glass at all, and the door to one unit had been kicked in, a fire-pit made in the living room. The door to another unit was opened, though still on its hinges, but the only thing within was a single stained mattress with a dingy sheet plopped haphazardly on the floor.

"Don't know if this is the work of your guy or not," the detective warned as they reached the landing to the second floor, his voice resounding in the gloomy, narrow confines of the stairwell, "but from what I've read of him, this is the type of place he likes to dump his victims."

Sara cringed as they passed an alcove that smelled like it had been used numerous times as a bathroom. "That's an understatement," she deliberately agreed, looking back at William. "He usually places his victims where he thinks they belong: in the trash."

"Gehenna," William remarked absently as he took in his surroundings. Sara's eyebrow rose, displaying her lack of familiarity with the term. "From what I understand, Gehenna was the closest thing the Hebrews had to a hell. Or it may have just been an ever-burning garbage pit on the outskirts of a city where they'd dump the bodies of the wicked to be burned along with the rest of the trash. It's hard to tell which came first, the story or the pit."

The local detective shrugged indifferently. "The religious wack-jobs are always the worst; they're so self-righteous. You can get a confession for the worst shit out of them easy, but it's still like they didn't do anything wrong. And that's not even considering they're getting their religion all wrong," he scrunched up his face as if a bad taste had invaded his mouth. "If only they'd read their Bible more often," he surmised with a wave of his hand and without a hint of irony. "At least the normal crazies have the decency to think, 'goddamn, I am truly fucked in the head and am engaged in some vile shit' every once in a while."

He stopped at a cross point in the breezeway, checking which hall to take before leading them down one.

"Anyway, we haven't ID'ed the body yet. We'll run fingerprints, check missing persons, but the estimated time of death is about 12 hours ago," he was explaining as William's phone started to ring. The agent recognized the number as Gina's, but the look Sara gave him suggested she'd be far too curious about this call if it seemed important. He dismissed it as a wrong number and ignored it. The detective renewed his report.

"The vic is female, and the examiner thinks her age to have been between 10 to 13 years old."

Sara stopped walking but only for an instant before regaining her stride. All of the Ghost's murders were horrific, but the younger victims hit Sara the hardest. If either William or the local detective noticed her reaction, they didn't acknowledge it. The local kept up the account, but she stopped listening. She could read it later. Worse, she could probably recite it along with him. They arrived at had once been a laundry room and found it crawling with the forensics team searching for any trace of evidence. The girl's body was being prepared for transport, but the examiners stopped when they saw the feds.

William and Sara looked over the scene and the body. Yet again they found nothing to give any clue about the Ghost's identity. "Well, what's the plan?" William asked her as the body was carted away.

"The official report won't be available for a while. I think I'll go with the body to the coroner's, be the first to hear what they have to say."

"If you're going with the body, it's being taken over to Armitage instead of county," The local detective interjected.

"Armitage? What's that; a local mortuary?" William asked.

"A mortuary, yeah. Oldest in the city."

"Why? What's wrong with the morgue?" Sara queried dubiously. It wasn't out of the question for a funeral home to double as a county morgue, but the city's coroner's office struck her as more than sufficient.

The local shrugged his shoulders as he lit a cigarette. "All I know is that the examiner on duty last night says the place got hit by an earthquake," he let out an unimpressed laugh along with a lungful of smoke. "If you ask me that particular egghead always struck me as bit too, I don't know, stressed. It's probably nothing that couldn't be cured by fondling someone a bit more alive than he's used to though." He said, greatly impressed with his own wit, as he scribbled the mortuary's address down for Sara.

"It's not far. Walking distance if you're into that sort of thing."

Her gratitude as he handed Sara the slip of paper was curt, though not as much as she wanted. With the detective gone, she turned to leave with her uncle. "What're you going to be doing?" she asked once they were outside of the complex.

William watched as they loaded the body into a van. "I think I'll check back in with Lowden. Maybe one of the Agency psychics got something new." He knew it was a longshot. He also knew Sara knew that too, but if Gina had anything for him it'd provide enough cover. "Otherwise, I'll head down to the precinct and wait for their report. Want me to give you a ride over to the mortuary?"

Sara shook her head. "If it's only a few blocks I can walk it."

"Then I'll meet back up with you later tonight unless I get anything."

Sara nodded her agreement and they parted ways. Once William got back to the car he listened to Gina's message. She knew about the latest victim but didn't have any further information that could help. As disappointing as it was, William wasn't sure what he was expecting really. *At any rate*, he thought, *I won't have anything to give Sara that could cause problems.* He started the car and pulled away, pointing the vehicle towards the police station, as a nasty feeling fell over him. He dreaded spending any time with that boorish detective, but there was something else, something out of place. The problem was more something *in* place that shouldn't have been there. Something about the crowd of people gathered outside of the apartment complex. The more he thought about it, the more he decided it was just contempt so many people would seek to find some entertainment from the loss of a little girl's life.

Soon he forgot the feeling completely. All he thought was how he was not looking forward to spending more time with that local detective.

He stood outside the complex and watched the police bustle about what they would no doubt call a crime scene. It was not something He did often, but from time to time He allowed Himself some pride in a job skillfully executed. It did vex Him how they could not see it was a simple act of nature. After all, what could be more natural than the retribution of the Almighty on a fallen world? If they could understand they might be useful allies, but He dismissed such thoughts. It was not His to question who the Almighty did or did not choose to carry out this mission.

He was surprised to see that one FBI agent here; the one who forsook her natural place in the world, the one who almost unwittingly helped Him out by charging the Hunter with His work. The thought of the Adversary's tool getting credit for His providential work galled Him greatly, but He could appreciate the irony of that affair. It was neither here nor there, He decided, since the Hunter was quickly released. It did throw the hound off His scent enough that it took quite some time before the Hunter posed any real threat again.

It was some time before the agent and her partner reemerged from the ruins. They talked briefly, then parted, he returning to their car and her walking off on foot. Interest got the better of Him and He followed her. He made His way through the crowd, brushing past her partner by inches. The older man looked right at Him- the wariness all too evident in his face as though he knew the very person they were looking for was *so close*. He took some enjoyment from that as He pushed through the throng of bodies.

Once free of the crowd He shuddered, hoping the action would remove their disease from Him. Although He was well aware of the general depravity of people, He could not understand why they found the misery and destruction of their fellows so engaging. If they wanted to lessen it, He could grasp that, but they never did. Instead they just wanted to see it, feel it, and breathe it all in. They acted as if it sustained them.

He supposed He shouldn't be surprised by that.

He waved those thoughts away; it was not His to fathom the denizens of this fallen world. He had His mission and that was all He need concern Himself with. He kept His distance from the female agent while keeping her in his sights. She stopped abruptly in front of a coffee shop and seemed to deliberate before going in. He walked past the front of the building, looking at her through the window as He passed slowly by, only to turn back and go inside. He skipped in line behind her. There was a restless energy about her, no doubt because of Him.

The lone barista was dealing with an intensely vicious and demanding customer, causing the wait for service to be that much longer. He took the opportunity to speak to the agent by making a disparaging remark about the customer, which she grimly acknowledged. He made a few more attempts at small talk, asking questions about her, nothing too personal though. Finally, He asked her for the time, which she brusquely provided, though He could not tell if she was annoyed by Him or the delay. He threw out a lame excuse for why He could no longer stand in line. She did not react in any way to His claim. She did not even look back at Him as He walked away.

He left the coffee shop and headed back to His hotel room, a tune about the blessings of the Almighty on His lips.

Sara was relieved the guy had decided to leave. She wasn't a stranger to having men try to strike up a conversation with her, to pick her up. It annoyed her for reasons more than the fact she didn't play on that team, but she typically just ignored it and went on with life. This one, however, galled her more than usual; there was just something off about the creep that left a pall hanging over her. She didn't think he was making a sad attempt to hook up with her; more like he was about to ask if she'd "found Jesus" or try an Amway pitch.

It was a relief when he left on his own, since Sara knew she was probably on very thin ice with this investigation to begin with. It wouldn't have been very helpful to her situation if she had to aggressively inform a random loser in a busy coffee shop that she was armed and perfectly willing to use deadly force if necessary.

Suddenly Sara realized she was having trouble remembering what the guy looked like. There was a vague sense of something physically off about the guy, but she was starting to draw blanks. *He had blonde hair,* she thought. *No! He had brown hair. What color were his eyes?* Sara had always been good at this sort of thing and both the Navy and Quantico trained her to gather and remember details at a glance, so she couldn't understand why recalling this particular person was so much trouble now.

The weight in the bag slung over her shoulder brought one thought to mind: The Ghost. She spun around to face the door, dropping the bag to the floor as she ran to leave the shop. Out on the sidewalk she drew her gun, scanning the people there in hopes of catching a glimpse of him. At the corner she saw him waiting for the light to change so he could cross. She ran and grabbed him as he started to step off the curb. He turned to find Sara's gun in his face.

"Down on the grou...!" She started to yell before realizing this was not him, just some confused and frightened guy suddenly staring down the barrel of her sidearm. Sara apologized, showing her ID and told him go on about his business; told the stunned and confused crowd around them to go about their business. She tried finding the Ghost once more as the sound of the man's hurried footsteps on the pavement faded behind her. People slipped passed her with a wide, nervous distance, her agitation alarming them as much as the pistol in her hand. She slipped the weapon back into her shoulder rig, recognizing that if the killer was still around she'd never find him now with an anxious herd of citizens doing all they could to avoid the crazy lady with the gun. Not even her badge and identification as an FBI agent helped with that.

She went back to the coffee shop, finding the people within were regarding her warily now too. She asked for the manager as she picked her bag up from the floor. She hoped that the Ghost hadn't been able to work his voodoo on the recordings here like with the earlier video. It took forever to get, but she also had a chance to ask others if they'd gotten a look at the Ghost. An hour later, she left the shop with a copy of the morning's recordings, a handful of useless descriptions, and her coffee. The last free of charge.

She pulled her phone and dialed her uncle. Before William could even get a greeting out Sara started talking. "I saw him! I fucking saw him!"

"Saw who?" he didn't get what she was saying at first. Then, realization hit. "You mean the Ghost? You saw the Ghost?"

"More than saw: I think the asshole was about to ask me out on a date."

"Where are you?"

"At a coffee shop not far from the mortuary." She'd have to

fill her uncle in on the full story later. "I got a copy of the recordings from the cameras at the shop. Can you get someone from local to meet me? I want to get this looked at as soon as possible." Over the phone Sara could hear William snapping his fingers at someone as he assured her he'd meet her there himself if he had to and hung up.

Sara got to the mortuary as fast as she could. She figured they were nowhere near finished with the initial examination but was impressed with their proficiency all the same. She discovered the head mortician had once been county coroner several years earlier. He was still rather young, so she doubted he had retired. Why he was no longer with the county she didn't know and didn't bother to ask. Besides, it wasn't her business and it wouldn't help with the investigation anyway.

She was looking over the preliminary report when William arrived. "The local detective *that* bad?" she drily asked her uncle.

"I think I might rather go on the date the serial killer was trying to ask you out on," he said with a rare smile. "What's that?"

"Prelim report on the victim."

"We think the prints gave us an ID on her: Rachel Wells, but we're trying to get in touch with her parent or guardian to identify the body for sure," William told her as he took the report.

"If it's her what do we know?"

"Eleven years of age; only known address puts her living in a housing project not far from the location of the body," he said as he skimmed the report. "We haven't been able to contact anyone, so uniforms are going to the address now."

"Eleven?" Sara shuddered. "He's killed as young as 13 before but not this young. Not that we know of."

"Did he ever try having a chit-chat with investigators before?"

"Also, not that anyone knows of. Plus, there's something off on his pattern. He would have started off with a few projects girl like Wells before going for someone from a well-off family like Walker. It takes more time for the heat to build on him that way."

"Something's changed about how he operates. Why?"

"We've never been able to determine what drives him in

the first place so that's impossible to tell. If we knew what's changed maybe that could tell us something."

William had one idea but couldn't tell Sara; not yet anyway. Although Salvia was believed to be in another location, he was currently in the city and there was a known connection between him and the Ghost. From reading Sara's files William knew the Ghost had a high level of confidence, and for good reason. Now he was pushing past arrogant and cocky. William wondered if the presence of Salvia and the Ghost both being here might hold the answer. Fearing it might distract her, William didn't want to let Sara know about Salvia just yet. He made a mental note to read up about the last time the two were in the same location.

William also speculated if the new piece he put into play himself was associated to these new developments. Looking at the reports, William was surprised at the detail Gina gave him about the new victim. The night before, she barely had any control over her abilities. Today she was giving a thorough description of a murder victim she had yet to physically see. With everything they dealt with on a regular basis, many in the Agency had come to believe nothing happens without a reason. William mostly disagreed with that. Usually things *did* just happen for no rhyme or reason- outside normal cause and effect, of course- or were simple coincidence, but there were moments where the confluence of elements screamed otherwise.

Over the years, William had been in more than a few of those moments. He was getting the feeling this may be another one of those situations now. Such occurrences were often unpredictable. Some happened quietly, others were explosive. Some were over quickly, others took years. However, they always left people changed forever and not always for the better. He had to wonder how this one would leave them when it was all over.

Chapter 8

It was late in the evening and Gina had spent the afternoon trying out some of her new talents. She could lift things with her mind easily enough now, but delicate handling was still a bit beyond her. For the moment, the amount she could lift wasn't much yet, a few pounds at most, but she figured she might be able to work up something heavier with some effort. She hadn't tried reading people's thoughts yet- it felt too invasive, and she feared messing things up greatly- though she managed remote viewing to a degree. While she couldn't cast her perceptions too far away, she was able to spy throughout the building.

Gina briefly peeked in on her father filling out order forms and Michelle painting henna designs on the hand and arm of a client's small child. Gina watched Marcella coach a college girl on how to breathe before she pierced the girl's bellybutton. In another studio Jacob worked on the child's mother; having completed the contours he briefly struggled with his foot pedal before starting in on color. In the next room Bruce was putting the finishing touches to a patron's back-piece he'd been working on for over a year. It crossed her mind to peek into Dez's apartment, but she decided against it. She succeeded at "seeing" out to the sidewalk, some of the side alley and the roof, but not much further. It was even more frustrating that *seeing* was all she could do. None of her other senses would work remotely.

At least, *so far* that was all she could use. As she watched a few pigeons on the roof she believed she could hear their cooing. Maybe. If she had, it was extremely muffled, indistinct, so she couldn't be sure.

Figuring this was her cue to attempt something else, Gina decided to give reading objects another chance. She started on the old coffee table her parents gave her when she first moved in to the apartment. It was ancient- scratched up and badly needed a new finish- but sturdy. She placed her hand on the table, her fingertips lightly brushing up against the surface at first before her palm settled on the top. The wood grain gave the table some texture. As shallow as they were, the dips, valleys, and peaks were easily discernible. Now she began to feel every whorl, curve, and swoosh of the grain on her skin. She felt the distributed weight of the objects sitting on its surface and the books and magazines stored in the nooks below the table top. Slowly, the various tableaux of all that had happened near the table began to flood into her, playing out in her mind and becoming indistinguishable from her own memories.

She felt people prop their feet on her, place a drink or plate down on top of her, even sitting on her. It tickled some as dice from one of the many games her brother and his friends played rolled across her as they used the table. It hurt when the table was dropped in the hallway as she was moving in, blunting one of the corners. Gina became mildly embarrassed when some of the more enthusiastic times she and Bruce had sex, as viewed by the table when it was passively involved, started mingling and contrasting with her own recollections. The awkwardness, however, was mostly because the table was obviously more committed to truth than Gina in this instance. She thought to herself *Oh man, that face he's making... he was such a dork... ohmigod, that face* I'm *making! Did I really think* that *was hot?* She knew right then the next time she saw Bruce was going to be embarrassing. Well, a little more than usual for her part, at any rate.

She skipped past those moments and found others, even expanding the table's perceptions out to the whole apartment. She walked through memories of her, Quinn, and Suz in the mornings after a late night out; laughing and talking about nothing as they ate cereal and drank coffee. All the moments when Gina cheered Quinn up after the latest of a long line of asshole boyfriends broke her heart, or her jaw. The first night Suz moved into the flat below; her desperate knocking on the door when she came up to Gina's, nervous because she'd never really been on her own or felt safe before. They held each other close, not speaking, until they drifted off to sleep.

Gina had never even told Quinn, or anyone else, about that night. She couldn't say why, though. It was just something she was never willing to share.

The memories went further back, she saw her parents buying the table at a second-hand shop and taking it back to the crummy studio they lived in when they first got married. All the nights they sat on the floor at the table eating take-out and talking about how their life together would go. It was difficult for Gina to see her mother again, looking so young and lively, but it alleviated those final memories of her withering away from illness.

A knock at her door caused Gina's thoughts to disentangle from the table's memories. It took her a moment to remember where she was, an undertaking made slightly more difficult by the fact so much time had passed. The sun was lower in the sky, casting long shadows in her apartment. Angie stood nearby, still as a statue, looking uneasily at the door.

"Do you need me to hide?"

"Relax," Gina answered quietly as she made her way to the door. "It's not like anyone else will see you." Gina opened the door a crack and saw Quinn in the hallway before opening it further.

"Hey, scary lady, you feelin' okay?" Quinn asked as she wrapped her arms around Gina. "I stopped by the shop first and Papa Frank said you called in."

"Yeah, I'm good now," Gina answered with a convincing smile. "I just had a hard time getting to sleep last night."

"Oh yeah? Your 'hard time getting to sleep' wouldn't have anything to do with our new friend would it?" Quinn put her bag down on the counter on her way to the fridge to grab a beer. Shocked that Quinn could be seeing the ghost, Gina looked with confusion towards Angie, who could only shrug in mutual confusion. "Don't think I haven't noticed those glances you've been sending Dez's way, little missy," she gave Gina a teasing wink over the bottle.

"Hey, you never said you and the potential serial killer guy were 'involved'!" Angie shouted from the other side of the room, her face full of scandalized fascination. Gina locked a "shut up" look on the shade as she answered both questions.

"Dez and I haven't done anything." This was said addressing the universe as well, just in case.

"Yet!" It was disturbing enough how both Quinn and Angie- living and dead- said it at the same time, but Angie's reverberating voice took it above and beyond unsettling. Both sporting the same leering expression certainly didn't help matters either.

"Anyway, I hate to say it, but you do sort of reek, lady," Quinn noted as she took another swig of her beer. Waving her hand before her face she continued. "Why don't you take a shower then we'll go get Suz and we can get a bite to eat before going to Demon Aether to watch Dez- who you have nothing going on with, at all."

"Oh shit! That's tonight."

"Yup!" Quinn said. "Now go and get ready, young lady!" Gina headed to the bathroom as Quinn settled down on the couch, pulling a magazine from a stack on the floor. Angie followed Gina to the bathroom but stood just outside the door.

"Are you gonna tell her about all of this?"

"Not yet," Gina whispered back. "I'm not even sure I understand it enough that I could explain it to myself." She looked back at her friend sitting on the couch. "Besides, Quinn's pretty skeptical about this sort of thing. I doubt she'd believe me much right now."

Angie nodded her head. "I'll be up on the roof if you need me," she said as she left the apartment, disappearing through the door.

"Just out of curiosity- and remember that I love you regardless of the answer," Quinn yelled from the couch, her mouth twisted, and brow scrunched in puzzlement. "But why are all your clothes tied in knots?"

The examiner put the report together quickly, which may have been spurred by Sara's persistence to hurry things along. William expected it to be shoddy and piecemeal but was impressed with Dr. Morgan's competency under pressure. The report needed some work. Still, the details were all there and it was enough for Sara to work with for the time being. William noted Morgan's clear aversion to manipulating the facts and near pathological need to detail what he saw and nothing less or more, regardless of how uncomfortable it may be.

With the report in hand, Sara poured over it to squeeze out every last detail in the hopes there would be *something* to lead her to the Ghost. Once it became apparent this would not be the case, she would compare the new data to all she had so far and see how it fit, hoping it would lead somewhere. William figured he'd find Sara passed out at the table in the middle of her files again tonight. He wished he could keep her from giving in to her preoccupation but, as much as it pained him to admit, he was going to take advantage of that tonight.

Leaving Sara in the hotel room with a box of half-eaten pizza that would probably breed penicillin long before she acknowledged its presence or her need to eat, William headed towards the south-side of the city.

He drove into the suburbs just past the university. The last time he was here was roughly 20 years ago. The houses were on the verge of ancient back then and still looked the part now. At the time it wasn't the best neighborhood for a young couple with a small child to settle down and raise a family, but the Shields could have done a lot worse. Now the place looked different; the houses were still antiquated but most were in some state of refurbishment if not completely restored.

William found the address he was looking for. It had been painted a different color and had a few additions built, but, it was the same house. A fact made more apparent once he spied Frankie

Shields in the garage working on a car- just as he had been two decades ago when William last saw him. His hair was salt-and-pepper now, instead of the full head of jet black it had been, and his gut had gotten noticeably flabby. Still, even from across the street William could see Frankie was the same man he had been then. As before, he did not expect this conversation to be easy.

He was about to get out of the car when a young boy and girl came into the garage from the house. The boy had a spiky red mohawk and his frame told William he had to be Frankie and Flora's son, Trevor. The girl was lanky and blonde. William assumed her to be Cinnamon, Frankie's niece. Thinking he might be able to hear a bit of their conversation, the agent rolled his window down a little.

"... off to?" Frankie was asking.

Trevor answered with something that sounded like "ether" but the rest was too quiet. "... going to get Jen first though."

Frankie gently moved to make Cinnamon put whatever she had picked up and started playing with down, which caused her to drag her cousin away towards an old green Jeep with its top removed. The pair waved good-bye to Frankie as a tall blonde woman, who William figured was Frankie's sister, April, entered the garage with two cups.

"Play nice," she yelled as they pulled away.

Frankie straightened up as the woman handed one of the cups to him. They talked briefly, Frankie pointing to something under the hood of the giant red Caprice Classic every so often for emphasis. She nodded her head as he did. Before long she went back into the house and Frankie bent back under the hood. William supposed this was as good a time as any. Politely, he stood just outside of the garage door. He was about to knock on the door frame when Frankie crawled out from under the hood to reach for his cup, pausing when he saw the agent standing there.

"Frank Shields?" asked William, already knowing the answer. He looked William over, a hazy recognition on his face, then discontent once he definitely placed the face.

"You?" Frankie grumbled as he reached for a heavy wrench. "I thought I'd never see you again."

"I had hoped for the same thing," William answered honestly.

"Then why are you here?" Remembering the reason why he last saw William, his heart skipped a beat. "They're not after Gina, are they?"

"No," William said, his hand out, palm down, to calm the man. "But there have been... complications."

"Complications?" The large man plopped onto a stool by the workbench. William noted this put Frankie closer to a revolver that was partially hidden in a cubby hole.

Asking for permission first, William stepped into the garage. "There's a case I'm working on... a serial killer's using the city as a playground."

"Yeah, I've heard about that. What's it got to do with Gina?"

"This killer is... special."

"Special?" Frankie's lips moved up and down, like he was testing the word out and not liking the taste it left behind. The memory of their previous conversation flooded into his mind. Frankie stood up from the stool. "Special? You mean like Gina?"

"I think so." Frankie Shields was a big man, but he was also fast. More, age hadn't affected that one bit. William had no time to react before the man covered the distance between them, grabbed him and shoved him hard against the car. Tools fell out onto the floor with a loud clang.

"Is this another one of your *experiments*?" He hissed, the last word with a sneer.

"No. This one is completely nature's fault as far as I can tell," William kept his voice calm and even, hoping it would placate the man threatening him with a wrench.

"Frank? Everything okay out there?" April yelled from inside the house. "Do you need any help?"

"Everything's fine, April," Frankie said as he let go of William, keeping him in a burning stare. "I'm just making a mess out here. Don't worry about it." He started picking up the tools and was silent for a long moment.

"So why are you here?"

"Because I need Gina's help. I think she can help put the killer away."

"Are you asking for permission? Gina's a grown woman. Not much I can do if she wants to put herself in danger like that." He said it breezily but there was a waver in his voice expressing his concern, as well as anger. "I'll have to trust her to do what she thinks is right."

"It's already been done."

Frankie stopped collecting the tools and straightened up, turning to face William again. He repeated his question, articulating each word slowly and methodically. "Then why are you here?"

William gave an apologetic shrug. "After our last conversation I figured it was only right to let you know; from me, and face to face." The urge Frankie felt to bash William's head in was strong; his fists clinched and unclenched a few times. When he spoke next, his voice was low and even.

"She help you?"

William nodded an affirmative. "Some."

Frankie let out a deep breath, his head bobbed in acceptance and went back to picking up the tools. Not needing any further dismissal, William went back to his car. He hoped he would never have to see Frankie Shields this close again.

As far as appearances went, Demon Aether looked the same as any other independent little coffee shop that might pop up here and there around the edges of a college campus, only to be gone within a few years at best, However, it had been around since the mid-1960s, and no matter how the fashions and trends changed over the years it always managed to be quite modish. Being a meeting place for civil rights activists and other local subversives it held an esteemed locale in the city's history. At least it did officially. There were many in the city and surrounding areas who would love to see the place in flames because of that very history, and more than a few who had tried to make that happen.

Over the years it had changed considerably. Once it had a relaxed atmosphere with plush couches and chairs around small tables encouraging and facilitating intimate discussion or providing a quiet place to read or study or think when one wished to be left alone. All of this might still occur in certain corners of the place, but that atmosphere had mostly been left to history once the original owners handed the business over to their children, who were either enthusiastic but ineffectual or disinterested in the joint as anything other than a cash cow to be milked dry. Demon Aether would have gone out of business several years ago if not for the near-Herculean efforts of the managers, Nate and Wendy.

The general disinterest of the inheritors allowed the brother-sister duo to run the place as they saw fit, but they often had to deflect one of the owner's odd or impractical ideas to drum up business. As aggravating as the attempts to click with the younger crowds could be, he at least *tried* to help the establishment stay afloat. He was also able to deter his siblings when they threatened to fire Nate and Wendy whenever they refused to hand extra cash over to them at their whim. At any rate his ideas, misguided as they usually were, could be directed into workable plans with a little tweaking. During the afternoons it was still possible to unwind and have quiet conversations with people. At night, however, it was filled with people waiting to hear the night's entertainment, whether it be poetry readings, live musicians, or amateur theater.

Dez's set didn't start until 9:30, but he arrived nearly two hours early. This was mostly to get a feel for the place, but Nate was also going to show him around since he might pick a shift or two. In terms of sound quality, the stage set up in a small corner at the front wasn't the most ideal place in terms of acoustics, but it was the best for audience viewing and participation. The afternoon crowd filtered out as the evening bunch began to file in. With less than 30 minutes before Dez was to go on Nate started helping him set up the microphone when Gina arrived with Quinn and Suz. He waved hello to the trio as they mingled with friends and acquaintances. Dez noticed Quinn mainly stuck with the techno, electronica, and hip-hop groups as Suz gravitated more towards the goths, metal heads, and punks. Gina was a bit more of a social butterfly. She had a place in almost any group but didn't quite fit in with any of them.

The three eventually ordered drinks and wedged themselves onto a loveseat as Dez started his sound check. Since Demon Aether didn't sell alcoholic beverages, Gina snuck in a flask and spiked each of their drinks with bourbon. As subtle as she was, Dez still caught her and the two traded conspiratorial smiles. Gina's disappeared as soon as she caught Quinn eyeing the exchange.

"Don't think I didn't catch that, Little Miss Slick," Quinn started.

"Catch what?" Suz inquired as she dismissed an emo kid who had been bothering her.

"Our Miss Gina casting furtive glances towards one Mr. Dez," Quinn answered in a scandalous tone and nodding toward the stage.

Suz feigned dismay. "Oh my sweet lordy-lord! Our little girl, all grown up and chasing the men-folk! Say it ain't so, pa, say it ain't so!"

"I'm afraid so, ma." Quinn shook her head solemnly. "Though she swears nothing of the sort is going on," said as she laid a hand over her heart.

The two laughed as Gina sulked between them. "Seriously, nothing has happened. We're just friends," she hissed out between gritted teeth.

"For now," both said at once, which prompted more laughter from them and more aggravation on Gina's part.

"Yeah, he looks good, but... but I hardly know him," Gina replied blandly, hating the weak excuse even as she said it. She couldn't tell them the stuff she had learned about Dez from Agent Post. She was convinced he wasn't a deranged killer, but there was more to him than she was comfortable with; things he was hiding from her and everyone else. She didn't like that much, but she'd let it go for now and give him enough time to come clean on his own. Still, jumping into bed with Dez with all of that hanging over the situation struck Gina as a really bad idea.

"You don't have to get to know him," Suz assured. "Just that it wouldn't hurt to get to know certain *parts* of him is all we're saying."

Quinn threw a look over Gina at Suz. "We?"

"Fine. That's all *I'm* saying," Suz said as she shot a smirk towards Quinn.

Quinn nodded her thanks, but her gaze went distant as she considered things more. "Still... it wouldn't hurt if you got laid." All Gina could do is look at her with her mouth slightly open. "I mean, it has been awhile," Quinn supplied with a sheepish shrug of her shoulders.

"It's only been...," Gina was about to point out the thing she had with Bruce ended not too long ago, but quickly remembered they had kept it on the down low.

"Piss off," she muttered pathetically as she drank from her spiked cup. The booze she added to the coffee allowed her to regroup. "Besides, I'm just not big on hooking up like that." She now knew this was true a lot more than she did a few months before. "There's nothing wrong with it in general. It's just not my thing.

"I mean most of the guys around here down for that act like I'm not only obligated to do something about their erections, but I should be happy they're even considering me in the first place. Nevermind about whether I get anything out of it and, hey, since I'm not doing anything useful once *they've* gotten off could I maybe slink off to the kitchen and make them a sandwich before they get the hell out of Dodge? I can't think of anything further from hot than that.

"I'm fine with a guy wanting to sleep with me. It's not like there aren't guys I wanna bang too, but I don't think it's too much to expect them to treat me like a person instead of some sex-and-sandwich machine. It's not like I expect them to wanna know or care anything about me other than sex. Still, I don't think it'd hurt them to at least give me a little more respect and acknowledgment than they would the wads of used tissue piling up next to their bed."

"Is my sister on another one of her dating rants?" Trevor

141

teased, appearing behind the loveseat with Jen and Cinnamon in tow.

"That can only mean she wants to get her fuck on then," Cinnamon added, relishing the chance to get some retribution from the other night now that Gina didn't have Mason to deflect her efforts.

Gina quickly shot up and wrapped her arms around them. She also gave Jen an apology for the other night, which the young girl said was unnecessary and asked if Gina was feeling better. Quinn and Suz each hugged Trevor and Cinnamon and welcomed Jen as Trevor introduced her.

"What are you guys doing down here?" Gina asked as the three found seats. She slyly handed the flask over to Cinnamon.

"Quinn told Dad what you were gonna be up to tonight when she dropped by the shop. He told me, so Cinnie and I figured why not come down and see what all the fuss is about," Trevor explained, jerking his head toward Dez up on the stage as the sound check ended. Quinn and Suz snickered, especially since they had Trevor and Cinnamon firmly in their camp. Seeing Gina blush at the comment, Jen told Trevor to stop being mean to his sister. She figured her brother had to be in love since, when it came to playful jabs between Gina and Trevor, admonishments to be nice to either one generally resulted in escalation, not a cease fire.

Trevor waved the flask away, so Cinnamon passed it over to Jen as Nate hopped up on stage. Jen poured a little bourbon into her cup and handed it back to Gina as the audience quieted to a low murmur. Dez was given a short introduction and then wasted no time going into his first song.

At first a few patrons continued their conversations but even that quickly died down. It wasn't long before the only sounds not coming from the stage were espresso machines and the clinking of cups on tables. Just like on the roof, Dez's music and voice captivated his audience. Even those intent on hanging out in the smoking area crowded closer to the windows. Between songs Dez told stories. Some Gina and the others had already heard, with some embellishments added, but others they had not. Most of the songs he sang were covers of well-known or popular pieces, though they were well done with a care to make them his own in some way. The receptive crowd appreciated the covers. The originals, however, kept even the most reluctant listener on the edge of their seats.

Somewhere in the middle of the set, a pervasive feeling washed over Gina. She squirmed in her seat, eliciting a whispered and ribald comment or two from Suz despite her own manifest flash of disquiet. There was something off about the situation. In the middle of a shortened cover of "Waiting for the Miracle" Dez slipped up but recouped quickly. He hid it well, but Gina would swear he had the same impression that something was just not right. Still, no one else seemed to notice. The uneasy air quickly faded and Dez continued with no further trouble.

Normally He would be content to stay in His room for the night. After such a rewarding day, however, He felt deserving of indulgence more than usual. Over and over He held the events in His mind as He worked Himself up. The little temptress from the tumbledown playground would have been enough. Her protests at His indictments against her only proved her guilt. The game she was playing with that little boy said it all. It was obvious where that leads, and she knew it. Sure, it seemed innocent enough, but He knew better.

He left her precisely where she belonged- in the bones of a derelict monument to the fallen world. It was a place of congregation for the lowest of all the garbage people who blundered or sold their way into the grip of the Adversary. The site was perfect, with the gawking horde gathered to watch, wondering how anyone could do such a thing. Their blindness to their own culpability was the sick icing on the depraved cake. The thought almost made Him shudder to conclusion.

Then there was the agent. Her quarry right under her nose, conversing with her, and she was oblivious. Naturally, with her being a woman, she simply could not prove a match for Him. Not like the Hunter, who would ultimately lose by way of being a servitor of the Adversary. Granted, she eventually realized she "had" Him in her grasp, though too late. He derived some amusement watching her panic; that she almost shot someone else made it all the better. That thought brought Him to conclusion more than once in the last several hours.

The sun set some hours earlier, doing little to reduce the muggy air. He lay on His bed, His tick-marked skin tacky from more than just the humidity. Blood trickled from the fresh cut on His leg, right next to the one He made a few days ago. He used tissue to wipe the blood away then placed gauze over it. As He sat in the bathroom He felt the presence of the Almighty. It filled Him with joy and ecstasy like nothing else could, not even His rewarding treats or the sweet, seductive pleadings of the Adversary's minions as their lives were cut short by His hand.

He let the Almighty in, let It permeate His being and dominate Him. When the sensation was gone, He knew what to do. Dressed and ready, He left His room and followed the path laid out for Him. Even though it was not His place, He could not help but ponder what this meant. Rarely had the Almighty directed Him like this, and never this forcefully. He was always left to carry out and interpret the subtle signs of the divine mandate on His own. Was this another step toward exaltation?

He found Himself in front of a coffee shop. It was not soulless and commercial like the one where He had flaunted His presence to the agent. No, this place had some character, even if it was deficient. Music wafted onto the street from within. It took Him a moment, but He soon recognized the voice and melody belonged to the Hunter.

A few times when the Hunter was close, morbid curiosity got the better of Him and He would go to some dive or pit the Hunter managed to find purchase in to hear the superficially sweet songs. Like all else, they mocked the music He would hear when in the presence of the Almighty. Many times, He lost Himself for hours contemplating why the fallen spent so much time ineptly trying to emulate the gifts of the Almighty, even as they purposely rejected them.

Still, He could not fathom why the Almighty would lead

Him here like this. He slinked up to one of the huge storefront windows, ignored by all around and peering inside. He could barely see the Hunter on the other side of the glass. He watched for a moment, though the impression the Hunter was not the purpose of His excursion weighed upon Him.

He let His gaze slip over the masses within before stopping on a small group nestled in the back corner of the shop. There was a blonde girl who fit His normal considerations, yet something about her screamed the Adversary had long had its claws in her. Such a waste, He thought to himself. The other three girls huddled on a couch were far too fallen for His help as well, though there was something about one of them. He couldn't tell if it was the pale one or the purple-haired whore next to her. No matter, they were not His concern.

The final member of the group was a boy. Perhaps he could be saved? No, like the three girls on the couch, it would be a task for another of the Almighty's envoys.

He was about to give up, go back to His room and pray for further guidance, when He saw her. She was sitting at the table with the boy, blocked from His view until the boy shifted in his seat. She was willowy with dark hair. Even from here He could tell she had kind eyes. She was well within His purview to be saved; pure and untouched so far though not for long. Yet there was far more about her than that. She had a quality about her telling Him she was more than His typical mark. No, she was a different type of servitor of the Adversary, or soon would be. Whatever she proved to be- however she would soon serve the Adversary- could be the object of His next mission. She could be the key to His exaltation, a test to prove His worth.

But not here, not right now. For the present, He would lay-low and wait for the sign to pounce. He stepped away from the window to return to His room and bide His time.

But that did not mean He could not do something to keep the Hunter out of His hair for a little while.

The hotel room was starting to look like a stereotypical conspiracy theorist's workroom.

Although she had several apps and programs on her laptop that could do the work- and she used them to their fullest- she still hung documents, photos, reports and clippings on the walls. Many of them had handwritten notes scrawled in the margins or over areas of interest. It occurred to Sara that this might indicate she needed help, but she pushed the thought from her mind. She cross-referenced the medical report on the latest victim with her piles of previous information until William returned. Sara was beginning to wonder if her uncle had been sneaking out to see an old girlfriend or something and his faintly rumpled clothes only added to her suspicions.

"How was the 'air'?" Sara insinuated with a raised eyebrow, not looking up from the report.

"Humid," he answered dryly as he dropped the car keys on a nightstand. "Anything new?"

"Nope. So... what's her name?" William stiffened, fearing his niece had discovered his trip to the morgue with Gina the night before.

"Whose?"

"Whatever ex you've been slipping out to hook up with?" Her voice possessed a playfulness William hadn't heard in some time. He was beginning to question whether her moodiness over the last year was the result of her reprimand instead of her obsession with the Ghost. Since her run-in with the Ghost earlier in the day, Sara had been starting to act more like her old self.

"No ex," he smiled. "I just get restless in this heat." Sara nodded her head with a smirk. Before she could respond, her phone rang. Other than throwing out a "yeah" Sara didn't say anything to the person on the other end. She just grabbed pen and paper and jotted information down.

"Thanks," she flatly intoned as she ended the call. "That was local PD. An anonymous caller reported someone was harassing people at some café. Kids like to hang out there, so it could be our guy."

"Sounds like a stretch."

"It probably is, but it does sound like a place where he might scope out potential victims." With no other arguments, William grabbed the keys as Sara gathered her effects.

The destination was the ground floor of a rather unremarkable building. Other than the sign for the café, Demon Aether, and an alcove with an ATM, there was nothing recognizable to let anyone know the structure's purpose. Milling about the sidewalk in front of the shop was a small throng of people mostly in their late teens and early 20s.

"They all look a little old for the Ghost's tastes, don't you think?" William suggested as they moved closer.

"Maybe," Sara agreed. "I still wanna check the place out."

William and Sara started with the kids outside, asking if they'd seen anyone who fit the useless descriptions of the Ghost. Predictably no one had. As for someone being harassed, if that had in fact happened, everyone was unaware or being pretty tight-lipped.

"You go in and talk to the manager," William told Sara. "Maybe they have surveillance video."

"That'll do some good."

"It could at least tell us if he was here," he said to encourage his niece. "Let us know we aren't wasting our time."

"True enough," she replied with a half-hearted shrug. "What'll you do?"

"I'll take a look around the area out here a bit more, just in case." She nodded in agreement and left him with a "Watch yourself" as she slipped through the door.

Even with the people outside, there was no shortage of folk inside, either. When they got the call, Sara had been wearing sweatpants and an old Metallica t-shirt. Before they left she changed into jeans, hiding her gun under her shirt at the small of her back, so she didn't look too out of place as she would in her usual work clothes.

She slipped up to the counter, identified herself, and asked to see the manager. She took the opportunity to get a better look around while she waited. The mood was easygoing but with the various, and generally antithetical, social circles represented. Sara imagined the place saw its fair share of trouble. Whoever was bothering people, if anyone really was, probably wasn't the Ghost. Granted, there were plenty of young girls present who might fall within his criteria, but everyone asked was certain they'd seen no one with even the vague depiction supplied.

More telling, there was none of the witness ambiguity associated with him.

"Yeah man, good show." She heard someone behind the counter say. Sara saw the man she assumed was the manager. His clothing was like the patrons; however, he looked much closer to 30, if not a little over. "You'll have to play again sometime soon."

Whoever he was talking to was on the other side of the doorway. Sara couldn't see him from where she sat, and he talked low enough she couldn't hear him either, only enough to note the voice was male. The manager said his farewells with a handshake. "Let me know if you want that server job, too. We'll get you on the schedule."

Finally, he turned his attention to Sara. "Sorry about that. Name's Nate," he said with a guileless smile and handshake to Sara. "We get cops in here a good bit; been awhile since the Aether had a visit from the Fed's though," he added cheerily.

"Oh yeah, when was the last time you had anyone from the Bureau checking the place out?" Sara asked as she showed him her ID.

He squinted in thought for a moment. "79? Women's lib movement, if memory serves. Definitely before my time," he supplied. "Anyway, how can I help you?"

"The cops got a report there was someone pestering some of the patrons here a little earlier tonight. It might be someone we're looking for." Sara described the Ghost to Nate as best she could. "Has anyone like that been in here tonight?"

"Not that I've seen. We get people like that from time to time but not tonight. Sorry."

"No one's complained about being harassed?"

"Not that I've heard. Hang on." Nate asked the counter server and a pair of waitresses the same questions he had been asked. None had seen or heard anything either.

"I see some cameras around the place. Can I take a look at the footage?"

"Again, sorry," Nate said guiltily, rubbing the back of his neck. "A storm knocked out the computer the cameras record to a few nights ago. The cameras work but we can't save anything they record until that gets fixed," he explained quietly, hoping no one other than Sara heard. Seeing the irritation in her expression, he apologized once more. He even offered to show her, so she'd know he was telling the truth if she wanted.

"That's alright," she said with a defeated sigh. She handed him her contact card. "Call me if you, or anyone on your staff or customers remember anything else, or if you have any further information."

"Will do," Nate agreed, giving Sara another handshake.

Sara pushed herself away from the counter and the world stopped. Sitting less than 20 feet from her was the closest thing she had ever had to an actual suspect: Desiderio Salvia. He sat with a group of five girls and one other boy. The boy and two of the girls looked like they couldn't be older than 18, tops. The other three girls were in their mid-20s. Salvia looked fairly acquainted with the three older women. She quickly reached across the counter and grabbed hold of Nate before he walked away.

"The guy over there," she hissed, indicating Salvia with her head. "Salvia. Do you know him?"

Stunned by her sudden action and quick turn in attitude, Nate sputtered his response. "Well, yeah... Not really... I mean, a little. He played here earlier tonight. He might start working here soon."

"How long have you known him?" She let go of Nate physically but held him in her stare.

"A couple o' days," he said massaging his shoulder. "I don't think he's been in town much more than that. Those girls he's talking to could tell you more." Realization set in. "Aw man! Is he, like, some kind of criminal? I just offered him a job."

"Huh?" Sara had forgotten the manager's existence for a moment. "No. No, he's not a criminal."

Sara dismissed Nate as she watched the small group,

debating on how to handle the situation. Salvia was mostly talking to the younger blonde girl as two of the older women, the pale one with facial piercings and the purple-haired one, joined in on the conversation. She was too far away to make out what they were talking about over the din of the crowd. The older woman with black and white hair was talking to the younger dark-haired girl and the boy.

None of them looked like they'd be leaving anytime soon, so Sara ordered a coffee and found an out of the way table where she could keep an eye on them. Soon, there was a small commotion near the door though Sara couldn't discern the source. Looking somewhat panicked, the pale and pierced woman excused herself from the group and stepped outside. Sara briefly thought about following her before dismissing it.

Salvia was her target.

Chapter 9

Almost as soon as Dez sat down, he and Cinnamon started talking about guitars and music. Gina and Suz listened in and threw in a comment or two every so often, though it proved difficult. Quinn was telling Jen stories about Trevor from when he was young, particularly those where she and Gina tormented the boy.

"Is this how I am when I start talking about tattoos?" Gina whispered to Suz, nodding toward her cousin and Dez.

"Not at all, babe," Suz replied as she casually ran her fingers through Gina's hair. "You are so much worse."

"I should have known I was walking right into that one."

Suz patted her head as she turned to make another order with the waitress. The server asked Gina if she wanted anything else, but she was too preoccupied trying to convince herself that Angie didn't just, literally, walk through the door and the few patrons standing in front of it.

"Finally!" Angie yelped from across the way, oblivious to the upset living around her. "I figured I'd find you eventually!" She made her way towards Gina, people between them reflexively stepping out of the wraith's path, some vehemently so. She stopped short of Gina and her friends, looking around incredulously. "Holy shit! I can't believe this place is still here!"

With a fake smile Gina told the waitress that she was okay. "I'll be right back. I'm going to step outside for some air." She said it to everyone though it was mostly for Angie's benefit.

"Want me to come with?" Suz asked, her tone hinting she'd caught the strain in Gina's voice.

"Oh no, it's good," Gina told her with a placating hand on Suz's shoulder. "Besides, you just ordered something. I won't be long."

Outside, Gina found a spot off to the side of the crowd where no one was likely to hear her talking to the ghost. "Okay, what's the big deal?"

"All the little ghost girls just went fucking crazy!"

"Crazy?" Gina decided to interpret the shaky, jerky movement Angie did as a head nod. "Define 'crazy' in this context."

"They just started, like, crying or wailing," Angie shuddered, which made her blurry with exaggerated motion for a split second. "They all started pointing in the same direction when they did. I walked where they pointed -*not* a fun trip, by the way- and I found you here in their path."

"Why does that last part not surprise me?" Gina grunted. "How long ago did this happen?"

"Less than an hour, I guess. You know me and time ain't on a first name basis."

"That doesn't surprise me either," Gina sighed. "I got this weird feeling about that long ago. Like there was something wrong." She started biting into her lower lip. "I think Dez might have noticed it, too."

"Dez the maybe-but-probably-not serial killer you have a crush on?" Angie pointed back towards the café, ignoring the nasty look Gina shot her. "What makes you think that?"

"About the same time I got the feeling, he acted odd, too. Not much but I saw it."

"Who are you talking to?"

The voice came from beside Gina, from the narrow alleyway between the café and its neighbor. Gina scuttled away a step or two while turning to see who it was. She was afraid it'd be Nate or Wendy out taking a smoke break and she'd have to make something up on the spot, which she was never any good at. She found William there instead.

She was getting strange looks from some of the people milling about outside, though few lingered on her for more than a second or two. "What are you doing here?" Gina asked between clinched teeth. "You nearly gave me a heart attack."

"We got a call that someone was harassing people here and figured it might be our guy," he answered. "Now, who were you talking to?"

Gina groaned. "Sadly, you're probably the only person who won't think this is crazy, but I was talking to a ghost." Seeing the look on William's face, Gina feared he might think she was crazy after all.

"The Ghost?" he demanded in disbelief. "You mean the killer?"

This confused Gina for a moment before she realized what he was asking. "Huh? No! Not *the* Ghost but *a* ghost. You know, like, a dead person?"

"Living impaired," Angie insisted.

"Not on your life," Gina retorted to Angie.

"Sorry. Something about this place..." Angie hazily explained as her mouth frowned in uncertainty.

William still looked puzzled. "She's still here," Gina clarified, subtly jerking her head towards the spot where Angie stood.

"There's a ghost standing right there?" he probed in a slow, methodical tone. Gina nodded her head. "The dispossessed spirit of a deceased individual?" Gina nodded her head again, with an added uncertain shrug thrown in.

"When did you meet this ghost?"

"Last night," Gina answered. "After you dropped me off at my place."

"You didn't even know you had abilities until last night, right?"

The word "Yeah" left Gina's mouth slowly.

"But then you made friends with a ghost in the last 24 hours?" William shrugged at the impatient grumble that got him. "Okay. What does... *she*?" Gina nodded. "What does she say? Was she one of the Ghost's victims?"

"No, she died way before the Ghost started killing," Gina answered that question easily. Then she explained how there were ghost girls who had recently taken up residence around her apartment building. These ghosts were victims of the killer. Angie, the ghost present, was Gina's source of information.

"Let me make sure I have it right: this ghost friend of yours says the victims' spirits are still here but not of their own volition?" William summed up. Gina's head went up and down in short motions. "That makes sense, especially if they're hanging around Salvia."

"You mean Dez?" Gina spurted. "How does that even begin to make sense? Do you still think he's the killer?"

"No," William said as he waved the question away. "I don't think he's the Ghost, but he is tied to him. That hardly makes him any less dangerous, though. These ghost girls suggest some serious mojo is hanging over Mr. Salvia's head."

"Mojo?" Gina's face scrunched up as if the word left a sour taste in her mouth. "You mean like witchcraft?" William nodded his head. "So, magic's real too? Like hag-faced witches and wizards in pointy hats? Are there special schools with poorly enforced dress codes?"

"Nothing like that but it's exceptionally dangerous to deal with."

"So what kind of magic is on Dez?"

"Sounds like a geis."

"He's under bird magic?" she blurted with an uncertain look, afraid this might be where she found out Agent Post was an escaped mental patient.

"Not G-E-E-S-E but a geis. G-E-I-S." Gina bobbed her head but still didn't understand. "It's a type of spell. It could be in the form of a curse or a prophecy or a vow. I think it's the last one in Salvia's case."

Angie put her two cents in. "I'd say it was the first one," she declared to Gina. "He hasn't *seen* those girls," added with a nod toward William.

Gina didn't respond to the wraith, though she couldn't

disagree with her assessment. "What's the point of one of these... geis?"

"For starters, to break one means death."

Almost too afraid to dig deeper, she asked, "And the ghost girls?"

"They're probably the enforcers."

Gina took all that in. "So, if Dez doesn't do something he's dead?"

"Most likely."

It worried her how evenly William gave that answer. "And the ghost girls will be the ones to kill him?"

"Sounds about right."

"First one it is," Gina said to Angie, agreeing with her assessment. Turning back to William. "But one of them is...was...his sister."

"I never said a geis wasn't nasty business." William's shirt was starting to stick to him from the heat. "Neither is magic in general as far as I can tell. A geis is pretty formidable magic and there are very few who could actually pull one off. Whoever put this on Salvia is not just powerful but serious as well.

"Anyway, I think the geis in this case mandates Salvia hunt down the Ghost. His sister was murdered by the guy and someone like Salvia could feasibly track him down."

"What do you mean 'someone like Salvia'?" William started to elucidate but Gina stopped him. "No. Nevermind. I'd rather hear it from Dez himself."

He nodded at that, letting her know he understood. Still, he felt he should warn her at least a little. "You should stay away from Salvia. Even if he's not the killer, people like him are a danger in more ways than you can imagine."

Before Gina could say anything, the café door opened with Trevor stepping out to look for her. "Hey, sis!" he yelled once he spotted her. Behind him Suz, Jen, and Cinnamon followed. Gina waved to them.

"Well, anyway, thank you for your time, miss," William said in a suddenly casual tone. "If you can think of anything else, just give me a call. I gave you my card already, right?"

"Yes, you did," Gina said in a slow, deliberate tone.

"You have a nice night then." He nodded to the rest of them before going inside the coffee shop.

"What was that about?" asked Trevor.

"You never struck me as the type to go for old man action, Gee," Cinnamon remarked with a wide grin.

"Was he a cop?" came from Jen, her eyebrows knotted in concern.

"Yeah, he was a cop," Gina answered. "He just wanted to ask some questions. They got a complaint about some creep hanging around here."

"I guess it's a good thing we're going then," Jen said. "Besides, my dad is probably gonna be pissed if I don't get home soon."

"Your dad seriously needs to get bent," Cinnamon told Jen. Her reaction was of timid agreement.

"Yeah, just wanted to say 'bye' before heading out," Trevor explained as he hugged his sister. He let go of her and she hugged Cinnamon and Jen in turn.

"Trev-bear is gonna give me a lift over to the Loft," Suz told her as she wrapped her arms around Gina. "I'm meeting up with Chastity and Raven. We'll be there for a while. Stop by later if you're up for it." Gina said she might but knew that was unlikely. Secret government agencies, psychics, ghosts, and now magic were real. She didn't know if she wanted to get really drunk, really stoned, or just go to bed.

She figured why not all three?

She waved good-bye once more as she headed back into the shop with Angie behind her. She almost ran into William and a short, dark-haired woman as they were leaving. He seemed to be in a quiet but heated argument with her. Both abruptly piped down with Gina in earshot. As they passed Gina started to acknowledge William, who subtly shook his head.

"That looked fun," Gina said under her breath to Angie.

"Then that'll be a real party," the ghost retorted, nodding her head to where Quinn and Dez sat. Quinn looked apprehensive and unnerved, curled up as small as possible in her corner of the couch, while Dez just looked pissed.

Gina walked over and took a chair across from the couch they were sitting on. "What's wrong?" she asked as she sat down.

Quinn shrugged her shoulders, the look on her face screamed that she wanted to run away. Dez simply growled out, "Nothing." His jaw was clenched to the point Gina expected to be pelted by shattered teeth soon.

"Want me to see if I can do anything?" Angie offered from behind Dez. Gina gave a quick but tentative sign. The ghost held her hands over Dez's head for a moment before she recoiled as if she'd been jabbed with needles. She shook her head in puzzlement.

"I can't get through," she explained to Gina. "It's like he's... not right." Gina then nodded towards Quinn. Angie held her hands over Quinn, who soon looked less agitated, though hardly at ease.

"Nothing, huh?" Gina smirked. "Looks like something to me. So, what happened?"

"I'd really rather not talk about it," Dez answered. He realized he might be treading into jackass territory, so, in a conciliatory tone, he added, "I'm not gonna be good company right now. I know you offered me a ride home but if you wanna do something else, I can walk back to the apartment."

"I can go now; no problem," Quinn said. "Harris gets off work soon anyway. Want me to drop you off at the Loft?" she directed to Gina.

"Nah. I might go down there later but you can just drop us both off at my place."

"Then let's skedaddle," Quinn replied as she finished her drink.

"What the hell was that?" William demanded when they got into the car. Sara didn't answer; instead she just sat and fumed. William's glare didn't let up. "Why were you bothering with Salvia? You know he's not a suspect."

"I know," she responded through gritted teeth. "I wasn't

accusing him of anything."

"Then what were you doing?"

"Don't you think it's a little odd that, yet again, here's Salvia in the same town as the Ghost?" Her voice wasn't indicting. It was more like she was solving a math problem.

"You *still* think he's the killer?" William said with a laugh holding no humor, for the first time afraid as the notion his neice was hopeless took root in his heart.

"No, actually," Sara snarled. "Just the opposite if you want to know the truth! I'm fairly sure he *isn't* the killer now!"

"Then what...?"

"What was I doing?" Sara finished. "I admit, when I saw him, my first instinct was to slap cuffs on him and haul his ass in." Her voice was even now but with a flicker of a laugh underneath. "I knew that Salvia wasn't the guy though. I've known that for quite some time now. I didn't want to admit it, but I knew." Her breathing was hard and burned in her chest. She took a few steadying breaths.

"But I kept asking myself how he was able to track down a guy we can't even successfully get a picture of? Salvia's got motive to hunt the Ghost down. Plus, he seems *damn good* at getting close to the fucker. Far better than we are, anyway. So why work at cross-purposes? Why not bring Salvia on-board to work with us?"

William contemplated the idea for a moment. "What'd he say?"

"I didn't get to ask him," Sara replied, a sour smirk on her face. "The second he saw me, he really wasn't much for talking. Not civilly anyway." She shrugged her shoulders. "Can't say I blame him. I'll come back down here tomorrow and get the address where he's staying. So long as the Ghost's here, I'm betting Salvia won't run for nothing. Maybe with a little time to cool off, he'll actually talk to me."

It was the best workable plan, which was good since it was the *only* plan they had. A better picture of who and, more importantly, what Salvia was had been forming in William's head. If what he suspected was true, it could be dangerous for Sara to partner up with him without knowing what she was getting into.

"I think I may know how he's tracking the Ghost but I'm not 100%." William began. "I'd need more information to be sure. If I'm right, he might help but it could come at a steep cost."

"What do you mean?"

"Just that if I'm right, dealing with Salvia could be riskier than you could ever imagine or handle," William explained. "I need some time to know what we're getting ourselves into and how best to approach him. Not to mention how to protect you if things go south."

"Is this another one of those ghosts and goblins things?"

"Something like that," William replied. "Look, I know you're not fully on board with that yet, you'll just have to trust me on this one."

"Okay," Sara agreed. "I'll trust you. Can't say I'm convinced yet, but there has been some stuff I really can't wrap my head around." She took a long moment to gaze out the window. "But I'll follow your lead on Salvia. Find out what you can and tell me how to work it."

William put his hand on Sara's shoulder and gave it a tender squeeze. He started the car and pulled off.

Quinn pulled her battered Corolla to a stop in front of Gina's apartment building. A few kids, four strong and possibly having gotten drunk way too early, were standing in front of the tattoo shop. Despite the store's lowered lights and barred doorway one of the young men was pawing at the door shouting, "Hello!" to the mindless laughter of his friends.

"Hey, are they open? Do you know?" the one girl in the group asked Gina as she got out of the car. Her voice was slurred, lazy, and patronizing. Gina glanced once at the store then once at the kids to make sure they weren't just being annoying and asinine.

"Really?" Quinn scoffed from the car though Gina barely heard her incredulous comment, so it was unlikely the kids did.

"Judging by the lack of lights, locked bars, and the sign

that says, 'Sorry, We're Closed', I'd say not," Gina responded as she held the seat up so Dez could climb out from the back. With the immediate bristling in reaction to having the obvious pointed out to them, she determined the kids were probably the right combination of drunk, stupid, and superior enough to be trouble.

They clearly didn't find Gina imposing. Two of the boys took a step towards her, their faces stony and promising violence. When Dez stepped out from the car, it was a different story. He didn't have a strong or powerful build. In fact, he was rather on the skinny side and was far from intimidating. Still, he stood over six foot and his composure suggested he could probably do some damage in a fight. While a three-on-one fight would unquestionably go against Dez, the kids would hardly come out safe and sound. This was enough to make them back off and head over to the club a few blocks away, throwing a few feeble and immature comments over their shoulders towards Gina and the others.

The little wave Angie gave from the door suggested she might have had a little to do with the turnaround as well.

"What the...?" Dez started once the group was well down the street. He seemed more amused than upset by the encounter. The anger over whatever distressed him earlier mostly gone.

"Fucking Tantric trash," Quinn groused with a roll of her eyes.

"Tantric's a club a few blocks down," Gina explained to Dez, jerking her thumb down the cobblestone road where the kids ran off. "They generally cater to the bored and brainless."

"Sounds like fun," Dez sneered as he headed towards the building entrance.

"Hey," Quinn called softly to Gina. She waited until she was sure Dez was out of earshot before continuing. "Call me later- or sooner if you need to. Let me know everything's cool, huh?"

Gina promised she would and ran to catch up with Dez. The stress from the tension at the coffee shop called for the use of the building's old elevator instead of the stairs. Neither talked on the way up and at the third floor Dez made his way to his flat with little more than a mumbled good-bye to Gina. The brusque farewell was more from weariness than ire. She was about to pull the wooden door for the elevator down when he stopped her.

"Hey, about before," he started. "You and Quinn have been nothing but nice to me and I shouldn't have acted like that to the two of you."

"It happens," she brushed any hard feeling aside. "Look, it's pretty obvious there's something going on, and, well, I've got some beer upstairs. Put your stuff up and meet me on the roof in a few. We can talk about it, okay?

"If you're up for it, you know?"

He took a moment to think. "Yeah, okay. Only if it's for real this time," he said with an easy smirk.

Gina took the jab in stride. "I deserve that. For real this time. See ya in a few," Gina smiled as she pulled the door down and sent the elevator up to her floor. In her apartment she put her bag away and kicked off her shoes. She thought about getting her pipe but decided against it and went to get the beer from the fridge.

"Something to say?" she asked as she pulled several bottles from a case. Without looking, Gina knew Angie was standing in the doorway. A disconcerting sight since the door was closed.

"He seemed more than a little pissed earlier. Very possibly violently pissed. You know nothing about him except that he's barely told you the truth since you've met him. He's connected to a killer and is under some bad juju," the ghost iterated, ticking her points along the fingers of her skeletal hand. They didn't *quite* move like normal fingers. "That about sums it up, I think."

"Concern noted."

Angie stepped fully into the apartment. "I know you don't want to hear it, but I think that Fed was right. Maybe you should think about staying out of Dez's business." Gina let out a harsh, disbelieving laugh. "Hey, I get it- damn the Man and all that- but he had a point. This is some serious stuff. I'm *dead* and it worries me."

"You're right," Gina shrugged. "I hardly know anything about Dez and I have no idea how much of what he's told me about himself so far is bullshit. I know even less about the Fed. However,

161

part of what little I *do* know about either of them is, between the two, the Fed is the only one of them who has attempted to kill me at some point in my life."

Confusion spread on Angie's face. "What? When?"

"Back when I was little. Before my mom and dad took me in," Gina explained. "He was supposed to kill me as part of some cover up or something, but he didn't. He helped a nurse there get me out instead."

"It sounds like he's got your interests in mind then."

"Maybe, but that doesn't mean I can trust him or his advice," Gina said as she eyed the closed apartment door and considered her bottle-laden hands.

"But Dez...?"

"I'm only going to talk to Dez; see if I can get him to come clean about all or some of this." Seeing that Angie was still unsure, she added, "Besides, it's not like I'm helpless. Apparently, I'm a super psychic and I have a ghost sidekick that he'll never see coming who will be keeping an eye out for trouble."

"Sidekick?" the wraith huffed, her arms crossing her chest.

"Fine. Buddy or partner or whatever," Gina corrected herself. The handle on the apartment door twisted and it swung slowly open, ostensibly all on its own. She fixed the shade with a satisfied smirk as she hopped through the opening. "We'll fight crime and they'll make a movie or cheesy daytime cable network drama," she conceded as they left the apartment, the door closing on its own behind them.

"Okay, but I get to be Lacey," Angie conceded.

"Only if I get to be Starsky," Gina agreed.

On the roof Gina found Dez waiting for her. All about him were the ghost girls; their faces as stern as their posture was rigid. She had noticed before how whatever constituted ghostly flesh on the girls waned and rotted to some degree. Now she was really seeing the extent. Some were missing large patches of skin on their corpus with bone and muscle exposed. One girl took a lazy look at Gina; her eyes were disturbingly large and round in bare sockets.

It was an unnerving contrast with Dez, idly leaning against the ledge, eyes closed softly and his peaceful demeanor in the center of it all, seemingly oblivious to the horror show all around him. He opened his eyes at the sound of Gina opening the mini-fridge and putting the extra bottles inside. "I was gonna knock on your door, but I heard you talking to someone," he said. "Figured I'd let you talk to whoever it was. It sounded important."

"It was just a friend who was concerned about earlier," she explained as she popped the caps off a couple of beers before handing one to Dez. She plopped down in a plastic chair, holding still and quiet for a moment to determine if she heard one of its legs crack. Satisfied she hadn't, Gina leaned back, sliding down in the seat just a little as she stretched out some of the stress gathering in her legs and back. She noticed a thin layer of sweat on Dez's brow and was starting to wish that she had changed into a pair of shorts. Still, her pants were light, baggy, and stopped mid-shin. She was glad she'd kicked her heavy shoes off in her apartment.

"Are you in a better mood now?"

He took a swig of beer and let the chill of it cool him before answering. "Yeah. Again, I shouldn't have acted like that back there."

"It happens," she brushed it off, again, as she slipped her socks from her feet. She rolled them up and tossed them onto the table. Wiping off the fuzz left behind, she continued. "What did the lady Fed say to piss you off so badly?"

"How'd you know she was a Fed?"

"Because I know the guy who was with her," Gina answered flatly. She reckoned if she expected him to be honest, it wouldn't do for her to start by lying her ass off. "Okay, Trust Tree time. I think I know a lot more about you than you probably wanted me to."

She wasn't sure if the twitch in Dez's body meant that he was about to lash out or run away, but he did neither. Instead he just stayed very still. The tension soon gave way to something that looked like relief.

"Like what?"

She took a deep breath. "Like I know about your sister."

She couldn't help but glance over to where the girl's shade

stood, just to the side of Dez. She was staring intently at her brother, although, she briefly turned toward Gina. Her face was gaunt, the skin pulled tight over the skull. She opened her mouth like she wanted to say something, but no words passed her lips. Just the wet ripping sound of her cheek splitting apart. "I know she was killed by that sick psycho fuck who's now killing girls here."

Dez's jaw was set tight at Gina's words. His initial instinct, the one he had lived with for so long, was to tell her to fuck off and mind her own business. If it had been someone else he probably would have, but there was something in her voice. More to the point, there was a *lack* of something in her voice. There was no accusation, no angle being played or intrigue. There was just empathy and kindness. She wanted to help. "Trust Tree? That's true. That's why I'm here. I've been looking for the guy ever since."

"Why haven't you tried the cops or those Feds?"

Dez laughed softly. "Yeah right!" His laughter rose a little more. A ghastly chorus of laughter spread through the ghost girls to match Dez's.

"Oh, that the sort of thing that'll set a movement back 50 years," Angie nervously tittered to Gina as the wraith regarded the girls. As far as Gina was concerned, the shade's own staccato, demented trill was neck and neck in creepiness with the grim snickers from the murder victims.

"As far as he's concerned, this killer, the cops and Feds couldn't find their asses with both hands in their back pockets."

"Yeah, I sort of got that," Gina admitted, doing her best to ignore the jeering geists around them. "What about the rest of your family? Are they dead too?"

"Dad is but my mom...," he hesitated. "My mom may as well be. It might have been better for her. In some small way I think she is."

"Tell me about them."

"Like I told you before, they were musicians. They met in New York. Dad was fresh off the boat from Jamaica, but my mom had been in the States from Portugal for a year or two. Dad said he fell in love immediately, mom said it took her a while. Most of their friends said she was just playing hard to get but I think there might have been...political issues involved." A weary smile crossed his face. His sister tried to say something again, but her cheek only tore more.

"They didn't make a lot of money with their music, just enough to keep things comfortable. Mom was from old money, though it was hard to tell. Besides, she left that behind when she met my dad. From what I could tell, she had to, but we were happy.

"Then Lucy was killed..." Dez's voice faltered and darkened. "It was before that really. Not long before that, dad was down in Seattle, doing a few shows there. My mom would've been with him but there was nasty flu going around. Lucy and I both had it, so she stayed to take care of us. On his way back, they said his car hit an icy patch...ran off the road. It was three weeks before they found him. Mom just...broke," his tone was as distant as his gaze.

"*Then* Lucy was killed." His voice was tight, constricted. Gina moved gently to his side, taking his hand in hers. She couldn't decipher the lingering look his sister gave her.

"Anyway," Dez said suddenly, with a forced lightness to his voice. His hand wiped at a tear forming in his eye. "I had to get out of there. The cops were useless, so I figured I'd try my hand at finding the guy."

"How?"

"I have my ways," he answered after taking a long pull from his beer.

"Care to elaborate?"

"You'd only think I was crazy," he laughed softly. The sound lacked anything resembling humor. "Or, crazier."

"You'd be surprised."

He shook his head, a small smile on his lips. "I've shared. Your turn."

Gina swallowed the last mouthful of her beer. She tossed the bottle into the garbage can, the disturbed air sending a slight whiff from where she threw up in it the night before. She headed over to the fridge to get another.

"Fair's fair," she conceded. "Shoot," she invited as she took a new bottle out.

"How do you know all this?"

"The other Fed, the guy?" she started, sitting back down in the plastic chair. "He showed up here last night. At first, he was asking questions about the girl, the first victim, from a few days ago." Gina's gaze slid over to the blonde. "He said I could help with the investigation."

"How?"

"You'd only think I'm crazy." A slight smile worked its way across Gina's face when she realized she had unintentionally copied him.

"I'm sure they make straitjackets in both our sizes."

"You weren't exactly share-time with how you thought you'd do a better job finding the guy than the cops," Gina pointed out.

"I know," Dez's tone became serious. "I want to tell you. I think I could. Maybe I will one day but...for now...just believe me when I say the less you know about it, the better."

Gina considered that for a moment before accepting it with a reticent nod. She took a sip of beer. "I'm not really sure how helpful I was anyway," she continued. "At any rate, he told me I should probably be careful around you. That you were dangerous." If Dez was going to respond, to agree or disagree, Gina didn't give him a chance. "Anyway, they don't think you're the killer. Not anymore at least."

There was silence between them as he pondered that detail. "Earlier, at the coffee shop, that lady Fed tried to talk to me. She was the one who accused me of being the killer, said I killed my own sister."

Gina nodded and gave a consoling half-smile. "I know," she spoke softly.

Dez eyes fell on her then, both annoyance and surprise lay within, though that swiftly faded into simple acceptance. "I figured she was just going to make more trouble for me. I'm close to the guy now- I know it- and I just couldn't stand the thought that she was going to make me lose him again." He was quiet once more as he collected his thoughts on this new information.

"I think she wants to find him just as badly as you do."

"Maybe."

"You could help each other out."

"Maybe."

"If you decide that you do want to hear what she has to say, I can get you in touch with her," Gina offered. "Just...don't mention me if you do."

"Why?"

"The guy Fed. He said it was best if I stay off her radar." As she spoke, Gina realized this would only lead to questions she wasn't ready to answer. She quickly added, "For my own safety, and that's all I can really say right now." That answer was obviously unsatisfactory to Dez. He took it all the same.

"Let me sleep on it. I'll know what I wanna do in the morning."

"Fair enough," Gina granted. They drank their beer and talked into the morning hours though they never really said anything. The ranks of ghost girls, standing silent, circled them. Angie curled up somewhere off to the side, eventually fading from sight as she seemed to fall asleep or whatever ghosts did. Gina found it worrisome how she was getting used to that madness.

However, she might have reevaluated her comfort level had she noticed the new addition to the number of ghost girls.

That was a bust. He hoped the agent would sidetrack the Hunter again, but that did not happen. Instead it seemed she was looking to cooperate with the Hunter rather than stop Him. Although He could not fail, it was no less bothersome.

This distraction could not have come at a worse time, since He now knew the objective for His advancement in His service to the Almighty. She was perfect; she was obviously warped by the Adversary, yet the taint had yet to be sparked. She had degeneracy not present in any of the others with the notable exception of the Hunter's sibling. That one's corruption was already triggered before He found her. It was probably in her blood, but this one was not yet in its thrall. He reveled in ending the human filth the Adversary would inevitably corrupt. They were ultimately incidental in the grand scheme, though, and thus of no real significance. He wanted to make a difference. He wanted to eradicate the more essential soldiers of the Enemy.

Then there was the unknown: the young woman the male agent talked to outside. They seemed to know each other in some way, though she showed him some measure of distrust. He did not know what she was about. She had power- that much was obvious. The very air around her seemed to bend and warp to her gravity. She had truly been gifted by the Almighty, even if she was in danger of using it for ill designs. She was of the Adversary to be sure, but she seemed unwittingly so. He felt a kindred spirit with her. What a coup it would be to deliver her from the grasp of the Enemy, not to mention what an excellent soldier and ally a former foe would make. The idea of converting her to His side excited Him and it would be nice to have a partner in His mission. Still, this was not for Him to determine, though, it certainly would not hurt to ask. He had been a faithful servant after all.

He would, of course, need to keep an eye on her, just to make sure she *could* be salvaged. He asked some of those milling about outside about her and discovered enough to start with. She was already somehow mixed up with the Hunter. So even if it proved fruitless to save her, as much as He hoped otherwise, she could be an effective avenue to him.

All of this was irrelevant if He could not keep the Hunter off His trail until His work was finished; until His exaltation. The Almighty would protect Him, to be sure, but it would be expedient to do something to damage any possible alliance between the agent and the Hunter. It would take some doing to make her suspicious of the Hunter again, though hardly impossible. He would just need to find the right enticement to encourage a change of mind.

If he could not, the possibility of enlisting the local law enforcement to his purposes might make the Fed's assistance unnecessary.

Walking along, deep in these ruminations, He found Himself once more in the district of the city He visited briefly on His first night. Surely, He could find someone who fit His purposes here. There were so many targets He could have taken a blind swing and cut an acceptable mark. He made His way through the crowds and clichés searching for the best one, and then he saw her. Her hair had a few fresh bright pink streaks through it now, but she was definitely the girl He had seen on that first night.

Her friends were nowhere to be found. Her face was a sad mask, lacking the garish make-up from the last time. Her eyes were rimmed red from tears. She was alone at a table in a pizza parlor, a half-eaten meal on the table before her. She stared and picked at her food with a fork. He went in and ordered a cola and sat down at a nearby table. He managed to start a conversation with her, learning her sadness was because a boy she liked rejected her when she refused to sleep with him. He was able to cheer her up some. She was just happy there was someone who understood her pain and sympathized with her.

Truth be told, He really did. He developed newfound admiration for this young girl. Despite His initial assessment, she was proving to be a Lot in this Sodom. For once He truly grieved when He slit her throat open, among the other things He did to her, in the parking lot after He walked her to her car. He assured Himself she would understand in the end and accede her place in the Almighty's grand scheme.

He left her in the backseat, observable enough to be found in due time. He took a thick tuft of her hair, making sure to also get plenty of the bright pink streaks. Finding this among the Hunter's possessions would surely cast doubt and suspicion back onto him and He would be free to do as the Almighty wished without distraction.

Chapter 10

"My niece tells me we have a new friend," Wilhelmina Murray- Mina to her friends- greeted Gina as they ran into each other by the mailboxes.

Mina owned the seamstress shop on the second floor of the building and was Marcella's aunt. Both were black sheep in their wealthy, influential, and powerful family, as well as all but disowned. Said family had members on more corporate boards, city councils, religious convention committees, and state legislators throughout the country than many people realized. There was even a governor in the family history, and Marcella's own brother was likely to be another, if not more, in the future. Because of their "choices" in life, both women were considered an embarrassment to the family. Both had legally changed their names to separate themselves from the namesake, though Marcella had only replaced her last name- adopting Murray as well- instead of her full name like Mina.

"Yeah, you'll probably meet him soon enough. He's staying in one of the third-floor apartments," Gina replied. "How was the cruise?"

"Boring!" Mina said with a dramatic sigh and a flip of her dark bangs. She was well into her 50s, but she could easily pass for much younger. "A lot of bites but no one brave enough to seal the deal as usual. There was one promising couple, but you know my thoughts on that."

"Well stiff upper lip and all," Gina encouraged with a smile. "Good to have you back." They said their farewells with a tight hug and Gina darted through the door into the tattoo shop.

Inside Michelle and Marcella were drinking coffee and talking about some new movie or television series. The door to the storeroom was open and she could see Jacob moving about, gathering supplies for the studios. The door to Frankie's office was closed but she could tell he was inside. Gina said hello to the ladies up front and yelled a greeting to Jacob in the back as she made a beeline to the coffee pot. As she fixed her cup, Frankie came out of his office with Suz in tow. They were laughing about something, but it was clear to Gina there was an undercurrent of irritation in her father's disposition.

"Hey," Gina saluted, mildly surprised to see her friend here. "It's not even noon yet. I wouldn't expect you to be up for another few hours or so."

"It's a strange day to be sure," Suz returned with a knowing look as she put an arm across Gina's shoulders. "It was good talking to you, Papa Frank," she said to him. "And to you ladies," was directed to Michelle and Marcella. She then guided Gina back to the latter's room. Inside, she pushed the door closed.

"Really, what's up?" Gina asked as she put her bag down on a counter.

"Quinn left me a message about what happened at the Aether after I left last night," Suz explained mildly. "I just wanted to make sure everything was alright."

"Yeah. Everything's cool."

"Cool, huh?"

"There's nothing to tell really. Dez thought someone was trying to stir up some shit while we were outside, and it pissed him off."

"Honest?"

"As honest I can be right now. It's his to tell you more than that."

Suz accepted this with a coquettish half-smile that was at odds with the skeptical gleam in her eyes. "Fair enough, so long as you're fine," she conceded. Her face brightened up. "Got anyone lined up early today?" Gina laughed before poking her head out and asking Michelle what her day looked like. Gina had no appointments for another few hours. Suz slithered out of the jacket she had been wearing and plopped lightly down in Gina's chair.

Fixing Gina with an exaggerated and flirty glare, Suz pulled her shirt off over her head, tossing it to lay over her coat. "Then I am your canvas this morning."

Dez told Gina he'd sleep on the idea of working with the Feds, which he said with total honesty even though he failed to actually sleep. Dez agreed with the advice given to Gina that she stay off their radar and, with that in mind, he used a pay phone at a nearby convenience store. He also planned to meet with them away from the apartment too. It turned out that finding a phone was easy enough, but the real trick was finding one that worked. This search took most of the stifling morning, extending into the overbearing blaze of the mid-day sun before he eventually accepted it as a fruitless quest.

"Post," the man answered from the other end once Dez gave up the search and picked up a pre-paid phone. The man's voice was rough and weary, like he expected the Apocalypse itself to be calling.

"This is Dez Salvia," Dez started cautiously. "A mutual friend suggested we might be able to help each other."

"Perhaps," he replied after a noticeable pause. "I'll let you discuss that with my partner." William handed the phone to Sara.

"This is Post," she said into the phone.

"It's Salvia." He could hear her taking a deep breath.

"I'm glad I was able to make my intentions clear last night, despite the reaction..."

"Yeah, whatever," Dez cut her off. He ran the back of his hand across his brow, dragging the sweat aside more than wiping it away. The heat was wearing on him. "I've been convinced we might be able to help each other catch- what do you call him- the

Ghost?"

"Convinced by whom?" Even over the phone Dez could hear her eyes narrow into detective-mode.

"No one you need to worry about," Dez spat out, kicking himself over such a slipshod mistake. "Do you want my help or not?"

"I do," Sara declared, maybe a little too quickly. "Give me the address of where you're staying, and I'll meet you there as soon as I can."

"What's wrong with now?" Dez asked, wanting to meet with them immediately and somewhere public, before he lost his confidence in this proposed alliance.

"Because right now I'm standing over the body of the Ghost's latest victim," Sara told him, her voice crisp and matter-of-fact. "Killed last night. She's 16; or was. Throat slit and a whole mess of other details I'm sure you could recite just as well I can."

Dez's breathing came hard at the news, more sweat formed on his brow as his heart pounded, and the phone started to crack in his grip. "Okay," he said after exhaling. "Meet me at this address." He rattled off the whereabouts of his apartment. "I'll see you when I see you," he told her before ending the call.

He had been watching the building all morning just hoping to see her once again, maybe even working up the nerve to talk to her. He really needed to concentrate on His exaltation, finding the target again and dealing with her. Still, He had a hope He could render His soulmate from this one before then. He was not sure what being exalted entailed, it was feasible it would leave Him as something other than human. If that turned out to be true, He felt it would still be nice to hold on to some small portion of His humanity. There was nothing that could do that like true love.

He watched as the Hunter left the building around mid-morning. This was cause for some concern. He knew the Hunter and His potential companion had some sort of relationship. Seeing the Hunter leaving the building she lived in raised the question of what their association was exactly. The servitor clearly had wormed his way into her life. What else had he wormed his way into? The thought angered Him greatly. He no longer wanted to simply kill the Hunter. Instead, He wanted to slowly eviscerate him over a period of several hours.

And now He was going to do so, whether it was His task or not.

His thoughts of the Hunter evaporated when He saw her a little later. It was brief. She popped out from a door at the edge of the building, stopping to talk to that "woman" who wasn't fooling anyone, only to disappear into another that led into a tattoo shop. Her occupation was no doubt iniquitous, scarring and marking bodies for the Adversary. Despite that, it was not so unforgivable if repentance was heartfelt. Besides, He told Himself, the best agents for the Almighty would be those who initially worked against Him.

He did not know how long He had been lost in thought about her and their future life together when the Hunter returned. He went past the tattoo shop, waving to someone within, and straight into the door on the edge.

Someone in the shop must know where the Hunter made his hideaway, but that could tip him off. He had the strands from the girl still on Him. This could be his opportunity to remove the Hunter from play and frame him for His work. He held the napkin which was wrapped around the girl's hair and felt another twinge of regret in killing her. Granted her death was for a greater purpose and would not be wasted, she was still salvageable. He wished He could have found another more deserving, but...well, surely, she would understand what her sacrifice was for and accept it.

He spent some time weighing His options before deciding to risk inquiring about the Hunter at the shop. He crossed the street and went in. There was a young couple sitting on a couch in the waiting area, a young girl looking at jewelry through the display case, and a sandy-haired young man standing at a computer screen with a dark-skinned woman. They were looking at tattoo designs and He noticed they wore matching rings on their fingers. She acknowledged His presence and, with a lingering touch of her shoulder, he left her side to go talk to the girl looking at the display cases. He had hoped He might get a chance to talk to her...no, Her...but He would settle for this for the moment.

He gave the woman a story. He was supposed to meet with the Hunter to work on a musical project but had lost his address. He remembered it was in this building though. She proved helpful and gave the information easily. He thanked her and made His way up to the third floor. At the door marked 3A, He could hear water running on the other side. He tried the handle, finding it was locked. He was good at picking locks, so this proved no obstacle.

Inside He started looking for a good place to plant the evidence. He settled on a worn Army surplus backpack near the bed when the water abruptly stopped. The bathroom door swung open and He found Himself eye to eye with the Hunter again. Those dreadful eyes that gave Him the sense of plummeting helplessly through space made Him freeze in place. A stunned look on the Hunter's sharp and airy features was slowing drained to rage. He choked His own fear with righteous anger.

Instinctively, His knife flashed towards the Hunter's neck.

"I think we are done," Gina sang as she straightened up from leaning over Suz, whose back was now adorned with a delicate design of full, curvy lines and dots that unfolded down the length of her slender body and stopped just above her rear. Suz sat up, straddling the chair, and checked the new work in a mirror that covered one wall of the studio.

"I like," she said with a purr. Gina's gloved fingers dabbed ointment over the work before covering the area with several bandages.

"You know the drill," Gina started as she explained the after-care procedure while Suz pulled her shirt back on, silently reciting the lecture in perfect sync along with her friend. She had heard it before and knew it well. Gina knew this just as much as

176

Suz knew that wasn't going to stop Gina from repeating it.

"How much do I owe you?" Suz asked as they walked out of the room and into the hallway.

"Pfft," Gina replied. She held an amused look on her face but a sensation like one from the night before washed over her again. Remembering how Suz seemed to feel it last night as well, Gina tried to gauge her friend's expression, but it remained unchanged. "Not a cent," she quickly added.

Suz smiled and shook her head as she pulled some cash from her bag. She popped into Frankie's office and held the money out to him. "Papa Frank, could you please make sure your obstinate daughter takes this for her work?" She thanked him when he took the money and assured her that Gina would take it.

Michelle was hanging up the phone as they came out to the front. "So what project is Dez working on?" she asked when she saw Gina.

"Project?"

"Yeah, some guy came in a minute ago looking for him, said they were supposed to work on some music project," Michelle explained. "Sounds cool."

"Did he give a name?"

"Um..." Michelle's cheerful face fell. "No. No he didn't." It wasn't like her not to get a name.

"What'd he look like?"

"Well he..." Michelle's expression screwed up in further confusion. "You know, I can't really remember." She gave a light laugh to banish her growing uncertainty, though it didn't work. "Funny, he was just in here and..." she said pointing to a spot in front of the counter.

"Did you tell him which apartment was Dez's?" Gina's voice strained slightly with distress as William's words about the Ghost came flooding back to her.

"Yeah. He knew he lived here so I just figured..."

Seeing the troubled look on Gina's face Suz demanded, "What's wrong?"

"I don't know."

"Is this an 'as honest as you can be' moment?" Suz

murmured quietly. Gina bobbed her head.

"Did I fuck up?" Michelle asked with worry on her face.

"I don't know," Gina answered. Her anxiousness only increased when Angie stepped out from the studio, her expression equally uneasy. Gina ignored the phantom's frightened, desperate appearance and started to run out of the shop. Suz roughly grabbed her arm and pulled the shorter girl to face her.

"Here! You stay here and calm down," Suz told Gina. A fire burned in her eyes and an odd pitch was behind her voice. "I'll go and make sure everything's cool. Okay?"

"Sure," Gina assented, somewhat calmer now, no longer sure why she was so fretful a moment ago or why it was so important that *she* go to check on Dez.

"Be back before you know it, babe," Suz gave an easy smile as she headed out of the shop, quickly disappearing around the corner.

Gina went back to her studio and closed the door behind her. "Problem?" she asked the ghost.

"You could say that. There's a new one up there."

"Another one? Since when?"

"Don't know. I just noticed her up on the roof, right before they started that wailing and pointing thing again. And I mean *really* wailing. They're pitching a serious fit up there."

"Where were they pointing?" Gina's stomach started turning with fear once more, afraid she already knew.

"Straight down," Angie responded.

From more than half a block away William saw the girl going into the doorway leading up to the apartments. At first, he thought it might be Gina before realizing that this girl was too tall and too thin to be her. She disappeared into the building and he pushed her from his mind. He pulled the car up to the curb in front of the tattoo shop.

"Charming," Sara wryly remarked while taking in the place and the surrounding block.

"You were expecting the Taj Mahal?"

"I was expecting something a little less 'I'm a sick, murderous asshole'," Sara noted as she got out of the car.

Rounding the car and stepping up to the curb next to her, William commented, "I thought you were over Salvia being the Ghost?"

"I am," Sara replied with more annoyance than she meant. "I was just going for a little levity." She took a step into the doorway, a cool breeze flowing over her and making her pause for a little relief from the heat. She turned to apologize to William for blocking the way when she noticed her uncle was lingering out on the sidewalk.

"Coming?"

"Think I'll hang back," he answered. "From what you said, he may be a little skittish. Best not to come on too strong."

"Suit yourself," she shrugged as she moved down the hall and toward the stairs. "But I don't want to hear any more bitching about the heat." From the stairwell she heard a woman shouting something a few floors above. There was a promise of violence in the scream. More, there was something wholly... well, *inhuman* was the only word she could think to describe what she heard. Sara broke into a run up the remaining stairs as she pulled her gun from the holster on her hip.

The Hunter quickly jumped back a step, the blade coming within a fraction of an inch from his throat. The attack was too wide; He was too eager for the kill. It not only gave the Hunter time to recover, but a fighting chance as well. The Hunter kicked out, his foot connecting with His side. It did not hurt too much, but it drove home His need for care with this opponent.

The Hunter was boxed in by the alcove leading to the bathroom, leaving him little room to maneuver. Seizing that advantage, He made two quick stabs. The first was easily dodged, but it was meant to set the Hunter up for the second, which sliced into his left shoulder. It was not a deep wound, only giving the

Hunter some concern. He made a few more strikes at the Hunter; none connected, not that they were meant to. They were just to keep the Hunter off balance, so He could inflict a killing wound.

The knife went high, but He quickly pulled it back and went low to cut across his gut. It would not kill the Hunter outright. Instead, it would make his death long, suffering, and damn hard to avoid even if he did manage to get help. The tip of the blade just bit into the Hunter's abdomen when he weaved to the side, allowing only a shallow nick on his stomach. The move surprised Him, and He had no time to register what happened as a fist slammed across His jaw. Blood filled His mouth and His knife skittered across the floor, which He ignored when He saw the Hunter going for something in the backpack. He crashed into the Hunter, smashing him against the wall. The Hunter slid down the wall into a sitting position, his breath coming in harsh gasps and coughs.

He smashed His knee into the Hunter's face once before retrieving His knife and closing in for the killing blow. From outside in the hall He heard someone, a woman, calling for the Hunter. To make sure he did not go anywhere or recover before He could deal with this interruption, He brought His foot down into the Hunter's face. The back of his head bashed against the wall and his body slumped over.

No doubt startled by the noise, the woman called the Hunter's name again, alarm in her voice. With His knife in hand he decided to greet her. He stepped out into the hallway, assured of his actions, but His determination faltered the moment He laid eyes on her. It was the purple-haired whore from the coffee shop. He assumed what He felt from her was just proximity to Her. Now He saw he had been very wrong about this one.

The night before there was nothing unusual about her appearance other than her exceptional, if twisted, beauty. Now her mouth twisted into a wide and misshapen gash filled with wicked needle-like teeth. Her eyes burned with an awful intensity from sunken hollows making it almost impossible to keep His gaze on her. Her wickedness was simply so pure, unadulterated. For a single, terrifying moment, He believed he might be looking upon the face of the Adversary itself.

Try as He might to shake such a silly fancy from His thoughts, He couldn't ignore how overwhelming was the woman's presence. Her horrible intensity seemed to fill the hallway. Arcs of fire and electricity snaked down around her arms and hands. He could do nothing but feebly hold the knife out and demand she stay away from Him.

Such commands did no good though, not even those in the name of the Almighty. She approached Him with a malignant purpose; He could do nothing but retreat. He heard another voice, another woman, yell for Him to halt but He ignored the order. A gunshot echoed through the narrow hallway and He jumped to the side. The glass in the window shattered as a second gunshot sounded. He took a quick glance and saw the female agent, gun drawn, at the other end of the hall and the fiendish whore was low and flat against the wall, now as she appeared the night before and holding Him in an evil scowl. He hastily pushed off from the wall, rolled out through the window and onto the fire escape beyond.

Once He was at the next level down He did not bother with the ladder, opting to hop over the railing and dropping to the sidewalk below. He regained His footing and headed toward the alley, only to find Himself facing the male agent, who already had his gun in hand. Before the agent could bring his weapon up, He struck out with His knife. The blade cut across the back of his hand; the gun fell and skidded down the sidewalk. He took a few more swipes with the knife at the agent, forcing him to stumble and fall over the doorstep. The agent grabbed the front of His shirt to keep from falling but it ripped open and he lost his grip. Deprived of His aims, He would have liked to take out His frustrations and kill this agent.

A glimpse of Her through the window to the tattoo shop, however, stopped Him. Her pale blue eyes bore into Him and Her expression was one of revulsion. He could not do this in front of Her, not now at least.

The female agent was at the ground floor now, gun drawn and level with Him, and ordering Him not to move. He sneered and disappeared down the alley before she could take a shot.

Cops came and asked questions, but Sara pulled rank. Still, she kept them around just for show. EMTs arrived soon after and saw to Dez and William, eventually taking both to the hospital. It was almost an hour later when Sara decided she could remove the cuffs from Suz.

"So, mind telling me what you were doing up there?" It sounded like a request, but Gina noticed Sara had the same ability as William to make an order sound nicer like that.

"I was going up there to check on Dez," Suz replied as if she were stating the obvious and rubbing her wrists.

"And the stun gun?" Sara asked holding up a large evidence bag, the item in question inside.

"The guy pulled a knife on me," Suz replied incredulously, as if that should be enough of an answer. Sara's raised eyebrow disagreed. "Naturally I was gonna taze the fucker until he pissed himself twice. Maybe three times for funnies."

Sara regarded Suz for a moment before ripping the seal on the bag and returning the stun gun back. "Can you give me a description of the assailant?"

Suz rolled her eyes. "You took two shots at the asshole. You know what he looked like." The statement drew the attention of a couple of cops milling about out on the sidewalk by the open shop door. Seeing nothing really of interest, they went back to their conversation.

"I just need corroboration," Sara lied. She could no more pick out the Ghost if he was alone among a line-up of Easter Bunnies. She doubted this witness could say what he looked like either, but there was a procedure.

"Let's see," Suz mockingly tapped her chin in thought. "He had short brown hair, almost shaved and he was about my height. He was pretty skinny, too. He was wearing a white button-up shirt and dark pants. And, let's see, what else? Oh yeah, *he had a big fucking knife he was threatening me with!*"

Sara had stopped writing and stared at Suz, unbelieving

the confidence in her voice as she relayed the description. "You mean you actually...?" She quickly recovered. "You said he was wearing a white shirt with dark pants?"

"Yeah," Gina cut in. "And, he had all these little scratches on him. On his skin."

"Scratches?" Sara reiterated.

"When Agent... um, your partner, grabbed him. The guy's shirt ripped open a little and he had a bunch of cuts, like tic marks."

"Do you agree with the description she gave?" Sara asked Gina, pointing over to Suz.

"Yeah. Sounds right."

"You saw him too, right?" She turned to Michelle. "You agree?"

"Maybe," she slowly answered. Her voice was tired and strained, prompting Jacob to hold her tighter. "I can't really say."

Sara pondered this for a moment, her face braced in deliberation. Finally, "See you two in there for a moment?" It wasn't a request. She guided Gina and Suz into Gina's studio and closed the door.

"Explain how you two are able to give a precise account of a killer that no eye witness, over the course of at least *seven years*, has *ever* been able to consistently describe." Amazingly, Sara managed to simultaneously yell and keep her voice calm and even.

Both girls looked at each other, then back to Sara and shrugged their shoulders in unison. She studied their faces for any hint of deception or duplicity. "Either of you ever see my partner before today?"

Suz shook her head but Gina spoke up. "I saw him last night down at the Aether."

"And?"

"He just asked me a few questions. Said that someone reported a creep or something."

"No other time?" Sara demanded of both. Her eyes lingered mostly on Gina, deeply too, but cut over to Suz as well. She frowned and shook her head.

Sara took a deep breath before she swiftly brushed between

them to leave. Gina subtly held her hand out and brushed it against Sara's bare arm. Images flooded Gina's mind: she saw Sara as a young girl spying on her uncle, as he stood before a mirror, blankly studying the horrible gouges that ran across his chest and back; saw her as a teenaged girl who wanted nothing more than for her father to show any trace of pride in her and her accomplishments, but resigning herself to accept the muttered, flat congratulatory platitudes; in a bar with loud music, Gina knew Sara's heart raced as an eye-catching woman placed a hand on her knee.

"Okay. I may need to ask you further questions later. Make sure you keep yourselves available," Sara commanded from the open door before leaving. Outside the door she turned back and addressed Suz. "Word of advice, if you wanna actually do anything with that stun gun, you might want to make sure the battery's charged. That one's dead as a doornail."

Gina and Suz looked at each other once Sara was out of sight. "Well, I think I'm in love," Suz said deadpan.

"Oh yeah?" Gina responded. "Then I guess we'll have to work out a timeshare or something, 'cause I saw her first. Did you notice she was shorter than me?"

"Was she? It's sort of hard to tell from up here," Suz remarked, resulting in a light smack in the shoulder from Gina.

Despite their appearances, Dez's injuries were not that bad. Still, fearing a possible concussion, the doctors insisted on keeping him overnight for observation. William's hand only needed a few stitches, but his shirt was ruined.

"I liked that shirt," William swore as he slipped on the fresh one Sara brought. It looked identical to the ruined one.

"It was a white button-up like all the rest of your shirts," Sara pointed out. "How could you tell one from the other enough to actually 'like' one more?"

He gave her a smirk, either ignoring the question or conceding the argument. "You talk to Salvia yet?"

"Yeah. I think he's on board," she answered, not really as certain as she sounded. "I did as you told me. Made no demands. Made no promises or offers that I wasn't very certain I could, and would, keep. Made sure they would be one-time deals and worded right. Never said thank you, so on and so forth," Sara counted out on her fingers as she leaned back to peer down the hallway towards Dez's room. She couldn't begin to fathom the litany of dos and don'ts her uncle gave her, but he was adamant she follow them to the letter. Which she did.

Then she saw Gina at the nurse's station. "What's with that chick?"

"What chick?"

"The one from the tattoo place. The dark-haired one with all the stuff in her face?"

"I guess they're friends," William offered with a shrug of his shoulders. "Or friend- friends."

Sara raised an eyebrow at her uncle's attempt at middle-school lingo. "I doubt he's been in town long enough to make friends like *that*." Dez was far from Sara's cup of tea, anatomically speaking, but, if pushed, she would grant he was mildly attractive.

Gina was about to knock on Dez's door when she glanced down the hall. Her pale eyes found Sara staring at her. A shiver ran down the agent's spine; her instincts told her there was something *off* about Shields.

"I mean, she told me what the Ghost looked like." She crooked her head back to her uncle, placing severe emphasis on her next words. "What he *really* looked like. That friend of hers too, the one with the purple hair and stun gun," she mulled over that for a moment.

"Salvia too, for that matter," she curiously added as her attention returned to the hallway.

"Hmm," William responded. He really wasn't surprised about Gina or Dez being able to see past whatever trick the Ghost used to avoid detection or description, but the other one he didn't expect. He made a note to look into Suz when he could. "Well, I've told you Salvia wasn't exactly human. He likely has some talents that help in that arena."

185

"Sure," Sara replied, far less dismissively than she would have a few days ago. Some things weren't adding up with normal math, leading her to consider the paranormal spiel given to her by her uncle and Lowden wasn't total bullshit. In light of the strange events of the last few days, she was willing to give it a place in the discussion at any rate. She wasn't buying into it completely just yet though. Gina disappeared into Dez's room and Sara turned her attention back to William.

"I know what you said but that doesn't explain her or her friend?"

William wasn't ready to give Sara information on Gina Shields and he didn't have any at all to give on Suz Reily. "Maybe the stress of the fight kept the Ghost from working his typical hoodoo," William suggested, hardly buying it himself.

Sara shook her head, rejecting the idea. "No. If something like a fight was enough, then why did it never not work before when he was killing any of those other girls?"

"Maybe none of them ever put up a fight like Salvia did," William offered.

"You need to look at the file on that one girl from up-state New York then," Sara replied. "The Washington girl. She put up one hell of a fight. Enough of one that he decided to let her go." The thought of the Ghost getting beat down by a 14-year-old girl brought a wry smile to Sara's lips. "Not a single clear eyewitness description of the Ghost; from her or anyone else. There was another one in Boston, too, but it wasn't as dramatic."

"Well, when you catch him you can ask the Ghost why someone else was able to see him right," William said as he walked with her out of the room, the upbeat lilt to his voice not as fake as he thought it'd be.

Gina was somewhat tempted to see if she could throw a person down a hall with her mind when she caught the other Agent Post watching her from another room further down the corridor. She didn't like getting the stink-eye from anyone in general and getting it from someone who might be bad news for her even less. Instead she knocked on the door and entered after she heard Dez answer. Now the blood had been cleaned off, he didn't look as banged up as he did when they carted him off.

"Do you have some mutant healing factor or was it just not that bad?" Gina quizzed as she put some magazines down on a bedside table.

"Just not that bad," Dez grumbled with a nasty edge in his voice.

"So... that was him, huh?"

"Yeah, and I let him get away." His face turned darker. Through gritted teeth he muttered, "Again!"

She looked at him laid up in the bed. "I'd hardly classify this as letting him get away." She plopped down in a chair, taking notice of what was on the television. It was some reality show with a cast who, whether it meant to or not, made a convincing case that pre-hominid antecedents still walked among humanity. Fortunately, the volume was way low. "Don't know if you noticed, but you did end up in the hospital. Somehow, I doubt that's where you'd be if you just 'Good day, sir'd him."

"I guess so," Dez grudgingly accepted.

"How long are they keeping you here?"

"Overnight," he said pointing to his head. "I might have a concussion."

"So, I saw Agent Happy McShortybitch down the hall. She talk to ya?"

"Yeah. I'm gonna work with her. Bring this to an end," Dez mumbled. He focused intently on the television. "Maybe."

"Hey, you have 'ways', remember?" she said with a playful yet grim laugh.

"And they really helped, didn't they?"

"No reason to get all broody, Batman," Gina rolled her eyes. "He ambushed you coming out of the pisser. Plus, he had a knife. You were unarmed but *he* was the one who pissed himself and ran. Sounds like point goes to you, dude!"

He started to wave her away but dropped his hand. "Look, just let me seethe for a while?" Dez asked. "It's how I process."

"Alright," Gina granted, waving her hand at him as if she were swiping the conversation aside. She stood up from the chair. "I need to get back to the shop anyway. Give me a call and let me know when they're gonna let you leave. I'll swing by and give ya a lift."

Dez nodded. Appreciation showed on his face and in his eyes, though he didn't say anything.

Gina left Dez to chew himself to pieces over the confrontation. She hoped he'd see it as optimistically as she did, which made her wonder why she saw it that way at all. Dez could have been killed and so could Suz for that matter. She didn't find it all too surprising a guy who killed young girls for jollies turned out to be a coward when faced with people who could and would defend themselves. It did scare her, though. The idea that he could just walk right into her home so easily wasn't something she wanted to think about. On some level she supposed she already knew that, but today just solidified it like a brick to the head.

Gina knew she'd never forget his face, never forget those eyes.

That's when it hit her. Today wasn't the first time Gina had seen those eyes. She recalled the dinner a few nights ago when she had a hallucination of Jen killed, her throat slashed and blood pouring out. Those dead eyes stared into Gina's as...well, that part Gina actively tried to forget. Gina remembered that the apparition had tick marks all over its body, just like the killer. Had that been a vision of the future, and not just a disturbing nightmare? If so, was it the really-real future or just a possible future?

How the fuck does the future work?

She was lost in thought as she passed through the hospital's doors, the heat pulling her from her absent thoughts, but not in time to keep her from bumping into someone. "Sorry..." Gina started to say before she saw that it was William.

"How's Salvia?" he asked conversationally.

"Fine. They're keeping him overnight though. How's your hand?"

"Just a few stitches," he said with an easy grin, regarding his bandaged hand. "Good as new in no time."

"Great." Pleasantries out of the way, Gina continued, "I think I might know his next victim."

William stood dumbstruck at the claim. He stuttered, trying to find words. "Did you...How?"

"I don't know, maybe I'm psychic or something," Gina answered, rolling her eyes, her arms flying out sideways.

"Of course," William muttered. "Who is it?"

"I think it's my brother's girlfriend."

"What's her name and address?" William asked as he pulled pen and pad from his jacket.

"Jennifer Holt. Not sure where she lives though."

"I can find out; have patrols increased in that neighborhood," William proposed as he took the name down. "Don't know how much good it'll do though. When did this information come to you?"

"A few days ago."

"And you're just now telling me this?"

"Well, it was right before I met you and I thought it was all crazy train and then you told me I was some government created super psychic and I was thinking *you* were all crazy train, so I wasn't gonna be all: 'hey, dude, go check my brother's cute teenaged girlfriend out'!"

"Your command of the narrative is astounding."

"Fuck you."

A car pulled up to the curb in front of them. Sara was behind the wheel. She and Gina glared at each other. Gina didn't need to be psychic to tell suspicion surged from the agent and it was all directed at her.

"I guess that's your ride. I'll try to get that address for you. Save you some effort," she told William as she walked away.

The drive back to the hotel room started out peacefully. Sara went a full half-block before she quietly spoke up.

"So, to reiterate: who is that chick?" When William went several moments without answering she asked again, this time much more assertively.

"I heard you the first time," William told her a bit sharper than he meant. "I was just giving you a chance to drop it."

"Drop it? Why would I drop it?" she demanded. "Who is she?" Sara glowered at her uncle sideways. "Wait. Is *that* who you've been sneaking out to see?" The accusations ran several levels deep.

His silence was enough of an answer for her. "It's a tad unconventional I suppose, but hey, whatever floats your boat, Uncle Will."

"It's not like that," William softly countered.

"Then what's it like? Who is she?"

A memory of pale blue eyes looking back at him through a closing door ran through William's mind. "Someone who doesn't need to be involved in this."

"Too late for that," Sara snappishly retorted. "Salvia pulled her into this somehow."

"It wasn't Salvia," William corrected. "Not entirely. I'm starting to think there was no way she could have avoided it." Sara went back and forth between watching the road before them and looking at him. She didn't want to push her uncle too hard, but she was in no mood for contemplative moroseness, especially if it wasn't going to answer her questions.

"And that means what?" They pulled into the hotel parking lot and found a space in front of their room.

"I'll tell you about it later," William said. Seeing the glare Sara gave him, he added, "I promise. For now, you'll have to trust me."

"That's pretty hard to come by right now."

"I know," the regret in his voice was genuine. "I'll do what I can to change that but for now I think we should concentrate on the Ghost." His phone rang. He looked at it and saw Gina's number flash across the screen. The timing was perfect and terrible all at once.

"Speaking of which, we may have a lead," he told Sara as he answered the call.

The stench of sweat and blood permeated His rented room. The landlord pounded on the door, yelling about complaints. He gave the disgustingly fleshy little man a thick wad of cash to ignore all those complaints, for a little while at least.

His side was discolored and sore but not a concern. His jaw was feeling a little better now that He had yanked out the teeth dislodged by the Hunter's punch. Perhaps the adrenaline masked it before, but the female agent managed to land a shot on Him. Fortunately, it missed the bone and imbedded in the meat. Try as He might, He couldn't keep from screaming as He dug the bullet out from His skin.

Unsurprisingly, his cries brought the landlord back, only to be sent away again with another large stack of bills. It was enough even to make him ignore the knife heating up on the hot plate and the yawning, bloody wound on His shoulder. The repellent man gone, He took the knife from the hot plate. Steeling his nerves, He pressed it against the gash and held it for what felt like hours. He did not hear any screams issue from his mouth, though His raw throat told Him there had been plenty.

The landlord hammered on the door again, the room rattling with each blow and his throaty voice bawling obscenities. He tired of the man's greed and paid him permanently. It was a tight squeeze to wedge the landlord's lifeless, corpulent body into the closet. Along with the cash He had given before, a heavy key-ring was found in the man's pocket. They might prove useful, so He took them as well.

Now He could concentrate on the real task at hand.

Chapter 11

Dez was discharged from the hospital early the next morning. Instead of calling Gina, he walked back to the apartment. When she found out, she was pissed though only long enough for her to make a comment about "stubborn-ass people". The rest of the day continued with an eerie normalcy until Quinn busted into the shop. She had obviously heard about the events of the previous day.

"You're staying your dork-ass at my place tonight, little missy," she told Gina matter-of–factly. She was compulsively worrying the old scar on her hand with the fingers of the other. Quinn always did that when she was anxious. "No ifs, ands, or buts."

"Sounds like you're in trouble now, girlie," the gangly old biker in Gina's chair said in a juvenile voice teetering with a laugh whistling through the spaces where a few teeth were missing.

Gina lifted her rotary from the cartoony bat she was inking onto his forearm and looked him in the face. "Stay out of this, Bobby, or I'll make the bat into a pretty, pretty butterfly." When his laughter didn't subside quickly enough she continued. "A pretty, pretty *pink* butterfly." Bobby stopped laughing.

Turning to Quinn, "I'm fine. Anyway, I doubt that asshole will come back here."

"You don't know that," she moaned, pushing a strand of bleached white hair from her face.

"No, but I think it all the same," Gina replied as she started back on Bobby's tattoo.

"Then I'm staying here with you," Quinn shifted.

"No, you're not! You've only got a few nights to get ready for Quentin's thing. If I stay with you or you with me, you'll never work on that." The rave was going to be a big opportunity for Quinn and Gina wasn't going to do anything to mess it up if she could help it. Besides, the rave was just as much the reason Quinn was playing with her scar as what happened with Dez.

"She makes a good point," Bobby interjected.

"Shut up, Bobby," Quinn snarled.

"He's right. I do make a good point," Gina said, looking up with a smug smile. Before Quinn could say anything else, "Seriously, I appreciate the concern, but I'll be fine." Quinn started to give another objection before Gina cut her off again. "If it makes you feel any better, the guy's looking to hurt Dez, not me."

Quinn considered that for a second. "That *does* make me feel a little better," she conceded. "Still, I'd feel more better if Suz or Michelle or Marcella or someone stayed with you tonight."

Gina glared at Bobby from the corner of her eye. The old biker kept his mouth shut. "Well, Suz has to work tonight and I'm sure Michelle and Marcella have plans of their own."

"I'm free," Bruce said as he passed by Gina's room.

"No, you're not, Bruce," Frankie yelled from his office before Gina could reply. It sounded brusque and cranky, which was honest, but humor also dripped from her father's comment. At any rate, it saved Gina from saying it in the less assertive, awkward voice she would have used. The memories from the table coming back to her made her squirm a little, and not just from discomfort.

Looking to get her mind on anything else, Gina quickly turned her attention back to her friend. "Seriously, I'll be fine. No need to worry." She knew the last part fell on deaf ears. "Besides Trevor picked up my pull list today and is dropping my comics off tonight. He'll hang out for a while since I'm making dinner," Gina offered. "He'll probably bring Jen with him."

She knew he would because Gina told him to. When she gave her address to William, he reminded her the cops probably couldn't help too much and suggested that Gina keep an eye on Jen as much as she could.

"That reminds me. Is Quentin's party all ages?"

"I think so. At least it should be until midnight, but I'll ask," Quinn took a deep breath and let it out slowly, bringing the discussion back to the original topic. "Okay. I think you're stupid, but okay," she relented. She looked at her watch. "I gotta go. I have to be at Dead Robot in ten minutes."

"Dead Robot? I thought Howie gave you the next few days off so you could work on Quentin's deal."

"He did but today's the day of the week when new stuff comes in. I told him I'd come in to help with that at least."

With that, the two said their good-byes. Gina knew nothing she said would put Quinn's mind to rest. Not that Gina could blame her friend. Quinn's history caused her to take this kind of thing seriously. The thought of trying to use her abilities to calm Quinn's apprehension crossed Gina's mind. She dismissed it as quickly as it came, though. Even if she was sure she could do something like that, the idea of doing it to a friend, especially Quinn, struck Gina as wrong. She even felt bad about letting Angie do so the other night, as much as it might have been needed. She sighed and went back to work on Bobby's tattoo.

There was a long moment when the only sound in the small studio was the hum of the machine. "I am free tonight," Bobby cut into the purring silence with a conspiratorial whisper and a shit-eating grin smeared across his face.

There was neither hide nor hair of the Ghost for the next few days, while Gina did what she could to keep Jen in her sights as much as possible all the same. Getting her and Trevor over for dinner at her place, taking them to the movies and whatever else she could think of as an excuse to hang out with them. It wasn't much of a chore since Gina found the girl pleasant company, though she was surprised Trevor wasn't upset at having so little private time with Jen. When she brought it up with him, Trevor simply explained, unlike him, she wasn't ready for things to "go there yet". Trevor didn't want to pressure Jen into anything she didn't want to do and being around others helped in that regard.

Quinn let Gina know that, as suspected, the party was indeed all-ages but only until midnight for anyone under 18. This would be one more way she could keep an eye on the girl. At least this would be fun. The sun had barely set when Trevor arrived at Gina's with Jen, Cinnamon, and Mason in tow. Having been to one of Quentin's gigs before, Gina advised them to dress as lightly as possible, which the summer heat made easy. She was glad to see they followed her recommendations. The boys had gone for simple with Trevor in baggy pants made of a thin material, an A-shirt with an opened button-up over it, and flat soled low-top sneakers. Mason had long shorts, an over-sized tee shirt with some sort of alien graphic, and a pair of white trainers he referred to as his "Tenth Doctors".

Cinnamon went for simple, as well: baggy shorts, a tight grey tee shirt with a still image from the movie *Thelma and Louise*. She also wore a pair of black and white sport sandals she borrowed from Gina some months ago. "You were supposed to bring those tonight because I was gonna wear them," Gina scolded her cousin. She grouchily accepted Cinnamon's apology and picked out a pair of scuffed and battered boots to wear instead. It was probably for the best since Gina doubted she'd do much dancing tonight.

Jen had on a pair of slippers, short-shorts showing off her long spindly legs, and a white button-up shirt with a short tale. For herself Gina went with a thin tee shirt with short black sleeves and purple body with a golden Yvonne Craig-style Batgirl logo. She mulled over throwing on pants now she was wearing boots but decided to stick with her baggy black capri pants. She thought about doing something special with her hair, not seeing much point. She had a chance to get Michelle to touch up the black earlier in the day and her hair tended to frizz for a day or two afterwards, especially in the heat. Whatever she did would quickly end up a tangled mess, making her effort hopeless. Thus, she just let it fall where it would.

The kids seemed as excited as she did, although, she expected theirs was due to anticipation of something new, while hers was because she knew there was a sick, murderous fuckhead gunning for one of them. She had already downed a couple of shots of bourbon, though her nerves were still on edge. She briefly thought about taking her pipe to the roof, only to decide against it. She didn't want to be *too* out of it.

Dez showed up a short time later, which helped her relax some. Just as she had with Agent Post, Gina told Dez she believed Jen was the Ghost's next target. She managed to weasel out of telling him *why* she thought this, the idea of getting a step ahead of the Ghost intrigued Dez enough not to ask too many questions. Dez kept the kids company while she finished getting ready.

"Is Suz meeting us here?" he wondered from the couch. Gina didn't hear the question over Trevor and Mason's banter about the latest issue of some comic book, so Dez stood in the alcove outside the bathroom and asked again.

"Yeah," Gina answered. Her voice was heavy with curiosity. "She should be here soon. Why?"

"No reason." Dez tried to make his answer as indifferent as possible, to no avail. Gina had seen Suz leaving Dez's flat the day before. Suz had her usual carefree airiness yet Gina couldn't decide if Dez looked like a kid caught with his hand in the cookie jar or someone who had been shown several levels of hell all at once. She didn't ask what was going on since it was none of her business, and she wasn't going to jump to any conclusions.

Now, however, was different. Gina gave Dez a sly look. "No reason, huh?" Then in a low, teasing sing-song voice she chanted, "Dez and Suz sittin' in a tree..."

She might have been justified in being angry with her friend- Suz not only knew Gina was interested in Dez, she was encouraging a hook up. However, Gina had truthfully insisted she wasn't planning on making any move on him. There were too many questions Gina wanted answered before doing that, about both him and herself. If Suz was interested in Dez, and Gina had thought she might be, she saw no reason to be mad at either of them if they got together. Especially since her own inaction was intentional.

Besides, Dez was likely in far more danger than Suz as far as that relationship was concerned.

"No, no. It's nothing like that. I...," he started, his objections seemingly sincere, before a knock at the door interrupted him.

Mason opened the door, fumbling for a hello as Suz waited for him to invite her in. She was decked out in a small black dress that tried really hard to be mid-thigh in length though failed completely. In practice it was more of a skirt with a flap barely covering Suz's front, using a pair of slim, horizontal straps to cover the back and another even thinner pair over her shoulders to hold it up. She completed the look with a pair of mid-shin gladiator sandals. Her bright purple hair, decorated with glittery gel, was pulled up into two slinky tails starting high on her head and bangs making a perfect line above her brow.

She smiled as she patted Mason on his cheek in greeting, sending him further into gibbering idiot territory. Gina took a sideways glance at Dez and was shocked that the mildly sexually repressed teenaged boy seemed to be better composed than he was in her presence. Suz gave greetings to the other kids as she made her way towards Gina and Dez. He mumbled out a quick "Hey" to her as he went back to the couch, giving her as wide a berth as he could manage in the process.

The two women squeezed into the tiny bathroom and helped each other get ready after a quick drink. Gina noticed odd glances between Suz and Dez, finding it getting old pretty fast.

"Okay, he said nothing's going on," Gina began in a whisper once they were in the bathroom, meeting Suz's eyes in the mirror. "But obviously something is. So: spill."

"He's right. Nothing's going on," Suz explained in a casual tone. "Nothing like *that* anyway. He and I just had a little chat about what happened the other day. It was completely friendly," she insisted, hand over heart.

"As well as clothed," she added after a suitable beat.

"Then why is he acting so anxious around you?"

Suz's lips curled on one side into a smirk as one eyebrow

rose. She turned her head to the side, as she often did when a wicked thought crossed her mind. "If I *had* to guess, I'd say it was because I told him what would happen to him if you got hurt because of him," she opened her mouth into a wide toothy grin that could have been joking pride or just a check to see if she had lipstick on her teeth. "I put particular emphasis on what would happen to his lower intestines and what they would be wrapped around."

"And here I was thinking it was something unseemly."

"What's a few threats of torture and death between friends?"

"The glue that holds it all together, I'd say," Gina remarked as she stood up a little straighter. She inspected the both of them and declared, "I think we are done."

Suz made a final inspection, purring out as she wrapped her arms around Gina's neck. "Perfection fucking achieved, babe."

They gathered near Gina's kitchen for a final drink, posing for pictures as they downed them. Cinnamon wanted to continue her conversation with Dez from the other night, so she and Mason hopped a ride in Gina's car. Though five or six in the Mustang was possible, four was already a tight fit. With that in mind, Suz grabbed a ride with Trevor and Jen in his jeep. Once the seating was settled, with Trevor following Gina, they headed to the north side of the city.

No one noticed the rusted heap pulling out from the alley across the street and discreetly tailing them.

When he first breezed into town many years earlier, Quentin bought several old depots and storehouses on the edge of the rail tracks dividing the city between north and south. The structures had been abandoned many decades before in a time when the city first suffered economic decline, and most were in a state suggesting the desertion was abrupt. To date, his concentration had been mainly limited to restoring only one of the buildings, the largest of them all.

It was a three-story squat eyesore with a crumbling diarrhea-green brick façade. Within it, the renovated sections blended well with its former derelict charm. The first-floor housed a bar and a small lounge area, though it was mostly dedicated to storage for the time being. Quentin had talked of setting up a kitchen on that level, just as he talked about a lot of things that were slow to develop.

The second story was open space, serving as a dance floor. A top-of-the-line sound system had been installed and the acoustics in the place were surprisingly good. One end of the floor had a small bar, the other a tiered stage area. Quentin had yet to book any live bands for the place, despite talking about doing so. Until then he kept the entertainment limited to DJs. Few had been to the third floor, which Quentin reconditioned as a second home. His primary residence was an unassuming house in an affluent area outside the city, though word was he slept here more often than not.

Gina had only been to the warehouse once before, to Quentin's first party. It didn't look like much then, and many thought it'd be closed within a year, but she knew this was hardly Quentin's first rodeo. Quinn thought the place would do well, too. "At the very least it'll be some competition for The Loft and The Orpheum. Both places'll have to step it up somehow," Quinn had asserted with no small measure of anticipation over the possibilities.

If it does do well, maybe Quentin can get them to fix this goddamn road, Gina thought, her teeth rattling in her head, as her car rumbled down the busted street as she tried to avoid the larger potholes. The deteriorated road became less of an issue once they pulled up to the short line of vehicles being directed into several parking areas. As they crept to the lot entrance, Gina noticed a black sedan with a younger woman and an older man inside.

Subtle. She softly elbowed Dez in the passenger seat beside her and nodded her head towards the other car. When the Mustang pulled even with the sedan, the four of them exchanged cautious glances before the occupants of each car settled into ignoring those in the other.

The parking lot was little more than a cleared-out space of grass and barely crushed gravel. Across the street another lot had already filled up. It was several more minutes before they made it inside. The place was surprisingly packed for such an early hour. It didn't take long for Gina to realize most people here were underage; almost everyone she saw had black X's on the backs of their hands. In the lounge, the music was pumped in but at low volume. With all the various conversations going on, Gina couldn't hear well enough to tell if it was Quinn spinning yet or not. She didn't have to wonder long, though, since after wrapping Gina, Suz, and Dez simultaneously in a massive bear-hug, Harris confirmed Quinn was on as they spoke.

Up on the second story they found the dance floor crammed with dancing bodies. The stage was darkened with a warm grotto of light where Gina could see Quinn hunched over some decks and turntables. She had a single headphone, detached from the headset, held to her ear while she fiddled with various buttons and settings. She was wearing a white halter top and a pair of baggy black jeans. Her face and neck were covered in white, highlighted by black lipstick and eye shadow. Her black and white hair was pulled back into two ponytails, one on either side of her head.

Gina wanted to run onto the stage and squeeze her friend tightly; however, Quinn was in the aloof persona she would often adopt to get up in front of a crowd when she didn't have a booth in which to hide; when she was visible for all the world to see. The last thing Gina wanted to do was mess up her friend's chances, so she restrained herself. Such a curb proved easy as Gina began to feel the pulse of the music and excitement and passion of the crowd. It was like the night at The Loft when she met Dez. She could feel the raw craze driving into her, pushing at her core just as she gave it fuel to burn. They grabbed bottles of water from the bar and powered their way into the teeming mass of revelers.

In the crowd Trevor, Mason, Cinnamon, and Jen soon drifted away from Gina and her friends, joining with other kids they knew from school, though Gina kept them in her sights. Harris plowed through the dancers with his wild motions to greet others he knew, leaving Gina, Suz, and Dez to themselves. The music was drum and bass, the lyrics and rhythm of "Cruel Summer" flowing into the undercurrent to complement the composition. With no hesitation, Suz took hold of Gina, pressing herself tightly against her friend, their bodies running side to side and up and down. Gina had no intentions of dancing tonight but the music, the energy of the masses; the pulse of Suz's body against hers swarmed her passions, causing her to match her friend's grinding pace. As the words of the song, lamenting being alone made their way past the thumping beat, Suz gave Gina a smile, landing a quick peck on her cheek before letting her go and melting into the crowd.

Looking about for the others, Gina found the kids still nearby. Trevor and Jen danced closely. Mason and Cinnamon awkwardly attempted to dance with each other while *not* dancing with each other. Dez was near them, making dance-like motions so he wouldn't seem out of place but not so much he would lose sight of Jen. Gina slid over to him and took his hands, placing them on her hips, her arms wrapping over his shoulders, shocking him out of his surveillance.

After a moment his expression relaxed. "I thought you were with Suz." His meaning clear, as well as the slight envy it invoked in him.

"Told you; we just goof around like that. It doesn't mean anything." His face told her he didn't buy that completely but wouldn't press the issue. "Just like I'm goofing around with you right now."

"Right now?" his gaze wandered back over to the kids.

"Yeah, right now," she said as she pressed closer to him. His head snapped back to her. His voice hovered in the back of his throat, words not really forming, but Gina cut him off before they could.

"Relax. We're just two friends having a good time before having to deal with a psychotic shit-stain who's looking to get his jollies by killing my brother's girlfriend." She backed away from him, a wide smile on her face. She fell into the crowd, pulling him along behind her and making her way towards her brother and the others.

Grabbing her arm tight, Dez stopped Gina short before reaching them. "How can you be joking about all of this?"

"Because I have to be," she shouted over the music. "I can't explain it right now but trust me. I know this is serious, like 12 miles of yellow caution tape serious. Look, he's gonna come, no doubt about it, but getting all twisted up in knots waiting for it isn't gonna help when he does."

They stared at each other, the mob sweeping around them, neither saying a word nor backing down. Finally, she broke the silence. "Look, broody's your thing, I get it. That's cool with me. But you just look like an ass- not to mention a total pedophile-watching Jen like a hawk. And, oh yeah, you probably stick out enough that when he *does* come, he can easily avoid you. He doesn't know that we know who he's after so let's not send him smoke signals now. We can keep an eye on her without being so obvious about it."

"If that's the case I'll do better by the door then," Dez replied. There was no anger in the statement, just an admission of limitations. He gave her a fast pat on the shoulder to show no hard feelings and dissolved into the horde. She sighed as she watched him go before turning back towards the kids, dancing her way over to them.

It was easy enough to discern where they were going. He drove past the club and parking lot and found a dilapidated shed where he ditched the landlord's car, then made His way back on foot. There He blended into the crowd waiting to get in. He was among so many who begged for His attention, He was sure this was the Adversary sending lessor minions to distract Him. He prayed to the Almighty to give Him strength in His time of need. Still, His hand inched towards His knife, hidden away in a sheath under His light jacket. A few people gave Him looks, not that odd since His clothing made Him so out of place, but no gaze lingered on Him for long. While He waited for admission, He looked about for the Feds. He knew the Hunter and She were here, making it likely the agents were as well. He saw the police milling about here and there, more than a few cruisers slowly driving by or conspicuously parked, but no sign of any other law enforcement. He relaxed a little, keeping His guard up all the same.

Inside were displays of corruption and degradation. Lust and excess, among other sins, were easily and wantonly indulged here. He expected such a display, having braved places like this before, but it was still alarming. In general, He didn't care for music, finding it to be a feeble parody of the divine. He could only imagine the sounds being pumped through the speakers having been vomited up from the deepest levels of the Pit. It seemed the music's only purpose was to invite people into pressing and rubbing themselves against each other.

He made it up to the second floor with no problem, blending into a darkened corner as the Hunter took up a position by the very door He walked through just an instant before. He took a second to study the Hunter; his face still showed bruises from their confrontation and he held one arm stiffly, the arm He slashed. His own arm and side caused Him to wince when He moved, if the Hunter was still weakened he would not pose as much a threat should he stand in His way. He looked for Her and His target, finding neither of them. He assumed they were somewhere within the squirming horde. As much as it disgusted Him, He slipped in among them.

He squeezed through the clammy, sticky mass of bodies bumping and choking about Him. The stench of alcohol, lust, and general human filth assaulted His nose. An occasional hand brushed Him below the waist, the contact causing a physical stir. It was all He could do not to lash out right there. His anger was doused and replaced by horror when He caught sight of the infernal whore from the Hunter's apartment. Her appearance was back to normal, or what passed for it, and she pranced about between several different people, both men and women. He was able to duck out of her sight before she saw Him and had to take a moment to let His fear of her pass by. After His senses returned, He realized it was a good sign. The whore was unlikely to let Her too far out of her sight, meaning She was probably nearby. That reckoning was quickly proven correct.

She was dancing amongst the target and a few others. He kept out of Her view but stayed close to them. Moments later the target said something to the blonde girl before both started making their way out of the crowd, mollifying Her before they left. He followed them out and stopped just at the edge of the mass, watching as they went through an opening marked "Bathroom". He looked for the Hunter, who was still at the door, his concentration tightly staying there. After a few moments of consideration, He left the concealment of the crowd and made a beeline to the opening.

Beyond it was a hallway. At the far end a stairwell but a pair of doors were before it marked "Men" and "Women". He hung about outside the two doors. One guy left the men's room and a group of young girls came out of the women's room, their giggling almost drowning out the music. He cautiously slinked into that bathroom.

From around a corner He saw the target standing before the mirror, her attention fully on her reflection as her long fingers worked tangles from her sweaty dark hair to bring back some life to the damp, matted mess. The blonde was speaking from one of the stalls, her vocabulary infected with the vilest words ever to spring from humanity's imagination. He glided up behind the target, His knife at her throat before she even knew He was there. He held a finger to His lips, telling her not to make a sound. A tear was already at the corner of her fearful eye. The toilet immediately behind them flushed and the hinges screamed as the stall door was slung open. The blonde saw what was happening, yelled an obscenity at Him and what she would do to His manhood. Knife still at the target's throat, He popped the blonde in her foul mouth with His free hand, stunning her into silence. Cupping her face in His hand, He slammed the side of her head into the stall's frame. She crumpled to the floor, vulgarities prattling faintly from her mouth.

He dragged the girl from the bathroom and down the stairwell at the end of the passage. At the first landing he heard voices in the hall behind them and picked up His pace. He found a door leading out of the building at the bottom. As He was about to take her out, a cop stopped them. It was not much of a complication, though, since the cop bought the lame story He supplied, even held the door open for them. The target appealed to the cop for help, tried to get him to see the danger she was in, but it was to no avail. The knife at her side kept her pleadings small and subtle and, as with many who meet Him, the cop felt an overriding need to be away from Him as quickly as possible. Outside, free of the thumping music and the Adversary's slaves, they crossed the lot under cover of darkness towards one of the old storehouses.

There He could take His time with the final assignment and glory in His exaltation before turning his full attention to Her.

Other than taking a quick scan of the revelries, with some hope of catching a glimpse of Gina and the others, Dez had barely taken his eyes off the door. With every new person who walked through anticipation built up within him. But this keenness was finding competition for Dez's attention. When he looked about the crowd, he couldn't help but think of Gina; her body against his on the dance floor, the smell of her sweat, the softness of her waist in his hands. Stopping the Ghost was his top priority but going back out there to be with her was putting up a damn good fight.

He had been on his own for quite some time now, never really getting to know anyone or making any friends. In fact, he was pretty lonely when it came right down to it. Still, it wasn't like he went without should certain needs pop up. Dez rarely had any issues finding someone willing to keep him company for a night or two if that was what he wanted. But a night was all they ever were to him. If it became a conflict between them and his pursuit of the Ghost, the chase won out every time.

And as much as he told Gina otherwise, not everyone he left back in Vancouver meant so little to him. One person, who held a special place in his heart, from back home tugged upon him greatly, even though he knew their time had long past. Still, the memories he had of them took a precedence in his thoughts that none had ever worked their way to replace them where Dez's affections were concerned.

But it was dawning on him the same could not be said of Gina Shields.

Lost in thought, Dez didn't notice Harris walking over from the bar. He jumped when the big man yelled his name out over the music from just a few inches away. Without a word Harris held out a bottle of beer to Dez, a second bottle for himself in his other hand. Dez took the beer with an enthusiastic nod.

"Dancing not your thing, man?" Harris asked as he leaned up against the wall next to Dez, pushing his sweaty blonde hair from his face.

"Only when the mood hits me," Dez coolly replied. He liked Harris, but the guy was nothing but a distraction right now.

"I get out there and I just look like a guy badly failing motor development classes," he said, not taking any notice that Dez was hardly paying him any attention. "Still, Quinn'll drag me out there anyway," he carried on as he took a swig. "Not that I can complain. She's a good woman and I'm lucky she wants anything to do with me. If it makes her happy, I'll gladly look an ass every now and then."

He saw Dez wasn't looking at him, so Harris nudged his shoulder. "Gina's a good one too. I'd be out there looking an ass for her as well." This caught Dez's interest more than the bump.

"I'll be honest with you," Harris persisted before Dez could say anything, "I didn't know what to make of you that night at The Loft, and I sure didn't know about leaving Gina alone with you at her place. But Quinn said that if Gina gave you her seal of approval then you were solid in her book, which makes you solid in my book.

"Look, I saw Gina dancing with you earlier. I don't know why you're over here and not out there with her, but I'd say that's an equation you might want to try adding up again."

On one level Dez wanted to put his fist in Harris's face. Harris was right- he sure as fuck didn't understand why Dez was watching the door and not dancing. Dez was looking to net the sick fuck who killed his sister and destroyed his family, a psychopath who had done the same to countless other girls and families over the years. At the moment, standing here watching the door and not dancing, seemed like the thing that would most likely make stopping him happen.

On another level, Dez had to admit Harris was right, which still made him want to put his fist in the man's face. He had been thinking about the night he met her. Dez had certain abilities, often simply called tricks, as did others like him. These tricks tended to be unique according to the individual, often influenced by heritage, but not always. Some started out with more than others, though it could be easy enough to learn more over a lifetime- if one were willing to pay the price. One of Dez's natural tricks, the one allowing him to track the Ghost, led him to The Loft that night. It was almost a clear, direct, and bright line highlighting the path between it and the bus station. Once inside, he saw Gina at the bar.

Initially, there was hardly anything special or remarkable about her, yet there may as well have been a neon sign flashing "TALK TO THIS ONE, MORON" over her. It unnerved the hell out of Dez how it had been so unequivocal. So explicit. Usually whatever authority fueled it would drag him through a Goldbergian series of humiliations and misadventures before it would get him to anything remotely useful. In the end, Dez knew these powers were accurate, fickle as they were, and he'd be better off following without question.

Not only was it so unexpectedly direct, there was the weirdness when Dez tried putting a spin, another of his tricks, on his part of their conversation. Although it usually worked better when he told a story or sang, he could put emphasis on certain words and compel people to do as he pleased. He wasn't sure of how far he could push a person, but he knew it was harder to get a person to do something they weren't inclined to do in the first place. The night they met Dez didn't want to push Gina into anything bad, just maybe be more disposed to help him out in whatever way she was supposed to. It didn't sit too well with him, but he wasn't going to risk disappointment when these unpredictable forces were being so obliging. In the end his distaste didn't really matter as Gina simply shrugged his impulsion off. It was more than that, really. Gina didn't just wave it off. Something within her ripped the impulsion to shreds and threw it back in his face. Dez almost pissed his pants when he felt it.

What really unsettled Dez about Gina's ability to resist his push is, outside of his family and those within their community, the only other person he'd met who could do this was the Ghost. Granted, the Ghost could only resist it, which was disconcerting enough. She kicked it out of her head without even noticing what she did. All it accomplished was making her look at him like he was a complete weirdo, or at least an amusement. Fortunately, she seemed to think he was just making a pathetic, if harmless, pick-up attempt.

Whatever was going on with her, Gina took him in and her father gave him a roof over his head, as temporary as that may be. Appreciation and obligation was important, vital really, to Dez's people. Gina's friends and family accepted him easily enough, though Suz scared him in ways Dez couldn't even begin to quantify. He knew immediately he did not want to get on her bad side. On top of that, it was Gina who pushed him to deal with the agents and revealed the Ghost's next target. How she pulled that off was unclear, but he wasn't about to start looking at gifts of fate too closely.

He was close to bringing an end to all of this and it was because of Gina. That fact alone put her in a singular class in his mind. Lately, though, his thoughts of her were starting to go other places. Places he couldn't dwell on right now, bringing him back to wanting to put his fist in Harris's face.

"I'm sure the advice is well meant bu..." Dez's comment skidded to a halt in his throat as a commotion near the bathrooms caught his attention. Harris noticed Dez's gaze and followed it. Both ran over to see what was going on and found Cinnamon staggering out of the bathroom, holding onto the wall for support. There was a thin line of blood running from her nose and lip and a large spot on the side of her head where her blonde hair was stained red. The small group of girls going in as she burst out was giving Cinnamon plenty of space. She saw Dez and Harris and pushed herself from the wall to get to them but fell over. Dez caught her and gently sat her up against the wall.

"Go get Gina!" Dez yelled to Harris. Not needing to be told again he disappeared around the corner. To Cinnamon, "What happened?"

"Cockbite had a knife. He took Jen." Her voice was weak and groggy.

"Where?" Dez shouted but the girl could do nothing more than shake her head. Suz was suddenly there at the girl's other side.

"I ran into Harris. He's getting Gina and the others," she explained as she knelt down and took Cinnamon from Dez, clasping the girl in her arms. Her eyes had a disquieting intensity, just as they did when she came to talk to him after the incident at his apartment. "I believe you have business to take care of," she said to Dez, her voice even and weighty.

With that Dez stood up and took off. If the Ghost took Jen from the bathroom, then he likely took her down the stairs at the end of the hall. If there was a backdoor it would be easier for the Ghost to get her out that way, but his trick was telling, no screaming at, him to leave by the front instead. Believing it best to follow its guidance and hoped its recent simplicity was holding as he ran down to the first floor, surging past the cluster of people, and onto the street.

Muffled as it was, the music pounding from inside the club was beginning to grate on Sara's nerves. She never cared for dance or techno or much of most types of music outside of rock and metal bands, and that was about it. If she ever listened to anything else it was because of some collaboration between a rock band and someone from another genre, like when Anthrax covered Public Enemy's "Bring the Noise" with the rap group joining in.

She had a slight grunge phase around the early to mid-90's, but she tried not to reminisce on that time though that had little to do with the genre.

Then again, her problem right now wasn't so much the music but how she had to rely on others to get her job done. More to the fact, the *people* she was relying on were her problem. Salvia wasn't much of an issue. He'd shown an ability to track the Ghost time and time again, and he wanted to take the Ghost down as much as she did. If he got the chance and took it, her only regret might be it wasn't her who put a bullet in the psycho's head.

The problem was the other two. She didn't know what to think of them. It rattled her some that William had no idea about the one named Suz, not even bothering to throw out a guess. Still, he didn't appear concerned about her. If she was a threat, Sara was certain her uncle would pick up on it. Besides, it was Gina who really riled Sara up. She couldn't put her finger on the reason why, either. William pointedly told Sara to leave her alone, which only annoyed her and made her want to do the exact opposite.

Why's he being so closed off about Shields? Sara darkly wondered as she closely scrutinized the people waiting to go inside.

She pushed those thoughts out of her mind for the moment. It was hard enough sitting here waiting for someone to call her in without these distractions. She reached into the box nestled between her and her uncle to get another doughnut. Normally Sara avoided the things like the plague. It wasn't that she didn't like them but that she liked them too much. But coffee and doughnuts made things better when there was nothing to do but sit, watch, and wait. She saw William's head vaguely bopping in rhythm to the music. She noticed his foot tapping, too.

"None of that!" she scolded.

"What?" William asked, genuinely unaware of what he was doing.

"None of..." Sara pointed her finger at William's head and wiggled her fingers up and down in a circular motion, "...that. Keep it up and, before you know it, you'll be justifying spandex as a lifestyle choice." She handed him a doughnut and grabbed

211

another for herself.

"Not at my age," he said, realizing what she was getting onto him about now. He took the confection and was taking a bite when he saw Dez burst from the front door and look about frantically before disappearing around the side of the building. "Salvia!"

"I see him!" Sara yelled as she flew from the car. "I'm on him; you check out the inside!" She charged without looking back over her shoulder to see what her uncle was doing. Her hand already under her jacket and taking hold of her gun. William tried to stop her but knew that wasn't going to happen. Sara was already across the street, unconcerned about the cars honking at her, and had disappeared inside the darkened area Dez had dashed into before the older agent had exhaled.

Barley following Salvia's blurry form in the gloom, Sara caught up to him once he slowed down by the discard hulk of an ancient box car just outside one of the abandoned storehouses. The gravel at their feet was interspersed with thick patches of tall, skinny grass and the rusted remains of leftover machinery.

The building itself was roughly three stories high with a tall concrete base and wood siding. There were gaping holes in the building's exterior walls and most of the front was taken up by a large steel shutter with sizable blotches of rust. Next to it was a standard door, now wide open and barely hanging from its hinges.

"Salvia!" the agent whispered as she came up behind him. In the dark she scarcely noticed he jumped slightly at hearing her voice. "Is that where they are?" she asked as she crept up to the ancient hunk of detritus he crouched behind.

"I think so." His attention was drawn strongly to the building. As if to confirm, they heard Jen scream from inside. Without hesitation, the two ran up to the smaller door: Sara on one side, Dez on the other.

Sara already had her gun in hand. She glanced at Dez. "You got a weapon?"

"Yeah." Dez pulled a knife from one pocket, flipping the blade out in the process. From another he produced brass knuckles and easily slipped them over his fingers with a practiced flicker of his hand. It was crude, but Sara had to admit it possessed a certain style. At that moment, she knew it would be more difficult to bring the Ghost in alive if Salvia got ahold of him first. The man wasn't looking for justice, but retribution. Sara didn't know much about Dez but based on what little William had told her she couldn't say that was surprising.

From the cover of the doorway Sara noticed the dilapidated structure still had electricity. Dim lights shone from the back of the structure. She could hear the girl's protests from the second floor. She was crying and scared, but she wasn't going quietly. She could hear the Ghost cursing the girl, asking her why she couldn't just accept her place in whatever scheme he had cooked up.

"Alright," Sara said to Dez. "Behind me." She slipped into the murky shadows and he followed.

Gina was starting to worry about how long Jen and Cinnamon had been gone. Between Dez at the door, Suz making her rounds, and the excitement of the dance floor, it was hard for her to get too anxious about it though.

Quinn was weaving the beat and lyrics of "The Metro" into her own drum and bass compositions. Gina was goofing off with Trevor and Mason, hopping on her brother's back in a mock effort to put him in a sleeper hold, when she noticed the crowd parting in advance of someone moving hastily through it, only to close in as they passed. From her better height on her brother's back, Gina studied the cause, seeing a pair of singed and broken cardboard angel wings sticking out over the top of the mob heading right for her. She slid off her brother's back, leaving the boys to go about their amusement. As the cluster of people before her broke apart, Angie fell to Gina's feet.

"What the hell is going on?" Gina said as low as she could over the reverberating bass thump. She tried to subtly help Angie up, seeing that her body had rips and gashes all over, some looking quite severe. From them an oily vapor spewed out, the same as earlier in her apartment, evaporating almost immediately but leaving a strangely sweet smell in its wake. The wraith's form was even more erratic and unstable than Gina had seen it previously. "What the hell happened to you?"

Angie briefly went into a series of gesticulations Gina could only guess were coughs or convulsions, though later she promised herself she'd do her level best to forget what she witnessed. Afterwards Angie acted a little better, though still rent and leaking vapor.

"The girls!" She juddered once more as her voice shattered. The geist regained some control, but her voice sounded like breaking glass. "The sister tried to keep the others under in line, but they went crazy. Swept me up in their rush... almost tore me apart dragging me along. Last time they got like this..."

Angie's head abruptly shook back and forth, her body convulsing as it seemed to dissolve. So fast did it happen, Gina could only see a blur separating from the rest of the shade's body. It finally halted, but the miasma escaping the wounds was getting thicker and heavier. The ghost looked pitiful, unsure if she could stay focused enough to speak again.

She didn't need to. "He's here," Gina finished the ghost's warning as she looked about for the girls, unable to see anything over the dancing throng. "Are you going to be okay?"

"I'll be fine. Just need to rest a sec..." That was all Angie got out before her body liquified into a puddle of unctuous fluid that pooled at Gina's feet before quickly soaking into the floor.

"You okay, sis?" Trevor had an arm around Gina's shoulders, pulling her tight. "You look like you've seen a..." Gina held her hand up to cut Trevor off. She loved her brother but if she let him finish that sentence, she believed she'd hurt him badly.

"Yeah, Gee, you're looking pretty pale," Mason said, the consoling expression on his face scrunched up into uncertainty. "Um, -er."

"I have to take care of something. You and Mason find Harris or Suz and stay with them."

"What about Jen and Cinnamon?" Trevor asked, but Gina didn't get to answer as Harris, pushing revelers aside, almost hurdled into her. He was panting and flushed.

214

"Cinnamon's hurt... by the bathrooms... Dez is with her, Suz too," he took a gulp of air, started to say something else but just took in more air. Catching the complete lack of mention of Jen, Gina felt it safe to make certain assumptions. As such, she knew he was probably right about Suz being with her cousin, but now wrong about Dez. She had to find him or the agents, or both.

"You two," Gina pointed to her brother and his friend. "Go with Harris and see to Cinnamon. Stay with him and Suz. Do *not* leave their side." Trevor was about to protest or, more likely, bring up Jen. Gina had no answers for the latter and didn't want to hear the first. "Stay with them. Do not leave their side," she reiterated, a force added to her voice telling the boys these were not suggestions. She didn't have time to shove her way through the multitude of people. She reached out with her mind and planted the notion that the crowd *really* wanted to get out of her way. To her surprise, it worked. As with Angie earlier, they simply stepped out of Gina's path, only to close back in behind her.

When Gina was out of sight, the boys followed Harris off the dance floor and over to Cinnamon. As they did Mason inquired to Trevor, "Dude, when did your sister become a Bene Gesserit because she totally broke out the Voice."

Once off the dance floor Gina made for the stairs, gently shoving people out of her way. She got down to the lounge area and saw William talking to a pair of cops. His back was to her; she took a step towards him but was stopped when an icy hand grabbed her arm. She turned and found Lucy's shade. The decay Gina noticed the other night had advanced considerably. The flesh now receding from her forehead and brow, leaving her eyes as large greyish orbs in boney sockets. One side of her lips and cheek were gone, giving her a permanent toothy half-grin. There were slashes and gouges across her corpus leaking the same vaporous material, much as Angie had though not as extensively. As usual, the ghost girl said nothing. She just pointed towards the back door, her face a mask of supplication.

Gina wanted to assure the girl she was getting someone to take care of it, that it'd be alright, but she didn't really know how. Besides, she honestly didn't know if it was the truth. She looked back to where William was still giving orders to the cops. A few more cops had joined them, and Quentin was there, too. It would be simple enough to take a few steps and tell the agent what was going on, if he didn't know already.

Simple, yes, but not what she did.

When she moved to get William, Lucy held Gina's arm tighter, the shade's face set with a desperate plea. Gina tried to let her know she was getting help, but the ghost simply let go of her arm, dejected anger in her eyes. With that, Gina took a deep breath and nodded for the shade to lead the way instead. The girl smiled and took off towards the back of the club with Gina in tow. She ran through the doors and across the darkened field. Gravel, which would have been difficult to run through in the sandals she meant to wear, crunched under her boots as she sidestepped hunks of discarded machinery. There were several possible destinations, but Lucy led her towards the one surrounded by the mass of ghost girls.

Even before she reached the building Gina could tell the shades were agitated. She paused at the door, the nearest ghost girl violently snapping her jaws. The action wasn't directed at Gina- at least she didn't think it was- but it unsettled her all the same. Looking inside, she wasn't sure what she expected to see. A small part of her hoped, maybe, she would come to her senses and go back to get William and the cops.

That part would have to get used to disappointment.

It wasn't completely dark inside, which left Gina mildly disenchanted for some morbid reason. A cold anger drifted over her from the surrounding ghosts as Gina wavered at the broken threshold. With a last look at Lucy and the girls, she took a cautious step across the doorsill, somehow certain a knife or hatchet or machete was going to come slashing down into her neck at any moment. When that didn't happen, she took another step inside, followed by another.

It was then her heart abruptly skipped. The disconcerting

silence was brutally smashed when Dez shouted a warning, Jen screamed, followed by a gunshot as all hell broke loose right above Gina.

Without thought, she broke into a run towards the stairs at the back.

On the upper level, Sara and Dez found stacks of moldy boxes as well as broken down and rickety crates and pallets stacked across the floor amid a maze of abandoned machinery and frail shelving racks, with more along the walls. From about the middle of the room, on the far side of a larger heap of forgotten freight and equipment, they heard Jen's muffled cries. They eased up to the pile, Sara signaling to Dez to make his way around from the far side to cut off the Ghost's escape routes.

Once he was in position, Sara swung around, quickly checking the nooks between the shelves on her left as she did and bringing her gun level over the girl. Jen was face down on the ground, her shoulders jerking up and down in time with her sobs and hands finger-laced behind her head. The Ghost, however, was nowhere to be seen. The sound of Sara's steps made Jen prop herself up, the hope of rescue on her face.

On the girl's other side, Dez came into view, his weapons at the ready. Sara saw his eyes go wide in surprise. "Behind you!" he yelled, his warning mixing with the girl's terrified scream.

Sara spun around, knowing the killer must be bearing down on her. What she saw was human-shaped, but she could only make out a vague blur. In spite of this, she was able to see the knife cutting through the air, its blade aimed at her neck. The attack missed, Sara twisting to the side just in time, but the knife caught the barrel of her gun. With a fast wrenching motion, it twisted in her hand so the round she fired off just skirted past the Ghost to hit a rusty shelfing rack instead. Old jars and cans fell from the frame, scattering contents across the floor as the whole thing collapsed with a deafening cacophony.

Over the noise and decades of dust and grit now spread

about the area in a thick cloud, Sara tried bringing her weapon level again to get another shot. Knowing he couldn't bring his knife back for another strike quickly enough, The Ghost pressed his lead by slamming his knee up into Sara's stomach. She reeled away from the surprising strength of the blow and tripped over Jen, her gun flying from her hand and landing somewhere off to the side. Dez was there to catch her, having to lose his own blade in the process. He dropped Sara softly to the ground and rushed the Ghost.

The knife came in level with Dez's eyes. Adrenalin rushing through him and instinct taking over, his hand shot up, snaring the Ghost's arm as the tip of the knife came too close to his face. With the brass knuckles, Dez smacked the Ghost in the side, hearing a wet crack as ribs fractured. With a garbled, shrieking curse and yanking his arm free, the Ghost fell away. Dez went in for another hit, this time to the Ghost's face, but he was overzealous and missed the knife cutting in at his leg. The blade sliced across his calf and he fell to the floor.

Pouncing onto Dez's chest, the Ghost delivered several stabs to his hounding enemy's torso, the knife splattering blood with each thrust. He took care not to cut too deeply, hitting nothing important, only wanting to keep Dez in pain, bleeding, and out of the fight. It was enough to sate the Ghost's hatred for the moment. He spoke of how he wanted Dez alive for a little while longer.

How he wanted Dez to watch him do to Jen what he did to Lucy.

He turned back to Sara, who was recovering, though she had barely found her breath again and painful coughs shuddered through her body. She was stumbling towards her gun as he made his way over to her. Noticing her moving about, the Ghost glanced over at Jen, who seemed to be trying to hide under the pallets, before turning his attention back to Sara. He managed to slam his foot hard into the agent's back before Jen swung a loose board she had found at the Ghost's back. The beam raked across his lower back, stray and rusty nails tearing into his flesh. The decaying plank broke from the force of the blow.

Staggering away a step, blood gushing from his back, he ignored Sara for the moment and turned his focus back to Jen. She was still stunned at her own actions and unsure of what to do now that she never even saw the backhanded smack he delivered to her jaw. The blow knocked her off her feet and she fell back, crashing into the pallets and crates. The girl, unconscious, remained still on the ground.

The agent was still clambering for her gun, though slower now. He reached down, grabbed her by her jacket, and turned her roughly to face him. Unlike the Hunter, The Ghost wanted her dead immediately, but he also wanted her to be looking into his eyes when it happened. His gleeful smirk turned into howling rage when Sara drove the blade of Dez's knife into his gut. Slamming her back to the ground, the killer frantically wrenched the knife out, tearing at his stomach more in the process. Tossing it aside, he smashed his foot into her arm, side, and belly several times, catching her once or twice in the head.

Once he tired of that, he pulled Sara up towards him, his own knife raised high. With her last bit of strength, she spat out a wad of bloody saliva, hitting him just below the eye. He smiled and brought the knife down, aiming right for her throat.

Except neither the knife nor his arm would move. He tried again and again to no avail. It was like someone held him back. He turned and found Gina standing several feet behind him, her hands held out before her in a grasping position. Her face was scrunched in intense concentration. He didn't know how, but he knew she was keeping him from moving his arm.

Realizing his was looking at her now, Gina took a sad, shuffled step towards him. Her heart was pounding hard enough to burst through her chest and sweat poured down her brow. Her legs were weak and felt as though they could buckle at any second. She thought it was a moment when she should say some witty or bad ass one-liner, like in a comic book or movie. All that ran through her mind, however, was how much of an idiot she was and how they were all going to die. The bravado and zeal that made her run out here had evaporated.

Honestly, all she felt now was a strong inclination to piss

herself.

Carelessly dropping Sara from his grasp, the Ghost regarded Gina for a moment as he lowered the knife. She didn't know why he was staring at her like that, with his eyes slowly pouring over every inch of her. It would have been one thing if he'd cut her heart out as soon as he saw her. But this- him just *staring* at her- was fucking terrifying.

Finally, coolly and evenly, he spoke. "I don't know what I ever saw in you." There was a flash of confusion that played over his face, which likely matched the one on hers. Just as quickly, however, his confusion was replaced by chilly anger.

He was fast; Gina barely ducked under the knife, scrambling to keep him in front of her. He spun back around, instantly bringing the knife down on top of her. She scuttled away. With the knife dashing close to her face, she was scarcely able to keep her balance. Her foot stepped on one of the broken pieces of Jen's plank which slid out from beneath her. She dropped to one knee and impulsively raised her arm. She didn't know why, it was like some other part of her suddenly took control.

To both their surprise, Gina blocked the Ghost's attack above her, stopping the knife though the tip of the blade sliced across her forearm and was only inches from her collar. She slid her hand down and, now with both hands, pushed back.

It didn't take her long to realize she didn't have the physical strength to shove him away, and she struggled mightily to just hold his knife in place. Heart pounding and mind racing, Gina didn't know what to do. The Ghost was stronger; much stronger. He'd overpower her soon enough and she couldn't think of any way to escape. Through a busted-out window Gina could see flashing lights- William and the cops getting closer, but she knew they'd never get there in time.

They might catch the Ghost- they might not- but she'd still be dead.

Out of the corner of her eye she saw Sara's gun. It was lying on the floor just a few feet away, but it might as well be on the other side of the world for her predicament. Her arms were going numb, quivering under his strength, and the knife edged closer to her skin. Some calmer, disconnected part of Gina's mind remembered she had the ability to pull the gun to her. But that required a hand to catch it, and she was already losing this struggle using both hands. She could use her powers to hold him or push him back, but Gina could barely keep him from killing Sara just a moment ago. And that had probably been boosted by the bravery she felt earlier, which had long taken its leave.

That's when she noticed the glass, nails, and various sharp broken parts from the crashed shelves. Gina reached out with her mind, lifting the improvised shrapnel and heaved them with all her psychic might. They raced across the room and lanced into the Ghost's back like a pin-cushion, piercing him down along his spine and hamstrings. He staggered back, screaming in pain and fury. A small measure of her earlier daring returned, and Gina smacked the knife from his hand. She followed this up by swiftly planting her fist in his nose. It was her left hand- her off-hand- so her punch was clumsy and graceless, but it was the only crack she saw to take. A sharp pain shot up Gina's arm from the blow, it was like hitting metal.

Gritting her teeth against the pain, she reached out for the gun. It sailed through the air, landing perfectly in her hand. Her fingers tightening around the grip as the Ghost bowled into her, knocking her to the ground. Knocking the air from her lungs.

He was on top of her, his hands around her throat. Having his knife back didn't matter; he would choke the life out of Gina and feel her neck crunch in his hands. She gasped for air that never came as tears ran from her eyes. Her vision darkened at the edges as tiny starbursts flickered here and there. To make it worse, strange images that could only be from the Ghost's life were floating through her mind. She was vaguely aware he was cursing her but nothing he said made any sense. Point of fact, nothing was really making much sense to her now. A strong urge to just go to sleep washed over her, but she vaguely felt like she had something she really needed to do before she could.

Through the haze, Gina gathered the strength to raise the gun, slipping it in under his arms. Its weight was shaking in her hand, but she weakly pressed the barrel to the Ghost's chin and squeezed the trigger. The top of his head exploded as the bullet speared through it, dragging bits of brain and skull and blood along behind it and spattering them over the floor and walls. Gina was remotely aware some splashed onto her face, could taste it in her mouth. Her ears rang from the report. Had her world not already gone dark she would have been blinded by the muzzle flash.

The Ghost's grasp fell from her neck, and she worried about little else other than the air hurrying back into her burning lungs. His body slumped atop her, his weight pinning her to the floor. Gina lay on the floor, her breathing coming in ragged, shallow gasps. Her throat seared with each inhalation. She was dimly aware of his blood streaming down over her face, trickling along her neck and into her hair.

The images crept back in and she knew she could no longer hold them back.

As she drifted off, she felt the body rolled away, felt the freedom for a moment before soft hands took hold of her. Long fingers wiping blood from her face, Jen's voice cut through to her retreating consciousness. The girl called out to her, distant and small, begging her to be okay. She was vaguely cognizant of people clattering up the stairs, lights sweeping about the room, and voices frenziedly shouting. She had a distant notion it was over now, that she was safe and, maybe, everyone was alive. The heaviness of the gun left her hand, tumbled from her fingers to clatter beside her. She could go home now, and her life could go back to normal.

Those were all sweet thoughts, but they couldn't compete with the flood of crazy rushing into her mind.

Chapter 12

The smell of salty air filled her nose as the light crashing of waves on a beach played a comforting melody. Her bare feet sank into the wet sand under her as it welled up between her toes. The air was warm though dry, not humid like Gina was used to. Her clothes didn't stick to her body and she didn't have a constant sheen of sweat on her brow. She found it pleasant really. It felt early in the morning and the sun was behind her. Gina had the sense she was somewhere on the West Coast.

Not far away, above the sounds of the waves, she could hear kids laughing and a radio DJ babbling, though about what Gina couldn't tell. The volume was too low and the radio too far away. Further down the beach there were a few large groups of people spread out along the sand; they paid her and the people she was with no mind, just simply enjoyed their day.

The party she was among, on the other hand, was quite a bit more serious. Several, 15 by Gina's count not including the few kids here and there, had lined up where the water washed up on the sand. As it swished in, the ocean water sprayed over their feet, washing over their ankles to seep into the hem of their pants or skirts. All of them had thin white robes over their normal clothes and held hands, a low hum radiating from their mouths. Two men and a woman had waded out into the water until it was up to their waists, though it would splash up closer to their shoulders at times. The woman held a baby in her arms, tucking it close to her chest when the waves threatened to wash over its head, beaming with happiness. The man beside her maintained a grim, surly look on his face. His eyes fell on the baby and the woman with barely concealed disgust.

The second of the two men was speaking, addressing both the couple in the water with him and the others assembled up on the beach. Over the waves, Gina had trouble hearing exactly what he said but between the snippets she could catch and the people in general she gathered this was a baptism. She realized some folks on the beach were talking quietly under their breath. These comments she heard clearly, as words like "whore" and "slut" were thrown with frequency and ease as they vented their condemnation of the woman's out-of-wedlock child. Conversely, there was much sympathy expressed for the man and suggestions his was a near heroic effort to wing in his wayward sister. As the preacher dipped his hands into the ocean and poured the water over the baby's forehead, a chill took hold of Gina, causing her to hug herself tightly, as an inkling of whom that infant would go on to become swept over her.

The noise and smells of the beach were soon replaced by the furious sizzle and reek of burning meat. Greasy smoke wafted past Gina's face, drawing her attention to a blackened brick searing in a pan on the nearby stove. Next to it a baby bottle sat in a pot of boiling water, the heated liquid bubbling over the top, making the flame sputter and hiss. Several broken dishes were scattered about the floor and a cabinet door had been pulled free and braced hazardously against a wall on the far side of the room. A gouge in the wall above it suggested the door had been thrown there. A baby was crying from a highchair at the table and a man and woman were in a heated argument in the other room.

Gina turned her attention towards the screaming couple, recognizing them as the man and woman from the beach. He had a coat draped over one arm and a suitcase in hand. She gripped his arm, making him drag her weight as he made his way to the door. She was pleading with him not to leave. At the door, unable to wrench his arm away from her, the man dropped the suitcase and coat. Gina winced as his hand slapped the woman across her cheek. The suddenness caused her to let go of him. She could do nothing more than hold her hand to her face and stare at him in stunned disbelief. For a moment Gina could see he was just as taken aback by his action as she was, which was soon replaced by regret, followed by resentment.

"Please," her voice was tiny. "He needs his father."

His voice wavered with scorn and loathing as he pointed at the baby. "That... *thing*...is not my son." His face greyed with animosity. "That's your doing, not mine."

With pure venom in her voice she spat, "You were eager enough at the time."

He glared at her with pure hate. "One moment of weakness..."

"One?" she asked with a dull laugh.

His face reddened, and his arm instantly reared back for another strike. She braced for the hit, but he held it there for what felt like hours. Finally, he let out a hard breath and lowered his arm. The word "Whore!" hissed out from between his clenched teeth before gathering up his suitcase and coat and walking out of the house. She hugged the doorframe as she called after him, begging him to come back.

The baby continued to wail.

Years passed before Gina. She saw the baby grow into a young boy, increasingly isolated by the cruel barbs and snipes from other children, along with the scowls and disdain from every other adult he knew. However, it was from his mother- through her bitterness and hatred at life- where his true horror originated. It was usually taken out on the boy. The more she kept him near, the more she resented him. But she could never let him go. Never let her shame escape her. Mother and son became trapped in a never-ending circle.

There was a little white church in the middle of a large clearing, surrounded by thick trees and bushes. A gravel parking lot, occupied with many shiny new cars and a small glade of lush green grass, was next to it. Again, it was a warm day, made more enjoyable by a light breeze, and Gina found herself on the edge of the clearing. A boy about her brother's age was hunched within a thicket of dense shrubbery, spying on groups of other children milling about on the green. Some were younger children, watched by their parents as they amused themselves on the playground. Nearer to the woods were older kids, boys and girls, closer in age to the boy. They were dressed well in slacks and button-ups and skirts and sundresses. They were light and bright in color; making Gina think it was probably Easter time, though not being very religious herself she couldn't be sure.

She noticed the boy was mostly watching one person, a girl, more than anyone else. She was pretty, with copious curls of black hair, milky-white skin, and deep blue eyes. She wore a sleeve-less white dress and white sandals. In some ways, Gina thought she herself might have looked like the girl when she was that age, though the young woman was quite a bit taller and thinner than Gina. It was hardly surprising the boy in the bushes wasn't the only young man whose interest she attracted. There were several boys around her, each clamoring for her attentions. She also seemed high up on the food chain with the other girls too, with many of them seeking her approval.

After some time, the girl apparently decided she had enough of the boys, dragging the other girls away with her to sit at several picnic tables. Her closest friends sat with her while the lesser girls congregated at other tables. The boys dispersed into various groups to do whatever interested them. Some took up a football and tossed it around, while others gathered to exchange dirty jokes, talk about what the girls might look like naked, or brag about sexual exploits they hadn't had but knew no one would call them on. Another group snuck off closer to the woods to sneak cigarettes. The boy ignored all of them except her. He stared at her as if she was the only other person in the world. Gina wondered if the girl even knew this kid existed, doubting it strongly.

And if the girl didn't before she would soon enough to the boy's humiliation.

Gina jumped when a hand burst into the bushes behind them, grasping the boy and yanking him out. He was pushed down and held to the ground by a large woman. She wasn't tall, but Gina supposed she outweighed the scrawny boy by nearly a hundred pounds. Her hair was cut close to her scalp, with spots where it looked like it had fallen or been pulled out. Her reek suggested it had been some time since she last bathed. Her clothes, wrinkled and fetid, supported that notion. He struggled to get away from his captor, a seemingly easy objective given that the woman was ungainly and put little effort into holding him down, but he seemed resigned to her subjugation.

"I told you," the woman foamed in a ragged voice as she snatched him up from the ground, her hand constricting over his collarbone. "I told you that you were to stop thinking about that girl. I know you have-I *heard* you thinking about her this morning. And last night! Don't think I haven't! She's nothing but a little whore! All of them are!"

He started to protest but she slapped him across the back of his head. She slapped him again and again, each time harder than the last. Gina could see the palm of her hand turning bright red from the hits. He cowered at her feet as she hit him, the whacks resonating among the trees. The kids from the glade noticed what was going on but, instead of getting their parents, they watched and snickered as the obese woman beat her son. The one laughing the loudest, Gina noticed, was the girl in the white dress.

"Pathetic, wasn't it?"

The laughter and the beatings had all stopped. The children, the boy and his mother were all gone now. Gina was alone in the woods, with the little white church in the clearing and all the shiny cars still in the parking lot. She looked about to locate the source of the voice. The Ghost stepped out from around the bushes. She was somewhat relieved his head didn't have the gaping wound she inflicted, but his appearance scared her all the same. She took a few scrambling steps away from him. Her immediate reaction was to run but she stopped herself. Gina felt stronger here, like this was her turf somehow. She saw no need to fear him.

Besides, he's dead she uncertainly assured herself. *Right?*

"Sorry, I had to stop it before it got too maudlin. That dirty secret with the parents, the sad little upbringing, it's *too* textbook.

'Honestly, I'm not a bad person, I'm just misunderstood'," he said the last part with a wretchedly contrite tone, wide frown, and a pleading gesture.

Gina tried to keep her breathing steady as she spoke. "I would've thought you'd wanna make me feel sorry for you. I mean, you did some pretty sick shit."

"Me?" he dissembled, his face scandalized. "I did absolutely nothing. *He* did everything," the Ghost explained, jerking his thumb behind him, seemingly towards someone yet there was no one else around. "*I* merely... advised."

"And you're not the Ghost or whatever your name really is?"

"Not at all."

"Then enlighten me: who the fuck are you?" she asked, her arms crossed over her chest to defend against her growing doubt.

"I don't really have a name. They get... restraining." The scene transformed into the playground and he was sitting in one of the swings, his legs lazily pushing back and forth. She was in the swing next to his. Without thinking she jumped to her feet, putting several steps between them, which seemed to amuse him.

Gina shook off the initial alarm of the change. With a huff she snarled, "That's whimsically cryptic. Then *what* are you? Or is that 'restraining', too?"

"Well, I think you would call me a demon."

"So... he was possessed or something?"

"Of course not! That's much too messy!" he said with a dismissive wave of his hand. "Like I said, I merely made some suggestions. He wanted to do all of that anyway, and with the way Little Miss Pretty over there laughed at him, can you blame him?" The question was sympathetic in delivery while derisive in undertone. "No, I just told him he should follow his dreams. That's the American way, right?"

"That's pretty selfless of you. I'm sure you got nothing out of it."

"I got plenty out of it. I had loads of fun, better standing among my peers. Really, who doesn't want the same for their efforts?"

"And the girls he killed? The families ruined by it all?"

"I said I had loads of fun and better standing among my peers."

"Doesn't fly. He might have been a sad sack of shit before you came along, but that doesn't mean he would have done any of this without you pushing him. Not to mention all the help you gave him, making people not be able to see what he looks like and all."

"That's where you're wrong, dolly!" His voice became an angry snarl. "I gave him no such help. Like I said, I only gave him encouragement to follow his heart's desire. The 'now-you-see-me-now-you-don't' act was his and his alone."

He sounded sincere, sounded like he was telling the truth, but Gina couldn't bring herself to buy it. She couldn't help being suspicious.

"Aren't demons supposed to be big liars?"

"Not at all. We're honest to a fault. But, maybe that's a lie." His face lightened as he yielded some. "Okay, have it your way. I *might* have given the poor guy a bit of a reach around. But, honest Injun, he had some power. Could make himself invisible- or close enough- and given what you saw, wouldn't you? That's what drew me to him in the first place."

A nasty smile grew across his face. It was a little too wide. A little too mangled. "That's what drew me to *you*."

"Me?"

"That's right. You." He stood up and started circling Gina. "He was fun, but he lacked to be honest. Not to get your ego up or anything, I just happened to catch wind of you by accident. If he hadn't ended up in that little 'burb of yours, I probably never would've known you existed. Hate to break it to ya, but you're not that bright a light just yet."

"You're not fucking with the Jenga tower of my self-esteem," Gina sneered with diminishing bluster.

"Come on, doll, turn that frown upside-down," he cooed. "Sure, it was chance but what a chance it was! His performance was pretty limp, if you know what I mean. But you..." Without warning he was right behind her, slapping his hand onto her ass and squeezing tight, fingertips digging deep into her flesh.

"I bet you could go all night and then some. Am I right?" When she got over her surprise at the move, Gina took a swing at him, but he let go of her and danced away, laughing loudly.

"That's what I mean. You got moxy! You got spunk, and I wanna give you mine!" With inhuman speed he stepped in close, grabbing her wrists and pinning them to her sides. His face was a hair's width from hers. "And you've got all the power I want."

He took in a deep breath, his face melting into a mockery of a human being, as a growl sprung from deep within him. His mouth became a wide and uneven fissure gashed into his skin. Multiple irises with misshapen pupils wedged past each other across his eyes. He locked his lips onto hers. She tried getting her hands free to push him away, but their flesh was melding together; she even tried pulling her whole body away from him, but her face seemed fastened with his.

Thin, ropey tongues pushed into her mouth, working slowly down her esophagus. His mouth was slithering over her nose, making breathing impossible. She bit down as hard she could. He began to scream and whimper as her teeth slowly cut through some of the extremities. She felt blood fill her mouth. It wasn't hot or fluid, instead it was cold and acrid- almost congealed- and it left a stinging film in the back of her throat. He ripped himself away from her. She thought for a moment he might take her skin, her face, with him. A booming crash from somewhere in front of her loosely registered and her hands and arms tingled and pricked.

She felt more than a little light-headed.

Gagging furiously, Gina spat out the portion of the tongues she'd bitten off, her stomach turning as she watched them- all greenish-black and reedy- twist and thrash on the ground. As she choked the blood out her mouth, a sad crumbling sound, more like an afterthought, of wood and brick made her look up. There was a gaping hole in the side of the church, the interior obscured by a thick cloud of dust. A figure stumbled out, grabbing the opening's side for support. The mortar broke off under his weight, though it held long enough for him to regain his poise.

The demon wiped the thick inky blood from his mouth and

chin with a hand that had become a twisted claw. A few of the tongues wriggled just outside of his mouth, slinging gooey gore for a second before slithering back into his mouth. His face set into a hideous grin, which seemed to run vertical as much as horizontal, as he whipped the blood from his hand, staining what remained of the pristine walls with the rancid stuff. Gina expected him to rush her again, but he kept his distance. An unsettling laugh escaped him.

"Cute, dolly, real cute. You're a lot stronger than I thought you'd be."

She spat more of his blood from her mouth. "Yeah, I'm real fucking adorable," her voice was rough as she tried to keep from coughing or vomiting, some of the blood still pooled in the back of her throat. "You wanna try that again?"

His only answer was a distorted smile.

"You're said you just made a few suggestions," she growled, repeating his claim back to him. "I suggest you slither your ass back to wherever you came from before I decide to give you a few new assholes." It was a bluff. While she felt stronger in this place, she wasn't sure if she could really do anything if he attacked her again.

"Fair enough," he accepted. Starting with his feet, his body began to break down into a bubbling pool of fetid black similar to the blood. As he melted to the ground he continued. "Not to sound clichéd but I will try again. Like it or not, your ass belongs to me." Several of the thin snaky tongues ran along his lips, leaving a trail of greenish-black mucus across his evaporating face.

"I just hope I'm not too late to the party," he threw in casually.

"What's that supposed to mean?" Gina roared. She really hated ambiguous bullshit.

His laugh was more of a gurgle, his face dissipating into the churning puddle. "Let's just say you really should learn to pick your friends better." With that he was gone.

She looked around at the churchyard, wondering how she was going to get back home, realizing she didn't actually know where she was to begin with. No solution or path popping out at her, Gina lay down on the merry-go-round, idly kicking herself in circles, watching the fake world spin above her.

The sterile non-smells of the hospital hit Gina before anything else did. She opened her eyes slowly, shutting them quickly as the light proved too much. Her groaning alerted April, sitting in a chair by the other bed where Cinnamon lay sleeping. The younger girl's head was almost fully encased by a large a bandage.

"Gina?" April started, her fingers lacing with Gina's. Her voice was almost breathless with relief. "Gina, are you awake?"

She tried opening her eyes again after a moment, this time the light wasn't so harsh or painful. "Yeah," she croaked. A faint memory of the bitter blood made her gag. "Can I get some water?"

"Sure," April said as she poured water into a small cup. She held it up to her niece's mouth, until Gina could wrap her stiff fingers around the plastic without crushing or spilling it all over herself. She tried with both hands but the splint on her left arm made it nearly impossible to use. April filled it back up after Gina downed the liquid in a few fast gulps. The second glass gone April offered to fill it once more, but Gina shook her head. She looked over to her cousin in the next bed.

"Cinnamon alright?"

"A few stitches," April said. "No worries of a concussion. Doctors gave her something to help her sleep. Besides, I doubt I could have gotten her to leave until you woke up anyway."

"Sorry she got hurt under my watch."

"Don't beat yourself up, sweetie," April smiled tightly, stroking her niece's hair to sooth her. "Besides, you and your friend Dez were the ones who led those FBI agents to the bad guy and saved Jen."

Gina gave her aunt a quizzical look and briefly wondered if she had woken up in Bizarro World. Granted, she was still a little out of it, but she knew that wasn't how it happened at all. She was about to correct the story when she caught a glimpse of William just outside her room.

All you need to know about the Agency is that you need to stay off their radar.

William's words from the night she met him, really met him, flooded back into her head. *I'll do what I can with that.* She figured he'd had a hand in rewriting this bit of history. Though, she noted, this wasn't the first time William Post did that for her.

"I guess you're right, April," Gina smiled. "Where's Papa?"

"He was down at the nurse's station earlier having a 'discussion' with the Holts."

Gina acknowledged her aunt's tone with a wince that had nothing to do with the pain she was in. "Jen's parents?"

April nodded her head. "They're a little intense, wanted to press charges and all. Frank was cool about it until they started talking bad about you and Trev and Cinnie. That agent..." She turned away, pointing to where William was standing outside once she saw him. "He stepped in. Not sure what he said to them, but the Holts dropped it. They weren't happy about it though. Frank needed to cool off after that, so your brother took him to pick up your car and take it home."

"Is Jen okay?"

"Other than the fact they sent her home with her parents, she's fine." Gina wanted to find out more, but they were interrupted by a soft knock at the door. William stood in the doorway.

"My apologies, Ms. Pratchett," he said to April. "Would it be okay if I had a word with your niece?" Once more there was his flair for asking permission in a way that informed it really wasn't a request. "If she's up to it, of course."

April looked sideways at Gina, who merely nodded her head. "I'll be outside if you need me," she said as she walked out. "You'll let me know if Cinnamon wakes up."

"We sure will," William politely assured as he closed the door. He turned to Gina. "How're you feeling?"

"Mystified. Perplexed," she answered slowly. "Bamboozled even."

A small laugh left him at that as he sat down at her

bedside. "Flippancy's always a good sign." William noted her voice, while low, didn't possess the raspy or strained tenor of someone who had almost been strangled to death. She was simply whispering so as not to wake her cousin in the next bed. He glanced down towards her throat. Before she was carted off to the hospital, there were angry black and purple marks welling up about Gina's neck and collar. Now they had faded to a deep blue.

This gave him a bit to consider, but when Gina noticed the look that had fallen over him, he could see the worry building in her. Hoping to distract or alleviate, William quickly turned his attention elsewhere. "I heard your aunt giving you the official story of what happened."

"Did you break out one of those flashy-thingies like they had in those movies?" Seeing that William didn't get the reference, she added, "I mean, you're sort of a Man-In-Black type, so I figured maybe you got some alien tech somewhere to use on people's memory."

"You mean extra-terrestrials?" he said uncertainly. Gina nodded her head slowly, wincing slightly at the pain it stirred up. "Those don't exist." After a second, he amended himself, "At least, if they do, they're not coming here that we know of."

"So, just monsters then?"

"Just monsters." He gently smiled. "It seems enough in my book."

Gina gave a small grin in return. "Can't argue with that. She took a more serious turn. "Then how did you get all of those cops to agree with the 'official story'?"

"Not that hard," William said glibly. "We just used the standard techniques of persuasion: threats and bribery. It won't hold if someone gets curious but, they usually don't. Near as I can tell, people would rather not know for the most part. Especially if it's easier for them to *not* know."

"How's your partner? The Ghost was wailing on her pretty hard when I got there."

"It'll take some time but she's a lot tougher than she looks. Some cracked ribs but no internal bleeding. She'll be back on her feet in no time," William answered. Gina didn't need empathic resonance to feel the pride swirling around William as he talked about his neice, nor the deep worry for her contradicting his praise. "Honestly, I think she's sore more about not being the one to pull the trigger than she is from being kicked in the gut."

"I'll be sure to let her get the next one." Gina couldn't remember ever saying anything so sincere. "What about Dez?"

"Salvia lost a lot of blood and it'll probably be a few weeks before he can really walk. More before he does so comfortably, if ever," William said grimly. "He'll pull through but, in more ways than one, this is a fight that'll stay with him for some time."

With all of that out of the way, William decided it was his turn to ask a few questions.

"So, what happened? Not in the warehouse, Sara filled me in on that for the most part." He scooted the chair closer to Gina's bed, as he pulled a notebook from his pocket. "When we found you, you were comatose. What happened *after* you blasted the Ghost's brains across the floor?"

"I don't know," Gina started. "Remember when I told you about the vision that let me know he was going to go after Jen?" William nodded his head. "It was like that except I think I was seeing his childhood or something." She told him all she'd seen, including being groped by something claiming to be a demon.

"A demon?" he asked incredulously, looking up from the notes he was taking.

"That's what he told me, though he said he didn't possess the Ghost or give him any powers, just nudged him in certain directions. All the freaky shit he could do he did all on his own for the most part."

William shook his head again. "A demon? That's not exactly the strangest thing I've come across, but it is a first for me. Maybe others in the Agency have. I'll have to look into it more."

"Think he was telling the truth about being a demon?"

"It's certainly within the realm of possibility. Like I said, I'll have to look deeper before I can say anything for certain."

"It said that it wanted to ride me since I'm stronger than the Ghost was," Gina said, her face reddening with embarrassment. It sounded way too boastful, as well as a touch perverted, for her taste. "It also said I should learn to pick my friends better and implied..."

Seeing where the warning was going, William stopped her cold. "Whatever it said, you should ignore it. Your friends and family give you strength." Gina really wanted to believe his words.

Still, William thought back to what Sara said about Gina's friend, Suz. Demons might lie, but he'd bet they told the unadulterated truth when it worked better than any falsehood they could cook up. And there was something off about Suz Reily that William couldn't figure out.

Cinnamon stirred in her bed. She opened her eyes and looked at over at Gina in the next bed. Drugged and groggy, she looked up at William, her eyes blurry and red from sleep. "Fuck sakes, mom; your hair looks like shit. Kill your stylist for doing that to you." Then she rolled back over and fell asleep.

William laughed. He looked back to Gina as she was kneading her leg now, wincing with the effort. It had escaped her notice at the time, but she remembered her impromptu missile attack hit her a little as well. Her skills definitely needed practice.

"Be careful with that," William advised. "Those nails and everything didn't get too deep, but they did have to stitch a few up. You don't want to rip them open. I'll let you get some rest and let them know you need something for pain."

He stood and walked to the door. Stopping he turned back to her. "You did good tonight," he softly said to Gina as he opened the door.

"I'm just glad it's over," Gina mumbled. "It is over, right?"

He looked at her in the bed. It made her seem small and child-like for a moment, bringing back memories of a little girl from so long ago.

"Sure."

He realized she meant *all* of it, not just the Ghost, making his statement a lie. Whoever the Ghost was in life was dead, but whatever it was that goaded him was still out there. And it had a taste for the girl. While reports on tonight's incidents mentioned Gina's involvement in only the most minimizing way possible, he was right that it wouldn't hold under close scrutiny. Someone would eventually get a clearer picture of what happened and add it all up. Whatever happened after that depended on who asked and what they wanted to do with the information.

Then there were all the other horrors out there in the world, which she'd likely attract. Power such as hers simply didn't go unnoticed. Salvia and the wraith she mentioned a few nights before were proof of that, as well as just the beginning. Despite their reputation for falseness, this demon *could* have some knowledge or insight into the future and gave a warning.

Still, William didn't see the harm in letting Gina have one night to sleep easy and think otherwise.

A nurse came in a short while later and checked the wounds on Gina's leg and the splint on her arm. It turned out she fractured her wrist and two fingers with her clumsy punch. She was given a sedative and drifted off to sleep.

She was met by the old dream, but it was different this time. She felt in control, enough to make it all the way down the seemingly endless hall. At the end she came to enormous double-doors, the rumbling from something desperately pounding on them vibrated through her body. Gina figured she knew what she'd find behind them and opted to keep them closed. She'd have to face it at some point, the fire and the screams and, especially, *her*. Knowing who she was now, Gina was no longer scared of what the bad-brained woman would do, but of what she would mean to Gina.

Mostly Gina was afraid the woman would simply mean nothing to her.

She went to another part of the dream, the one recently dominated by the man with no eyes. It had now lost the surreal elements. A woman with deep dark skin swept into the room where Gina was playing. She heard all the commotion in other parts of the facility but paid it no mind. It couldn't hurt her, so it was irrelevant. The woman scooped Gina up, except her name wasn't Gina.

She was called 178.

The woman held 178 tightly in her arms and told her everything would be alright. There was a man at the door. He had a gun, and he raised it when he saw the nurse and 178. The woman didn't see him. She tried to calm 178 down though, in reality, she was trying to calm herself down. Subject 178 could feel the woman's heart beating so fast. She told the woman it would be fine, they would live and go somewhere sunny, but her words couldn't penetrate the woman's fear. She just smiled at 178, but her heart raced all the same.

Behind them the man trained his gun on them, but it didn't stop moving when he wanted. His face twisted in confusion and sweat beaded on his brow as he smoothly placed the gun to his own head. His struggle played out as a whimper seeped from his mouth and he pulled the trigger. The woman screamed and dropped to her knees, huddling over 178.

An outer door burst open and another man in a dark suit entered soon after. With barely a look he assessed the room, picking out priorities and targets. The woman held 178 tighter, turning her back to the man in the suit, putting herself between him and the girl. She told the child not to look, to close her eyes, but 178 craned her neck so she could see over the woman's shoulder. The man was just a few steps away. He studied the situation, voices buzzing in his earpiece. His eyes meet with the child's peering out over the woman's bobbing shoulders. Subject 178 whispered in the woman's ear.

He never raised his gun. Instead he grabbed the woman's arm and spun her around. He dragged them out into the hallway, the woman begging and pleading, pointing out that 178 was just a child. The man took them to a door, said it led to safety. Subject 178 waved good-bye as the doors shut, but the man in the suit never saw her gesture.

It didn't matter. She knew she'd see him again.

Next, she was in a car. Warm sun filtered through the back window and bathed over her. She had never seen the sun until the day before. Not personally. She had glimpsed in the thoughts and memories of others, but she had never seen it with her own eyes.

Had never felt it on her own skin.

She leaned over the back seat and gazed out the window. They were just off the side of the road in front of a small greasy hamburger stand. The smell of fresh burgers made 178's mouth water. She didn't know what the smell was, what a hamburger was, but swallowed down the saliva filling her mouth all the same. Across the highway were a line of tall, thin trees with long, fan-like leaves sprouting out from the top of their trunks. Past those was a beach with sand so white the sunlight reflecting off and hurt 178's eyes. Further out was the blue ocean. She had seen images like this before as well, in other people's minds and memories. She felt from them how fun it was and she wanted to run out and play in it.

The woman, still in her tidy nurse's uniform, was at a payphone. She was talking to someone, her voice simultaneously excited, thrilled, and scared. She wasn't on the phone long. She then went to get some food from the hamburger stand. As the car pulled back onto the road, 178 took her first bite of the burger. As she ate, she smiled at the woman, ketchup and grease running down her chin and onto her shirt.

Then she was no longer 178; instead she was back to being Gina. It was Memorial Day and she realized it was just a few months before her mother died. Gina had moved out some months earlier. Between working and no longer living at home, Gina rarely saw Flora Shields much anymore, making this holiday that much more enjoyable. Her father was getting the grill warmed up while April was in the living room keeping Trevor and Cinnamon occupied. Things weren't going so well for her aunt and cousin, so Gina was grateful to hear them having some fun. Flora and Gina didn't talk about anything, didn't even say a word to each other. They just sat at the table on the patio drinking lemonade, secretly spiked with bourbon, from large mason jars.

She woke up and the sun was spilling in through the window to her room, making it much too bright. Her father was in the chair next to her bed, his head in his hand, eyes closed. Frankie looked up when he heard Gina stirring in the bed. "Hey, baby doll," his eyes brightened with his relieved smile. "Sleep well?"

Gina stretched her arms and back as much as she could, a yawn escaping her. "Surprisingly, I did." She looked over to the next bed. "Where's Cinnie and April?"

"Your cousin's in there getting dressed," he said, jerking his thumb toward the bathroom door behind him. Almost on cue a hissed "Fuck" slipped from the closed door as something clattered about on the floor within. "April's signing some paperwork. You ready to get out of here?"

"Without a fucking doubt!" she beamed at her father.

Frankie smiled again. "April brought you some clothes to change into," he said as he stood up, pointing to a bag in another chair. Gina assumed it also had the clothes Cinnamon was putting on since it was already opened and looked like a tornado had gone through. "I'll go let the nurse know. Get the process started."

He started to leave but Gina stopped him. "Papa? At some point... we need to have a talk." Her voice was small, and she felt like she was five.

He looked at her. He still had a tender smile on his face but there was something in his eyes telling Gina he already knew what that talk would be about. "Sure, baby doll. Whenever you're ready for it."

With that he left the room.

Chapter 13

For the next several days Quinn and Suz all but took up residence at Gina's apartment. A couple nights, Michelle and Marcella dropped by for a beer or two and to make sure Gina was doing okay. Jacob swung by one afternoon on his way into work to check in. Bruce did as well, though he didn't knock, just left a note and two bulk-sized boxes of Nerds (her favorite candy) at her door. A number of others came by, called, or sent their well-wishes through someone.

She even got a call from Jen late one night. It was hurried and mostly consisted mostly of quiet series of "thank you" being repeated several times. Gina wasn't able to say anything or ask how the girl was doing, though, as Jen hung up so quickly. Trevor said she had been "grounded for life plus a few decades", so Gina didn't feel slighted by the abrupt end.

Her family spent quite a bit of time there was well, often to bring Gina groceries or meals. Her kitchen hadn't been stocked this well since she first moved in. She tried a few times to have that talk with Frankie, though they were rarely alone. It was just as well, she had no idea how to tell him about any of it anyway. Still, the way he looked at her, she'd swear he already knew what she wanted to tell him.

For the most part when Frankie did talk, it was about taking Gina, Trevor, and Cinnamon to a gym he used to visit back when he was into boxing. There were also plans to take them to a gun range, so they could learn to handle weapons. April wasn't too keen on these ideas when it came to her daughter, but she was eventually worn down by Frankie and Cinnamon. Gina wasn't too hot on the idea at first, either, but eventually came around to it. She even started looking forward to it.

It was nearly a week before she heard from Dez. Gina tried to see him at the hospital a few times but every time she went he was sleeping. It was like he hadn't slept in years. He called her one night while she was playing a board game with Quinn, Harris, and Suz.

"I think they're letting me out tomorrow morning."

"You think?"

"Well, they said I could leave but they advised against it."

"If there's the chance that..."

"I know it'd probably be best if I stayed but I *need* to get out here. I'm going crazy and I wanna sleep somewhere that doesn't remind me of a high school chem lab."

"Okay," Gina told him what time she'd pick him up. The next morning, she found him waiting for her on a corner outside the hospital. She was sure that if it hadn't been for the knife wound on his calf, he'd have walked back to the apartment. He still looked pallid and weak. When he talked it seemed like he had trouble catching his breath.

She helped him up to his apartment. "I know you said you wanted to leave the hospital, but...," she started as she eased him down to the couch.

"I'll be fine." He saw the extreme doubt in her face. "Really."

"Okay. Need me to get you anything?"

"I think my phone's around here somewhere, maybe in my bag. Can you get it for me?" Gina found it and handed it to him.

"Anything to eat or drink?"

She could see the thought of having something other than hospital food appealed to Dez. His face actually took on a healthy glow for a moment, but then his expression fell. "I didn't have much food here in the first place. Anything I did have might not be all that good anymore." Gina checked and found he was right. Other than a single can of Coke and a small bottle of mustard, there wasn't anything in his kitchen that looked mildly edible. She brought him the soda.

"I got plenty of stuff at my place. I'll bring something down." He accepted the offer as he took a huge gulp of cola. She returned a few minutes later with two large sandwiches, a bag of chips, and another soda. Through the door she could hear him talking to someone. She couldn't catch enough to know what Dez was saying, but his tone was swirling with so many emotions.

She knocked on the door before letting herself in. Dez ended the call as Gina set the food down on the table in front of him. He put on a pleasant air when he mentioned how great it all looked, but she could tell he was angry, frustrated, and more than a little hurt and sad. She figured he was talking to someone from home, his mother perhaps, to tell them the man who had caused so much damage to their family was finally gone. If that was the case it would appear the retribution they sought had little curative merits.

She left him to the food and his thoughts after telling him to call her if he needed anything. He said he'd probably sleep more once he finished stuffing his face, mentioning how good the food tasted. This time, though, Gina sensed his praise included gratitude for more than just the food.

The next day Gina went back to work. Frankie said she didn't have to, that she could take more time, but she was getting restless. She spent most of the night before rescheduling clients whose appointments had been canceled, ensuring she would have a busy first day back. Simply returning to something normal helped take her mind off things. She even opened the shop early to accommodate someone. For a few hours she forgot she now lived in a world where there apparently were ghosts, demons, psychics, and hoodoo, and who-knows-what else.

For a brief time, she could ignore being a part of that.

For a few hours all that existed in Gina's world was the hum of her machine, that weird, staticy ding the autoclave made when it was finished, and gabbing about nothing really with whoever was in her chair. Even when the customer said nothing at all, the silence had a normalcy to it Gina feared would soon be in short supply, whether she ever used her abilities again or not, whether she ever crossed paths with anything strange again.

The fantasy lasted only a few hours. It was late in the evening and the sun was low in the sky. It filled the front room with a peculiar orangey glow and washed it in a heat that made it difficult to stay awake. Gina had someone in her chair almost non-stop all day, but now she had an hour or so to kill before her next appointment. No other customers or regulars were in the store. She sat up front, lazily sketching pictures of a horrid and ragged man with several long tentacles for tongues hanging from his mouth with a small army of ghostly and broken girls. Michelle and Marcella were there too, the former painting a henna design on the latter's hand and arm, talking about nothing and everything at once. Every so often Gina put her art pad to the side to munch on a few small chocolate muffins Michelle had made as a "Welcome Back" gift. Frankie was in his office on the phone with some old friend. Bruce and Jacob were in the back kicking a footbag back and forth, an occasional enthusiastic praise or affable admonition making its way to the front.

Outside, a cab pulled up in front of the store. An elderly man dressed in an old-fashioned suit, slate grey with a red tie, and matching heavy overcoat and bowler hat stepped out from the back, telling the driver to wait for him. He studied the store front and the door on the edge of the building for a moment before walking into the shop. He was incredibly tall and slender. His skin ashen and wrinkled and, when he removed his hat, his grey hair was thin and brushed back from his face giving him a prominent widow's peak. He looked positively ancient thanks to his wizened face, but his deep green eyes hinted at a cerebral vigor. In his hand he carried a leather briefcase that, though in excellent condition, looked as archaic as the man himself.

The man asked where he could find Desiderio Salvia. He was polite and had a certain charisma to him, but the bizarre factor was through the roof. Michelle noticeably flinched at the request but Gina, not sensing any danger from him, told him which apartment was Dez's. With that he graciously bowed his head and left for the flat. He came back down a few minutes later, once again tipping his hat to Gina from outside as he got back into the cab. The car pulled away and that was that.

Michelle and Marcella, when telling the others about the guy, just found him odd and amusing. Gina, on the other hand, found him to be a portent to the weirdness now in her life for good.

She didn't have much time to dwell on that though as the bell over the door rang once more and a young woman stepped in. Her expression was nervous and eager, she could barely contain herself. She timidly approached the counter and asked for Gina, she was the next appointment. The girl apologized for being so early and explained she could wait if Gina was busy. Gina gave her a smile and took her back to her studio.

For a little while longer, life could be normal.

William and Sara returned to DC once they were certain the local PD was on board with the official story. There were one or two cops who resisted at first, which was usual according to William, but they fell in line soon enough. For the most part, few truly bought it, but even fewer cared. The real story opened far too many questions with answers they'd rather stay ignorant of, especially the ones the press would want to ask.

Initially Sara was angry the Ghost was dead. She wanted him brought to justice the right way. Eventually, she began to see there would have been no way, despite her boxes and tomes of evidence and material on him and all he did. None of it, not a single bit of it, would have been worth shit in a court. No witnesses, no physical evidence, no video or photographic evidence. Nothing she had would have gotten them a trial, much less a conviction. All it would have gotten her was the privilege of watching the Ghost walk away to kill again and again and again. She came around to accepting it. Her goal of stopping the Ghost's killings had been met, and how it ended was probably the only resolution possible.

She didn't know what to think of the whole demon angle

her uncle had presented. It came from the Shields girl, which was another factor Sara wasn't sure about. The last week or so convinced Sara her uncle and Lowden had not been blowing smoke up her ass with all the paranormal talk. She couldn't even begin to rationalize the thing with the video recordings, or the fact she saw the Ghost just appear out of thin air. She tried to tell herself she was just hallucinating when she saw what Shields did with the nails and she must have just picked Sara's gun up instead of it flying across the room into her hand.

Her attempts were ultimately in vain though. She could only deny reality for so long. When she brought this up with William, he didn't tell her anything more, just asked she not mention Gina and what she could do in any report or to anyone else.

Sara rested for a few days before she and William were to meet with Lowden again to go over the details in more depth. Her body hurt way too much to do anything physical, so she spent her time combing through the internet for background on the supernatural. She quickly decided most of the information available was complete garbage, either propagated by people too bored with their humdrum lives yet too boring to do anything worthwhile about it, or invented whole-cloth by folks smart enough to come up with it but too blinkered not to fall for their own nonsense. What very little remained was utter madness (though Sara was beginning to realize that hardly precluded it from being legitimate) or had an impressive validity. Still, she held back from admitting any of it had a positive association with reality.

When the day came to debrief with Lowden, William picked her up. They went over what they would say and how to answer certain questions that were sure to come up. The subject of Shields' anonymity loomed large in their run-through. This wasn't the time for it, but Sara knew she needed to have a profound talk with her uncle about this girl and his obsession with her concealment. Likely, she'd have to do some serious digging on her own.

At Lowden's office the director was as enthusiastic as

before at seeing Sara again, especially in light of her injuries. Although she had healed a fair amount over the last week or so, her left eye was still swollen with a yellowish-purple bruise and a nasty scar ran along her brow. She had gotten to the point where she could elevate her left arm over her head without too much pain, but she couldn't hold it there for long or lift much weight with it. Normally she would have dressed more conservative for such a meeting. Instead, her condition had her default to something far more comfortable, though she took steps to look as professional as she could muster.

"I won't take up too much of your time," Lowden began, looking intently at Sara. "I want you to concentrate on getting on the mend as quickly as possible." He took a glance at the official report and then had them give a brief rundown of what in reality happened in their own words. Every so often he'd interrupt to ask a follow-up question or two.

"This information regarding demon involvement is a new development. We've been wondering about those but never had anything concrete. This was provided by Salvia, correct?"

"Yes," William and Sara said simultaneously, though Sara was a little slower than William.

"Salvia. What do we have on him or his people?" William had been asked to look into Dez further.

"His involvement was due directly to the murder of his sister, Lucile Salvia, in..." Sara supplied as she checked her notes. "June 2007."

"There is the possibility that binding magic was used on Salvia, placed by someone close to him, to compel him to find the Ghost," William provided. "Magic that included the spirits of the killer's past victims and would result in Salvia's death if he took too long or gave up trying."

"That requires something or someone powerful," Lowden pointed out. His apprehension over the implications was painted across his face. As was his fascination. "Do we any ideas about that?"

William shook his head. "It's doubtful Salvia even knew of its existence or, if he did, what its true purpose was." William flipped through the files, pulled out a dossier, and handed it to Lowden. "Personally, I believe it was his mother, Amália Lourdes Salvia, who placed the geis on him." Lowden looked at the profile for a moment as William handed another to Sara. "Given what I found on her, I believe she has power and motivation enough to do so.

"As for intel on Salvia's people, that's difficult to come by. Further, while we've known of their existence for some time, we're not sure how much of what we know is useful or accurate," William continued. "There are similar communities across the world, that much we can be certain on. They have an impressive ability to be insular even while integrating themselves within the surrounding populations and maintaining a remarkable diversity."

"Any threat of invasion or infiltration?"

"Low levels at best. The incidents that do occur appear to be strictly to keep human authorities and politics from interfering with their own. There's nothing to suggest they have any malicious intent towards those outside of their communities, not on any large scale at any rate, just a few isolated incidents here and there, usually involving individuals or small gangs.

"If we have to deal with them, there seem to be intermediaries and procedures we could use. There are precepts and precautions that need to be heeded, though. Otherwise there is danger of easily provoking them or inviting a load of trouble."

"Interesting," Lowden remarked. "Now, there's one thing that I'm still not clear on. Who is this Gina Shields person?"

"She's just some girl who ingratiated herself to Salvia as far as we can tell," Sara offered calmly.

"Salvia's profile does show that he has some ability at manipulating people on an emotional level," William pointed out. "His ways seem mundane, but most likely are preternatural by nature though we don't know their extent or quality. He could be at his peak, or he could get more powerful with them over time."

"Enough so that she walked into a confrontation with a serial killer?" Lowden was unconvinced. "From my understanding a person's self-preservation factors a good deal into such influences."

"Usually, though not always," William replied. "If they're powerful enough or the victim susceptible enough, a lot of damage can be done. Again, Salvia's methods probably aren't the typical psychological or social means, and we don't fully know his experience with using such abilities or how receptive Shields might be to those techniques," William suggested. "It'd hardly be the first time we've seen something that drastic. That episode in Juneau back in 99, for example?"

"Don't remind me," Lowden grimaced as he waved his concerns away. "I haven't been able to enjoy a Billie Holiday song since." He took another look over the reports and his notes to make sure he'd covered everything. "Well, one last thing and I think we'll be done here."

His eyes fell on Sara. "Still think it's a bunch of nonsense?"

Sara cut her eyes over to her uncle, then back to Lowden. She took a deep breath. "The more I look into it there are some things I don't think can be explained so easily. Some things make a little more sense but... there's so much that's just complete drivel. It's near impossible to separate fact from the fiction."

"To say the least," Lowden conceded. "We still have problems in that area even though we've been operating for over 60 years now. Still, I've read your file, Sara. I know that, even at its best, what the Bureau has to offer is beneath you. I think you know it too. I can't believe this hasn't piqued your interest, at least a little.

"And your father was one of our top agents. He left a legacy I think you could easily meet." William stiffened at the mention of his brother, but Lowden could see the effect of that dangling carrot play out over Sara's face.

"What about the Bureau? I'm on suspension."

"That can be taken care of," Lowden said with a dismissive smirk. "Of course, you won't start until after you've been signed off by a physician. You'll have plenty of time to get better." His smile became more candid. "As well as to think it all over."

"Maybe," Sara said. "I could use a few more days to think it over."

"Understandable," Lowden said with a warm smile. "It's a

big step and I wouldn't want you to take it lightly," he assured as he stood up to see them to the door. Lowden shook William's hand and gently patted Sara on the shoulder as they left. With a fond farewell he told Sara to take it easy and get better.

Once Sara and William were down the hall and well out of earshot, Lowden looked to his receptionist. "Rachael, dear," he said to the young woman. "I need you to find any information you can on a Gina Shields. It may require some of our... alternative methods. I'll get you what you need for that." He glanced at the clock on the far wall and sucked in his breath. "You know what, it's lunch time. They'll probably be cranky right about now. I'll get what I have together and send it your way and you can start on it in the morning. How's that sound?"

She gave him a knowing smile as she nodded her assent.

It had been a long day and Gina had another to look forward to tomorrow, and the day after that, and for the next few days after that. Still, she found it gratifying. She would have taken the stairs, as she usually did, but she was beat and went for the elevator instead. She ran into Mina, whose arms were loaded down with reams of various fabrics and other material she was taking out to her car. Gina helped with that as much as she could, her wrist and hand still bound up and her leg hurting. She wished Mina a good night once they were done and rode the elevator up.

On reflection, she stopped it at the third floor to check in on Dez. She hadn't heard from him since the day before and there was something way off about the man who visited earlier. Her hand was raised to knock when she heard notes being plucked from a guitar. They stopped when she thumped the door. A moment later Dez answered. He still looked worse for wear, noticeably limping and still wan of color, but he no longer needed the crutch to walk and he was far from the greyish color of the day before. Strangeness stomped right back in, full force.

She could only stare at him at first before she stuttered, "Well, I was swinging by to check on you, but it looks like you're doing okay now." He flinched at the bite in her voice.

"Yeah," his face reddened, relatively at least. She gave him credit for being somewhat self-conscious about it. "I can explain that."

"Can you, now?" Gina's brow raised in wariness. She was certain that he *could* explain it, she was just doubtful he *would*. Then again, she wondered if she really wanted him to.

With an invitation to enter, she slipped by him but opted to lean against the kitchen counter instead of finding a place to sit. That way if he started with his mysterious act again, she could leave in a huff with greater speed. They stood in silence for what felt like forever.

"Well?" Gina shattered the quiet.

"Okay. The truth." He went over to the coffee table and picked up a small wooden box from it. He handed it to Gina. It was lacquered, with a single hinge on the back. A knot-work design covered all sides except the bottom. Other than the velvet inlays the inside was empty, though it had a sweet scent.

"That was quite illuminating, Dez!" Gina said as she slapped the box back down into his hand. "Thank you, that clears everything right up!" She started to leave but he continued.

"That man who visited earlier, he was from back home. He brought me the box; it was from someone close to my family...a reward for..." he put the box down on the counter. "There was this apple in the box and..." he searched for what to say next, but nothing came to mind.

"An apple? That what the kids are calling it now-a-days?" Gina mocked. *Oh great; tall, white and spooksome completely smoothied his melon.*

"Fuck, this is all gonna sound crazy."

"Gonna? Whatever, man," she wrote off his claim. "You're in luck because 'crazy' has lost a lot of punch for me lately."

He considered that for a moment. "I guess I have more than a bit to do with that," he sighed. "Okay, I'm not entirely human."

"Clarify," suspicion burst into her mind as images of ropey-tongued mouths danced in her head.

251

He scratched the back of his neck, mostly so he didn't have to look at her. "I'm fae-blooded."

"That means what? That you're part Tinkerbell?"

"Something like that." He didn't like the reference but if that helped move things along he wouldn't object. "There aren't many True Fae left now, not that there were a lot to begin with, I guess. As far as I know, no one's seen one in decades, but there's tons of fae-blooded and my family's among them."

Gina didn't respond at first, staying quiet for a stretch. When she did react, it was with manic laughter that went on for an uncomfortably long spell. All the weirdness and insanity she experienced over the past week she had locked up in the back of her head and it was catching up to her now. The outburst was inevitable. It came down to laughing, crying, or going on a murder spree. Crying seemed passé and the spree would be just too emo for her, so laughter was the only option.

When the laughter died down, Gina wiped away the tears spilling from her eyes. "That's rich! That's just fucking awesome. Suddenly a serial killer targeting my brother's girlfriend became the closest thing to normal that's happened all week."

Through still-bleary eyes, she looked at him. Hoped to see some hint that this was just a shitty joke. Instead, she saw his hair now had fiery-golden streams running through the earthy dark strands. She understood that now, with this knowledge, she was starting to glimpse the real Dez; to see through whatever obfuscated his true nature.

A few more spasms of laughter escaped her. Once she mostly regained her composure Gina said, "I've been processing a lot of weird lately and now I have to add faeries to the mix, so I'm gonna ask that you just skip to the apple. I'm assuming that's why you don't look so horrible today?"

"Yeah," Dez replied. "Fae-blooded aren't as powerful as True Fae, nowhere close, but we do have some tricks."

"I take it these are the 'ways' you mentioned before?"

He nodded his head. "As different as they are, some just come naturally to us but others we can learn, if we're willing to pay the price."

He picked the box up from the counter and held it up before putting it back down. "Some of us have the power to enchant things and my family knows a few. It's usually food or drink, to give them restorative qualities." He pointed to the splint on her wrist. "I wanted to save half for you, I more than owed you that, but it was an all-or-nothing deal. Plus, I was also told that it wasn't exactly free, as so little with us is. Whoever ate it would owe the maker in return."

"Owe them what?"

He shrugged. "No telling. It may not be as steep as it would be-a small favor most likely-but..." His leg started hurting again. It may have been better and mending faster, but it was far from healed. He grimaced as he lowered himself to the bed. "You've done too much for me as it is. No way I was gonna let you walk into that, no matter how much it might've helped you up-front."

He put his leg up on the bed; it felt much better without weight on it. With the relief, she could see his features shift some; become thinner, longer. He closed his eyes for a moment, and when he opened them they were like a star-filled night sky.

"Besides, you're an outsider. They'd take advantage of you in any way they could, especially once they saw that you have tricks of your own."

"Saw that, huh?"

"Didn't see anything," he shrugged, not looking at her. "But somehow you knew Jen was his next target and you knew where to go to save our asses." He didn't mention what he felt the night he met her, when he tried to grease the way a little. Dez had no idea what Gina had going on, but he had to admit it scared him more than a little. "I know you aren't in any way fae, but I've seen a lot of crazy shit out there over the last few years. I don't know what you are, and I don't have any right to pry either. But I know enough to know you ain't exactly the average girl."

"You'll have to forgive me but I'm not in a sharing mood right now," Gina sighed. "But yeah, I have tricks and those were some of them." Her shoulders felt heavy. "It's been a long day. I'm going home." She pushed away from the counter and opened the door.

"We okay?" Dez asked from the bed.

"Don't know. Maybe," she looked back at him, a tired smile on her face. It didn't feel right. Not right now, at least. "Probably."

"For what it's worth- I am sorry."

As the words left Dez's mouth Gina felt the balance of gravity shift between them in her favor. Instinctively she knew she had something to hold over him, like a debt, and one that he could never weasel out of without severe repercussions. It unnerved her to have such power over someone else. She wanted to reject it but felt something such as this so freely given could not simply be discarded, nor could it be so effortlessly fulfilled.

It made her want to slap the shit out of him. Instead, she closed the door behind her and took the elevator the rest of the way to the fifth floor. Inside her apartment, Gina kicked off her shoes as she made her way to the bed, plopping face down onto it. Sleep took her almost immediately.

The garbage truck made a ton of racket as it lifted a dumpster up and spilled the contents into its hold. It was early morning and the sun wouldn't be up for a few hours more. Most people were still asleep and would blanch at the thought of being out working at this hour, but Darnell Lewis liked it. He had been at his job picking up garbage for the city for 15 years now. It gave him a decent life and supported his family well enough. It had its low points for sure, like when he and his crew found that dead girl's body the other week. For the most part, though, he liked it.

He was sifting through loose bags, hoping to find something salvageable, before throwing them in the back of the truck when he glanced up at the tattoo shop across the street. He had been on this route for years, so it wasn't his first time noticing it, but every time he did he had to wonder what would possess someone to do something like that to their body. The very idea of tattoos, not to mention whatever else they did in there, just gave Darnell the heebs.

The truck's driver, Ray, lowered the dumpster back to the

ground too hard, as he always did. It wasn't likely to really harm the receptacle, but it could damage things surrounding it. Darnell looked up to yell at Ray about it, again, when a shape rose up from the shadows. He thought it might be Alan, the new kid, but he was messing with cans further down the alley. Figuring it was probably a bum, Darnell put his hand on the can of mace he kept on him in case it was a wild and wooly one. He found himself staring into eyes that were beyond wrong. He wanted to cry out for help, but he couldn't speak. The words stuck in his throat.

A voice filled Darnell's head, telling him things he didn't want to hear, things that this entity would make Darnell do. He blacked-out for a moment. When he came to, he was laying in the pile of trash bags he had been going through. Ray and Alan were leaning over him.

"You okay, man?" Ray asked as he looked Darnell over carefully.

"Should I call for help or something?" Alan suggested uncertainly.

"No, man," Darnell said as Ray helped him up. "No, I'm alright." He felt light-headed, started to fall back and grabbed Ray's arm for support as the other men held him up. Feeling better, Darnell waved the others away. "I must have just slipped on something."

"Well..." Ray started, looking at the back of Darnell's head. "I don't see any blood, so you must not have hurt yourself too bad." He studied his colleague once more. "Sure you okay?"

"Yeah," he answered. "We only got another block or two left. Let's get that done and we can call it a day."

That excited the other two and they left Darnell to go back to what they were doing. Darnell picked up a few of the trash bags and started walking to the truck. He looked over his shoulder, back at the tattoo shop, which no longer interested him. Instead, he slowly shifted his gaze to a window on the third floor that was slightly cleaner, newer, than the others. His eyes lingered there for a moment before he lifted them further to the fifth floor. He didn't know why but he became keenly fascinated with that level. For some reason Darnell knew something on that floor was very important to him, though he didn't have the foggiest idea what it could be.

As he tossed the bags into the back of the truck, a second iris with a misshapen pupil squeezed its way across his eye.

The dream came again. It wasn't as horrific as it used to be. Still it jolted her awake, the dread it typically filled her with was blissfully missing though. Gina searched for her phone, tapping about her nightstand before realizing that it was still in her pocket. She pulled it out and checked the time. It was around 4 AM, meaning she'd been asleep for almost six hours. She hadn't eaten anything before she went to bed and her stomach was growling.

She tossed a couple Hot Pockets in the microwave and let them heat up while she went to the bathroom. By the time she was done, the microwave dinged to let her know her food was ready. She dumped them onto a plastic plate, grabbed a soda from the fridge, and her pipe off the counter. With all of that in hand, she headed to the roof.

The humidity was still evil, but the heat wasn't too stifling. A light breeze offered the first hints that colder weather was on its way, though still months away. She ate her Hot Pockets and slouched in the chair as she pulled from the pipe. She let the smoke linger for a moment longer than normal, blowing it out in a thin cloud.

Maybe it was because she was rested now, but her aversion to all the craziness, though still present, was far less than it had been. She was still uncomfortable with her abilities but, with time, she might understand them better. Then there were the others. Even with her literal absence of a life, Angie hadn't exactly been unpleasant to be around. Gina found she missed the ghost's presence. Similarly, the whole fae-blooded thing Dez had going on wasn't so much a problem to her, it just happened to be the unfortunate straw that broke the camel's back. She still liked him, in more ways than one, but this would be another thing she'd have to weigh.

She still didn't like the idea of some shadowy government agency, even if its purpose was to monitor the paranormal. She knew it had a hand in making her, and that involved some monstrous measures. William and, to a degree, Sara might be okay but the whole thing reeked to Gina.

And she didn't even know where to begin with demons being real.

She closed her eyes and listened as a siren went off in the distance, cars went down nearby streets, and a garbage truck going about its route clattered down the alley across the road. She heard people leaving the club down the lane and a ghost needlessly clear her throat. Several days ago, Angie making any noise, even if it was to politely let Gina know she was there, would have made the living girl jump out of her own skin. Now it was almost as normal as her phone ringing.

"I was wondering what happened to you," Gina said, a happy smile crossing her face as she turned to look at the wraith. The grisly markings of Angie's death were still present, but they didn't seem as substantial as before. They almost looked like they were healing. Even her tiara didn't appear as melted and her wings seemed less bent and broken.

"Like I said, I just needed to rest a moment."

"A moment?" Gina laughed, which made her cough. After a minute, she got enough air back into her lungs that she could speak. "Angie, it's been like a week since you just..." Gina moved her hands out in a bursting motion. "Like, dissolved."

"A week?" Angie cried, her form shifting oddly. She sat down in one of the chairs. "I guess that *could* be why everyone had left the party."

"Ya think?"

"How is everyone?" Gina gave Angie the gory details: the killer was dead; Sara and Dez were messed up but alive and on the mend; Jen was safe from being murdered but her parents were still in full freak-out mode. She also told the ghost about the killer being goaded by a demon, or something claiming to be one anyway, and Dez being fae-blooded.

When Gina finished filling Angie in, the wraith was

dumbfounded. "Wow! I know you miss out by being the first one to pass out at a party, but that's pretty wild."

"Don't beat yourself up too much. You did get taken for a ride by a storm of pissed off ghost girls. Near as I could tell they messed themselves up pretty badly, too."

"Speaking of which," Angie looked around expectedly. "Where are they? They still around?"

"Haven't seen them since that night. Good too since they were starting to look a little ripe," Gina said as she took a draw from her pipe. "Couldn't say where they got off to, though."

"Job done. Maybe they moved on."

"Moved on to where?"

"The great wooly hereafter, I guess," the ghost shrugged her shoulders absently. "What about you? What are you going to do?"

"Me?" Gina thought for a moment. "I think I'm gonna go back to bed." She hopped up from her chair. "You probably still have nowhere to go so you can sleep over if you want, so long as you don't keep me up."

"No, I mean... oh, really? Thanks... but no, I mean about all of..." Angie moved her arms up and down to take in all of Gina. "This? The mega psychic stuff and me and what not."

"Oh that?" Gina considered it for a moment. "I doubt I could do anything about it now. Hell, if I ever could that ship definitely sailed a long time ago." She took in a deep breath and tucked her lower lip under her teeth in thought. She was silent for some time before, "I can accept it, but I don't really like it. Still, 'with great power comes great responsibility' as a wise person once put it. Whether I like it or not, I guess it's a fact and I'll just have to live with it," she explained as she headed back down to her apartment.

"So," Angie prodded as she stood up, following Gina down the stairs.

"Yeah, I guess I'll just have to be a fucking superhero," she said with a dry smile as she slipped her good arm around Angie's nearly-intangible shoulders.

ABOUT THE AUTHOR

J Shaffer grew up in Birmingham, AL and still lives there, spending a dreadful amount of time watching movies, reading books, and playing games. Also, writing stories that are probably a cry for help. On the up-side, they're a dog-person but like cats and most other animals too.

Dress

The shutter tile on the wall clock turned with a booming finality, echoing harshly throughout the silent morgue. From his desk it occurred to Dr. Francis Morgan he had never really noticed the sound before. Then again, he thought, he had never needed a distraction from his work before. Glancing up at the time, he groaned when he saw it was nearly 2 AM. He let the cheap pen he was using slip from his fingers and rubbed at his eyes while giving in to a deep yawn.

"We got a body coming in. I put a fresh pot of coffee on," Bryce said, trying and failing to stifle a drowsy sigh of his own. The younger medical examiner was a vague shape until Morgan's bleary eyes were blinked cleared. He was leaning against the door frame, arms slowly folding across his chest. "It should be ready in a minute."

Morgan tried not to think how extraordinarily appealing Bryce Morris looked at that moment; even in the drab sea green scrubs the man was wearing. It'd always been beyond him to see the clothing as anything more than practical, certainly not lascivious. Doubtless, however, it had more to do with the person in them than the articles themselves.

Bryce's dark hair was a slight mess, matted close to his scalp from sweat. It was, thankfully, a slow night so the young man had busied himself the last few hours cleaning the entire morgue,

263

a task the janitorial staff seemed reluctant to accomplish in a thorough manner. In the confines of the office, it was hard for Morgan not to take in the man's scent: an oddly stimulating mixture of cologne, perspiration, and bleach.

It caused a treacherous stirring in the older man. He wanted to tell Bryce that coffee wasn't what would wake him up right now. If his associate really wanted to help he'd have already lost the scrubs and clambered down under the desk.

Instead he simply smiled, dispelling such notions from his mind. "Thanks, Bryce. That's probably what I need right about now."

Morgan didn't want to think these thoughts about his subordinate. He never had a problem being professional before. On the other hand, he'd never had as thorny a personal-professional relationship with anyone like he did with Bryce. The complications started the moment they met a few years earlier.

Morgan's sister had just died, suddenly taken through misfortune. The two of them were close, had been all their lives. For her to just be gone like that- it hit Morgan hard. After her funeral he dropped into a bar to drown his sorrows. Turning to alcohol like that wasn't a habit of Morgan's but he felt the circumstances would allow for it this once; and getting trashed seemed just the perfect thing to take his mind off the whole thing.

Until, that was, the handsome young man approached him at the bar. He introduced himself and they flirted for an hour before catching a cab back to Morgan's house. Quite some time has passed since he had a night like that- picking up a stranger and just fucking for hours and hours- and even longer since he honestly enjoyed one.

Of course, the interruption to his pain proved fleeting, shattering completely a few days later as Morgan was reintroduced to Bryce as his new subordinate. Neither had known this when they met but it didn't make things any less awkward. The whole situation was inappropriate from a professional standpoint, especially in a city that had a rather unforgiving and biased conservative quality. If their prior relations were to become known the best they could hope was for the whole thing to be kept politely quiet while one or both looked for employment elsewhere.

Even if they had found themselves in a more tolerant environment, the two agreed any romantic relationship between them was ill-advised. Of course, Bryce seemed to have gotten over the initial discomfort far faster than Morgan. Not surprising since his dance card always seemed full, not to mention his younger years shielding him from the greater sense for discretion than had been the case for Morgan's younger years.

In the end, Morgan hoped it was just weariness and a need for interruption causing his current rousing.

"Is that the Brandy Wilder report," Bryce said, his gaze dropping to and narrowing on the paperwork spread out across the desk. Whether he did so out of professional curiosity or to simply pass the time wasn't clear. What was clear, however, was the fact his question wasn't a question. Bryce already knew the answer the second his eyes fell on the document sitting before Morgan.

What was also clear was his annoyance. He didn't even bother trying to hide it. Nor did Morgan bother hiding his feeling on the matter, letting it shade his response. "What else would it be?" he answered mordantly.

It was the fifth time he had worked the report up since the girl's death nine months ago. The concluded cause of death- drug overdose- made Wilder's father far from pleased. This was hardly the first time in Morgan's career someone, usually a relative, disputed such findings. Death had a funny way of letting people know their loved ones had deep closets that were chock-full of skeletons. Sometimes death was the way they found out the person they thought they knew possibly never even existed, and it was so easy for denial and betrayal to take hold in such cases. The preservation of their memories required a scapegoat, a filthy liar who was out to malign their lost loved one. As a coroner, it was a role Morgan found himself playing many times over the course of his career.

However, none of those next of kin had been the District Attorney or someone equally influential. Someone who could bring a ton of grief crashing down on his head, and the power to make it count.

Brandy Wilder had a history of drug abuse, a fact which caused no end of trouble for her father. Shortly after his first election to D.A.- a win based on a strong record of convictions for drug-related crimes, no less- it was all over the news when his daughter was arrested during a raid at one of the city's housing projects. Media arriving on the scene had recorded her doped up antics, which not only made the local headlines, but had made national news.

When Wilder later used his position to get his daughter cleared of charges, provided she go into rehab of course, the media crucified him. Worse, rehab did little good for Brandy and her behavior continued to be publicized. Wilder managed to get re-elected two more times since then but it was always close. The last one was by a hair's-width and likely only because Brandy managed to stay out of the papers. Seemingly, she really was on the road to recovery.

Then, on a cold January night, Brandy Wilder was found in her apartment, new puncture wounds in the pit of her elbow and a needle with traces of heroin in her hand. She had been dead for at least two weeks before anyone found her so cause of death was difficult to determine, but the evidence was quite clear. The amount of heroin she seemed to have used in her last moments might not have killed her during her aggressive party days. However, if she truly did cleanup- only to relapse- she wouldn't have been able to handle the quantity she needed in her days of heavy use. It would have been an easy oversight- simple force of habit- for Brandy to make.

Unfortunately, it was an election year and it was going to be another tough campaign for Wilder. The last thing he wanted was to have his daughter's death used against him. Thus Morgan, as county coroner, found himself in his office spending over sixteen hours today rebuilding his report of her death for the fifth time.

"Any changes?"

"Nope," Morgan grumbled as he picked up the pen to continue. "If he's so worried about his re-election Wilder would have been better off accepting the findings and dropping it back in January. The voters probably would have forgotten about it by now. I doubt Clark would use a family tragedy against Wilder, but the DA using his pull like this is a different story; especially five times trying to get a different result.

"He done nothing but assured he'll have haunt him right up to election day."

"Election's still two months away; plenty of time to have you do a sixth or seventh," Bryce noted breezily as the coffee pot gurgled behind him. He pushed himself from the door frame. "Two sugars, no cream, right?" he said over his shoulder. Morgan smiled and nodded his head.

The outer doors to the morgue burst open; a gurney with a body bag was pushed through by an EMT. Following them was a cop whose expression plainly said he wanted to be anywhere else except here. Not for fear or apprehension but simply because he found this part of his job tedious. Bryce told the technician where to put the gurney, Morgan moving to follow them since the cop shoved his paperwork into the former's hand.

"So, what's the story?" Bryce asked, eyeing Morgan helping the EMT move the body over to a vacant table.

"Deceased is a 23-year-old female. Collapsed at that club down near 1st," the cop explained, his tone bored.

"I know where you mean," Bryce replied. The timbre of his voice was disdainful. The place- Tantric- had barely been open a year but its seedy repute was firmly established in the minds of anyone who knew its disreputable owner. Ironic in light of Morgan's recent activities as said proprietor was one of Brandy Wilder's more well-known cohorts.

"Yeah?" The cop's shoulders didn't move but the shrug was there anyway. "Well, according to her ID her name's Jessica Wright. Apparently, she was fine one moment then she just dropped dead. Friends said she hadn't been drinking anything except water the whole night. She wasn't on any medication that her friends knew of and none were on her."

The cop actually shrugged then. "'Course that doesn't mean someone else couldn't have done it for her, but I'll leave it up to you to figure all that out," he impassively uttered.

Despite her friend's claims an overdose was a possibility. One of the ample reasons the club in question was of ill-repute were the bartenders selling various date rape drugs along with drinks. Even if she kept to water, someone could have dosed her all the same.

"Has her next of kin been notified yet?"

The cop shook his head, as he waited for the noise of the EMT wheeling the gurney out to die down. "The friends didn't know how, and she didn't have it on her person. It might be on her phone, but if she has one it wasn't on her. She was a student at UAB. You can call their admin office to get that info." This was emphasized with a jerk of the cop's head; the morgue was on the edge of the collage's campus, so this was common.

Paperwork signed and a copy of it in hand, Bryce turned to the body. Morgan already had gloves on and was unzipping the bag as the cop left. "You're not on the clock tonight," he reminded Morgan as he tied a plastic apron at his mid-section and grabbing some gloves for himself.

"I know but right now anything is better than looking at that report," the older man said with a measure of exhaustion in his voice. Ignoring Bryce's good-humored scolding, Morgan pulled the plastic away from the girl. In the harsh light of the morgue Jessica's skin had taken on a bluish shade made worse by an off-putting combination with her flax blonde hair. Her expression was distant, more so than most fresh corpses. It was like her body just shut down, switched off, and went back to the default, factory setting.

She looked like she was waiting for someone to press a button and turn her back on.

Sighing, Morgan started with the preliminary examination asking: "Anything worthwhile on the response team's report?" With a finger he opened her mouth some and peered inside. Then he ran his hands slowly down her neck, checking for obstructions.

"It suggests aneurism," Bryce said, reading it from the clipboard at her feet as he pulled gloves on over his hands. His tone hinted doubt.

"You disagree," Morgan stated as he checked her chest and torso for abnormalities.

"Possibly," the younger man offhandedly replied as he went to work the body bag out from underneath her. "That's probably what it is but I'd rather examine her myself first though." Morgan smiled: a similar sentiment could have come from his own mouth.

"Then I leave our guest in your capable hands, Dr. Morris," he cheerfully said, straightening up and stepping away from the table. Fatigue washed over him as he did. "It's probably for the best if I call it a night anyway."

Bryce smirked at Morgan. "Then I bid you a safe drive home, Dr. Morgan." The M.E. removed the girl's shoes, white pumps with a short heel, and placed them in a large plastic bag. They were probably just right to emphasis the shape of her leg but low enough to dance comfortably in.

Now he had taken his coroner's hat off, Morgan took another look at the girl on the table. Jessica Wright had been a pretty girl; not exceptionally beautiful but she likely had her fair share of second looks. She had a long, willowy body and her hairline gave her a perfectly heart-shaped face.

Bryce turned her over slightly to unzip the back of her dress. As he pulled it down Morgan noted how nice it was. It was white, form-fitting and with thin shoulder straps. Several rows of cream-colored tassels of varying length formed an intricate, weaving pattern down the torso. Morgan thought it would have been right at home on a flapper during the Roaring Twenties, though modified some to fit more recent fashions.

He pushed these thoughts from his mind, stepping away from the slab and its occupant. He tossed his gloves into a bin as he went to his office to gather his things.

Once he made it home he slipped out of his clothes, stripping down to his underwear, and slipped in between the sheets of his bed. His thoughts briefly lingered on Jessica Wright. It seemed strange to him until he realized it wasn't her but the dress which had piqued his interests. Something about it seemed so familiar.

As he lay there, tossing and turning, unable to sleep, Morgan's unusual fixation with the dress was edged out by memories of his sister.

"It surprises me this county can ever get anything done, let alone right. We keep getting people like Williams on the Commission," Richard irritably complained as he chopped a large ravioli in half and impaled it with his fork. His criticisms against the Commissioner from District 3 were only matched by his gripes about the Commissioners from Districts 2 and 4. When it came right down to it, Richard didn't seem too fond of District 1's Commissioner either. "That woman thinks money grows on trees, at least when it comes to what she wants. Otherwise she wants to tighten the purse strings."

He grumbled as he chewed the ravioli, swallowed hard and smirked. "We know that's my job!" He looked across the table at Morgan, expecting the specific reaction that was his part of this long-standing joke between the two. When he was instead met with a distant, glazed over stare, Richard's expression fell. He reached over the table and nudged his friend. "Hey, earth to Fancy. You in there, Fancy?"

The nickname drew Morgan from his haze, almost hearing it in his sister's voice. He saw the worry cross Richard's face. Morgan let out a nervous laugh in an attempt to waylay the concern. "Sorry. I had a long night and not much sleep."

Richard's face brightened up some. "That so? What's his name?" When it was met with a hard look from Morgan he went a different route. "It wasn't the Wilder deal again, was it?"

"What else would it be?"

"Jesus Christ jumped up Allah will that man not let it go," Richard sneered before letting out a flabbergasted huff of a laugh.

"I can't really blame him...," Morgan mechanically started before Richard cut him off.

"Blame nothing," he spat. "Look, I like Jack Wilder... and Brandy was a sweet girl when she wanted to be... when she wasn't doped up to her gills on what the hell ever..." Richard tightly shook his head side to side. With a great exhale, he continued, "... but he's gotta deal with the fact that his precious little angel was a junkie and the sooner the better."

"I know," Morgan grudgingly agreed. This was far from the first time they had this exact conversation.

"Besides, he's going up against Clark this year," Richard continued, not hearing his friend. "That guy's gonna hammer him with this like there's no tomorrow and Jack'll be a blithering pile of shit before it's over with."

"I know," Morgan said again. "But it's not like I can tell him no. Not without inviting a world of trouble at any rate. You know what Jack's like when he doesn't get what he wants. And you never know *what* Jack knows and doesn't know."

Richard looked as though he was going to use the comment to revive his rant but all he said was, "Yeah. Yeah, I know." He stabbed at the other half of the ravioli and popped it into his mouth. Morgan used his fork to push at a cherry tomato in his salad.

"It's more than just the Wilder deal," he eventually admitted after a long silence. "I've been thinking a lot about Lily lately." Richard's face went stony as he put his fork down, his attention fully on Morgan now. He had been afraid to say her name, knew his friend could clam up at the mention of his sister. Even now Richard still blamed himself for her death.

Richard had been Lily's husband for nearly 25 years when she died from an embolism. The cause was concluded to be a large but unnoticed air pocket in the syringe she used to administer her insulin shots. Lily was diagnosed as a diabetic at a young age and had been giving herself the shots for decades, so it was peculiar she would have been so careless. Her inattentiveness was accounted for when Richard noted she had taken one of his sleeping aids the night before. She had never taken one before, she likely wouldn't have known how, if at all, it would affect her awareness. Richard found her at the kitchen table the next morning, slumped over the back of her chair, staring at him with dull, lifeless eyes.

It was at the funeral when Richard confided in Morgan that he had suggested Lily take the medication. She had been having trouble sleeping for over a month leading up to her death. A bad turn in the stock market the previous year ruined their retirement funds, and it was looking like it did greater financial damage in other areas. They were on the verge of losing so much they had worked for together. The bleakness weighed heavily on Lily, seemingly more than Morgan would have believed possible, making her a nervous wreck.

Neither she nor Richard had mentioned any of their money woes to him except in the briefest of passing. This struck Morgan as odd: they often confided in him. In the end he attributed their lack of disclosure to Lily's normally stoic approach to such issues and Richard's pride and plain unfamiliarity with the subject.

"I thought that if she could get just one night's sleep," Richard had told him at the service, crying like a baby on Morgan's shoulder.

Now, in the restaurant, Richard was abruptly detached at the mention of her name. Knowing his best friend like he did, Morgan saw this as simply a defense mechanism; if Richard acted otherwise he'd break down into an emotional wreck right here in public. There was a long moment of silence before Richard spoke, attempting to put a distant air in his voice.

"What's brought that on?"

"I know you don't want to talk about her," Morgan apologized. Richard simply gestured that his friend get it over with.

"I'm not sure why. It wouldn't be her birthday anytime soon, and she didn't..." He nearly choked on the word when Morgan realized what he was about to say next. Death was his occupation but when it came to his sister he preferred not to acknowledge its existence. He regained his composure and soldiered on. "There isn't any normal reason why I might be, outside of simple absence perhaps, but for some reason she's been in my head."

Neither talked or ate or drank. They just stared at each other. It became uncomfortable for Morgan long before Richard cleared his throat and scooted his chair away from the table.

"Maybe you'll figure it out soon." He stood, yanked on his jacket, and gruffly adjusted his tie. "I've should get back to the Courthouse. The Commission's meeting later today and I've got to prepare to deal with Williams again." Forced as it was, his typical devil-may-care smile returned at the mention of his rival.

Morgan was sure it was fake; both the excuse to leave and the blustering smirk. Richard probably did have a Commission meeting later that afternoon, but he preferred to make an entrance and never rushed to get back. Still, Morgan wasn't going to push his friend, so he started to get up to leave as well. "Sure," he replied. "I'll get the check."

Lily had always handled their finances and emotionally was not the only way in which Richard had never recovered from her death. He usually had enough money to cover his necessary expenses, but Morgan knew his brother-in-law was drowning in debt. Again, the man's pride would never allow him to admit this truth. It also meant he would put up token resistance about who covered the check, but he always quickly conceded to "let" Morgan pick it up.

Instead, Richard's face turned exaggeratedly sour and his retort was far more forceful than usual. "The hell you will, Fancy!" Without waiting for Morgan to reply, he plucked out his wallet, producing a pair of hundred-dollar bills and plopping them on the table. "You've been up all night on a fool's errand for Jack "Ass" Wilder," he gave Morgan a mischievous grin. "This is my treat."

Morgan saw several more bills in Richard's wallet before it was flipped closed and vanished into an inner pocket of his jacket. The last two years the man was lucky to have two twenties in his pocket; a pair of hundreds would have been implausible much less several of them. More, now Morgan's mind was turned to it, the billfold wasn't one of the cheap ones Richard usually picked up. This one was nice: hand stitched and made of soft leather, and probably cost more money than Richard usually carried.

"Richard, where...," Morgan gaped, unable to speak for a few seconds. "Where did all of that come from?" Richard's grin faded, replaced by an uncharacteristic bashfulness. He let out a dismissive chuckle before talking.

"Well, I guess Lil...," he took a deep breath as he gingerly sat back down, acting as if he believed the chair would break under his weight. His hand worried at his chin for a moment as he steadied his breathing. "Lil always was the one with an eye towards the future. I never gave much thought to it, you know? Anyway, she had life insurance policies for the both of us and it got things back on track again."

"But the last two years? You had this and...?"

"No, no!" Richard franticly waved his hands in an attempt to ward off any hint of suspicion. "No, Fancy. I know what this must look like but believe me it's not the case. It took so long because Lil made changes to the policies a few months before she died, and the timing kicked off an investigation by the insurance company. You know how those guys are: quick to take your money but slow giving it back." His shame was replaced by his normal breezy attitude. "Anyway, they finally cut the check a couple weeks ago and it's all cleared the bank now. I've already got the big stuff paid off or up-to-date now."

"Okay but...," Morgan said, clearly glad for his friend's fortune- despite the context- yet still stunned at the cash on the table. Again, Richard gave a dismissive snort.

"Hey, if it wasn't for you, Fancy, I would've been out on the streets a long time ago," he rationalized. "And I don't just mean you keeping me afloat the last couple years. If I hadn't met Lil I probably wouldn't have got to where I am today." His cheer was replaced by an uncommon reflective distance.

"Hell, she got my shit together, you know? Without her the best I could have hoped for out of life was maybe getting the chance to pass out in dirty underwear in front of the TV after drinking a case of beer every night.

"And I only met her because you were able to put up with me as a roommate back in college, good buddy!" he said, liveliness returning to his voice.

"I get that," Morgan said, again pointing to the cash, "but it's not necessary. Use that for something you need to pay off or something for yourself, at least. You've been through enough and I was happy to help my friend *and* brother out."

Richard waved it away. "I am paying off something I need to pay off... or starting to anyway! I know I owe you way more than this..."

"No, you don't owe me...!" Richard held up a hand to stop Morgan's objections.

"Yes, I do," he said adamantly. His magnetic smile stretching across his face. "And this is just the first of many, Fancy; the first of many. Believe me I am going to pay back everything I owe you."

After lunch Morgan stopped by Wilder's office to drop off the latest report. He was grateful the man was in a meeting at the time; it might give him a few days before Wilder caught up with him to redo the whole thing. When he got home he ran a few miles on the treadmill, something he hadn't done in quite some time. His legs were like jelly as he shambled into the shower. Once he was dried off and wrapped in a heavy robe he tried to turn his brain off, drink some wine, and watch television, only to end up flipping through channel after channel of a cultural wasteland.

He still couldn't get his sister out of his head. He was pouring his third glass of wine when his eyes fell on a picture on the bookshelf. It was a window-style frame with several photos inside. With glass in hand he stepped over to the shelf, taking the frame down before plopping back down into his plush chair. He ignored that some of the red spilled out on the armrest, his attention on nothing but the photos.

There was one of his parents, both deceased, which he ignored for the moment. He studied the middle-left one, the one of him and Lily. It was taken the day she visited Auburn University for a tour of the campus. Morgan had been there two years by then, and to be closer to her brother was probably the reason she gave the place any consideration. It was a few hours after that picture was taken when Lily met Richard for the first time. Morgan and Richard had been roommates their freshman year, quickly becoming friends as a result. Lily was instantly enamored of Richard, as most women were, though he was taken with her in a way he normally hadn't been with other girls.

It was also when Richard learned Morgan's nickname of "Fancy," the result of a two-year-old Lily's inability to say "Francis" correctly. The moniker was swiftly adopted.

He opened the frame to pull the picture out. He wanted to hold it closer. Once the stubborn backing was prized away several other photos fell out onto the floor at Morgan's feet. He gathered them up and started sifting through them, laying out the ones he didn't want on the table. He came to another one that made him stop. It wasn't the one he was looking for, but it caught his interest nevertheless.

It had been taken at night and in what was obviously a McDonald's parking lot, the blurry yellow and red sign casting a hazy tint over them. A much younger Morgan stood in between Lily and her old high school friend, a girl named Connie. Richard was on the other side of Lily. The four were dressed up and standing arm-in-arm with each other. He flipped it over and read the scribbled description on back.

Richard, Lily, Fancy and Connie.
Jackson, Miss 1979

Looking up from the photo, Morgan mused inwardly at the passage of time since it had been taken: 27 years. Calculating how old he must have been at the time, he had some trouble believing he had ever been as young as 22. Looking at it closely he remembered why they were in Jackson that night. Morgan allowed himself to fall into the memory conjured up by the ancient relic of his past.

"Why not?" Lily demanded of her brother. She was lying on the couch, her head resting in Richard's lap, their hands idly wrestling. Although she was giggling due to his antics, Morgan knew she wasn't going to be distracted from her goal here.

"First, do we even have a car that can make the trip? Second, do we have the money to go? And third, it'd be an overnight trip and we don't know anyone in Jackson so where would we even stay if we were to go?" To him it was all very logical and airtight, thus there should be no way for his sister to muster up any response.

It took her all of half a second to obliterate his points.

"First," she said between chortles, "Richard's car can make it no problem."

"That's true, Fancy," Richard said unhelpfully. Lily winked up at him in thanks.

"Second, we have the money. Mom and Dad always sends us cash at the first of the month- which was only last week- and you never do anything, so I know you still have a lot left. And third, Connie transferred to Millsaps earlier this year and has a place off campus with a couple people she goes to school with. She said it's no problem for us to crash there."

Morgan sighed, knowing he was defeated.

A few months ago, he had taken a risk by coming out of the closet to his sister and best friend, telling them that he was gay. He had no idea what to expect but decided if he couldn't at least tell them then he probably couldn't tell anyone at all. He was relieved when both were quite accepting, though it took Richard a day to really wrap his head around the concept. As good a feeling as it was, Morgan still had no idea who else it might be okay sharing this with; and he certainly didn't know where he might find others like himself.

Not in Alabama.

Unbeknownst to Morgan, Lily had been talking to her best friend, Connie. Instead of Auburn, Connie ended up going to the University of Alabama in Tuscaloosa. He hadn't known she was now at Millsaps College over in Mississippi. The other girl had mentioned her house was not far from an openly gay club. It occasionally had problems with the locals, but so far had gone largely unbothered by the intolerant. Lily made up her mind, then and there that they were going to take a road trip. If a small club in

Jackson was the only place her brother could be himself in public, if only for a night, then they were going to Jackson.

Morgan appreciated her efforts, but the thought twisted his stomach. He didn't know any other gay men and had no idea what it'd be like to be around them. Despite coming out, the disparaging ideas about homosexuals he had heard all his life remained, swirling about his consciousness. All the horrible things he'd heard about them- about himself, even if he didn't realize it then- were still there.

The whole prospect of being around other gay men mortified Morgan to no end. Lily would hear none of it, however; casually brushing it all off as ignorant chatter.

The week's end came with Richard's truck loaded up and pointed towards the Alabama-Mississippi state line, and further to Jackson. It was late by the time they got to Connie's place, so they had a few drinks while catching up and meeting her housemates before crashing. The next morning, Lily decided she really didn't care for anything she had brought to wear for that night, so she and Connie left in search of something different. Still uneasy, Morgan spent the day smoking a few joints and drinking shitty beer.

In the end his anxiety was for nothing. The bar wasn't much different from any other they'd visited, with the primary exception of men plainly making out with other men and the like. Connie seemed to be something of a regular at the place, so the suspicious stares normally given to strangers were minimal. Ultimately, Morgan enjoyed the night immensely. In fact, it was one of the most memorable nights he'd ever had. He hooked up with someone from the club, though it didn't go too far. Morgan couldn't even remember the guy's name. Couldn't remember if the guy had even given a name, or if he had asked.

Over the couple years, they made a few more visits to Jackson though they eventually found other places a touch closer to them; places in Birmingham and Mobile; a few in Atlanta. Over the years the time he frequented such establishments became fewer and further between. By his early thirties he was lucky if he dropped in once or twice a year. It wasn't even in such a place he'd met his most notable tryst, Bryce. That had been in a regular bar catering only to those who wanted to consume overpriced alcohol and had the money to pay.

All the same, that night played out in Morgan's head as his wine-soaked brain was lulled into sleep, curled up in the oversized chair. The moment that stood out the most was when he and Lily shared a dance in the tiny area set off, possibly as an afterthought, to the side. There weren't many others on the floor with them, letting them freely move about easily. The image of Lily twirling in his arms echoed; the multi-colored lighting coloring her hair, the smoothness of her moves in high-heels, the tassels of her white dress shimmering with the shifts of her tiny frame.

The next morning Morgan woke up with a slight hangover. It had been some time since he drank that much, and he never had a head for wine to begin with. It probably didn't help he failed to drink any water or eat more than a few bites after the treadmill. He stumbled into the bathroom to shower, the hot water releasing most of the tension in his body. A much-needed act of self-sufficiency taking care of the rest.

He made coffee and cooked some runny eggs and several pieces of bacon, figuring what remained of his hangover could be chased out with enough grease. The empty wine bottle and glass were still on the coffee table. He cleared them off and noticed the photos on the floor in front of the chair, the one from Jackson prominently on top. He gathered them all up while studying that one again. That's when the connection, the reason, why this one picture stood out so much to him; why it affected him so when Jessica Wright, a stranger, was brought in a couple nights before.

She brought back memories of Lily. Separated by 27 years yet the two women wore the same dress.

Or, at least, a dress that was exceptionally similar. He had errands to run and decided he'd stop by the morgue on his way out. The urge to compare the dress in the photograph and the one now likely bundled up in a plastic bag in a storage box overwhelmed him. He carefully gripped the picture as he grabbed his keys.

When he got to the morgue he found Bryce and the new intern whose name Morgan couldn't remember off hand; Veronica or Monica? He made a mental note to refresh his memory soon. They were hunched over a body towards the back of the room. From here Morgan could tell it was a male who had met a messy end, probably a car accident. He waved to them as he went to the store room housing the personal belongings of their guests.

"Wilder's not making you do another report so soon is he?" Bryce halfheartedly joked as he appeared in the doorway. Morgan smiled and shook his head.

"Not yet, but there's no need to get impatient," he replied as he pushed a container back onto the shelf. He delivered the comment with a dead-pan voice, but Bryce caught the joke. "Where's the stuff from Jessica Wright?"

"Who?"

"The girl from the other night," Morgan explained. "Possible aneurism on the dance floor."

"Oh, her. It's gone."

"Gone?" The next container was shoved back onto the shelf with a little more rancor than Morgan intended. "What do you mean, gone?"

"We were able to contact her parents yesterday morning. They retrieved the remains and her possessions later in the afternoon." Seeing the distress on Morgan's face Bryce solicited, "Is something wrong? Did we miss a hold?"

Morgan waved the question away. "No, nothing's wrong. It was just something weird..." He took a steadying breath. "Did you determine cause? Was it an aneurism?"

"Not an aneurism," Bryce responded. His face a picture of haughty satisfaction. He enjoyed proving others wrong way too much. "She died of an embolism."

It took Morgan a moment to realize he heard Bryce correctly. "An embolism? How?" He didn't doubt Bryce's competency, but it was beyond unexpected.

Bryce shrugged his shoulders. "Significant air bubble in her heart. Not sure how it got there but that's what all the signs point to."

"Strange," Morgan murmured as he slipped past Bryce. After having spent a good bit of time thinking of her the last couple days, the fact Lily died of the same cause readily jumped to the forefront of his mind.

"It is what it is," Bryce off-handedly said over his shoulder, not knowing the meaning behind Morgan's comment, as he went back to the body on the slab.

Morgan ambled over to his office and checked his messages. Sadly, Jack Wilder didn't give him as much time as he hoped. The idea of filing harassment charges against Jack crossed Morgan's mind but was dismissed just as quickly. It would accomplish nothing except grief for him and Wilder would not only hold a serious grudge, he still had the pull to make life hell for Morgan.

Eventually, he consoled himself with the knowledge the election was only two months away and Clark had a good chance to win, especially if Wilder kept up this madness. Morgan could work slowly, take his time, and might never have to worry about it again after November. He gathered up the material for yet another report, waving good-bye to the others as he left.

The temperature was still well in the 90's outside but in his townhome, at this table, it may as well have been freezing. Morgan had sat there, vacantly, for the better part of an hour before the chill in his spine dissipated and he felt able to move once more. In one hand he held the photo from '79, in the other was a forensic picture taken in Brandy Wilder's apartment. Brandy was sprawled across her bed, face up and eyes blank. There was a syringe held loosely in her hand and a packet of whitish powder on her nightstand. Her upper arm had a length of surgical tubing wrapped around it.

Previously, that's what had always taken up Morgan's notice before. What caught his eye now, however, was Brandy's dress.

It was white, form-fitting and elegant. Off-white tassels making a complex, interlaced design spread over her upper body. As he suspected with Jessica Wright it was akin to the dress Lily wore in the almost three-decade old snapshot. It was possible they were different outfits, but Morgan found it hard to believe. He vaguely recalled Lily said it was handmade by some old lady in Jackson and the only one in the shop. After she died Richard gave away or sold most of Lily's clothes; Brandy might have acquired it that way.

Maybe?

Brandy was quite stockier and bustier than Lily. Enough so it'd be near impossible to let the dress out enough for her to wear it. Jessica, on the other hand, was of a similar build to Lily; the outfit would match her size with no problem. Unless Brandy had managed to adjust it to fit her. If that were the case Morgan had no idea if Jessica would have had the means or ability to alter it back.

He realized he was getting ahead of himself. He never knew what became of the dress after that night thirty years ago. He couldn't remember ever seeing it again. Lily could have lost it, or it might have been damaged beyond repair. It could still be among the things Richard kept, still in their house. Also, the '79 picture was of poor quality, taken with a cheap instant camera and the image degraded over the intervening years. The details were now faint and fuzzy. It could be they were only alike on a general level.

Morgan grabbed his phone and dialed Richard's number. It was a woman's voice that answered. They sounded perky, and young. Very young. Morgan hesitated, wondering if he dialed the wrong number. "Is Richard there?"

"Sure, hold on a sec," she chirped. He could hear her calling Richard to the phone. Richard's faint voice asked her who was on the phone; Morgan assumed he was answered by a shrug as no audible response came. There was music in the background too. It was far too recent and poppy for Richard's tastes, at least as far as Morgan knew.

"'Ello?" Richard's voice sounded drained. Drained, but also contented.

"Richard?"

"Fancy!" he happily bellowed, life returning to his tone. "What can I do you for?"

"Who was that?"

"Oh, no one you know, Fancy," the smile surely accompanying the comment was clear, even over the phone. Morgan wondered if it was just as lecherous in reality as it sounded through the receiver. Tension crawled up Morgan's neck muscles. On one hand, he was glad Richard was moving on with life; he had plenty of it ahead of him. On the other, Morgan felt some anger over this betrayal to his sister's memory, even if Morgan rationally knew that betrayal only existed in his own mind.

"I hate to bother you, Richard," Morgan started, trying to keep the resentment from his voice. He could hear water splashing. He banished the tawdry images from his head. "It sounds like you're having a good time."

"Nonsense! Hit me."

"This is going to sound strange, but do you remember that time we went to Jackson?" Morgan asked.

Richard made his usual buzzing sound as he scoured his memory. After a second or two, "You mean that first time in, what was it, '78? '79?"

"Yeah, '79."

"Yeah, I remember it. What of it?"

From what little he could gather Morgan got the impression his friend was having a much-needed good time. He felt like an asshole for ruining it by bringing up Richard's dead wife once more. Still, he needed to know. An admittedly petty part of him very much wanted to remind Richard of Lily.

"That night Lily wore a dress..."

"You mean that little white number," Richard interrupted. Given the topic his tone was uncharacteristically enthusiastic, though it called back to the lascivious young man Morgan met all those years ago. "The way she looked in that get up..." he finished the sentiment with a long, appreciative moan.

"You remember it."

"Don't think I could ever forget that."

"Do you know what happened to it?"

"Fancy, whatever you do in your own time is fine by me, but I think Lily was more than a touch smaller than you..." he answered with an unusually playful tone.

"That's not what I mean," Morgan blurted out with a snort, trying to stay in the lightness of the mood. "No, I was just curious as to what happened to it. Just wondering if it was one of the things you gave away."

"Nope," Richard said. "Lil loved that dress. If I gave that away I have no doubt she'd have sat up and smacked me silly."

"So, you still have it?"

"Nope," he answered again. "Lil's got it."

It took Morgan a moment to get what he just heard. "You mean you buried it with her?"

"Of course," Richard said. "That and a few other things. You know old photos and that raggedy-assed stuffed bear she had as a kid and would never get rid of. Those were a few things I figured she'd want with her in Heaven, so I put 'em in there with her."

Morgan dwelled on that for a moment. "You don't think there's any way it could have ended up in a thrift shop or something like that, do you?"

Richard's tenor took a brusque turn. "Hell no! Fancy, what's this all about?"

He debated on whether he should mention anything about Brandy Wilder or Jessica Wright to his friend. It still sounded crazy to him, so he decided against it. "Nothing, Richard. Just a wild hair I got. Sorry to have bothered you."

"No bother," Richard replied uncertainly. "Give me a call later in the week. We'll have lunch. On me."

"Sure," Morgan returned before he hung up the phone.

He went back to the table and stared at the photos. Since the dress was buried with Lily there was no way what was worn by Brandy Wilder or Jessica Wright on the nights they died could be the same one. Still, as irrational as he knew it to be, Morgan just couldn't shake the feeling Lily's old dress had somehow found its way into both girls' possession.

With a fast, second trip to the morgue it was easy enough to get the address for Jessica Wright's parents, though Bryce was more inquiring of Morgan's temperament this time around. It took a bit of fast-thinking- as well as pulling a little rank- but Bryce dropped his worried interrogation, unhappy about it though he was.

The Wrights lived far north of the city, near the state line, but the drive didn't bother Morgan. The sun was low on the horizon, casting long creeping shadows along the ground, by the time he got to the home. It was situated on a dead-end road and plain looking, though it struck Morgan that it was probably quite cozy if looked at in a better frame of mind.

Up close, however, he couldn't see it as anything but gloomy, like no one was home. From the outside, it as if it could only be occupied by ghosts and memories. Beside the front door an American flag hung limp and sad with no wind to rustle it. There were no vehicles in the short driveway, but a garage door sat closed at the end of it and an old red pick-up truck was parked off the side of the house. Coming to a stop at the end of the driveway, he thought he could see a dim interior light through one window, but he wasn't sure.

Stepping up to the porch, the air felt oppressive, like it a heavy rain was about to drop, though the sky was clear blue, and the sun shone brightly. He rang the doorbell and heard someone lethargically stirring about inside. The movement had a measured quality to it, like it was weighted down with dread. A moment later a woman answered the door, her teary red eyes and drained face making her look far older than her likely age. She looked Morgan up and down, studying him for a second before speaking. When she did, her voice was small and timid; guarded.

"Yes?"

"Mrs. Wright?" Morgan asked to be sure.

"Yes," she said again as a surly-looking man appeared

behind her. This was presumably Jessica's father.

"Ma'am, I'm Dr. Francis Morgan with the Jefferson County Coroner's office. I'm sorry to intrude but I need to talk to you about your daughter. Do you have a moment?" She looked back at the man before opening the door wider. They invited Morgan in, reflexively offering him refreshment. He thanked them but declined, he was intruding on their grief over something that was surely born out of madness; already risking upsetting or offending them greatly. He wasn't going to drag it out by accepting their decorum, even if it was merely an automatic act.

"I know this is a bad time and I won't take up too much of it," he told them as they dismissed the inconvenience. "There's something that's come up that suggests Jessica's death could be connected to a different case we have, an older one, and I'm hoping I might be able to get some answers."

"The other doctor told us she died of an embolism," the man said. There was more than just grief in his voice. A twinge of anger and suspicion popped in. "Did he lie?"

"No. Cause of death was accurate," Morgan quickly leaped to Bryce's defense, allaying their apprehensions. "We're not sure if these two cases are connected yet but it is something that needs to be followed up on just in case," Morgan said, hoping to keep from having to explain anything in greater detail. The man looked liable to punch someone and Morgan would rather it not be him.

"Chester Moore from the funeral home has already got her remains," Mrs. Wright supplied. "We can give you directions and call them and let them know you're coming."

"Thank you but that shouldn't be necessary," Morgan told her. "Actually, what I need to see are the clothes she was wearing the night she died. I believe my associate would have given them to you when you came down to the office."

Mrs. Wright excused herself as she went to retrieve the box with her daughter's personal belongings. She came back a minute later with a small cardboard box in her hands that she handed to Morgan. It had been unopened, the lid still fastened with tape stamped with the coroner's official seal. With her parent's permission, Morgan cut the tape with his car key and looked through Jessica's effects.

There wasn't much on her when she was brought in. Giving the manifest a fast scan, he saw the dress listed. He pushed aside her tiny purse, wallet, and small make-up case. He placed her shoes on the floor in front of him but didn't see the dress. It should have been readily apparent, but it wasn't there. The large plastic bag it had been placed in was there, sealed shut but empty. Morgan took it out to examine closer. He saw no holes or cuts in the bag, but the dress was gone.

"No one's tampered with this box before now?" he requested of Jessica's parents. Both shook their heads.

"It's been in Jessica's room since we got back yesterday," the girl's father grumbled. "Neither of us have touched it."

"Anyone else been by who might?" Again, they shook their heads in the negative.

Morgan checked both the bag and box once more, with a modicum of frenzy to his actions this time, yet still no evidence either had been tampered with or damaged. The Wrights started getting a little agitated. They tried to ask more about this connection to another case, but Morgan ignored them, which only served to heighten their distress.

Quickly placing everything back into the box, Morgan stood and hurried to the door. "Again, I'm sorry for taking up your time. I'll get out of your hair now. Sorry for your loss." He practically ran out of the door, down the driveway and to his car. The Wrights stood at their door, hollering questions to him as he went, still demanding answers as he peeled away.

He didn't get a signal on his cell phone until he got back on the freeway. By now Bryce would have already left the office but he tried there anyway. Monica- or Veronica, which ever- picked up. Making another mental note to remember her name, he asked for Bryce. She informed Morgan he had already left. Thanking her he hung up and tried Bryce's cell.

"Dr. Morgan," Bryce said his name with expectation.

"Bryce, are you sure Jessica Wright's personal items were accounted for?"

"Well, yes, I am doing just fine. How are you?" Bryce

287

huffed with annoyance. He didn't wait for an answer. "Yes, they were all accounted for and sealed in a storage box. Her parents took it with them."

"You're sure."

"Yes!" It was the terse tone Bryce always adopted when he felt his competency was being questioned. He exhaled. "Francis is there something wrong?" Bryce rarely referred to his superior as anything other than Dr. Morgan. It made him realize how worried the younger man must be if he used Morgan's first name.

"I'll be honest with you, Bryce. I don't know."

"Do you want to talk about it?"

"You'd think I was going crazy."

"Maybe, but it might help."

The way Bryce said it carried a heavy suggestion there could be much more than just talking between them tonight. It brought the tension still in Morgan's muscles to his attention. Weariness washed over him and there was nothing he wanted more than to spend the night with Bryce.

"Alright," he sighed. "Where do you want to meet?"

Morgan told Bryce about the dress and the strange connection between it, his sister and the two girls. As predicted the young examiner thought the whole thing was mad. After hours of going over every detail, Bryce finally conceded. "I suppose the dresses in these pictures are the same as the one Jessica Wright had on." There was a great amount of doubt in his tone. "I mean they look *similar*."

And that was the extent of it then. The matter was dropped between the two after that night. The rest of September trudged by with little out of the ordinary.

By late October the fascination he had had with the dress waned. His almost nightly engagements with Bryce contributed a great deal but the lack of additional leads in his search was what truly dashed it. There were avenues he could pursue but they all ranged from the absurd to the offensive. If there was a link, however insane it seemed, he'd never find it now the dress was missing. If there were anything to it, it was lost to him now. With the days turning into weeks, and eventually almost two months, the whole thing started to seem insane to Morgan.

Until the night the body of Susan Rollins was rolled into the morgue.

Rollins was found in her car parked in a deck near the Civic Center. No signs of violence to suggest a wrongful death. Once Morgan saw her clothes, however, he knew what she died of. The examinations confirmed it.

They pointed to an embolism, but Morgan knew it was the white dress. He knew it had something to do with Lily.

Recognizing he was upset about something, Bryce offered his company to Morgan. Nearly two months ago, when he had explained his bizarre idea about the dress Bryce indulged him but clearly didn't care for the subject. If there were to be any conversation now Morgan knew it'd be on this topic. As such he graciously declined the offer.

It might have been the liquor but that night his dreams were confusing yet vivid. He had the sense Lily was lying next to him, her ephemeral arms wrapping around his body, holding him to her. She whispered in his ear, her voice so small and cold and detached. Her words, carried by stale breath, coiled into his mind and consumed his dreams.

It started back in the bar in Jackson. Passively, he watched Lily danced, the lights playing on her hair, her smile glowing. It ran through her graduating from college and marrying Richard. All the important and happy things in Lily's life were laid out in front of him; the birthdays and holidays, her friends and family, Morgan and Richard.

Beneath them, though, were more troubling details. Her marriage was largely content and adoring, but Richard's passions could run to the destructive. There were fights, nasty ones, usually a result of Richard allowing setbacks to get the better of him; of him acting on reckless impulse and not taking a moment to think things through.

Such as it was two years ago when Lily told him about their financial misfortunes. Everything they had worked towards was under threat of ruin. She insisted they could turn things around; it'd take a little while longer than they had anticipated before they could retire, but they'd be okay in the long run. Although Richard seemed to accept her assertion, she knew deep down he was terrified. She just didn't know he was scared enough to force his sleeping pills onto her; scared enough to inject her with a syringe full of air so the money from the policy on her would take care of the setback. He propped her up at the kitchen table, laid her insulin bottle out in front of her and acted like he found her that way.

Sure, he regretted it as soon as he pushed the plunger down, but that didn't matter. It was done and there was nothing he could do to change it. If he had spent a moment to think about things he might have concluded it was foolish. Instead he was weak and cowardly and destroyed the best thing he had in his life.

At her funeral Richard had slipped the dress into her coffin, along with a few other things. He knew she loved it; she had worn it at one of the happiest times in her life. In his twisted, guilt-ridden mind this was a way to make amends with her, just saying he was sorry he killed her.

After that it was dark and cold, the very air grew heavy, bearing down on Morgan, threatening to crush him. In the darkness he could feel the rot and decay set in, consuming Lily's flesh just as much as the anger and resentment ate away at her soul.

Then he was in a Salvation Army shop with the dress. It hung on a rack for a week before some girl bought it. She was plain-faced with a mop of black hair, dull green eyes, and oily skin. She was ungainly and unflatteringly pudgy. Once the dress was on her, though, she came alive. Her hair was shiny and thick, her eyes bright, skin clear and pale. She seemed light as air on her feet and the plump parts of her body morphed into lush curves. She arrived at her prom alone but had the eye, probably for the first time in her life, of every boy she came in sight of. Unlike all the previous dances of her life, the girl never saw a dark and lonely corner of the decorated gym that night. She felt so vibrant right up to the point she dropped dead on the dance floor.

The dress was again in a consignment shop. It hung behind a counter until the cashier, angry at her boss for not giving her a raise, took it and several hundred dollars from the register as she closed the place up. She wore the dress for a night out on the town and was dead by morning. It played out like this a few more times before it got to Brandy Wilder ten months ago. After a night of drinking and partying she decided a nightcap was the perfect ending to her fun. The dress ended her before the heroin had a chance to take hold.

It was two weeks before she would be discovered, and Morgan could feel her putrefying inside the garment. He was aware of the corpse breaking down and fuming within. She was finally found, the dress removed. Freed. After months of mourning the Wilders gave Brandy's things away to a local charity, which was where Jessica Wright saw the dress as she sorted the stuff out. She sneaked it into her purse, hung it up in her closet, and promptly forgot about it. It stayed there for a few months until Jessica was invited out to a club by a guy she really wanted to make an impression on. She undoubtedly did just that since Jessica died while their tongues were in each other's mouths.

It was found by Susan Rollins at an estate sale. The surviving family raved over it when Rollins brought it up to pay, though none of them remembered the garment, much less attaching a price tag to it. Still, they sold it to her and she ended up dead in her car a week later.

Morgan woke up screaming.

Richard was awakened by the doorbell ringing and pounding at the front door.

His young girlfriend was startled by the racket and he absently reassured her, though he couldn't really muster a care if she calmed down or not. Just in case, he shoved a loaded pistol into the pocket of his robe before slogging down to see who was at the door. Curses at whoever had the temerity to pound on his door at three in the morning were leaving his mouth before he saw it was Morgan.

"Fancy, what the hell are you up to?" he commanded once he took a relaxing breath. "Do you know what times it is?"

Morgan pushed Richard back into the foyer. "Fuck the time, Richard, I know! I know what you did!"

"Baby, is everything okay?" the young girl quietly asked from the top of the stairs. Under different circumstances she was probably quite attractive but with sleep-puffy eyes, bed-head hair, and barely contained panic she wasn't much to look at now.

"It's okay, Katie, go back to bed," Richard gently instructed her, not taking his eyes off of Morgan. It took her a moment, but she pushed away from the wall to trod back to the bedroom. Ignoring her Richard turned back to his friend. "Now what's this all about?"

"I know what you did," he hissed in return.

"I know you know... now can you tell me what it is I did?" He was trying to maintain a sense of conviviality, trying to humor his friend, but there was growl in his voice that had never been directed at Morgan before.

"You killed her."

Richard's heart skipped a beat, stuttered over his voice. Shock and offense spiked through his tone. "Killed who?"

Morgan sneered. "Lily, who else? I know you drugged her and shot her full of air! You tried to make it look like an accident, all so you could get the insurance money."

Richard looked at his friend blankly, stunned speechless for probably the first time in his life. Finding himself, his face flushed red. "How dare you..." It alarmed Richard some when he realized his hand had slipped into his pocket, fingers wrapping around the grip of the gun. His hand and the weapon stayed in his pocket as he stepped up into Morgan's face.

"You need to leave. Now!" he snarled between gritted teeth.

Morgan stood eye to eye with his old friend. Finally, he

backed away to leave. Outside the door he turned back and said, "I know you killed her, Richard. I can't prove it, but I will."

"Fancy, I don't know what it is you're going through right now, but I didn't kill her. I'd never do something like that. I loved her and always will." Morgan started to object but Richard cut him off, yelling over him. "I may have pushed her too hard to take those pills, I don't know, but I do know I will always blame myself for her death.

"And to have you come to this house, where Lil and I built our home and accuse me like that..." He took a moment to steady himself, his breathing coming in hard gulps. "When you want help getting' over all this, let me know. Until then stay the hell away from me." The door slammed shut, the sound echoing to deride Morgan.

After a short time of staring at the closed door, Morgan walked away. He could swear he saw Lily nearby, an upsetting smile on her insubstantial façade.

The next two weeks Morgan did all he could to get the evidence to prove Richard killed Lily. He made all the requests to anyone he could think of, called in every favor he thought might help and a few that probably wouldn't. He even handed Jack Wilder a report stating his daughter died of a plain old heart attack instead of anything drug related.

None of it did any good. Richard filed a harassment complaint against Morgan and used his influence as Commission President. The pressure he was able to bring to bear against his old friend was immense.

Even his olive branch to Wilder hurt him more than helped. "Have you seen the Goddamned poll numbers?" Wilder scorned when he called Morgan the night after the latest report was dropped off. "Clark's up by 20 points! He's going to fucking win, and it was your bullshit about Brandy dying of an overdose that lost me the election to that... that..."

Morgan knew it was taking everything in Jack Wilder not

to use a racial slur so obviously dripping from the tip of his tongue in regard to Clark.

The other man took a deep breath. "Now you come to me with your dick in your hand wanting my help? Now you try to bribe me? Go fuck yourself, you goddamned faggot!" Wilder yelled before slamming the phone down.

The same falsified report was eventually used against Morgan.

He knew it was over, that Lily's murder would go unpunished, when Bryce recommended he stop. It led to a fight which ended any future they could've had together. He almost thought it a mercy when he was informed Richard would agree to stop his actions against Morgan on the condition he resign as County Coroner. He was cleaning his office out when Bryce appeared in the doorway.

"Need any help?" Those were his words, but his tenor was contrite. An apology for what he had said the last time they spoke.

Morgan smiled. "I'm almost done, but thanks." He put the last of his personal items in the box. "I hear they're bringing Jim Stein in to replace me."

"They are. He should be satisfactory," Bryce answered, his tone flat. He was being diplomatic; Morgan knew he hated Stein.

He picked up his box and moved to leave, pausing to lean in close to Bryce. "If they have any sense you shouldn't have to put up with Stein for long. If they aren't stupid they'll give you the job soon enough. I'd offer to put in a good word for you but..."

Bryce smiled at that. "What about you? What'll you do?"

"I'll be alright," he declared. "I've already talked to Warren Rice over at Armitage Mortuary. He's going to need a head mortician in a few months and says it's mine if I want it. I've got plenty put back to keep me afloat until then."

The younger examiner was about to say something before being cut off by EMTs rolling in a body. Since he was still, technically, Coroner for another hour Bryce let Morgan sign for it. Monica and Bryce transferred the corpse from the gurney to an examining table and went to work, saying their sad farewells to Morgan while they did.

As Morgan left the morgue for the last time he caught a glimpse of the white dress on the dead girl, and Lily standing over the body.